The Prosector

A. Lee Dellon, MD, PhD

Published by A. Lee Dellon, MD, PhD, 2022.

This is a work of fiction. Similarities to real people, places, or events are entirely coincidental.

THE PROSECTOR

First edition. May 21, 2022.

Copyright © 2022 A. Lee Dellon, MD, PhD.

ISBN: 979-8201204280

Written by A. Lee Dellon, MD, PhD.

ACKNOWLEDGEMENT

I wish to acknowledge the following people who helped review the manuscript for THE PROSECTOR; Joann Thompson Greer, Kelli Greer Sussman, Esq. and her husband, Alec Jarvis, Esq., Cindie Reynolds and her husband, Dan Dubberly, MD, Timothy W. Tollestrup, MD, Andreas Gohritz, MD and Elaine Lanmon, my graphic designer, who, in addition to helping create the Landsmann Family logo, helped to edit the text. Special thanks to Steven Lisberger, who has lived through a critical part of this story and taught me what THE STORY is really about. Finally, a loving thank you to that most critical of all readers, Luiann Olivia Greer, my wife, whose keen eye was finer than Spellcheck, and whose love and understanding gave me the time to complete this writing.

Cover Design by Elaine Lanmon, Graphic Design, Haltom City, Texas

Disclaimer

THIS IS A WORK OF FICTION. Therefore, the novel's story and characters are fictitious. Names, characters, and events are the products of the author's imagination. Any resemblance to actual persons, living or dead, or actual events is purely coincidental, with the exception that any public agencies, institutions, or historical figures mentioned in the story serve as a backdrop to the characters and their actions, which are wholly imaginary.

THE PROSECTOR

A. Lee Dellon, MD, PhD

(THE PREPARATION OF anatomical specimens so that others may learn from them is a special art, requiring the skill of a master surgeon, the love of learning and teaching, and the peace of mind to complete the work. The person possessing this unique combination may be called The Prosector.)

FRONTSPIECE

LANDSMANN FAMILY CREST

I

UNIVERSITY OF UTAH SCHOOL OF MEDICINE

SALT LAKE CITY, UTAH, 1914

FORMALDEHYDE

It was a horrible smell. It was not just in the air she breathed. Everything in the humid room smelled like the worst bottle of bad wine. And that was the *best* comparison she could come up with. Even the scarf she wore around her face to cover her nose did little to help that smell.

At least the odor was not that of rotted, decaying human flesh, which is what the air would be full of, if it were not for the formaldehyde that was used to embalm these people.

Olevia felt alone. Yet she was not really, alone.

She was surrounded by old men and women. Dead, old men and women.

Human cadavers surrounded her. Olevia was surrounded by dead people.

The dim ceiling lights shown over several rows of dull-grey, metal tables. Each table had a pan underneath it, used to collect "drippings" from the body that lay on top of the table.

There was one body per table. There were fifteen tables. Four medical students would dissect each body.

A cloth, once white, but now brownish, stained, and moist, covered each body. The University of Utah's Human Anatomy Course was nearing its completion, and each of these corpses had been uncovered, dissected, and then covered again many times. The room from Olevia's vantage point looked like a winter road with deep ruts in it, after cars had driven over the melting snow.

Each cadaver was a human body. A body perhaps whose former owner had been successful in life. More likely, however, thought Olevia, "not successful", as these were the bodies left "unclaimed". Bodies, which had become the property of the State of Utah, to be used to teach, for the benefit of its citizens. Ultimately, each was a body to be cremated.

But before those ashes were to be created in the flames of the incinerator, there was much that could be learned from that human body to benefit the living. There were secrets to be learned. Answers from the dead could be used to unlock the mystery of pain and suffering in the living. Olevia knew that this was the reason she was in this room, in this place. Olevia wore gloves to protect her hands. Already today, however, these gloves were permeated by the somewhat greasy, wet stuff that just oozed slowly from the tissues of the body in which she was working. She took the gloves off. She then adjusted the scarf that she wore pulled up over her nose, and put on a new pair of gloves.

She was a Doctor. Today she was doing research, in the "Anatomy Lab" of the University of Utah School of Medicine, in Salt Lake City, Utah.

She reminded herself that she was not really, alone. Besides the embalmed bodies, there was one other living body in the room. A body, living like her own, but that body, that other woman in the room, almost always went unnoticed at this time of day. She came in quietly in the late afternoon each weekday, to clean. Rumor had it that she had been there from "the beginning". She was more like a part of the room. She just blended in. Her dark brown pants, and loose-fitting shirt draped from her slender body much the way in which the moist loose skin from the cadavers draped over the bodies they once contained.

Olevia knew this woman's name. It was 'Chipeta". A strange name. A beautiful name.

Olevia knew very little else about her. As Olevia looked at the woman, kneeling in the corner of the room, scrubbing the floor, it seemed time to learn finally how this woman had arrived at this spot, this location, this point in time.

"Chipeta", Olevia quietly called out to the woman. "Can I talk with you for a little while?"

"Yes, Mam," replied Chipeta quietly, with a somewhat unusual accent.

As Chipeta stood up, Olevia judged that this figure in brown was about 5' 1" in height, about a head shorter than Olevia. There was ornamental beading on Chipeta's shoes, or were they moccasins? She also noticed that

Chipeta wore a beaded necklace, quite broad and worn tight to her neck. Chipeta's thick black hair hung over each of her shoulders in a braid, quite in contrast to Olevia's pale brown hair, which Olevia wore up tight in a bun at the back of her neck.

Olevia now pulled down the scarf from her face, revealing bright inquisitive dark eyes, and a kindly, caring smile. "What made you decide to do this type of work?" Olevia asked in a manner calculated not to be condescending or to create any concern about the housekeeping duties Chipeta did.

"Why Mam, I might ask you the same question," replied Chipeta without a trace of arrogance. "And Mam, I notice that when you speak you have an accent I have not heard before around these parts. Where are you from?" Chipeta added on to her first question.

Olevia noted that her voice sounded as if it came from a much younger woman than this woman's face would suggest. "Perhaps the exposure to the embalming fluids had taken their toll on this woman's skin," thought Olevia.

"Chipeta, you are correct," answered Olevia. "I am originally from Munich, a part of Europe that is now called Germany. I have tried hard to learn to pronounce English without a typical German accent, but sometimes I will say 'Zis' is what is happening, instead of 'This' is what is happening. And I have to be careful with other letters too, like 's'; 'Zo' I am very careful, instead of 'So' I am very careful, *und zo on!*" Olevia said with a humble smile.

Chipeta just stood quietly, trying to understand these sound changes.

Olevia continued, "I came to America to become a doctor. I was not allowed to pursue Medicine as a career in Germany. I came here to Salt Lake City looking for a relative. He supposedly took the advice of the Editor of a newspaper, the New York Tribune. That advice from the famous editor, Horace Greely, was to "Go west, young man. Go west."

"Well, Mam, perhaps you and I are more alike than you might think. I too was born in what used to be an Empire. But I did not have to "go west". I was born out here, in the West. This used to be the Empire of the Ute Indian Nation. I was born just over those Wasatch Mountains, she said pointing out the Anatomy Lab window. To the east of Salt Lake City, in

Uintah, on the Green River," said Chipeta, now standing and moving closer to the only other living being in the room.

Olevia noticed that as Chipeta stood, she almost expanded with dignity and pride as she spoke proudly of her ancestors. Olevia noted the almost round face, high cheekbones, broad nose, and high forehead. Deep-set eyes shone in a face whose skin was not really, red, but darker brown.

"What made you decide to do this type of work," Olevia said, repeating her original question.

"Doctor, with no disrespect, I tell you that my People believe that the bodies of our ancestors are sacred. We protect our burial grounds. We believe our Ancestors speak to us still, teaching us. This room is like a burial ground. But here the bodies get desecrated. They get torn apart. I like to think that when the daily assault on these bodies if over, that I gently care for them, covering them back up, in preparation for their final funeral fire," Chipeta replied, looking the Doctor straight in the eye.

Olevia was quiet for a moment, recognizing this strong attack on the very basis of what she was doing here. "Chipeta," replied Olevia, "as you have said, we may be more alike than you at first realize. I do respect these people. And, yes, they do teach us still, after they have departed this life. That is why I do my dissections. So that they may teach me what I do not know."

"Yes, Doctor, I do understand that. And I have observed that you are much more delicate with your work than those young men who are in here regularly tearing at these departed folks," replied Chipeta, quietly, seeming to give Olevia a compliment.

"Thank you, Chipeta," said Olevia, humbly. "When I search for something in the Anatomy, I must go slowly, so I do not miss anything. The human body has so much to teach us."

"Did you find your relative yet?" asked Chipeta. "This is a strange place to be looking, unless you believe your relative has died."

"No, I have not found him. However, I do believe he is departed now. He might have taught in this very place. He was an Anatomist, who left our home to do research he could not accomplish where we lived, in Munich. He was my Uncle."

"Well Mam, I have been employed here since the University of Utah started teaching Anatomy in 1905. The biology Department started teaching Anatomy right here in this very building. There were 16 students in that first class. Today we have 60. I have always loved history. I did not have much formal schooling on the Reservation, but the Mormons here in Salt Lake City, believe in Education, and encouraged it amongst my people. They supported our education especially if we converted, which I did."

"Vonderful," encouraged Olevia, slipping in a German accent again. "Do you get to know any of the students who dissect here?"

"Well, Mam, I come to work in the late afternoon and the students usually had all they can stand of the smell by then, and have left. But there was one young faculty member, I remember. I never did know his name. He came and did extra dissections in the evening. He was very gentle when he dissected. He seemed fascinated by the arms more than any other part. Perhaps that was your Uncle," observed Chipeta.

Olevia's heart skipped a beat at thought that Chipeta might have known her Uncle Albert. Instead of pursuing this subject further, she said, "Chipeta, I love history too, and I know that in 1912, the University of Utah did open a formal two-year medical school, which included Anatomy. At the end of those two years, its students had to seek the last two years of clinical experience at another medical school. I had the good fortune to go to a four-year medical school. It is named the Johns Hopkins University School of Medicine. It is in Baltimore, Maryland, way back East," Olevia went on.

"But why did you have to come from your home country to America to go to medical school?" asked Chipeta.

"There are so many prejudices in the world Chipeta," Olevia explained. "I am sure you saw the way the people from back east, the 'white people' treated your people. Your skin is a different color, but, as you saw with the Mormons, education is so critical to our understanding. In my country, Germany, and actually, in America too, it is very rare for a woman to be allowed to receive the education needed to become a doctor. Men were just simply prejudiced against women becoming professionals in this field. The men say that women are too emotional, and best suited to raising children."

"Yes," agreed, Chipeta. "Men think women should remain the squaw, home with the children in the Tee Pee, preparing food. Women were not permitted to become hunters and warriors."

Olevia continued. "My medical school, Johns Hopkins School of Medicine, opened in 1889. There were women even in its first medical school class, something almost unheard of in the medical schools of Europe." After sharing this information about herself, Olevia now felt she could ask her new friend some more questions.

"Chipeta, your name is musical and one I have never heard in Europe or in America. What does it mean in your native language?" asked Olevia, becoming intrigued by this hard working, usually quiet, woman janitor.

"I am named for my grandmother. Her name means 'white singing bird'. She was an artist skilled with beads and leather, and became married to the Chief of the tribe, Chief Ouray, my grandfather. She had great insight into people's character and advised him. She spoke Spanish and English besides our native tongue. Chief Ouray, and my Grandmother, even went to Washington, DC and helped negotiate the truce that ended the Indian Wars here in Utah," explained Chipeta. "Did you know the state of Utah derives its name from our Tribe, the Utes?" Chipeta asked proudly.

"No I did not know that. Thank you for this history lesson. Did you create that necklace with beads the way your ancestors did?" asked Olevia, impressed with the craftsmanship of the necklace.

"Yes I did it requires much careful use of a metal needle. In the old days my ancestors used a porcupine quill. The little beads we call 'seeds' but they are really painted glass. In the old days, before the European traders came to these parts, we did use painted seeds. The big beads we call 'pony beads', and use them for spacers. I usually tie one knot between every 3 seeds and put the pony beads end to end. We buy them already painted white. The strung beads I can then weave into a fabric and then sew that fabric on to my moccasins. You see the traditional straight pattern on my "mocs," she said, lifting up one foot to demonstrate. "I can just sew on new "leathers" to the bottoms when the bottoms get too stained from the floor and drippings of this Anatomy Lab."

Chipeta then asked, "Mam, I notice how well you use the knife and other metal tools for your dissections. You are very precise too. You could make beautiful bead designs for moccasins."

"Thank you Chipeta. I now do these types of dissections as part of my profession. I am not just a Doctor Chipeta, I am a Surgeon."

"Oh," replied Chipeta, not seeming to be aware of the difference. "Can you explain more about that to me, Doctor?"

"Sure, I can", said Olevia. "Well, the first woman was not admitted to the most famous University in Munich, my hometown, Ludwig-Maximillan University, until 1908. Women were not thought suited to become Doctors. Nurses, yes, surely. But, not Doctors. And, certainly not Surgeons. Chipeta, I trained to become a surgeon, and it is that surgical training you see when you observe me dissect," commented Olevia.

"I never knew there were woman surgeons," commented Chipeta. "Here in Salt Lake City, all our surgeons are men. I often wonder if my ability to knit and create beads with my instruments would permit me to dissect the way you do, but I would never be given the chance. What inspired you to become a surgeon?" she asked.

"The man I was searching to find, my Uncle Albert, injured his left hand in a chemistry experiment. He had been pouring an acid with his right hand into a glass beaker held in his left hand. Some of the acid spilled out on to his left forearm. The acid burned through his sleeve, through his skin, and down to the bone in the area just where the thumb and wrist joined the forearm," said Olevia using her right hand to point to the exact place on her own left wrist.

"Oh, what pain that must have caused," said Chipeta.

"Yes, Chipeta," Olevia continued, "I remember still, although I was only about 5 years old at that time, the horrible pain he had, and how long it took the wound to heal. He always wore a bandage around that wrist, to keep it covered. He would say that even the air blowing across the wrist would be so painful. He would not let anyone get close to that left hand. The pain of that injury changed his life, and, probably has determined mine."

"I remember such a man," interrupted Chipeta, excitedly. "That young man who worked alone at night, always kept a special cloth wrapped around his left wrist, even on the hottest of days. I thought it quite unusual."

"Chipeta what happened to him?" Olevia asked excitedly. "Certainly, that must have been my Uncle. What else can you tell me? What happened to him?" asked Olevia very intensely.

"Mam, what happened to him is a mystery. There are rumors, ... But I must learn more about you first, perhaps to help you understand," said Chipeta, putting off an answer to what she knew would be the inevitable questions.

UNCLE ALBERT

"Chipeta, walk with me over to the window, and away from the cadavers. It will help me remember more of my home as I look out the window," said Olevia. "I will tell you a little more about my Uncle Albert," said Olevia.

"That will be so interesting," encouraged Chipeta, as the two women walked towards the window.

"Chipeta, I remember sitting in the living room of our house in Munich, just across from the English Garden," began Olevia.

"I though you said you were from Germany, not England," challenged Chipeta immediately, proving she was paying attention.

"Of course, you remembered correctly. 'English Garden'— A strange name given to the largest park in my city. Its landscaping is more like that of the English countryside than formal European landscaping," replied Olevia, who then suddenly looked away from the window and down at the floor, her face clearly changing to a sad expression.

"Why do you look so sad when you remember a beautiful garden Doctor?" asked Chipeta.

"Chipeta," Olevia went on, shaking that painful shadow from her mind, "from the living room and bedroom windows of our house there were views of this beautifully landscaped area, created in the 'English' style, a relaxed rambling style, in contrast to the typically sculpted and organized gardens in Paris and at the palaces, like Versailles in France," Olevia said, bringing back more pleasant memories of the English Garden.

"Did your Uncle even have pain when he played with you in the English Garden?" asked Chipeta.

"Yes he did," answered Olevia. "He would talk to me about it when we walked. When we sat down in some quiet place, he would seem to be thinking, and would ask if I could think of anything to help his pain."

"What did you think of?" asked Chipeta.

"Oh, I was just a child, Chipeta. I would just put my head on his shoulder and gently rub his good hand," Olevia replied and then suddenly stopped talking and looked down at the ground again with an almost angry expression on her face.

"But why do you look so sad, or is it really anger? You had a vision. Something bad happened?" persisted Chipeta, with the insight of a Medicine Man from her tribe.

"My Uncle Albert had worked for the Frederick Bayer Company, the most famous chemical company in Munich," said Olevia, changing the subject. "Chipeta, perhaps you have taken a 'Bayer Aspirin' for a headache?" asked Olevia, now looking at her with a smile.

"Mam, our tribal healer would make us an herbal remedy from the dried leaves of Tobacco Sage and the Uintah White Water Lilly. These leaves would be boiled with Elk root to create a tea. After drinking this tea, my headache would go away, and sometimes I would have wonderful visions. Perhaps the Bayer Company should learn what was in those dried leaves!" commented Chipeta.

"Yes, you are right. Modern Science has much to learn from your Healers and their knowledge of medicine," observed Olevia. "None of the medicines we had then, except an extract from the Cocoa leaf, could help my Uncle Albert's pain. After his injury he went to study Anatomy at the Ludwig-Maximillian University. He took up the field of Anatomy because none of the famous Professors of Medicine, even in Vienna, the Medical Center of Austria, could explain to him why, he had such horrible pain. Horrible, even after the wound on his left wrist had slowly healed, leaving a painful scar."

"I still do not understand why your Uncle thought Anatomy would be the area to study instead of Chemistry?" replied Chipeta. "Didn't he want to find a stronger *drug* for his pain?"

"No, Chipeta, he wanted to find the *source* of the pain, an anatomic structure, and cut it out!" explained Olevia. "That of course was unheard of. No one would cut out a nerve. It was felt to be wrong. Doctors simply did not, and still do not, understand much about nerves."

"Chipeta, come and look at the wrist on this body," Olevia continued, moving to a nearby table. Olevia put on another pair of gloves and pulled up her scarf over her nose. Then she began pulling back the wet, moist, brownish sheet that covered the left hand and arm. "You see Chipeta where the student has removed the skin from the back of the hand and lower arm. Of course, you see the shiny white tendons that move the fingers, and the dark brown muscles that pull on those tendons to create movement of the fingers," Olevia said, pulling on the exposed extensor tendons to lift up the ghost like fingers so that they pointed at Chipeta.

Chipeta took a step back, almost as if the hand had come to life.

"Now come closer," encouraged Olevia. "Look at these small things that look like little strings. These Chipeta are the nerves. They are almost too small to see. Yet they are our connection to the world around us. They let us know we are being touched. The help us experience what the hand is touching and what is touching us. They connect our body to our mind. They tell us if something is moving in our hand, or if what we are holding is hot or cold. And . . . the nerves tell us about pain. Messages from nerves are the only way our brain can know if something is causing us pain," Olevia concluded.

Chipeta looked closely now. "Yes, I see them! All these years I watched but never saw. Those nerves are like the strings I use for my beading. They link every thing together into a web of sensation. This must be how we 'see' with our fingers, like how I can still do beading even with my eyes shut," she said with new insight into how her body functioned.

"Yes, Chipeta. And that is why my Uncle Albert knew he had to study Anatomy. Only through research into the human body could he come to understand the source of his pain. Through that research, through Anatomy dissection, he believed he could find the solution to his own pain problem, when no one else could."

"Are those nerves as strong as those tendons?" asked Chipeta.

"No they are not, Chipeta," answered Olevia. "Here, you pull as hard as you want on the tendon. It does not break, only the finger moves with more power," demonstrated Olevia. "Now you do it"

Chipeta did the same movement, "it is very strong," she agreed.

"Now pull on this nerve with the same force," instructed Olevia.

"It is just pulling apart," said Chipeta her eyes widening I amazement.

"Yes, the nerves are delicate, and must be handled very gently so we do not injure them. Especially in surgery on our patients," commented Olevia.

"Thank you for sharing this story Doctor Olevia. I am beginning to understand the story and the mystery about your Uncle Albert's disappearance and his search into nerves. Can you share any more with me from your childhood with him?" asked Chipeta.

"If you find this interesting Chipeta, then yes I can", said Olevia as she covered the exposed hand and arm back up, so they would not dry out.

Olevia removed the scarf from her face and moved again to be closer to a window. She took off her gloves and cracked open the window to get some outside air. She looked over at the western slope of the Wasatch Mountain range, to the colorful trees and red sandstone, bringing her mind and memory back to a time she spent with her Uncle Albert in Munich.

"We spent much of my childhood walking in the English Garden, in the Spring, in the Summer, and in the Fall. I would hold his left hand, as nothing was allowed to touch his painful right hand and wrist. Not even the sleeve of a shirt could touch that area. In the winter, Uncle Albert taught me to ski in the mountains in nearby Salzburg. His left hand and forearm remained without a glove even in the mountains in winter. He told me that the cold put his left hand to sleep. This seemed to deaden his pain. Uncle Albert told me 'No feeling, no pain'. He preferred numbness to pain. When the frostbite would wear off, however, his pain returned seemingly worse than before. Only cocaine then would relieve his pain," said Olevia, completing her story.

"Doctor, even as a little girl, you must have wanted to help him, give him relief somehow," observed Chipeta.

"Yes, I always felt there had to be something I could do to help my Uncle, even if the Doctors couldn't. I felt helpless, frustrated. I hated feeling that there was something I could not do. As I got a little older, Uncle Albert would tell me that rubbing his neck and shoulders was helpful at relieving the stress from the pain. I could not bear to see my Uncle Albert suffer. But what could I do?" said Olevia sadly.

Again, a dark memory became exposed from somewhere deep in her mind, and Olevia moved into the more recent memory of Uncle Albert.

"Chipeta, one day Uncle Albert just simply packed up, kissed my father, his twin brother, and kissed me, and said 'good bye'. He said he was going to America 'in search'.

"In search of what?" asked Chipeta.

"None of my relatives could ever answer that question for me," replied Olevia.

JARED BENSON

"Doctor Olevia", said Chipeta, seeing how those early memories of Uncle Albert seemed to be disturbing, "What are you doing research on now in the Anatomy Lab?"

Shutting the window and moving back over to the table, at which she had been dissecting, Olevia, put her scarf back up over her nose. "Come Chipeta, and I will show you," she said with excitement. They walked back to the table where Olevia was originally working.

"I have been dissecting the groin, the area between the place where your belt would rest and the pubic bone," Olevia said as she put on yet another pair of gloves. Olevia demonstrated the groin area of a man to Chipeta at the table where she had been dissecting before their conversation began.

"Doctor, I know this word 'groin'. I have seen words on the black board and heard students talking. I am good at languages too, like my Grandmother. I do not know the real name of the language, like 'Spanish', so I just call it Anatomy Language," said Chipeta proudly.

"That is good to know. The groin is such a strange body area to most people. They know it only on the right side as where the appendix is," said Olevia, dramatically lifting the previously dissected abdominal wall up and away from the abdominal contents to show the appendix and the right side of the colon. "This is where it would hurt if the appendix were inflamed or burst. If it burst," said Olevia, pulling the appendix away from the colon enough to cause it to tear, "then death almost always follows."

"I hope there will be drugs to fight the horrible infection and inflammation that follows the appendix bursting," commented Olevia, "but today we do not have these. Perhaps those drugs will be created by my own father, Alexander, working at the Bayer Company, she whispered aloud. Then, as she lowered the abdominal wall, she pushed those memories of childhood away. Olevia focused upon that right groin area. Groin pain was her challenge for today.

"Chipeta, this is also the region in which a hernia would form. When I was a medical student at Johns Hopkins Hospital, the Chief of Surgery, Doctor William Stewart Halsted, devised the best approach to repair a hernia. A hernia is a weakness in the muscle layers that lets a loop of intestine force its way through the muscles, over this ligament, the inguinal ligament," said Olevia. "Halsted's operation." Olevia continued, "was a method to tighten structures to narrow the opening of this weak area."

Olevia now demonstrated this to her with the cadaver. "If I put my finger over this ligament, that goes from the hip bone to the pubic bone, called the 'inguinal ligament', and if I grasp a portion of the loose small intestine, and pull it through this space, called 'the external inguinal ring', then a hernia is created. This type of hernia is called an 'inguinal hernia'. Sometimes the intestine will force its way into the scrotum. The intestinal loop can have its blood supply cut off by the pressure," Olevia explained, squeezing the loop of bowel with her fingers. "Then the intestine would die and then the man or woman would die. Similar, to the death after a ruptured appendix."

Chipeta watched all this with great interest. Doctor, can I put on gloves and touch those parts, too, like I did with the tendon and nerve?"

"Yes, of course, if you wish to," replied Olevia.

"Doctor, my people developed these same swellings sometimes. Especially the young men," said Chipeta, putting on a pair of gloves, and reaching in where Olevia had demonstrated the hernia place to be. "They say it came on after lifting heavy stones or trees while clearing a field. In the older days, after moving a buffalo they had killed from horseback. Yes, I can feel that place... Doctor, Thank you for allowing me to do that," said Chipeta pulling her hand out of the abdomen, and removing her gloves. "Our Medicine Man would treat these swellings by having a wide leather belt made to fit over the swollen place, to force it back down and keep it inside," offered Chipeta sharing her ancestral knowledge.

"Yes, excellent," said Olevia, realizing she now had a new 'colleague' with whom to share knowledge. That same approach is used still today, and the device is called a 'truss', worn by men usually who do not want an operation or who are too sick to have one. "But without a strong inside repair, as described by my Professor Halsted, the hernia would recur, that is it would often come back."

"Doctor, if this is so well known, why are you still doing research on it?" asked Chipeta.

"Halsted's successful operation for long lasting hernia repair spread world- wide. With so many new surgeons doing that operation, complications developed. Painful complications," said Olevia.

"Doctor, did you ever see this pain problem in your surgery training?" asked Chipeta.

Before answering her, Olevia started to look around the room at some of the other tables, as if searching for something.

"What are you looking for Doctor? Can I help?" asked Chipeta.

"Chipeta, when the students were in here and all the covers were off on each table, I saw one older male cadaver that had a scar in the groin area, as if a hernia repair had been done. It was amongst these tables in this corner," Olevia said pointing to a corner of the room near the window. "Let's uncover some of these and perhaps we can do some research together."

As they went together and uncovered one cadaver body after another, and then recovered it, Olevia continued, "Chipeta I had not seen this painful complication after hernia repair at Johns Hopkins Hospital when Halsted and his young surgical students, the residents, did the surgical repair. I have thought about this. Perhaps it was because the surgeons I was watching operate were so gentle when they operated, tying each bleeding vessel with fine suture material, and carefully closing each layer. Today we call this the 'Halstedian surgical technique,'" replied Olevia, and then stopped as the next cadaver she uncovered had a white, thick scar in the right lower part of the abdomen, just where Olevia had shown a hernia would occur.

"Chipeta, this is the body I saw. See that scar," Olevia said, pointing to the white line, which was a long straight line with smaller cross lines, representing where each stitch had been tied. "Well, Chipeta, now that I am in my Surgical Clinic in Salt Lake City, instead of studying in Baltimore, I often see patients whose hernia did not come back, but these people, who have no hernia, have a scar just like this one, but these men in my clinic are disabled by groin pain. And it hurts them if you touch the scar or even near the scar, and they have lost feeling in this area of the pubic hair," demonstrated Olevia pointing to the base of the penis.

Chipeta seemed lost in thought, and then said, "Doctor, the scar has a memory of the pain it has suffered."

"So here is the mystery requiring Anatomy research," Olevia explained further. "They have hernia pain and no hernia. They have numbness and yet experience pain in the numb area. Touching further up, that is here, towards the iliac crest," said Olevia pointing to these places as she taught Chipeta, "causes pain to be perceived down here towards the groin and base of the penis. These people can not sit with their hip flexed, they have difficulty walking, working and having sexual relationships with their wives," Olevia said, ending her explanation of the mystery of groin pain after a hernia repair.

"Doctor, what do you think can cause this pain if there is no hernia present," asked Chipeta, who clearly was following this line of reasoning. "Can just the scar itself mean something painful to people? If you remove the scar, can you remove their pain, or the memory of pain?"

"I have come to believe that a nerve, the ilioinguinal nerve, which goes through that hernia opening, gets stuck in the hernia repair site. This stuck, or injured nerve, is what causes the pain, and yes, a scar somewhere along the path of that nerve is responsible for the pain. It is where the nerve is injured," Olevia went on.

"Chipeta, I know now from my earlier dissections how to find this nerve up here, away from the hernia surgery. If you look for it down here, where the surgery was done, then that little white nerve just blends in with the white scar of the hernia repair. How about you help me, and we will try to find it together on this body right now?"

"I am ready to help you Doctor," said Chipeta, pulling on another pair of gloves, just as she had seen the medical students do.

Olevia already had taken a knife and was cutting through the thin abdominal wall, through the skin, down through a thin layer of fat to the white shining layer that covered the muscles below. "This is the fascia of the external oblique, the connective tissue attaching a muscle from the flank to the rectus muscle, that goes up and down on the front of the body," said Olevia. "Now the nerve we want will be going in this direction from this bone," she said pointing to the iliac crest, "to the exit of the inguinal canal," she said pointing to the scar. "During the tightening of the deep tissues to close the exit so the hernia does not occur again, that nerve gets injured."

Olevia now used her knife to slit the white thick fascia of the external oblique open. "My research is to learn how to find this little nerve in an area away from all the scar created by the hernia repair, and then to remove that nerve in order to stop the pain. "Chipeta, you grab this edge with this clamp and pull it towards yourself, and with your other hand, pull the other side away in the opposite direction."

"Yes Doctor. Like this? Am I doing it right?" Chipeta asked?

"Yes, you will make a good surgical assistant. Perhaps I will take you to the Operating Room with me," she said with a wink at her new friend.

Chipeta just grinned from ear to ear.

"Now we just look beneath this opening for a whitish brown or yellow embalmed string-like structure that should be the ilioinguinal nerve, as it lies below the fascia and on top of this dark brown muscle, the internal oblique," Olevia explained, searching.

"Doctor what is that?" said Chipeta with an excited voice, letting go of the fascia with one hand to point at something.

"You have the eagle eyes of your ancestor hunters, Chipeta," said Olevia. "Yes that is it. Not very big is it? And see if we gently lift it and follow it, the nerve goes directly down into that hernia scar."

"But what is that other little line," asked Chipeta, pointing.

"Yes, Chipeta, I see it. Yes, it is another, even smaller nerve. Very hard to see in this cadaver. Good for you. This one has been described before; it is called the iliohypogastric nerve. Let us pull on it and see where it goes?" said Olevia excitedly.

"The old scar is moving again, Doctor," said Chipeta.

"This is wonderful observation. It means that pain in that scar can come from two different nerves, not just one," explained Olevia.

"I am beginning to understand," replied Chipeta. "So, you operate like this. You find this nerve. You then cut this nerve to disconnect it. Then, no nerve signals get through from the scar. Then there is no nerve pain. And there is numbness instead of pain."

"Yes, exactly. Chipeta, I am so impressed with how quickly you understand and accept this new knowledge of Anatomy and how it can help us to help people in pain. But doing this surgery proved not to be so simple for me," responded Olevia in a now sad voice.

"Did you try this surgery and it failed?" asked Chipeta.

"Yes. In an attempt to help such a patient, whose hernia had been repaired by a Surgeon of good reputation in Salt Lake City, I operated on the man again to find that ilioinguinal nerve. That man, Mr. Jared Benson, gave me permission to try to find that nerve and remove it. I operated on him, but not like we just did. Not knowing this approach when I first operated, I re-opened the original hernia repair site. I could not find the little white nerve in the white hernia repair scar. The thick scar is the same color as the nerve. I made a new incision up higher, and found the ilioinguinal nerve coming into the hernia repair scar. I removed that nerve, but he did not get any pain relief."

Chipeta just nodded as if she could picture this.

Olevia went on, "My surgery failed. My patient awoke from surgery with the same pain. Now, Mr. Benson had been very depressed prior to my surgery. The failed attempt to relieve him of his pain made him even more depressed. When he did not come in from the farm at dinnertime last week, one of his children went looking for him. The son found his father hanging by the neck in his barn. Jared Benson was dead. I learned of this the next day, which was just earlier this very week. I have never had a patient who died related to surgery that I did," Olevia said dejectedly, finishing her story.

Chipeta was just silent. Then said, "Doctor, even though this Mr. Benson did not die during your surgery, you clearly feel responsible for this death. What did you say to his family?"

"I did not have an answer for his family. Was I wrong in my assumption about the cause of his pain? Was I wrong to operate on him?" Olevia asked, repeating the question she thought was on Chipeta's mind.

"Doctor, can Anatomy ever be wrong?" asked Chipeta.

"Anatomy has many variations. Not all people are built the same way. Perhaps, yes, there can be another nerve, not just the ilioinguinal nerve. Maybe another nerve is involved. Although I love Anatomy, abnormal or unusual Anatomy can also be the Enemy," responded Olevia.

BACK ON THE HORSE

"Doctor, will you be afraid to do that surgery again?" Chipeta asked Dr. Landsmann.

Olevia turned quietly away from Chipeta and walked over to the Anatomy Lab window. It was now almost dark outside. The house lights were coming on. The sky, over the Wasatch Mountain range, was a beautiful evening color. Olevia removed her scarf and her gloves. She took a deep, a cleansing breath, and turned to look at Chipeta.

"When one of your young Ute men would fall from his horse, learning to ride, what advice did your tribal elders have for him?" asked Olevia.

"They told him, and if necessary forced him, to get back up on that horse and try again until he had mastered riding. Our Ute warriors became excellent horseman," answered Chipeta quickly, proudly.

"Yes, and that is the right approach whenever learning a new technique, be it a sport, a hobby or a profession. Well, Chipeta," said Olevia, "I have been thinking back to the pioneers of surgery whom I observed at Johns Hopkins Hospital. I remember the stories of how the first Neurosurgeon, Dr. Harvey Cushing, operated on patients for brain tumor. Each patient surely would have died of that tumor. No surgeon had ever successfully removed a brain tumor and had the patient live. Each of Dr. Cushing's first ten or so patients did die during or immediately after surgery," said Olevia retelling this story.

"Oh, my," said Chipeta.

"Should Cushing have stopped after his first patient died?" asked Olevia. Should Cushing have stopped after his tenth patient died? Cushing persevered with his research until he found the right approach to operate on the brain. This took laboratory research into the fluids that surrounded the brain and research into measuring the pressure of that fluid around the brain. That research finally permitted a patient to live after brain surgery. Today those techniques are being taught to new surgeons who are now operating on the brain successfully," said Olevia somewhat upbeat as she finished this story.

"Doctor," said Chipeta, slowly. "I know how hard it is to be a pioneer, as you are trying to be. The early pioneers in Utah, the first white settlers, fought with my ancestors. Seems there is always someone to fight against the Pioneers. Seems to me that you are going to be a Surgical Pioneer. Are you a fighter, Doctor?"

Olevia remained silent, looking to the Wasatch Mountains, as the sky darkened. Perhaps looking for inspiration in the beautiful but fading colors. "I am a hard worker Chipeta, and I will stand up for the ideas that my research proves are right, but I somehow never thought of that as fighting,"

Chipeta continued, "My parents told me about the stories of the Mormon Pioneers, and other Pioneers who came out here, to Utah, to live. They had so much to learn. So many died. So much we each had to learn from each other, Mormons and Utes and the U.S. Army.

"Well, Chipeta, that of course was real fighting," agreed Olevia.

After a pause, Chipeta continued, a little sadly, "Right here, where this Anatomy Lab is, used to be the old Army base, Fort Douglas. Colonel Connor was in charge. When the Army came, in 1862, they fought with my people, originally to protect the mail carried by the Pony Express. By the next year, due to loss of land to the Mormon settlers, our tribes were pushed further up North. Our tribes lost land used for agriculture and hunting. In the winter, my ancestors were starving. They began to raid the camps of the settlers. It was at that time that Colonel Connor went north to 'punish' my people. In 1863, he massacred my people at the Bear River, and that is still called today 'Connor's 300-man campaign'. He had 220 Calvary and 80 more men with his artillery. He defeated one of our Ute tribes, the Shoshoni, and my distant cousin, Chief Sagwitch and his son were badly wounded but survived to tell the story. Colonel Connor was promoted to General, today, we all do live together in peace."

"It seems that often death must be the price of progress," Olevia said philosophically.

"And you Doctor, does that mean you will do the same operation again?" asked Chipeta.

Olevia listened quietly, seeing the parallel, as Chipeta understood it. Then Olevia said, "As saddened as I am by the death of Jared Benson, my patient, I am still convinced that my theory about the ilioinguinal nerve and groin pain is correct. That is why I forced myself to come back to the Anatomy building today. Together, you and I did find a better approach to locate a second nerve that I must also remove when I do this operation the next time," Olevia said smiling. "In the next surgery for this problem, I will make just one incision, but up here, away from the first surgery, and . . . I will look for two different nerves, not just one."

"So, you are back here with the dead and have learned another of their secrets?" said Chipeta, also smiling. "I am honored to have shared this sacred experience with you."

"Yes, exactly. What could I do differently? In this dimly lit room, with all its smell, I must continue to dissect. Chipeta, I too, like one of my teachers, Harvey Cushing, must persevere through failure. Research into the human body is the answer, the source of truth for the surgeon."

Olevia wiped a drip of perspiration from her nose. How long, she wondered, would it take tonight for the formaldehyde to evaporate from her nostril hairs?

"Can I help you search for secrets again, Doctor?" asked Chipeta.

"Sure, if you wish to," Olevia said. As she put on yet another pair of gloves.

"Doctor, will you really let me see an operation on a living person?" asked Chipeta.

"Would you like to learn how to assist at surgery?" asked Chipeta.

"Oh yes, Doctor, if that were ever possible for someone like me," Chipeta said humbly.

"I will see what I can do," offered Olevia, who now observed her own fingertips. They were wrinkled, puckered like the skin of a prune. She used to have beautiful soft hands, perhaps hands someone would want to hold again, one day. But not today! Today her hands were cold and smelled like bad wine. She wiggled her fingers into the new gloves, picked up her dissecting instruments, and dug down, more deeply, into the mysteries of the groin: into her research.

"Chipeta," Olevia said, "Let us see how many cadavers have the two nerves separate from each other in this location."

What Olevia might find during her dissection excited her, motivated her, and, might be the secret that she sought: how to solve groin pain after a hernia operation.

Her Uncle Albert's quest, like her own quest now, were probably similar: Find the location of the nerve or nerves that transmitted the message of pain and find a way to stop that message by dividing the nerve or nerves sending the pain message.

CIRCUS OF PERGAMON, 190 AD

"Doctor," said Chipeta, "Do you know that I also am responsible for cleaning the office of the Director of the Anatomy Lab?"

"No, I did not really know what else you did," answered Olevia.

"Well Doctor, now that I know you and I both share a love for History, maybe you would stop working for a little, let your fingers regain some feeling. Come with me to the Director's Office. There are some wall displays that I just know you will love," suggested Chipeta to her new friend.

Olevia smiled inwardly. "Ok Chipeta, my back is starting to hurt anyway from bending over this table," she said as she took off her gloves, pulled down her mask and started to walk towards the door with Chipeta.

They walked down a hall that went next to the Anatomy Lab, and approached what Olevia knew to be the office of the first Professor of Anatomy at the University of Utah, Ephraim G. Gowans, MD. A sign in Latin hung over the entrance way to the administrative offices: *Mortui vos Liberabunt.*

"Chipeta, I love that sign. It is what anatomic research is all about," said Olevia.

"Please tell me what it means in that other language," asked Chipeta.

"It means 'the dead shall set you free', translated Olevia, as she and Chipeta opened the door and entered the small administrative area. "And it is such a co-incidence. The motto of the Johns Hopkins University, where I went to medical school is so similar, *"Veritas vos Liberabit"*, meaning "The Truth shall set you Free." If we equate them, for example as in mathematics, we perhaps get a solution that says 'The Dead are Truth," said Olevia philosophically.

"Doctor, you know so many languages," commented Chipeta, "and now look at this one," she said pointing ahead of them.

"It is the custom in Europe, where I grew up, to have instruction in Classic Languages, such as Latin and Greek," replied Olevia. "A lot of the names you hear in the Anatomy Lab are derived from these two languages.

Chipeta, watching Olevia's reaction, and said, "I knew you would like to see this. Looks like our Anatomy Lab but it is from a fight in ancient times. Perhaps from a time before even the Utes roamed this land."

Olevia looked intensely at the picture and could see a gladiator lying on a stone table, his head tilted to the right from the sword blow that created the large gash in the left side of his neck. Blood no longer spurted from the carotid artery, which now was exposed, continuing slowly to drip blood into the wound. The gladiator's evidence of life, his blood, was being covered with fresh sand as the Circus, the arena, was prepared for the next fight.

"Chipeta. Perhaps this is how you should clean the floor of our Anatomy lab, with sand," Olevia said, jokingly, pointing to the painting.

"I could not put dirt on the floor, Doctor," Chipeta said seriously.

"Chipeta, that was what they had back in those days. So in this drawing, the area where the two men fight, men who were then called Gladiators, in the time of the Romans, that floor is covered with sand. The Roman, which is to say the Latin word for sand is *harena*. We pronounce it 'arena.'"

"Thank you Doctor for explaining this to me. You must have been an excellent student," said Chipeta with a smile. "What does it say in those small, complicated words at the bottom of the painting?"

Olevia noted now that the illustration of the gladiator had footnotes. "It says that Emperor Commodus, who became Emperor of Rome after Marcus Aurelius, had continued building in northeastern Turkey, at Pergamon, until a huge Temple had been constructed. Such a city required an appropriate Circus to amuse its citizens. In the late second century after the birth of Jesus Christ, 200,000 people lived in Pergamon, on the shore of the Eastern Mediterean." Olevia then pointed to the center of the seated area and said, "Here is the Emperor Commodus, in the center of these seats with the canopy to protect him from the sun. He is probably discussing the next gladiator fight to begin in the arena. They called this whole round theater a 'Circus'."

Chipeta then asked, "Who is this man taking care of the injured gladiator? Is he a surgeon?"

Olevia studied the footnotes at the bottom of the page some more, and then answered, "He is the Emperor's Chief Physician, Galen of Pergamon. He was a doctor. Back then, Chipeta, a doctor did everything. There were not separate specialties, like surgery. There were not actually many true operations that were done. That knowledge did not exist. It was not even understood how the body functioned. The doctor tried to stop bleeding, help wounds heal, and try to line up broken bones."

"Doctor, why would Galen's picture be in an Anatomy Lab?" Chipeta asked.

Olevia actually had read about Galen, and could answer this question. "Galen was an observant man, and had a questioning mind. He tried to learn about the human body from simple inspection and manipulation of the gladiator's wounds. Even if Galen's goal was to learn how to better help other gladiators in distress, and even as the Physician to the Emperor, Galen was forbidden to dissect, or cut into, a dead gladiator. He was forbidden to do then what we do every day in this Anatomy Lab. He was not allowed to do what you saw me doing today, and what you see the medical students doing."

"That is amazing. How did we then get to this point where there are Anatomy books and all students are required to study by dissecting?" asked Chipeta.

Olevia then walked over to another illustration that was labeled "Role of the Church in Anatomical Teaching through Dissection."

"Chipeta, that is such an interesting question and gets right to the point of how important it is for students to be able to do what you see happening so 'normally' here today," said Olevia.

"For example, Chipeta," Olevia said, "the word 'dissection' in Latin means 'to cut into pieces'." Then, reading from the illustration in front of her, she continued, "In the year 150 AD, Roman law forbid the dissection of humans. In the Roman Empire, where the Pope played a central role in the thought process and morality, the human body was sacred, and not allowed to be studied after death. The human body could not be cut open, even by a physician, trying to understand how the body worked."

"Doctor, how could this Galen then learn how to help people who had been injured?" asked Chipeta.

"Galen had no books on human anatomy to guide him," answered Olevia. "There were no books yet written on human anatomy. So Galen wrote his own book that showed what he had learned about anatomy from his own observations of the injured gladiators."

"Doctor, then you are going to have to write your own observations of anatomy to teach other doctors how to help people," suggested Chipeta.

"Yes, Chipeta, that is what I will have to do. Write so others can read what has been learned. This is important Chipeta because there just always seems to be someone who is against introducing new knowledge," said Olevia

"What do you mean, Doctor?" said Chipeta.

"Well, here is an example right on this chart of the history of the Popes and their influence on human dissection," said Olevia pointing to the dates on the chart.

"Pope Eleutherius, who was the Pope from 175 to 189 AD, and his successor, Pope Victor I, who was the Pope from 189 to 199 AD, were against dissection. They were the Pope's during Galen's time as Chief Physician to the Emperor."

"Why were the Popes against dissecting if that was needed to learn how to help people who were injured and suffering," Chipeta kept inquiring.

"Chipeta, here is an historical note, at the bottom of this chart, that may answer your question," said Olevia, who continued then to read aloud, "the Popes were concerned about the dead person's body being resurrected."

Before Olevia could continue reading further, Chipeta interrupted her, "What is resurrection, Doctor?"

"Chipeta, it is like your ancestors going up to the sky to be with the Great Spirit. In ancient times in Europe, this concern over resurrection was not a purely Catholic concern. The Orthodox Jews of Palestine believed that their dead bodies would rise intact to enter the Kingdom of God upon the day the Messiah returned to Jerusalem. The devout Jews insisted on being buried intact, as the Prophet Isaiah had written in the Old Testament.

Thy dead shall live, thy dead bodies shall arise,

awake and sing, ye that dwell in the dust,

for thy dew is as the dew of light, and

the earth shall bring to life the shades (Isaiah 26:19).

Chipeta observed, "Yes, Doctor, you are correct. My people, the Utes, also believed in burial and the after life. This is why we keep our burial grounds sacred."

"This history about the Popes continues," said Olevia. She continued reading: "The Papal Bulletin of Pope Boniface VIII, who was the Pope from 1294 to 1303, gave a reason for not permitting dissection. This reason was that during the time of the Crusades, the knights and royalty, who died in the Holy Land, had to be sent back to their homeland to be buried. They had no way to preserve the bodies.

The bodies were usually dissected, by disembowelment; their flesh separated from their bones, and their bones boiled. These bones could then be sent back home to Europe and England for burial."

Olevia read on, "Pope Boniface VIII wrote,

> "As there exists a certain abuse, which is characterized by the most abominable savagery, but which nevertheless some of the faithful have stupidly adopted, We, prompted by motives of humanity, have decreed that all further mangling of the human body, the very mention of which fills the soul with horror, should be henceforth abolished."

"What happened," Chipeta asked, "if someone did dissect a human body?"

Olevia answered, "Chipeta, it says here, in the end of this foot note, 'While the Pope did not use the term 'dissection', the meaning of this pronouncement was taken to include that it was sacrilegious to mutilate the human body, even for science, even for finding new knowledge. By Papal decree, 'mutilating' the human body was punishable by excommunication from the Catholic Church."

"Dissection was considered as mutilation?" Chipeta asked. "I understand this. What the medical students do in here is more like mutilation, compared to what you do Doctor."

"In an interesting way, Chipeta, Galen, standing in the Circus at Pergamon, could watch the dissecting instruments of the arena. These were the sword, the knife, the axe, and the trident. He could watch the gladiators dissect each other. Gladiators were permitted to do this work on each other, on the living, yet Galen, the Physician, was not permitted to do this on the dead."

Chipeta then asked, "What is this showing with the pictures of monkeys?" pointing to the next large panel of the display.

"It says that the Pope had no moral prohibitions about dissecting non-human animals. This is the reason why Galen experimented on live animals, called vivisection. What Galen could not discern from the gladiators, he tried to learn by dissecting 'apes'. Barbary apes were available to him from North Africa. These animals are actually monkeys and not apes. They lived in the mountainous regions of the Barbary Coast of North Africa, which we today call Morocco," said Olevia, pointing to a region of a map, that showed both North America and Africa. "Galen believed that these 'apes' would be quite similar to humans."

Chipeta moved in front now of Olevia to look at the next part of the display. "I have looked at these for many years, but have never read them, Doctor. You are helping me to understand so much. Although I am a good talker, my ability to read is not so good. I can see this says 'Research'. But what research did Galen do, Doctor?"

"I am happy to help you read this Chipeta," said Olevia. "It says *'Observations from Galen's Vivisections'*, meaning what Galen learned form operating on living animals.

1) To study function, Galen was the first to tie cords around nerves, establishing that they served motor function, since the parts that were past the tied cord would stop moving. This was similar to what Galen observed on the gladiators when an injury occurred in the leg to a nerve.

2) To study consciousness, Galen observed that, when he divided an artery in the sides of the neck, there would be loss of blood from the divided artery, and consciousness could still persist for a while, a long

with persistent function. This was similar to what Galen observed on the gladiators who, when pierced through the heart, remained conscious and clear in their thoughts until their heart was still.

3) Galen was the first to distinguish nerves from tendons. From the injured but living gladiators Galen identified tendons, and could prove their function by pulling on them to see the fingers move. He observed nerves but knew only that if they were touched while the gladiator was still alive, extreme pain was perceived. He made these same observations in his vivisection on the Barbary Apes.

"Thank you Doctor," said Chipeta. "That is just what you showed me with the tendons in the Anatomy Lab earlier today."

"Yes, exactly. That part of what Galen taught is still true today, as you and I could confirm with a simple experiment."

"And what is this last section with the big drawing of the heart. That heart does not really look like the hearts I see in the Anatomy Lab," remarked Chipeta.

"Yes, you are right," said Olevia looking at the final panel in the display. "On this side, it shows a drawing of a heart, and says that the earliest Philosophers, like Aristotle, from the Macedonian part of Greece, who, lived in 384-322 BC, considered the heart as the 'seat of wisdom'. Galen thought differently. He thought that blood moved from one side of the heart into the other side of the heart through little openings that he could only imagine, and therefore the heart supplied food to the muscles of the body. Galen believed the brain was the 'seat of wisdom'."

"But doctor, today we do not believe the heart supplies food to the muscles," observed Chipeta.

"Chipeta, this is the way with the history of ideas. Galen was a good writer. His books were translated into many languages. They were considered 'truth' for the next 1300 years, but that is enough Anatomy history for today. One day you and I can come back and start with this next section, with the title Vesalius, 1543. He wrote an Anatomy book based upon dissecting humans, the way you and I were doing today."

"Thank you Doctor, for teaching me. Now I must continue my work for tonight," Chipeta said walking back to the Anatomy Lab.

"Good night Chipeta. I will let you go back to your work. Thank you for showing me this History of Anatomy. You have today been a student who has taught her teacher. These readings reminded me that established religion was the earliest impediment to surgical knowledge. Dissecting another human is what a student must do to learn anatomy," said Olevia.

Then as she walked out the door, Olevia turned and said to her new friend, "I enjoyed talking with you Chipeta. Our talk reinforces for me my choice to be a Surgeon. Our time together here today reinforces that surgery requires dissection of the living, which is surgery. Direct observation at dissection leads to understanding, and then, perhaps, to truth."

"Chipeta", Olevia concluded with confidence, "My next patient with pain after a hernia repair will get relief of that pain through surgery because of what we found here today."

CONNOR CORNER STORE

Walking home from the Anatomy Building, Olevia breathed in the fresh air. It was just turning Fall. The building with the Anatomy Lab was located just half a mile from the foothills of the Wasatch Mountain range. Looking directly ahead as she walked east was the opening to Red Butte Canyon.

She could look up to its height, about 8,000 feet above sea level. She could see the red sandstone, from which the canyon received its name. She knew that when the Mormons first settled Salt Lake City, in 1847, they quarried this strong stone for their earliest buildings.

Olevia loved this walk to her little house, on the corner of Red Butte Canyon Road and Connor Road. As the formaldehyde begin to evaporate from her nose with each consecutive breath, the recent memory of her arrival into Salt Lake City began to block out the dimly lit environment she had just left.

She had gotten off the Pullman coach car arriving at Union Pacific Station, Salt Lake City, Utah. The porter brought her luggage from the baggage car. She followed him through the beautiful station, recently completed in 1907. It was constructed of red sandstone. There were beautiful stained-glass windows. On the ceiling, was a portrait of Promontory Summit, located just north of Salt Lake City, showing the golden spike being driven into the track at the completion of the transcontinental railroad. She turned back to look at the front of the station as the porter let her out, and looked up to the see the large, shield-shaped, Union Pacific Railroad emblem, right over the front door.

Olevia was coming to town to look for place to live, but wanted to see where she was going to work first. She had been hired to work in the new medical school.

As Olevia entered the taxi, she asked the driver, "Do you know where the new University of Utah Medical School is located?"

"Yes Mam," he replied. "It is where the new buildings are going up near the old U.S. Army barracks at Fort Douglas."

Olevia remembered the driver as being slim, with a long grey beard, sitting up straight as an arrow. She remembered asking the driver, "Why was there a need for an Army fort out here?"

"Used to be called Camp Douglas. Set up to protect the U.S. mail moving along the old overland route. Protect the telegraph, too. Sometime after that they decided to name it a Fort. Don't know why. But it hasn't been used much and the new Medical School has put some of its people into those old buildings," the driver said knowingly, and proud of himself for knowing it.

"Very interesting," commented Olevia to the driver. Olevia could see now as she walked, how this memory from her first arrival into Salt Lake City was coinciding with some of the stories that Chipeta had just told her.

"I know the University of Utah has been around a long time," Olevia remembered asking the taxi driver. "Seems strange to just now decide to build a medical school," she asked, interested to see what his local knowledge of the place was.

"Well, Mam," he replied politely. "We only have about 600,000 people here in the Salt Lake Valley. The old Salt Lake County General Hospital has some pretty good people, mostly trained back East. Guess someone decided we ought to start training our own doctors out here. About time I'd say."

The taxi driver took her down Fort Douglass Boulevard along the row of the original soldier's barracks. These were two-story, red brick buildings with chimneys in the center, pointed triangular gables at the corners, and white wood-outlined balconies across the entire front of the building. There was green grass in between each building and ample lawn in the front. Driving past these, the taxi driver pointed out the officer's quarters, which were individual homes, again with red brick and white wood moldings. Further along were the stables for the horses. There was also a beautiful gazebo, again, of white wood.

The taxi driver slowed down as he approached the southeast corner of Fort Douglas, and stopped in front of what was clearly a cemetery.

"Why are you stopping here?" asked Olevia, suspiciously.

"You seemed interested in the history of this area, Mam. No extra charge to you for this little stop," the taxi driver explained. "Here is where the first soldiers, who died in a fight with the Shoshoni Indians at Bear River, are buried. That massacre killed 350 Indians, the most ever on a single day by the U.S. Army. It was in 1863. The stone monument is for General Patrick Edward Connor, the commander at that time. We are proud of the fact that later, the 24th Infantry Regiment was stationed here. It was one of three Negro Regiments in the US Army at the time. The '24th' left to fight in the Spanish-American War in Cuba and distinguished themselves. Many who died in that fight are buried here.

"Were you in the military," Olevia asked.

"No Mam. I was not in the military, but I am a member of the Mormon community here in Salt Lake City. Our community welcomed those Negro soldiers and the members of the Military became part of the culture of our city. There are more than 1300 soldiers buried here. One day, Miss, you might want to walk through and read the tombstones," said the taxi driver as he finished his impromptu tour.

At the mention of the name 'General Connor', Olevia smiled, because today she lived at the corner of Red Butte Canyon and Connor Roads. And today, Chipeta told the story of the fight at Bear River, and Colonel Connor being promoted after winning the 'Campaign of the 300'. She smiled again as she thought *the General is still remembered. Therefore, he is still alive.*

This made Olevia think of her family home in Munich. Her family motto, the motto of the Landsmann family was 'to be remembered is to live forever'. This motto was written in Latin on the Landsmann family crest. As the story of General Connor is retold, and as she approached the street with his name on it, she appreciated again that, religious beliefs aside, the very act of remembering someone does give that person a form of immortality, and that person does live on, even if only in memory.

Memorandum est Vivere in Aeturnum, was the Latin form of the Landsmann motto.

As Olevia now continued walking towards her own home, she realized how thirsty she was from the Anatomy Lab dissection and the dehydrating formaldehyde. She walked into the Connor Corner Store for a drink.

"Hey there Olevia" called out a cheerful female voice from one of the little wooden tables in the corner. "Come on over, you look a little pale, and down!"

Olevia smiled warmly as she walked over to the table and sat next to a colleague. Jennie Ross, a Canadian woman doctor who specialized in delivering babies. Olevia and she had become friends, both sharing inquiring minds and having to defend themselves continually in the male-dominated medical environment.

"You stink", said Jennie. "Have you been spending more time studying with your departed friends?"

"Yes. Good guess. Your nose is not only beautiful, and long, it is also well-educated. I'm on my way home to shower, but I am so thirsty. That root beer in a frosty mug you're drinking looks good. I'm going to have one too," said Olevia, waving to the waitress who was on her way over to their table.

Jennie's usually pretty, smiling face now took on a serious expression.

"The rumor is spreading already," said Jennie. "One of your patient's hanged himself. Salt Lake is still a pretty small place, especially amongst the medical communities."

"Yes, it is true. I am sure this is all that the male Surgeons need to start after me again. They still cannot believe these little nerves can cause pain, and that a Surgeon, and especially a woman Surgeon, can find them and remove them safely from the body," replied Olevia, happy to have someone to confide in.

"What were you trying to find in that man's lower quadrant anyway?" asked Jennie. "From what I hear, he did not have a new hernia nor did he have appendicitis. The other, as you call them, 'male Surgeons', say you had no reason to operate on that patient, and that is what the kindest of them say. I have been told, that some of the men think you have the need to castrate your male colleagues, and you were symbolically just getting back at a man when you did that surgery!"

Olevia's mouth fell open. She took her eyes off Jennie's beautiful face. Olevia was just quiet for a moment. Then she looked back up to her friend. Looked her squarely in the eyes.

"Jennie, you deliver babies. But you are also a Surgeon, a woman Surgeon. Sometimes you have to open the woman's abdomen to save the baby if the delivery is complicated, right?" asked Olevia not answering her friend's question.

"Yes, I do" replied her friend, "but what does that have to do with a hernia repair?"

"And Jennie", Olevia hurried on, wanting to make an important connection, "You have to open the abdomen down low near the pubic bone when you operate to remove tumors of the uterus, right?"

"Yes, I do," replied Jennie again, not following Olevia's train of thought.

"Have any of your patients come back to you months after surgery with pain down near their scar?" asked Olevia, her brain finally making the connection she was looking for.

"Some of the women do have pain. Actually most have a lot of pain for while, and then it goes away. But in some, yes, they have pain wearing their clothes. They have pain when their scar is rubbing up against their husband, and so they won't sleep next to him. Is that what you mean?" answered Jennie, her long hair now moving forward off her ample breasts, as she leaned forward.

"Yes. Exactly. That is what happens to male hernia patients too, about ten percent of them in my experience out here. So, Jennie, why do your women patients have pain after they are healed from your surgery?" asked Olevia, trying to help Jennie follow the same approach to helping a woman patient with pain.

Jennie suddenly sat up straight and pushed her root beer to the side. "Is that what you were trying to do with that hernia patient? Relieve his post-op pain?" she asked.

"Yes, exactly", said Olevia. "That is what I was trying to do to help that poor man, Jared Benson."

"Mr. Benson had so much pain. He could not even drink to try to kill his pain, as so many do, because he was a Mormon and did not drink alcohol. He could not work his farm. He told me that he could not sleep close to and hold his wife because when his groin scar would touch her it hurt him so much. He could not play with his children," continued Olevia.

"No wonder those surgeons are so upset with you. They have never even thought of that approach. No one has cut out an injured nerve to relieve pain after a hernia surgery. Now if you were successful what would they say? But you failed," said Jennie.

"Mr. Benson was already so depressed from the pain after his hernia repair, that the failure of my surgery to relieve his pain just pushed him over the edge!" explained Olevia.

"There is no answer to any of this in our books or teachings," said Dr. Jennie Ross, seeming now to understand the problem and the connections Olevia was getting at. "You think that some of these little nerves to the skin are at fault? We do always cut them of course with our incisions. Are you saying that in some people, those little nerves get caught up in the scar and create pain?"

"That is exactly what I think, Jennie. Our anatomy books do show these nerves to the skin. They do *not* show us how we are to find them at surgery. None of our surgery textbooks, or teachers instruct us how to remove those injured nerves. In fact, in the now world-famous writings of how to repair a hernia, written by my own teacher, Dr. William Steward Halsted, in the Bulletin of the Johns Hopkins Hospital, with wonderful illustrations, the ilioinguinal nerve is not even shown once!"

"What made you think a nerve was the source of Mr. Benson's pain and that you could find it?" asked Jennie, brushing her long dark hair away from her eyes so she could see Olevia more clearly. In contrast, Olevia had short brown hair, closely shaped to her head, a haircut more likely seen on men.

"Jennie, if you perceive pain, that sensation can only be transmitted through a nerve. The question then becomes, which nerve, or nerves sends the pain message to the brain after hernia surgery?" explained Olevia.

Olevia noted the movement Jennie made to move her beautiful long hair away from her pretty face and noted looking down from that pretty face to Jennie's loose blouse, how it flattered her rather large chest. Olevia glanced down at her own outfit, a tight thick shirt outlined her rather thin frame, and her shirt was tucked into her pants.

"Ok, Olevia" said Jennie, following her logic. "Then you have to find the nerve and cut it, right?'

"Yes, exactly," answered Olevia, "And then what to do with the live end of the nerve which will still be there attached to the spine?" continued Olevia with her inquiring, research-related, question. "If we cannot answer these questions, then we may create more pain by cutting the nerve."

"Your perfume Olevia," Jennie said trying to interject some fun into this sad conversation, "*Fragrance of Formaldehyde*, suggests that your body is consumed with lessons from the deceased. You have literally invested yourself with the concept that only their bodies hold the answers, the secrets, THE truth you are looking for. Please find a new perfume," Jennie said with a warm smile, and reached out and touched Olevia's hand.

They each ordered another root beer.

"Today in the Anatomy laboratory, I began to view the Anatomy book, as the Sacred Text for doctors, especially for those doing Surgery," said Olevia. "The anatomy described in that book is God's truth about how we are constructed. Jennie, what if there is something we need to know that is not in that book? Did God forget to put a nerve into the human body? Is the anatomy book wrong? Perhaps those great artists who interpreted the findings of the human body at the time, just overlooked, or did not see a little tiny nerve that is really there?" questioned Olevia. "What did you find today, during your Anatomy Lab research dissection?" prompted Jennie.

"Well," replied Olevia, "I found the exact pathway the ilioinguinal nerve goes that is causing the pain most of the time in patients who have had a hernia repair. And, Jennie, there are probably usually two nerves, the ilioinguinal and iliohypogastric nerves."

"Nice. How did you find it?" asked Jennie with interest.

"I found it not by opening where the first surgery would be, the place where a hernia would be repaired, or where you sewed up the abdomen after delivering a baby or removing the uterus, because these little nerves would not be distinguished from the scar itself," explained Olevia. "So, I went higher up, and opened the top layer of the abdominal wall covering, which you know is the thick white covering of the external oblique muscle, and, right there, just under that layer, lying on top of the muscle, the internal oblique muscle, was the ilioinguinal nerve. The very nerve I found in my patient, Jared Benson. But next to it, was a second nerve, the iliohypogastric nerve. I did not find it in Jared, because I operated where the previous surgery was, and was content to find just one nerve when I operated higher up. Now I know from my research today how to plan a better operation for the next time someone like Jared Benson comes to my clinic."

"Wonderful" said Jennie, "Problem solved."

"No. Not really. I believe my findings today in one cadaver. How often is the anatomy like that? Is it always the same on each side? You may know, they both come from about the same place in the spine and can separate from each other. It is important I think to look for two nerves there and not just one," Olevia said thoughtfully. "And I must repeat the dissection on many more cadavers to learn better the variations. I started to do this, but it was just getting too late."

"Ok," said Jennie, following this line of reasoning. "Then you will just have to look for two nerves," and she took her hand back from where it had been touching the back of Olevia's hand and resumed her grasp of her own root beer glass.

Olevia was quiet for a minute and took another sip of her root beer. "I have to question really, the future," Olevia said with a pause. "Can I bring myself to do this operation again on someone in pain knowing that failure and death occurred the first time I did this operation. Will any male surgeon even refer another patient to me? I am honestly worried about my future here at the University."

SKI JUMP

The two women surgeons finished their drinks and left the Connor Corner store. They walked close to each other, a clear bond between them. They faced similar obstacles and criticisms. They knew that they each suffered the same insecurities about their role in the Man's world of Surgery and faced the same prejudices about the work they had chosen for their life. There was strength in their bond together.

Jennie Ross lived near to where Olevia lived and as they walked east along Connor Road she offered, "See that big 'U' written on the side of the west-facing slope of Red Butte Canyon?"

"Sure," Olevia said. "It's huge. Why do you point it out?"

"You never asked me why I am working out here in Salt Lake City," said Jennie, encouraging a question from Olevia

"Ok, then Jen. Why did you decide to practice OB-GYN here in Salt Lake City?" Olevia obliged.

"Well, now that you asked," Jennie said, giving Olevia a wink, "I was born in Canada, and grew up skiing in the Canadian Rockies. There was no opportunity for a woman to go into 'Female Surgery' in Western Canada, so I applied and was accepted to the new Women's Medical College of Pennsylvania. You know – the one that used to be called the Female Medical College of Pennsylvania. They changed their name to that in 1867. They had their own Women's Hospital of Philadelphia, too, where I trained to deliver babies and do surgery on women. When I finished my training, there still was no place for me back home in Canada where I would be accepted to do what I was trained to do. Therefore, I came here to give it a try. There seemed to be a lot of pioneering spirit out here," answered Dr. Jennie Ross, Surgeon.

"What does that have to do with the big 'U' painted on the side of the hill"? Olevia interrupted her.

"That is the local ski jump!" she said with a smile, hoping understanding would come to Olevia. "They are developing lots of trails, up in the mountains, east of Salt Lake City", she went on to explain. "Try to imagine that slope covered with snow."

"I'm in!" said Olevia. "My father's twin brother, my Uncle Albert taught me to ski in the Austrian part of the Alps, Salzburg. I do miss skiing."

"Twins! I love twins," said Jennie. "They are so special, and there are so many great stories. They are very difficult to deliver safely, especially for the mother's safety," Jennie continued, now a Surgeon teaching a 'fellow' Surgeon.

"Why is that?" challenged Olevia. "Don't you just let 'Mother Nature' take her course?"

"Birth in the 19th century was a painful and dangerous process," taught Jennie. "When Queen Victoria gave birth to Leopold, her first child, in 1853, she was given a drug, a chemical used to relieve pain called Chloroform. They would not have had this drug at the time your father was born."

Memories now started coming back to Olevia. "My Father, Alexander, told me the story of how his mother died. Her name was Alexandra. My Father was named for her. Alexandra was my grandmother. My Father's Father was Jakob Landsmann. He was my Grandfather."

"What do you remember being told about their birth, the birth of twin boys?" asked Jennie the Obstetrician.

"My Grandmother died in childbirth," said Olevia, retelling the story. "She died in childbirth, as a result of an emergency C-section."

"Oh my," said Jennie, sadly, empathizing with Olevia. Then, Jennie continued teaching: "A baby being born headfirst into the world, had a good chance of surviving the delivery, and so did the mother, if the baby's head was not too large. If it was too large, the doctor delivering the baby could make an opening into the living baby's skull, breaking the bones, or craniotomy, in an attempt to get the baby out of the mother's pelvis. The mother often lived; the baby almost always died."

Olevia's eyes widened at this horrible concept.

Jennie continued, "If the baby came out in a different position and got stuck, the doctor delivering the baby could insert large spoon shaped instruments, called delivery forceps, placing them around the baby's head, to guide, if not pull the baby out. This often worked. Unfortunately, the spoons frequently tore the mother inside the pelvis or tore the vagina down into the rectum, leaving the mother to die from infection. The baby, if it survived, would likely have a deformed head and a paralyzed face."

Olevia just stared, almost in disbelief at these comments. Her gaze shifted to the big "U" on the side of the mountain.

Evan though her discussion was giving Olevia distress, Jennie continued with her teaching. "If the hand came out first and the shoulder got stuck on the pelvic bones, the doctor could insert a different-shaped forceps, to pull the baby out. The mother usually lived. The baby lived, but often had a partially paralyzed arm."

Olevia was still staring at the big 'U' on the hill. The side of the hill began to look like a pregnant woman from the side, with a huge slope up and then a huge drop. Her father's story of his mother's death was re-entering her consciousness. Somewhat in the distance now, Olevia heard Jennie, still teaching, continue.

"One egg or two? If there are going to be twins, would they be 'identical' or not. Two eggs can be fertilized to give non-identical twins. The twins would not look like each other. One could be a boy and one a girl. You could also have twins who were identical in appearance. They both must come from the same egg, one egg, not two. Twins can even be born stuck together: their one egg did not split into two very well. "

Olevia's mind now saw the ski slope split open to show two skiers stuck together in the air. "Wait" she said to Jennie. "Now I have heard of that, twins stuck to each other, but have never seen it."

"Yes," Jennie continued, her voice almost stuck in some pre-programmed lecture to a class of medical students, "This was first described in 1811, in Bangkok, in the country then called Siam and in the province of Samutsongkram. That country today is called Thailand. Two babies were born joined to each other by the cartilage of their chest bone, or sternum. They were genetically Chinese. They were both male. They must have been small at birth, and they were delivered vaginally. The mother lived."

"Yes, finally a happy ending to one of your stories," said Olevia. "And what did the mother name these twin boys?"

"That is a fun answer too," said Jennie, now smiling. "She named them Chang meaning "left" and Eng meaning "right", for the position they were in when you looked at them. The boys shared one large liver. They had two heads, four arms and four legs."

"Wait, "said Olevia. "I cannot really picture that. Can you pretend like you are Chang, and I will pretend like I am Eng? You come over and stand next to my right side, and let's pretend we are those two young men joined to each other."

Jen then walked over and put her left side against Olevia's right side, and they turned and looked at each other. They were two heads, 4 arms and 4 legs.

"Oh my, and I thought my anatomy stories were something special," commented Olevia, and was amazed at how good it felt to be pressed up against Jen's breasts.

"Yes, this is an amazing story. Do you want to hear more?" Jennie asked? At this moment a man passed the two women, who were pretending to be attached to each other, giving them a quizzical stare. Jennie responded by moving a little bit further away from Olevia.

"Of course," said Olevia. "Please continue the story," she encouraged, giving the passing man an equally quizzical stare."

"As young men" Jennie continued, "Chang and Eng were reportedly seen swimming in the ocean one day, and the captain of a passing boat pulled them out of the water. After getting a look at them, he offered their mother money so he could take them to the United States. Their mother agreed and the captain then took them to the United States, where they toured in a circus as part of a "freak show" with the P.T. Barnum Circus."

"We had traveling circus entertainers in Europe," said Olevia. "They were mostly what we called 'Roma people', Gypsies, from Romania. But no 'freak shows.'"

Jennie continued, "In time Chang and Eng earned enough money so that they could leave the circus. They became American citizens, took the last name of Bunker, bought land in White Plains, North Carolina, and believe it or not, each married a different woman."

"Impossible," said Olevia, in wide eyed astonishment.

"Yes, it is true," said Jen, "and they married two sisters who were not twins, Adelaide and Sarah Ann Hayes. Chang had ten children and Eng had seven. Chang and Eng would spend three or four nights at Adelaide's house and then three or four nights at Sarah Ann's house. They worked as farmers and were quite successful. Chang and Eng became the famous 'Siamese Twins', after whom all other twins were named."

"That is an amazing story," commented Olevia.

"Yes, and completely true. I even got to see a plaster cast made of their bodies when I was studying, because after their death, Chang and Eng's body was brought from North Carolina to be displayed at the Physician's College in Philadelphia where they made a plaster cast of the body. Then took out the liver, the only organ they shared, and preserved it. I got to see the liver too; it is larger than a normal sized liver," concluded Jen.

The two women continued walking down the street.

Olevia's mind now came back to the present. "Jennie, if the mother or the baby dies while you are taking care of them, can you be sued by the Lawyers?" asked Olevia, wondering about the family of Jared Benson, the man who had just hanged himself.

"Olevia, that does worry those in our profession of Obstetrics. There are now so many lawyers, looking for something to do. More graduate each year. Even if the mother and child live, but the baby is paralyzed to some degree, the parents blame the Obstetrician. Of course, as I just described for you, there are naturally occurring birth problems, that just are part of nature, and not the Doctor's fault. But perhaps sometimes we are to blame, too," Jennie conceded, honestly.

"Of late," Olevia confessed, "I have begun to worry about lawyers."

"In Salt Lake City," Jennie continued, changing the subject slightly, "there is lots of mining, the railroad is growing, and many businesses that need legal work. The Lawyers have not started on the Doctors," she paused, then added "yet".

Olevia, usually more upbeat, could not help but add, "Perhaps that day will come."

"Actually," Jennie continued, "I delivered 3 babies in the last 4 years, all for the Smith family. The Mormons you know try to increase their numbers. Charles Smith Junior, the father is a prominent lawyer here in Salt Lake City, and his father, Charles Smith Senior is a lawyer too, a Church High Priest, and a member of Congress. A very prominent family, and I have found them loving and accepting even of doctors!" Jennie concluded with a smile.

ONE EGG, OR TWO?

Olevia and Jennie walked a little further, approaching where they lived.

Jennie had been quiet, still thinking about lawyers and getting sued. Then her thoughts turned back to twins. Jennie continued questioning, now thinking more like an Obstetrician than as Olevia's friend. "What did your father Alexander tell you about his birth and that of his twin, Albert," Jennie asked, stopping, and turning to Olevia. "What did the doctor do to save them?"

"My father told me the story many times," replied Olevia. "I think it helped him to remember and accept the tragedy. You know my last name is Landsmann, and our family tradition goes back far into the Prussian empire. Our family has a crest, which I will show you sometime. The crest has a motto across its base, written in Latin, *Memorandum est Vivere in Aeturnum*", quoted Olevia.

"Something about living forever if you are remembered?" wondered Jennie aloud, her Latin scholar days having been long ago.

"'To be remembered is to live forever'. You were so close Jennie," encouraged Olevia. "My Grandmother's name was Alexandra. My father, Alexander, as I told you, is named for her. Perhaps my father, by repeating this story of his birth, helps my grandmother's memory to live forever. And now I retell the story, again perpetuating her memory, keeping her alive," said Olevia.

"My father said that after 8 hours of labor pains, and exhaustion coming, my mother's doctor told her that when he put his hand inside her womb, he could feel a baby and it was lying transverse, across the pelvis. It would not come out from that position. The doctor had listened with a wooden stick with an opening and a cup at each end, like the stethoscope we use today, and told my mother and father there were two babies inside. He could hear two sets of heartbeats, two distinct hearts beating. My father says that his father Jakob, my Grandfather, told him that my Grandmother had always been slender, and now her belly was so big and stretched it seemed you could see each movement the babies inside were making. You could see the uterine muscle contractions," recounted Olevia.

"Then what happened?" asked Jennie.

"The doctor, who was very experienced, my Father says, told my grandmother, Alexandra, and grandfather, Jakob, that he could not use the forceps to try to turn the baby or the womb would burst for sure and he would injure one of the two babies. My mother was happy to have two children. She and Jakob did not have any children. She wanted her husband's family name of Landsmann to live on, to be remembered."

Jennie just looked at Olevia, and watched her usually peaceful, pleasant face, become saddened. Jennie thought she could see Olevia's eyes start to water.

Olevia went on with the story. "My father said that to keep Alexandra's mind off the pain, my grandmother drank wine and continued to say, "One egg or two?"

"My Grandparents wondered what they should do. What could they do? What should they do? My father says he was told that his mother, Alexandra said 'the babies must live!' My babies must live."

"I am told," continued Olevia, "that Alexandra, my Grandmother, asked the doctor to open her belly and take out the two babies. Doctor, you must save my babies if you can," she said.

Jennie decided to force Olevia to take a pause here, as she could see this was an upsetting story for her to tell. Jennie knew from her own experience, that by retreating into a teaching mode, the Doctor could comfort himself and those who were listening. Then, Jennie began teaching again.

"Olevia, as you must understand, being a Surgeon, opening the abdomen in a living woman to remove a living baby, without anesthesia, had been done going back even into antiquity. It was believed that the uterus would contract and stop bleeding, and heal itself, and so it was not the practice to suture it closed. However, most often, the uterus continued to bleed, and the mother died, or she died shortly thereafter from infection."

Olevia lifted up her head now and looked at Jennie. "Yes, I know that is called a 'Caesarian section.'"

"Yes, exactly, and do you know why it is called that?" Jennie asked.

"No, not really," Olevia answered honestly, relaxing a little from her painful story.

"Well, supposedly it was named due to the method in which the Emperor of Rome, Julius Caesar was born in 100 AD," continued Jennie. "However, history says that Caesar's mother, Cornelia, lived to see her baby grow up, so this was probably not the way Julius Caesar was actually born. Under the Roman Law, or Caesarian Law, it was permitted to open the abdomen of a dead or near-death mother to attempt to save the life of the yet unborn baby. This ancient law is probably the origin of what came to be called a Caesarian Section, today's 'C-section.'"

"One egg or two," Olevia went back to the story of her Grandmother. "My Father said he was told that Alexandra kept repeating this. As Alexandra grew weaker, my Father said that she was given more wine to drink. I am told that my Grandfather, Jakob held his wife's head in his hands as he stood at one end of the kitchen table on which she lay. The Female midwife stood on the opposite side of the table from the doctor, to help him. As the heartbeats of the twins grew more faint through the stethoscope, the Doctor took a knife in his hand, and cut Alexandra from the top of her swollen belly to the pubic bone. With the uterus being so swollen with the babies, the skin was very thin and there was no muscle in the middle line of the cut," Olevia paused.

Then, she went on. "I am told that the Doctor pressed hardly at all and the swollen, basketball-sized, reddish-grey structure erupted out of Alexandra's belly. The Doctor quickly took the knife and made several tentative cuts into the womb. Blood squirted out, and then, with a final gentle cut, the knife went through to the inside sack filled with water. Blood and water gushed out, covering the doctor and the midwife."

"What do you see, Doctor?" gasped Alexandra, who was quickly losing consciousness.

"I see one large sac with two babies in it", said the Doctor, as he quickly opened the sac and began to clean the fluid from the twins so he could take them out.

"What else?" Alexandra cried out. "Are they alive? Do they look alike? Are they boys or girls?"

The Doctor now could get a closer look. "Alexandra they are both boys, and they look healthy, and, . . . and . . . ."

"And what?" Alexandra asked, now so softly.

"They are each holding on to each other's hand," the Doctor replied.

Alexandra smiled, as her eyes closed.

She drifted off to a peaceful, eternal sleep.

Her engorged womb never stopped bleeding.

AIR HEAD

Olevia had hardly fallen asleep when her bedside phone rang.

She was called to the Emergency Department of the Salt Lake County General Hospital to see a man with a head injury. She was told he had been skiing and that he also had a leg injury.

Awakening quickly, as her reflexes were used to doing, she got dressed and into her car. The shortest route was to just take 800 Street West to State Street and turn south. At this time of night, and ignoring traffic lights when she could, she would arrive at 2100 South State Street, the site of Salt Lake County General Hospital, in about 9 minutes.

She spotted the unique outline of the hospital as she drove down South State Street. It was made of white granite, carved from the Wasatch mountain not far away. It was just three stories tall but had much architectural detail. Instead of the building having square corners, the two corners facing South State Street were octagonal in shape and stood out from the straight wall that connected them. Each of these two octagonal structures had a balcony on top. In the center of the wall that connected the two octagons were pure white steps of marble going up to the entrance that had ten thin white marble columns supporting a sculpted canopy. There were rows of evenly spaced tall rectangular windows on each floor.

Olevia drove around to the back of the hospital to the Emergency Room entrance. She parked her car in *Emergency Parking: Doctors Only* space. Then she walked quickly through the doors of the Emergency room.

In the ER, Olevia's ears heard the sounds of the emergency room staff before even her eyes could locate the spot where they were working. Then her eyes confirmed the location of the patient receiving urgent care.

Olevia walked over to the center of the beehive of activity. Some part of her brain smiled at this term, 'bee hive of activity'. Utah was nicknamed the 'The Bee Hive State'.

Almost immediately, a large woman in uniform, with a red cross on her white smock, saw Olevia walking in her direction, and advanced to meet her.

"Hello, Hannah," said Olevia, recognizing the Charge Nurse, Hannah Ryan, by shape alone. Nurse Ryan was taller than Olevia, broader of shoulder, with ample hips, and short reddish-brown hair tied up beneath her white angled nurses cap. She was an imposing figure, and a presence here in the ER for more than a decade.

"Hello, Dr. Landsmann, glad you could get here so quickly," replied Hannah. "This young man is unconscious, and you are the best-trained Doctor to figure out what is going on. Ortho is already here as you can see, working on the broken leg."

Olevia now looked past Hannah Ryan, RN and into the center of the 'Hive'. She saw her patient lying on a stretcher with an oxygen mask over his face and an intravenous line pouring fluids into his outstretched left arm. A young Orthopedic Surgeon and a male assistant were already working on the boy's right leg.

Olevia knew that with so many accidents in the mines and the new ski slopes, there was always an Orthopedic Surgeon staying overnight in the hospital. That is how this Surgeon got to this patient ahead of her. She hated to be late to a party!

Many of the miners lost their legs from crush injuries or lived in pain the rest of their lives and were unable to work. Many became alcoholic, just trying to relieve their pain. Some took their own lives.

The nurse in charge, Hannah, relayed the critical information to Dr. Landsmann. "This young man is 28. He and his friend wanted to ski as early in the Fall season as possible. They drove up to Alta to do this."

Olevia knew that Alta was the first ski resort to be developed in Utah, and even though the lifts would not be running this early in the Fall, there had been recent snow. It was about a 45-minute drive. She knew that eager skiers could hike up the mountain and ski down. She had skied at Alta herself. The terrain in early Fall, when the snow base was not too high, could be tricky.

Olevia looked more carefully now at the young man. He lay on the stretcher, motionless. He was unconscious.

Probably a good thing, she thought, *as he was not feeling the pain as the Orthopedic Surgeon pushed and prodded to get the bones of his lower right leg back into position.*

Charge Nurse Ryan continued her history of the accident. "The friend, who was skiing with this young man, had helped to bring him down the mountain and called the ambulance. The friend, who was skiing just a few seconds behind him, told me that his friend was a great skier. He said that the two of them had been skiing off the trail and as they approached the tree-line they decided to continue through the pine trees. His friend who had taken the lead, tried to turn left to avoid a tree when his left ski hit a patch of ice, and he slid to the right. His right leg twisted."

At this description, the Orthopedic Surgeon stopped what he was doing and looked up. "His friend said the sound of bones snapping was 'crisp, like a shot in the otherwise still morning air,' and I can believe it. The leg took a lot of force to break like this." The Orthopedic Surgeon looked up, saw Olevia, frowned, and then just continued on, without an introduction, "his friend said it 'Actually it sounded like two shots close together'. And both the tibia and the fibula are broken."

The Orthopedic Surgeon now looked directly at Olevia and said "his friend also said he watched as his friend rotated up in the air, the right leg angled to the side, and then he saw his friend's head hit the tree." He assumed correctly that this new Woman Doctor's arrival signaled someone to care for the young man's head injury.

Hannah, the Charge Nurse, regaining control of the narrative, continued then, as the Orthopedic Surgeon went back to work, "The friend made a brace from a tree branch, and put this young man onto a larger branch to act as a sled. The friend said that he slowly dragged his friend down the mountain on that tree branch . At first his friend was awake and talking but stopped talking as they reached the bottom of the slope. When the emergency personal arrived, they transferred the injured young man onto a real stretcher to bring him to our emergency room. Finding that the young man had lost consciousness, and might need emergency head surgery, the ambulance brought him here to us, at Salt Lake City County Hospital. His friend was allowed to ride in the ambulance with him," said Hannah, completing her story.

Olevia was well-trained in head injuries. Even though there was not yet a recognized specialty of Neurosurgery, Olevia knew that one day there would have to be such a specialty to deal with problems in the Central Nervous System, the brain and spinal cord. Olevia was interested in the Peripheral Nervous System, the nerves to the rest of the body. But today, she would be a Neurosurgeon, operating upon the brain, or at least near the brain.

"Dr. Landsmann," said the Orthopedic Surgeon, who must have had heard her name from Nurse Ryan's greeting, "Why did the Charge Nurse call YOU to come in for the head injury?" He said, emphasizing 'you', which Olevia took to mean, 'you a Woman.'"

"I know we have not met before, Doctor," she said politely, putting on a hospital gown and gloves handed to her by Hannah. "During my training at the Johns Hopkins Hospital in Baltimore, I studied with Doctor Harvey Cushing. It is my belief that in time he will be given credit for founding the new ,surgical specialty of Neurosurgery. I have observed his technique and Charge Nurse Ryan has seen me do what is necessary in these situations. As you know Sir, opening the skull is one of the earliest operations ever done to MAN. Dr. Cushing gave me the knowledge needed to perform what I now must do." Olevia answered as politely as she could, attempting to assure the Orthopedic Surgeon that she knew what she was doing AND had the right to be doing it.

The Orthopedic Surgeon was not to be outdone by the show of confidence. "Thank you for sharing that, Doctor. Of course, I know about the operation called 'Trephination'. It is done, after all on a bone, the skull. I am a bone surgeon. I suppose even a Cave Man was able to take a tool and make a hole through the skull bone," he said with a smile that was more of a grimace.

Olevia could see his sarcastic, facial put down of her. He was not even wearing a mask. "Well, Sir, you will soon see that not only a cave Man but a modern Woman can do trephination. I would bet that the cave Woman did trephination too, depending upon how angry the cave Man made her!" she said, giving the attack right back to him. "The critical decision is not whether to make a hole, but where to make that hole."

"Good luck figuring that out!" said the Orthopedic Surgeon, who was continuing to manipulate the broken right leg.

Olevia now entered her teaching mode: "There are skulls from pre-historic times that have holes in them with smooth edges, demonstrating that some people actually survived that Cave Man surgery." Olevia then added, "Sometimes the trephination was done to remove broken pieces of bone. Most skulls that have been found, however had ragged edges to the bone, suggesting the person had died before the bone could heal. Those were probably trephinations done by the Cave Man. Perhaps if a Cave Woman, had done the surgery, she would have been more gentle in her approach than the Cave Man."

The Orthopedic Surgeon sort of grunted at this suggestion. "Thanks for the lecture in anthropology" he said and went back to his work.

Charge Nurse Ryan then asked, "Dr. Landsmann, how will you decide where to drill the hole?"

"I must carefully examine him and see what his Nervous System tells us," said Olevia.

Olevia began saying aloud what her physical exam was demonstrating. "This young man is unconscious but breathing on his own." Olevia then pressed on his chest and pinched his skin to create pain. "He makes no response to painful stimuli," she said. Then she looked into his eyes, lifting his eyelids. "On the left side, the left eye, the pupil has a normal size. When I shine light into it, the black area becomes smaller, which is normal," she continued. "On the right, however, the pupil is large, and does not respond to light when I shine in the flashlight."

"Is that telling you which side to drill the hole on?' asked the Charge Nurse, trying to learn.

"Yes. This is an ominous sign. His right arm has muscle tone, but his left arm and leg do not." Then Olevia felt the bruise on the right side of his skull; the bone was intact. To Olevia, the diagnosis was clear.

" Doctor," said the Orthopedic Surgeon, seemingly unimpressed with all this examination and muttering, "what have you decided from all of this?"

"Doctor, I believe that this young man has an acute, expanding, subdural hematoma. When his head hit the tree, the bone did not break, but a blood vessel did. It is probably still bleeding, and the pressure of the blood is increasing the pressure inside the brain. His brain will soon be damaged irreversibly!" concluded Olevia.

She then looked around, as if expecting disagreement. The space was quiet. Everyone was looking at her in amazement.

"This is a true neurosurgical emergency," Olevia stated for emphasis.

The Orthopedic Surgeon now turned to look at her again. "Doctor, what would happen if we just observe him for awhile, do not make a hole in his skull, and see if he will awaken on his own? I have seen that happen in many instances," he challenged.

Olevia replied without a moment's hesitation, "With this degree of intracranial pressure, he could stop breathing and die as the increased pressure within the skull pushes the brainstem down into the neck, compressing the centers that control his respiration, and certainly we do not want to see that happen," she replied.

Olevia now turned the questions back to the Orthopedic Surgeon working on the leg. "Do you need to go to surgery to fix the bones?" she asked.

"We have to get x-rays, but we think he can be treated with Professor Baldwin's non-operative approach, weights and pulleys, putting this leg into traction. We most likely do not have to open the leg," the young Orthopedic Surgeon said. "The answer is 'no, we do not have to go to surgery.'"

Olevia now noticed that the Orthopedic Surgeon was taller than she, with a slim waste, broad shoulders. He had a full head of hair, on his strongly masculine face. She assumed he must be from Salt Lake City originally, but he was clean shaven, without the beard worn by most of the Mormon men.

"Did you train with Dr. Baldwin?" asked Olevia. She knew that Dr. Baldwin was the first Chief of Orthopedic Surgery at the University of

Utah. Salt Lake County General Hospital was the hospital for the new University. Everyone knew that Dr. Baldwin felt the most conservative, non-operative measures to get bones to heal was the best approach. Dr. Baldwin's approach was almost always used first, especially if no bones were sticking out of the skin.

"Yes, I did," said the Orthopedic Surgeon, "why did you ask?"

"I must decompress this young man's skull immediately, and in the operating room under the most sterile conditions," Olevia said. "Can you wait to place him in traction until we get him into the operating room?"

"Yes, I can," answered the Orthopedic Surgeon, showing a new respect for her knowledge, confidence, and decisiveness.

While the operating room was being prepared, Olevia and the nurses rolled the young man on to his left side, while the Orthopedic Surgeon and a male assistant supported the broken leg. Supporting the leg was important to prevent injury to the blood vessels and nerves that went through the region of the fracture to supply the foot with circulation and sensation.

"What are you preparing to do now?" challenged the Orthopedic Surgeon.

"I must do an emergency lumbar puncture," she said, as she put a needle into the space next to the spinal cord and began to let the cerebrospinal fluid drain out.

"Why do you have to do that?" he continued his interrogation. "Have you detected a spinal cord injury?"

"No that is not the reason," Olevia said gently but firmly. "This will reduce the pressure in the central nervous system just a little. Not so much as to let the brain herniate, but once sufficient fluid drained out, I can inject air into this same space."

"I have never heard of this," responded the Orthopedic Surgeon. "Why would you want to put air into that space?" he questioned defiantly.

"One of my teachers," answered Olevia, now threading a thin tube into the wider metal needle, "Doctor Walter Dandy, another pioneer in Neurosurgery at Johns Hopkins Hospital, developed this technique. He called it pneumoencephalography," she explained. "The air will rise into the space around the brain, and show up on an x-ray, allowing us to visualize the pathology from the head trauma."

"I cannot even imagine that," replied the skeptical Orthopedic Surgeon.

"I appreciate that YOU probably can't. But it is the same as you looking at bones on an x-ray. Think of the air in the lungs that contrasts the rib *bones* to the other tissues. Dr. Dandy thought that air around the brain would allow different penetration of the x-rays and allow the brain to be seen better on x-ray. Dr. Dandy worked in the laboratory with Dr. Cushing and took over from Dr. Cushing. That happened just recently, 1912, when Cushing went to become a Professor of Surgery at the Harvard Medical School," explained Olevia patiently, as she worked with the syringe next to the spinal cord. "Did you know, Sir, that it was Cushing who personally took the first x-ray ever at the Johns Hopkins Hospital? He paid to purchase the x-ray machine himself, and had it brought over from Europe."

Now Charge Nurse Ryan, who had seen Dr. Landsmann do this procedure before, asked, "Doctor, should we start raising the head of the table?"

"Yes, slowly begin to do that," said Olevia, as she began injecting the air into the small tube that had been placed into the patient's spinal canal. The Orthopedic Surgeon and his assistant continued to stabilize the leg.

"That should do it," called out Olevia, "The air should have had reached the skull. Bring over the x-ray machine. Let's take the x-ray right here and then get on our way to the operating room as quickly as possible."

HOLE IN ONE

In the operating room of the Salt Lake County General Hospital, air gently blew in through an open window while a young nurse walked around spraying the room with carbolic acid to 'sterilize' the room.

The young man lay on the operating table, with a cone shaped device held over his nose by the left hand of a doctor who was serving as the Anesthesiologist. His right hand gently dropped a liquid into the small opening of cone. The larger end of the cone was held over of the young man's nose. The shape of the device allowed the liquid ether to vaporize so the young man could inhale the fumes and remain asleep.

Olevia knew that this young man, who was supplying the ether, was a surgeon in training. Another Male Surgeon in the operating room to observe her, she thought! She knew that, although William Morton introduced the concept of putting someone to sleep for surgery, using ether, in Boston in October of 1846, it was Oliver Wendell Holmes, Sr. MD, who coined the terms that were being used today. She remembered reading that Dr. Holmes, Sr. had written a letter to Dr. Morton, just one month after the historic operation in what was now being called "The Ether Dome" in Boston. Dr. Holmes at that time was a Professor of Anatomy and Physiology at Dartmouth Medical School in New Hampshire. Holmes said he wanted to 'share' in the great discovery. He created the term *anesthesia* and *anesthetic*, from the Greek word meaning 'lack of sensation'. Still today, in the early 20th century, she knew that there was yet no specialty of Anesthesiology. This too would occur one day she surmised, because young surgeons did not want to be doing this type of work. They wanted to be cutting!!

As Olevia mused over these historical thoughts, she observed that the Orthopedic team was placing pins and plaster around the right leg, to hook it up to a trapeze like device that would allow the broken bones to align. This required weights to be placed on the ropes to compensate against the pull of the tightened muscles.

As Olevia turned towards her patient, an assistant approached, carrying a large black piece of firm but shimmering material.

"Here is the developed x-ray," he said, approaching Olevia. Walter Dandy's Pneumoencephalogram, was ready.

"Please close the open window. We are going to be operating on the brain today," she asked.

Olevia looked at the x-ray 'film', made from celluloid, which she knew was the current version of the cellulose process developed in the Chemistry Department in her home city of Munich. She placed the x-ray on to the 'light box' next to the x-rays of the right leg.

Olevia examined the broken leg views. The leg had a spiral fracture of the fibula and a clean transverse fracture of the distal tibia, just above the ankle. She turned to look at the Orthopedic team. It was clear they had placed the right leg in traction, pulled the foot while keeping the knee held steady with a pin through the proximal tibia, and aligned the bones.

At this point an assistant came in with a second x-ray of the leg. The Orthopedic Surgeon turned to look at it, and then showed it to Olevia. "This post-reduction film shows the bones aligned quite beautifully. Now we just have to apply some plaster to maintain the alignment, and balance the weights," he said in the most confident of tones.

Then he turned to Olevia and asked sarcastically, "What does YOUR x-ray show?" He walked over to the light box to look at the pneumoencephalogram.

"This demonstrates the central part of the brain has shifted to the left due to a space occupying area filled with blood on the right side where he was injured," explained Olevia, pointing to the white and dark areas on the celluloid. "The blood is just underneath the skull and located right here. This is where I must open the skull," she concluded her teaching.

"Then, Dr. Landsmann, I think you enjoy giving lectures. But I assume this means that your diagnosis is confirmed. And, from the x-ray, it looks like there is a lot of blood under the skull. Congratulations," said the Orthopedic Surgeon, begrudgingly.

"Thank you, Doctor. Yes, he has an acute right subdural hematoma. And please be kind enough to tell me your name, Sir, my name is Olevia Landsmann."

"I am Dr. Levin Randolph," he said, giving a smile. "Pleased to meet you. Sorry I gave you a difficult time, but if you grow up out here in Salt Lake, as I have, you get to hear some pretty 'tall tales' and you learn to check things out."

"No problem, Dr. Randolph," Olevia said. "I get that response a lot out here. A Woman Surgeon is still rare. A surgeon operating on nerves is also rare. I believe there is much surgery can do to help people with problems in the Nervous System, and my research is related to that," she said humbly, continuing to stare him straight in the eye.

"Dr. Landsmann, your patient is ready for surgery," said the surgical scrub technician, who had completed shaving the right side of the young man's head and was now 'painting' the exposed bone with an iodine solution.

As Olevia completed washing her hands, putting on a clean gown, and then putting gloves on her hands, she observed the placement of the sterile sheets around the skull, leaving room for the Ether cone.

"May I stay and watch you do the trephination?" asked Levin Randolph, MD, the Orthopedic Surgeon.

"Certainly, it will be my honor. After all, the skull is a bone, and you are a bone specialist!" She said with a smile, which she knew no one could see as she was also wearing a mask. "Just put on a mask, scrub your hands and put on a pair of gloves. An infection in the brain leads to death very quickly. And today, in more modern times, we just call this operation a 'burr hole' and not 'trephination.'"

Olevia watched as Dr. Randolph did as she asked. "When did you start wearing these rubber gloves out here in the West?" she asked.

"Just recently actually. It seems like a really good idea. Infection in bone in the leg usually leads to amputation, and that often leads to death."

"Dr. Randolph, there is a great story behind the creation of those gloves. Have you ever heard it?" she asked watching him get ready to 'scrub in.'"

"No, never have. Just thought it was some Industrialist from back East finding a way to make more money," said Levin, reverting back to his sarcastic and demeaning tone. "Please proceed with your next 'lecture' Doctor."

Ignoring his continued sarcasm, Olevia just proceeded. "Our first Professor of Surgery at the Johns Hopkins Hospital, Dr. William Steward Halsted, was in love with his surgical scrub tech, Caroline Hampton. She had sensitive hands. The bichloride of mercury that we used to sterilize surgical instruments caused her to have a rash on her hands. Hands that Halsted liked to hold! He asked the new BF Goodrich rubber company if they could make gloves out rubber, and they did. So, Dr. Randolph, you were correct in that it was an 'industrialist from back East'. That rubber company started in New York State before moving to Ohio. The BF Goodrich Rubber Company gloves protected those hands of Caroline Hampton, and she could then assist Dr. Halsted better in surgery. And, of course, they could hold hands better in private! Today, more and more surgeons and scrub techs are wearing sterile gloves," said Olevia, completing the story.

"Thank you for enlightening me and letting me know that I was correct," said Dr Randolph curtly, hating to admit there was something about surgery that he did not know.

"May I have the scalpel with a number 15 blade on it," asked Olevia.

The nurse handed the scalpel with the small little blade, and Olevia made an incision in the scalp over the site where she believed the blood had collected inside the skull.

"Thank you," she said, handing the scalpel back. "Drill, please," she continued.

Olevia was handed the drill to make a burr hole in the young man's skull.

Just before she did, she turned to Dr. Randolph. "Levin, that story has an even happier ending. Hampton married Halsted in 1890."

Then Olevia, using a very small drill bit, pushed the drill gently with one hand so that the drill 'bit' into the bone as she rotated the handle on the drill, forcing its tip to move deeper into the bone. She did this for a few minutes. Suddenly, she felt no more resistance against the drill bit. She stopped drilling immediately.

"Why did you just stop drilling?" asked Dr. Randolph, sensing that Olevia had just made a mistake "Did you decide you are drilling in the wrong spot?"

"No, Levin," Olevia said with a sigh, "I just felt no more resistance against the drill, so I know I am through the skull. I stopped so I do not injure the covering of the brain, the dura. This means I am probably within the clot, in exactly the correct spot," she said as she withdrew the drill.

Bright red blood spurted out of the hole.

Dr. Randolph moved instinctively to cover the bleeding spot with a sterile cloth.

"It is ok to let the blood out," said Olevia, gently moving his cloth a little to the side, so it could soak up the blood, and not prevent it's coming out. "We want the blood to drain out in order to reduce the pressure on the brain," she explained.

Knowing that she had the correct location, she lengthened her incision and enlarged the hole with a bigger drill bit. Then made several more holes that created the corners of a square.

"Now what are you going to do," said Dr. Randolph, suspiciously. "Just make a lot of holes looking for more blood?"

"I am going to connect these small holes, and remove the piece of bone that they outline," she answered. Then she 'connected the dots' and with a small chisel was able to lift out the small square of bone and place it onto a sterile cloth.

The patient's blood pressure, which had been high, with a slow pulse, indicative of increased intra-cranial pressure, now began to normalize. "Blood pressure is now normal, pulse back up to 68" spoke up the young surgeon giving the ether, who had been using Cushing's method of charting the patient's vital signs.

"Levin," said Olevia, "I know you will think I can speak of nothing else except my Professors, but the observation that our "Anesthesiologist" made reflects the observations that Cushing make first in his patients during brain surgery, and then in the Animal Laboratory at Johns Hopkins. In fact, that chart the Anesthesiologist is using to chart blood pressure and pulse was started by Cushing. He found that when the pressure inside the skull, the intracranial pressure went up, the systemic blood pressure also went up, and the pulse slowed. Presumably this was a reaction the heart made to continue to pump blood into the skull in the face of that higher intracranial pressure. When that pressure is relieved, by the surgery we are doing now, the blood pressure comes down and the pulse comes back up to normal."

Dr. Levin Randolph just listened to Olevia in amazement. In the operating room, with a surgical gown and surgical cap and surgical mask on, she looked exactly the same as any Male Surgeon. She looked as much like a man as most surgeons did. In fact, he reminded himself, with her manner of dressing she looked more like a man than a woman even when she was not scrubbed in surgery. He was getting sick of her lecturing to him. He was not her student.

"Dr. Randolph," called Olevia, "These are the final steps in the surgery."

He just watched in further amazement as Dr. Landsmann, this Woman Surgeon, gently removed the rest of the clot from the top of the brain, stopped the bleeding, by placing a small silk suture ligature around the small bleeding artery on the surface of the dura, and then, replaced the bone flap, suturing everything closed again.

COMPARTMENT

He opened his eyes.

"What is your name?" asked Olevia.

"Edward Cannon," said the awake, young man, staring down the bed at his right leg. This leg, he saw was suspended painfully by cords from a frame over the bed. "My right leg hurts", he said.

"Open your eyes, while I shine a light into them," Olevia said, happy to hear her formerly unconscious patient speak, and to recognize that he had a right leg and that it hurt.

The pupil in the right eye now was the same size as the pupil in the left eye. Olevia wondered what changes had occurred in the previously paralyzed left arm.

"Lift up your left arm, and open and close your fingers. Squeeze my hand", she said.

Edward was able to do exactly as he was asked to do.

"Doctor, my right leg is really hurting, and my toes are tingling. And I'm really hungry!" said Edward.

"Yes. Well, you broke two bones in the right leg. The Orthopedic surgeon, Dr. Levin Randolph, will be here soon, and you can ask him about that leg. I will have the nurse bring you some breakfast," replied Olevia. "By the way, how is your head feeling?"

"A little headache on the right side. Is that where I hit the tree? I saw it coming my way but could not duck my head in time. My leg failed me," replied Edward.

"Yes, your leg did fail you. Then you bled inside your head. I had to remove some bone to let the blood out. You came close to dying, or to living and being paralyzed. Looks like things are coming along quite nicely now. You are a lucky young man. Do not touch the bandage on your head. The skull is now broken also, but by me, and it too has to heal without infection. After I removed the blood and stopped the bleeding, I replaced the piece of bone that I removed to let the blood out." She concluded her explanation and left his bedside.

Dr. Levin Randolph, the Orthopedic Surgeon and his assistant then came by while Edward Cannon was eating breakfast. "How do you feel?" Dr. Randolph asked.

"My right foot hurts and tingles and buzzes, and it is cold," Edward said.

"It will hurt, of course. You broke two bones. I put them nicely together for you. You will spend 6 weeks like this, in bed, in traction. Not bearing any weight on that foot. We will lower your leg and it will feel less cold. We will come back to see you in a few hours."

But by noon, Edward was crying in pain. The nurses had given him morphine and called Dr. Levin Randolph back to check the circulation in that leg. The nurse could feel that the foot was in fact cold.

Olevia came by again to check her patient and was alarmed to see him being wheeled out of his room with her new 'friend', Dr. Randolph, hurriedly pushing the bed up the hallway himself towards the operating rooms. Levin looked at her, sensing her alarm.

"Dr. Landsmann, Edward Cannon is quite awake. It is not his brain," said Dr. Randolph. "It is his leg. He has no pulse at the ankle. There must have been too much bleeding from the ends of the broken bones. The leg has swollen inside the cast. The foot is cold and pale. He has the classic signs of compartment syndrome! His leg will die from lack of circulation if I do not relieve the pressure."

"What will you do?" asked Olevia, hurrying up the hall after Dr. Randolph.

"We have to open the leg in several long cuts, and release the pressure. Similar to what you did for the increased pressure around the brain. He can lose the function of the muscles of his leg from this problem. The muscles die if circulation is not restored within 6 hours. He could lose the entire lower limb," said the Orthopedic Surgeon, as he continued pushing the stretcher quickly to the operating room.

Olevia ran to catch up with him, to help him push the bed with all the heavy metal poles and weights hanging from them. She looked at Levin now and realized that he was quite a strong man, and now quite worried. Perhaps he was in need of help himself right now, she thought.

"Dr. Randolph, permit me to scrub in with you. Even though I have never seen this procedure, I will do what I can to assist you," asked Olevia politely.

"Ok," replied Dr. Randolph, and then added, "But no more lectures, please."

He thought to himself, *I have no interest in teaching a Woman how to do an operation.*

In the operating room, Olevia watched, fascinated, as the plaster was removed, the leg taken out of traction, and the leg painted with iodine. The "Anesthesiologist" was back in place with his bottle of Ether.

Levin Randolph, now fully clothed for surgery, took an elastic bandage, wrapped the leg to the thigh, rolled up the end of the bandage from the ankle till skin was exposed up to the knee, so that the Esmarch bandage acted as a tourniquet.

Olevia, scrubbed and standing close to Levin Randolph, stood, quietly, observing.

"Number 22 scalpel blade and hand me the knife quickly," commanded the Orthopedic Surgeon to the scrub tech, without even looking at her.

The Scrub Tech did so as quickly as she could.

Without saying even 'thanks', Levin Randolph took the knife with the very large scalpel blade, and, very quickly, and firmly, with one long motion slit the inside of the leg, the side where the tibia had fractured.

Then, the Orthopedic Surgeon, moving to the other side of the operating table, where his vision could not see where Olevia's hand was holding and positioning the leg for him, just as quickly, took the #22 scalpel blade, and slit the skin on the outside of the leg, the side where the fibula had fractured. In doing so, he almost cut Olevia's finger.

She quickly pulled her hand away, the position of the leg shifted.

Levin Randolph stopped cutting, looked up at her, sort of smiled, said "sorry", repositioned the leg, and completed his incision in the skin. The slits went from just above the ankle to just below the knee.

Within her mask, Olevia's mouth dropped open in surprise. The scalpel blade she used was the much smaller number 15 blade, and she made her incisions so carefully. How appropriate she thought that Levin had to demonstrate his masculinity by showing that size mattered. His big #22 blade versus her smaller #15 blade. And, was that cut so close to her hand, really a mistake, or was it meant for her to get the "point"! He did not want her here.

"Moist warm towels, now, quickly," Levin Randolph appeared to just yell into the air at no one in particular.

"Here you are, Sir," replied the scrub tech preparing them and handing them to him as quickly as she could.

"Olevia, help me wrap the incisions with these moist towels. Then we will see what happens," instructed Dr. Randolph.

Olevia was stunned by the suddenness of these moves. She had never seen this done. But then, she thought, she had never watched Orthopedic Surgeons at work! As she maintained gentle pressure on the incisions, she asked, "What is that bandage called that you just used to wrap the leg. Our Dr. Cushing at Johns Hopkins started their use, for surgery on the hand. I have not seen that exact type used before," asked Olevia.

Dr. Randolph, much to Olevia's surprise, now clearly showed an academic interest in his work. He answered, "It is called an Esmarch bandage. Esmarch was a Surgeon, interested in military surgery. He became Professor of Surgery at Kiel, in Germany, and then was called to Berlin to oversee all surgery at the University Hospital. In 1870, when the Franco-Prussian war erupted, he was made Surgeon General of the Army."

He stopped talking, turned and looked directly at Olevia, and said, "I can lecture too, Doctor, even about European history."

"I love it," replied Olevia. "Teach me some more", she encouraged.

"Well, at the risk of your making fun of my pronunciation, as I can tell from your accent that you must be from Eastern Europe somewhere, I will say that from Esmarch's war experience, he wrote a textbook, *Handbuch der Kreegs...*" said Levin Randolph, fumbling for the correct word.

"*Handbuch der KreigcirurgischenTechnik,*" offered Olevia.

"I guess, if you say so," said Levin Randolph. "I know it means *Handbook of War Surgery Technique.* Today we use an 'Esmarch bandage' to exsanguinate an extremity before operating on it. This rubber tourniquet was invented by Esmarch to prevent bleeding during amputation." Levin then paused and concluded with "I suppose Esmarch had his bandage made much the same way your Dr. Halsted had rubber gloves made."

Mabel Ryan, the Circulating Nurse in the operating room, the Nurse in Charge of this room, had been observing the exchange between the two doctors, and tried to get them back on track. She said, "Doctors, there is no bleeding from the pale white leg. Does this mean the fasciotomy was not successful?"

"Dr. Randolph, Did you only cut the skin? Olevia asked.

"Yes," he replied, thinking, *only the patient's skin. I should have cut into yours.* Then Levin Randolph said, "Now I have to cut into the muscle compartments themselves to release the blood vessels and the muscles that are bulging." Then, from where he was standing, the side of the operating table next to the outside, the lateral side, of the leg, he again took the scalpel and its knife blade and cut through the thick white connective tissue covering of the muscle, the fascia.

As he did this, the scalpel came dangerously close to Olevia's hand, again, and she alertly pulled it away and gave him a cold stare.

"Doctor," he said to Olevia, "perhaps you should keep your hands further away from the surgical site," then turning to inspect his work, like an artist stepping back to inspect his canvas, he said, "I have released the fascia of the lateral compartment."

Almost in self-defense, Olevia's mind reverted to her Latin training. 'Fascia' meant bundle. In this case the bundles of collagen that created the strength in the covering of the muscles, is what he had just cut into.

Immediately dark purple muscle bulged out. There were two compartments on this side, Olevia remembered, the anterior and the lateral. She watched as Doctor Randolph then made another long incision in the second compartment. She now kept her hands very far away from where he was working. These compartments, Olevia knew, contained the muscles that lifted up the toes and ankles, dorsiflexion, and turned the ankle up and out, eversion. The Orthopedic Surgeon then went back around the operating room table to do the same to the posterior compartment, which held the muscles to flex the toes and calf downwards.

Olevia looked closely at the bulging muscle in the lateral compartment. Sticking out from beneath the cut white fascia on top of the purple muscle were two ends of a 3 or 4 mm white nerve. It had been cut in half by the long, quickly made, incision!

The Orthopedic Surgeon then unwrapped the Esmarch bandage. Now bright red blood began oozing from the skin edges, and muscle began to get less purple and become pinker. He then took sterile warm water-soaked sterile cloths and wrapped the leg.

"Olevia", he said. "Please hold these warm moist compresses in place while I watch the foot and feel for a pulse."

"The foot is turning pink," observed Mabel Ryan, RN, giving a sigh of relief. "Your surgery will be successful, the foot will live," Nurse Ryan continued.

The Scrub Tech relieved Olevia from her job, and continued to apply pressure, then finally changing to moist cloths with room temperature water. Then she assisted Dr. Randolph as they applied traction back to the foot. And waited for a new x-ray.

Doctor Randolph took off his surgical mask and smiled at Olevia, clearly happy at the result of this emergency surgery. "We are a good team," he said, trying to not let his true feelings for her show. "You brought his brain back to life from a bleed, and I brought his foot back to life from a bleed."

"And I also kept my own hand from a bleed," she said suspiciously.

"Sorry about that Doctor. You were not used to the Orthopedic surgical techniques we use. I thought you were more familiar with our procedures."

"What next?" asked Olevia, changing the subject.

"If the x-ray shows the bones are still aligned well, we will loosely stitch the skin back, and do this a little more tightly each day until the swollen muscle shrinks back. Then we let the skin close on its own. By then the bone will probably be healed too."

Olevia could not restrain herself from asking, "Do you ever worry about the nerves to the skin that may have been injured in the fasciotomy? For example, I am sure I just saw two ends of the superficial peroneal nerve in the wound," she concluded.

"Of course, we do not try to cut them. In this emergent situation, we just do what we have to do," Levin replied confidently. Then he looked at Olevia thoughtfully, "Should we repair that nerve?" he asked. "Do you want to sew those nerves back together now? Can you even do that?"

Olevia did not know what to say. She just looked at Levin for long silent moment. She hated to turn this Orthopedic moment of triumph into something negative, but she just felt this was an important point, perhaps one from which they both could learn.

In response to Olevia's momentary silence, Levin Randolph said, "I suppose there is no right answer then, except just not to cut that nerve in the first place. But preserving the limb must take precedence over a cutaneous nerve. I am sure you would agree Doctor."

"Here is the problem we face now Doctor," replied Olevia. "You and your Orthopedic Surgery colleagues must have injured nerves like this many times, and so you must know how often these patients come back to clinic with pain. Right?" asked Olevia.

"Yes, and some do come back with areas of numbness and pain along the scar when they do form a painful neuroma," answered Dr. Randolph honestly.

"If you were to send one of those patients to me, I would then remove the hurt nerve, and do something with the end still attached to the spine so that it does not grow back and form another painful neuroma. The patient would be happy to have a numb area of the foot instead of pain, right?" Olevia replied.

"Yes, that is right, and what do you predict would happen if you were to sew these two ends of the nerve back together that you just saw. We could scrub back in and do it right now, if you think it is the right thing to do," offered Dr. Randolph, challenging Dr. Landsmann even further, as he was beginning to think she was being critical of his surgical technique.

"There is just no science or research to guide us. Logic makes me think we should repair the injured nerve and tell the patient this happened. There are so many lawyers out there now, and angry patients are learning to find them. And yet, if we repair the nerve, and are successful it will regenerate, all the way to the foot. That is about 18 inches. The nerve can cause pain as it regenerates. We might be committing the patient to 18 months of pain, for which he will NOT thank you or me, even though we tried to help him. And the irony is, the treatment for a painful nerve is to go back and divide the nerve, so there we are back where we started," Olevia concluded.

"Dr. Landsmann, I am not sure what your answer is. Do we repair the injured nerve or not repair it," again challenged Dr. Randolph.

"Our responsibility as Doctors, as Hippocrates of Cos wrote in 600 BC is '*Primum, Non Nocere*,' First Do No Harm. Even though some small harm has been done to this leg, it is a complication of trying to save the leg . . . ."

"Please stop lecturing to me and just try to answer the simple question!" interrupted Levin Randolph forcefully.

"It is possible, Dr. Randolph, that we might make this complication even worse by trying to repair that nerve right now. My recommendation, then, Dr. Randolph is to continue to just let the leg heal and follow the patient over time to learn what will happen," concluded Olevia.

The Orthopedic Surgeon seemed both satisfied and mystified at the same time, and as he turned to walk away, shaking his head. He mumbled to himself. "*SHE* would not have even known how to do a fasciotomy. SHE has probably never even repaired a nerve!"

Olevia turned, watching him walk away. Immediately she decided to spend more time with Orthopedic Surgeons. "Dr. Randolph," she said to get his attention. Clearly not afraid of him, she continued, "May I come to your clinic and follow his recovery. I think your patients and their injuries create natural experiments, from which we both can learn."

Dr. Levin Randolph did not even turn his head to acknowledge her question. He just kept walking.

ACID BURN

Jennie and Olevia decided to have another root beer together at the Connor Corner Store. They each had enjoyed so much their discussions with each other the week before. They each realized they had someone they could trust and confide in. They planned ahead to take time off and met for lunch. Their drinks came first. But they never did eat anything.

Olevia decided to ask Jennie a personal question. "Do you think you will ever get married?"

Somewhat taken aback by this simple question, Jennie was quiet for a moment. Then she said, "Yes, I would like to get married. I care for so many loving and lovely young couples, and deliver their babies. So, yes, I would. For sure, but . . . will I ever find someone who would marry me! I work all the time. Like you. That is why so many male doctors are married to nurses; nurses are who they see most days and who understand how hard they work. The nurse is there, being sympathetic to them during their times of stress. It is not likely that I will marry a male nurse!" She concluded with a smile. "How about you?"

"There was a medical student who sat next to me in Pathology Class at Johns Hopkins, during medical school. They sat us alphabetically. I was an 'L', Landsmann. He was an 'M', Mabey. Ezra Mabey. He sat to my right." She recalled also, now smiling, "when you and I were talking about skiing, well skiing is not the only reason I decided to come out to Utah." Olevia explained, "Ezra is from Salt Lake City."

"Really! Nice. What is going on? You never talked about Ezra before?" asked Jennie.

"I could tell that Ezra was very smart. Of course, everyone in our medical school class was very smart. But he knew so much and did so well in school. At Hopkins we were encouraged to always be 'one up' on each other. Knowledge was the key. In fact those words are so close to the motto of the Johns Hopkins University, *Veritas Vos Liberabunt*. I once told him that I knew in Latin that it meant "The truth shall make you free." To which Ezra added, "Yes I know that, and did you know it is a direct quote from the New Testament, Book of John, chapter 8 verse 32?" He had me at that. I came to learn he was a Mormon, a member of The Church of Jesus Christ of Latter-Day Saints."

"Then you two were in competition from the time you first met?" quizzed Jennie anxious to learn more.

"I suppose so, but at that time it was friendly. For example, there was the time we were examining the skull of a man who died from a pituitary tumor. The man was a 'giant', you know, from too much growth hormone. My Professor Harvey Cushing, at 'Hopkins', you may already know, was the first surgeon to attempt to remove this tumor," said Olevia.

"Oh my. No, I did not know that," said Jennie. "The pituitary gland is deep in the brain behind the eyes. What surgical approach did he use?" she asked.

"He did it through the nose!" replied Olevia with a smile, sticking her little finger up her nose to illustrate. "The pituitary gland, as you remember, sits in that little scooped out piece of bone, just behind the nose, the *sella turcica*." Olevia now had to smile inwardly, as she knew this meant 'Turkish Saddle', in Greek, not Latin.

"What did that have to do with Ezra?" reminded Jennie.

"Ezra used the skull to ask me if I remembered the names of the twelve cranial nerves from back when we took Anatomy, the year before. I rattled them off, and so then he asked me how I could remember them so easily. I told him the memory device we learned at my dissecting table from a classmate who was from Massachusetts," said Olevia. "In Massachusetts, my classmate said there was a man named Oliver Wendell Holmes who was both a lawyer and a doctor. And he also liked poetry. Jennie, you probably learned the same memory rhyme as me."

"Not sure I even know what you are talking about," confessed Jennie.

"OK. I know you are just trying to be humble, wanting to hear me recite it."

"Well then," go ahead, said Jennie, sipping her root beer.

Olevia smiled, and said out loud, "Oh! Oh! Oh! To Touch And Feel A Girl's Vagina, AH!!"

"Ugh, yes," Jennie replied. "I thought it disgusting then. Now, as a Gynecologist, I find it even more disgusting. But it helps me still to remember the real names of those 12 nerves," said Jennie as she listed Olfactory, Optic, Occulomotor, Trochlear, Trigeminal, Abducens, Facial, Acoustic, Glossopharyngeal, Vagus, Accessory and Hypoglossal.

"Wow. So I am impressed," said Olevia, "but," she continued, returning to her Hopkins story, "Ezra Mabey was not to be outdone."

"What did he say?" asked Jennie, smiling with anticipation, learning about her friend's medical school romance.

"So crude and unlike you, is what Ezra Mabey said to me," Olevia answered. "Then he added," Olevia went on, "Oliver Wendell Holmes, Senior was the one who went to law school, quit to go to medical school and wrote these mnemonic poems. He became Professor of Anatomy at Harvard Medical School. It is his son, Oliver Wendell Holmes, Jr. who became the famous lawyer. Indeed, he is on the Supreme Court of the United States, right now. Then Ezra went on to say, you might have learned the more congenial mnemonic that Holmes Sr. also created."

"I told Ezra that I did not know that one," said Olevia. "Then he just smiled at me," said Olevia, and he quoted Holmes Sr., "On Old Olympus Towering Top, A Finn, And German Viewed A Hop."

"Did you like him because you finally found someone you thought was smarter than you," asked Jennie.

"He was that," admitted Olevia, "Ezra was Brilliant but Blunt."

"Jennie, I must tell you I am often conflicted about men. Seems the MALE of our species has caused me a lot of pain already," said Olevia, her face becoming saddened, almost dark in expression. Olevia paused, as if remembering things."

"What are you saying Olevia?" asked Jennie, totally surprised at the way the conversation was turning.

"I love my father and Uncle Albert, but Albert's pain brought great pain to my life, in ways I cannot really talk about now. When I dissect male cadavers, I sometimes wonder if I am taking out an inner hatred of men by cutting them with my scalpel. And yet, I care so much for my male patients, as much as for the female patients, and I have dedicated my life to relieving pain. I fear that these concerns will prevent me from every having a meaningful, long-term relationship with a man," concluded Olevia, seeming to feel relief at finally having expressed this to someone.

"Oh, my," said Jennie, just staring at her friend.

Not knowing what to say next, Jennie just seemed to say what was on her mind, "And how do you feel about women?" she asked.

Olevia looked at Jennie with a new interest. "Jennie, I wish I knew how to answer that. I have so much still to learn about myself," she said.

Not wanting to intrude further into these private thoughts, Jennie brought the subject back to where it began: "So, how do you think those feelings affected your relationship with Ezra Maybe?"

Olevia, thankful for this change in conversation, added, "While I loved the competitive academic discussions Ezra and I would have, I must admit that I liked him more for his interest in nerves. As you know, Jennie, I am very interested in nerves."

The waitress came over to their table. They each ordered another root beer in a frosty mug. Then Jennie decided to change the subject slightly, and continued, "Olevia you never told me you were so interested in nerves, especially so early in your career, even in medical school."

"It is a fascinating story and goes back to the twins I was telling you about, my father Alexander and my Uncle Albert," Olevia began her story. "My father told me proudly that both he and his brother were accepted, precociously, at age 5, into the best private Gymnasium in Munich. That is what the Bavarians called a private school. Not a Gym, a place to exercise, as the word is used in America. There, they did great in math and natural sciences. They had excellent language skills, and in addition to learning classic Latin, to improve and strengthen their minds, they learned French, so that they might communicate with the neighbors to the west of Germany. My Father said that in time, as his Father's company, Bayer Company, expanded marketing to America, he and his brother grew to be strong, competitive, and energetically loyal to each other."

Jennie now interrupted her story. "Olevia, I understand they were identical twins, and looked identical, but were their personalities also much the same?"

"My Father said their personalities were different in some ways," replied Olevia. "For example, my Uncle Albert was left-handed and my Father was right handed. Albert seemed to relate better to people while my Father concentrated more on his immediate work or play project. My Father says that they were mirror-image twins."

"What does that have to do with nerves," interrupted Jennie, who noticed that Olevia seemed to be drifting back in time.

"My grandfather, Jakob, would take his sons to the Bayer Company with him. My father remembers asking what the strange smells were. They easily learned to distinguish the fragrances of different chemicals and learn their funny names of the chemicals. My Father said it was easier to learn the words 'aniline', 'formaldehyde', 'acetylsalicylic acid' and 'sulfuric acid', as it was to learn the names of the dinosaurs, Tyrannosaurus Rex, Brontosaurus, and Triceratops. I remember my father making a joke: 'Was trichlorobenze a chemical or a dinosaur'?"

"That is funny," laughed Jennie, picturing an animal with three Chlorine molecules as the horns on top of a body represented by six carbon atoms linked in a hexagon.

Olevia continued, "With their great grades and abilities, my Father and Uncle were accepted to the best university in Munich, LMU."

"Does the MU part mean Munich University?" asked Jennie.

Olevia assumed her teacher's role again. "In 1472 Duke Ludwig IX of Bavaria established a University to bear his name. It began in Ingolstadt, a city on the Danube River, just north of Munich. When the French threatened Ingolstadt in 1800, King Maximilian I moved the University to Landshut, and finally in 1826, then King Ludwig I of Bavaria moved it into the center of Munich, where it was most usually referred to as 'University of Munich'. Ludwig-Maximilian University, or LMU, is often ranked as one of, if not the top, university in Europe. Not surprisingly, chemistry fascinated my Father and my Uncle. My Father said they had amazing teachers. One of them, Adolph Baeyer discovered how to create, to synthesize the plant dye aniline, critical for the dye industry for clothing. Dyes could now be created in a laboratory instead of extracting them from plants. My father said that their teacher, Baeyer, reacted phenol with phthalein to create phenolphthalein, which led to his identifying chemicals that gave off light from the chemical fluorescein."

Jennie now perked up. "Hey, I have heard of that. It is called fluorescence."

"Exactly," Olevia responded. My Father was very proud of the fact the Professor Baeyer was a Jew, and in 1905, Adolf Baeyer was awarded the Nobel Prize in Chemistry."

"So your name Landsmann is a Jewish name?" Jennie stated, more than asked. Then followed with "How does this story lead to your interest today in nerves?" Jennie continued sipping slowly on her root beer.

"My Father and his brother, my Uncle Albert, were hired by the company that my Grandfather Jacob Landsmann worked for, the Friedrich Bayer Company. My Father Alexander and my Uncle Albert were permitted to do independent chemistry research. They knew that creating chemicals and obtaining patents could lead to wealth. A French chemist had found an extract of willow bark that would relieve pain and headache. The Bayer Company had found a way to create that willow bark extract chemically. This weak acid, acetylsalicylic acid, was found to relieve many simple pains and fevers too," explained Olevia.

"Wait a minute," commanded Jennie. "Don't tell me that is how Bayer Aspirin was discovered, by your father's company!"

"Right again, Jennie," applauded Olevia, clapping her hands. "How clever you are. The Bayer Company mainly popularized it and marketed it, rather than discovered the chemical originally." Olevia paused, and then said, "Now can you guess this one. Bayer chemists did the same for an unusual chemical from a poppy plant. A British chemist first created the molecule from morphine, but the Bayer Company trademarked its name. What is that drug called?" Olevia quizzed her friend.

"You got me with that one," said Jennie.

"The Bayer company named it 'Heroin' and I know you know it is used to treat more severe pain. The company did not realize how addicting it was when they started marketing it."

"But what does that have to do with you becoming interested in nerves?" Jennie persisted with her original question.

"My Father and Uncle decided to work together. My Father would weigh out the chemicals, being more precise, and my Uncle Albert, being more creative, did the 'cooking'. Uncle Albert would mix nitric acid and sulfuric acid with benzene, heat them at 50 degrees centigrade to create nitrobenzene, or aniline. Aniline could then be mixed with oxygen and different metals to produce dyes ranging in color from yellow to purple to black. My Father then collected the products and took meticulous notes."

Olevia paused, and took a deep breath, and sucked in the last of her root beer. "One day, quite unexpectedly, Uncle Albert made a startlingly painful discovery. He was holding the beaker of sulfuric acid in his left hand, his dominant hand, pouring it into the glass beaker held by his right hand, to get ready to heat the contents for the aniline reaction. The sulfuric acid poured out too quickly, hitting the lip of the glass beaker, and splashed on to the back of his right wrist, just behind the thumb."

"Ouch" interrupted Jennie. "That must have been so painful, I shudder to think of that acid pouring on to my own wrist!"

"Oh, how right you are, Jennie," replied Olevia. "My Father tells me that the white laboratory coat Albert was wearing turned brown and smoked when the sulfuric acid landed on it. Then the acid hit my Uncle Albert's skin . . . . My Father told me that he was not far away from his brother Albert. My Father, Alexander, says he heard his brother scream. My father said it sounded like his own voice screaming. My Father said his own hand hurt, but only it was his left wrist, the 'mirror image thing', I suppose," commented Olevia.

"What happened next?" asked Jennie.

"My father said he ran to his brother who was moving to the water shower. They arrived simultaneous, and my Father pulled the cord just as Albert got his arm into position. The downpour of water washed the burned brown cloth away. My Father, Alexander, said that the next thing he did was to pull off the white lab coat so water could more directly get to the skin. He said it was hard to get the lab coat off as my Uncle Albert was screaming and moving his arm continuously, as if he were trying to shake the acid off of his arm."

"What did the arm look like when the lab coat came off?" asked Jennie.

"My Father, Alexander, told me that the skin looked a piece of bacon grilling on the stove. The skin was boiling with little bubbles, and then just dark pieces of skin falling right off the wrist area. The water pouring from the faucet just washed this all away, until white stripes, which I now know must have been the tendons, were exposed. My father said they turned grey and were spreading apart as if to rupture, and then my father said he could see bones and the wrist joint!" concluded Olevia.

"What did they do next?" asked Jennie.

"My Father Alexander told me that my Uncle Albert could not stop moving and waving his right hand around. So my father took a wet cloth and wrapped it around the wound to keep it covered, and they both ran to find the Bayer Company Nurse," answered Olevia.

Olevia, took another deep breath and continued, "Uncle Albert told me that his memory of this moment was the memory when his 'nerve' left him. He told me that he felt his 'stomach turn over'. He told me that he felt so many different pains at once. He said his mind was just lost in pain. He felt burning, but it was different from heat. He felt pain going up his arm and down into the back of his thumb. He felt pain deep in his wrist. He felt pain if he moved his thumb. He felt pain if he did not move his thumb," said Olevia and then stopped talking.

"Oh, my good Lord! How horrible! How that story must have affected you! I can see it in your expression as you tell the story," interrupted Jennie.

"My Uncle Albert would tell me this story many times, as I grew up, and he would not let me touch that right hand. He lived with that same burning pain from his thumb into his wrist and up his forearm. That pain never left him," said Olevia concluding.

Then Olevia added one more line, "Jennie, to finally answer your question, that story is how I became interested in nerves; through the transmission of pain in my Uncle Albert.

PHANTOM

Jennie and Olevia both rode the same taxi back to the Salt Lake City County Hospital. They were sitting close together. Their shoulders were touching.

Upon arrival at Salt Lake County General Hospital, Jennie went to her 'Ob-Gyn' Clinic and Olevia went to her Surgical Dressing and Wound Clinic.

"See you soon," said Olevia, with a smile and a wave.

"I hope so," said Jennie.

As Olevia approached her clinic, she could see a small line forming outside the registration room. There were people in wheelchairs and people with crutches. These seemed to comprise most of those she saw. They were mostly men.

As she walked past the line, she recognized some of her return follow-up patients. She went up to two of them who were talking to each other. They seemed similar in outward appearance as she approached them from the back. Both were young men, and both were missing one of their legs from the knee down. One had long reddish-brown hair, a bandana, and a red, checkered shirt. His name was Ammon Allred, and perhaps not surprisingly, red was his favorite color. The other had long brown hair in a ponytail, and a green checkered shirt. His name was Isaiah Call. They both had wide shoulders, and muscular arms, thick necks. Men who were used to hard work in the mines.

"Good morning gentlemen. What are you two talking about so intensely?" she asked them.

"Good morning Doctor, Mam," said the one in the red shirt, looking up at her from his wheelchair. "Well, we are having a friendly little dispute. I have been telling this guy how lucky he is to have no feeling in his missing leg. Sure, he's got a messy wound there, and an infection that you have been treating, but he does not have pain like I do," Ammon Allred explained to her.

"Doc," interjected Isaiah Call, the man in the green shirt, also looking up at Olevia from his wheelchair, "he just cannot understand what it is like to be paralyzed from the waist down, you know from that mining accident that I had." Isaiah continued, "I feel no pain, I'm paralyzed. I wish I had more feeling, or at least some feeling," he said, frustrated, took a deep breath, held his nose, and continued. "Doc, you gonna cut off some more dead tissue from me today? My stump is starting to stink again!"

Olevia gently moved the two wheelchairs apart, as if breaking up a bar room brawl. As she looked down at the big bandage with yellow oozing from it on the stump, she said to Isaiah, "Yes, I will continue to remove whatever tissue needs to come off. Soon. Here in clinic. As you said, you cannot feel anything due to your being paralyzed. But your bone was almost sticking out last time, and it may be that we will need to go back to surgery and formally remove more bone and try to get the healing started all over again."

"Doc," interrupted Ammon Allred. "Please be careful when you examine my stump. It hurts so bad when it is touched. I cannot even come close to trying on my artificial leg. Do you think you can re-operate on me?" he asked Olevia. She now observed his artificial leg, a wooden peg, sitting across his lap on the wheelchair.

"I know you are tired of hearing this," Olevia said as she turned her attention to Ammon. "As your friend Isaiah here says, you are lucky not to be paralyzed and to still have sensation in that stump, even if it is painful."

"Doc, you know I lost my leg in the same mine cave-in as him," said Ammon. "Why is he paralyzed and numb? I would be able to walk if it were not for this pain?"

"You know the answer," said Olevia. "He had his back broken. You did not have your back broken. Both of you had your foot and lower leg crushed. Since you did not break your back, your nerves are still sending messages from your stump," she answered, now in her teaching mode.

Olevia felt it was so important to help people understand about nerves. Information about nerves was poorly taught, even to medical students, who should be learning the newest advances in knowledge.

"But Doc, please find a way to make a least my stump numb so I can wear my fake leg and get around without this blessed wheelchair," continued Ammon Allred. "I would trade numbness for pain any day. And Doc, please give me some more of those pain pills, I need 'em a couple of times every day," he urged, holding his stump with both hands to illustrate his point.

Olevia turned to walk towards her examining and treatment room. Then she stopped and turned back. "Ammon, do you still have the feeling that your big toe is curled down, even though you have no foot?"

"Yes Mam," he replied politely. "Even times when I do not have pain, my brain plays tricks on me, making me thing my missing part is still there. My friends think I am going crazy. They believe I am losing my mind. Am I, Doc, losing my mind?" asked Mr. Allred.

"Well, let me answer you this way, because I did not know you before your mining accident. You might really be crazy," she said with a smile. "People in Salt Lake City often talk about miners as if they are a bit crazy, working deep underground in the dark. For me, I like to think of miners as surgeons working inside the Earth instead of inside the human body. You mine for veins, or streaks, of gold and silver that keep businesses alive and I 'mine' for streaks that are nerves, like electric wires, that keep people able to feel what is happening to them, even if what is happening to them is painful. You two men and I are doing much the same work. Surgery too, can be dangerous, and perhaps I will tell you a story about that one day," said Olevia.

"But, Doctor, excuse me for interrupting, Mam, that is nice us being alike and all that. But what about my missing toe seeming like it is still there?" Ammon, asked again, bringing Dr. Landsmann back to focus on his problem.

"Your situation was described in many soldiers who fought in the Civil War, about 45 to 50 years ago," commented Dr. Landsmann, now back on track. "There was a doctor from Philadelphia who was very interested in nerve problems and cared for many of the wounded soldiers. He was also a good writer and left us excellent case histories in his book that was published in 1872."

"What did he say," asked the other amputee, Isaiah Call.

"His name was Silas Weir Mitchel. He named your phenomenon 'Phantom Limb'. Your brain perceives a part of your body that is no longer there," concluded Olevia.

"Oh no! I got a phantom living in my leg, and I may or may not be crazy," answered Mr. Allred, trying to make the facial appearance of a crazy person.

"Doc," interrupted Isaiah, "I heard most of those guys in the Civil War died if they had an amputation. We are both living proof that you surgeons are doing something better. What is it Doc?"

"Yes, you are right, Isaiah. Perhaps 50% or half of the amputees died of bleeding or infection when they had a leg amputated during the Civil War," answered Olevia.

"I like your stories, Mam, it helps ease my pain. Got any other stories about amputations," said Isaiah Call.

"I can tell you about the most famous amputation in history. But it is not a funny story," Olevia said. "And it shows how surgery can be dangerous too."

"Yes, let us have it," both Ammon and Isaiah almost said in unison.

"Robert Liston was a surgeon who was born in Scotland in 1794, and went to Edinburgh University," said Olevia, beginning her story. "He first followed in the footsteps of John Hunter, a doctor, from London, and established himself as a master anatomist. Then he became a surgeon. Liston was good. He was fast. This was the time before anesthesia. When he became more well-known, he moved to London and set up his office. He got the reputation as being the 'fastest knife in the West End' of London."

"But what about the amputation story," asked Ammon Allred, anxious to hear the good part of the story.

"Ok. Ok," said Olevia smiling, "You want me to tell you about his world record?" she continued trying to get them interested in what she knew was a truly gruesome story.

"What record is that?" asked Isaiah.

"All any surgeon could do at that time in history was to operate quickly, and minimize blood loss," continued Olevia. "For amputation, Robert Liston used a circular knife that he could swing around the leg in a fluid motion cutting directly to the bone as quickly as possible," she said, lifting the peg leg from the lap of Mr. Red shirt, and swinging her hands around his stump in a circular pattern, to illustrate her point. "And then, with the bone saw in his other hand, he would immediately begin the final part of the amputation, sawing through the bone."

"How fast could he do the amputation," asked Ammon, grabbing his 'leg' again.

"The story is that surgeon Robert Liston was so obsessed with his time, that in fact he had an observer pull out a watch just before he began every amputation. 'Time me! Time me!' Liston would yell out to the audience," said Olevia, retelling the infamous story. "Just to help you picture this scene better, let me tell you what he would wear when he operated", she continued, dragging out the story.

"He wore his usual long frock black coat and top hat, the coat almost stiff from previous blood baths. He used his bare hands. The long, curved knife may never have been washed."

"That is horrible," interrupted Isaiah. "Was the patient usually drunk?"

"Yes, but despite the whisky the patient had been drinking for hours, the patient usually screamed out in pain. Robert Liston's time on the day he set the record was just 2 and a half minutes to remove the leg." Olevia stopped her dramatic movements as other patients in the clinic had turned to watch this private show.

"His record is for the fastest amputation on record?" asked Isaiah, trying to pay attention.

"No. Not really. His record is for the most people to die from an amputation!" announced Olevia.

"How can more than one person die from an operation," Isaiah quickly replied.

"In this most famous case ever recorded," continued Olevia, looking around now at her audience of many nearby patients in the Wound Clinic and enjoying her theatrical moment, "It is said that an aged doctor, standing by to assist the surgeon, had his coat tails cut by Liston's knife, and probably imagining a worse injury than just that to his coat, died on the spot from a heart attack. Another of Liston's assistants had two fingers cut off, and he died later of wound infection. Finally, the patient who had the amputation died two weeks later, from an infection in his amputation stump. One operation. Three deaths. That is the record held by Dr. Robert Liston," and she finished her story, while those around her looked up at her in silence, stunned.

Another patient, seated just behind her now spoke, causing her to turn around.

"Doctor," said a woman sitting with her hands holding a bandage at her side, "How was that surgeon punished for killing three people?"

"Yes, it would seem that something was done wrong," said Olevia, realizing that perhaps this was not the best audience to have described this operation. "Perhaps you should know that it was not only the surgical patient who had to be very brave during those times. The surgeon had to brave in those times, and even so today. Trying to improve the patient's care and create new knowledge is always difficult and brings its own problems," she tried to explain.

"But what happened to that Doctor," persisted the woman who asked the question.

"In time, Robert Liston was made the first Clinical Professor of Surgery at University Hospital in London in 1835. His book *Practical Surgery* was published in London in 1837 and in America in 1838. I even used his book to study from," answered Dr. Landsmann, as she then turned and walked towards the treatment room she would use for the rest of her Wound Clinic.

YOLK, ROSE AND TURP

Olevia left the waiting room of her Wound Clinic, and opened the door to her treatment room, where she would be seeing patients. She was greeted warmly by the nurse, who usually helped her with her Wound Clinic patients.

"Good morning, Dr. Landsmann," said Margaret Jefferson, a round-faced youthful woman, curly black hair, average height, slightly overweight, with a smiling black face.

"Good morning Margaret," said Olevia, "are you ready for some more of our ghastly wounds today?"

"Yes Mam. We have to help these folks," Margaret replied.

"Then please bring in the first person to see me," she asked.

Margaret came back in pushing a stretcher, along with a male assistant, whom Olevia did not recognize. He was taller than Margaret, strong in appearance, with a peaceful face that somewhat resembled Margaret's. On the stretcher was a man lying face down.

"Dr. Landsmann, this is Robert Collins, your first patient today, and this man helping in the Wound Clinic is my cousin Johnathan Jefferson. He has just started working here in the Salt Lake County General Hospital Clinics area," said Margaret.

Olevia observed as Margaret and her cousin Johnathan begin disrobing the patient. First, they put gloves on their hands, then they removed the patient's pants, and started to remove the yellow-brown stained bandage from the patient's buttock.

Olevia asked, "So how exactly are you two related?"

Margaret, clearly the more talkative of the two, answered. "Our fathers are brothers and are descendants of the U.S. Army's 24th Infantry Division that was stationed at Fort Douglass. You may know that the '24th' was an all-Black division that fought with distinction for the Union Army in the Civil War. They fought again in the Spanish American War in Cuba. Just about all the Black people you see in Salt Lake City are related to the '24th'."

As the final bandage was removed, Johnathan turned his head to look away from the sight of the deep hole going from the buttock down to a whitish base with surrounding yellow brown tissues.

"Robert," said Olevia, addressing the prone patient by his first name," remind me how long you have been paralyzed from the waist down."

"It has been two years now since my mining accident, and I keep trying to sit and lie so there is no pressure on that wound back there, Doctor, but it is just hard not to sit on it sometimes. I know it is not healing well. It drains and smells. I am sorry about that," said Robert, accepting the blame for his poor wound healing.

"Yes, we know, Robert, it is hard, even with the padding on your wheelchair. But I have some news for you today Robert. We are going to try something new. We are going to pour honey into that hole, that ulcer, today, and give you a big bottle to take home with you," said Olevia.

Now Robert turned his head and looked at her, "Really?" he questioned.

"Yes, really, but we first have to clean out a little more dead tissue," she said putting on gloves, and turning to receive some instruments from Margaret, as Johnathan stood holding a large basin into which the tissues that Olevia removed could be placed.

To distract Robert, she again began teaching. "Honey does seem like a strange way to treat a wound," Olevia began. "Did I ever tell you the story of a famous surgeon from about 300 years ago, named Ambroise Paré?"

"No" said both the patient and Margaret simultaneously. Johnathan looked at Dr. Landsmann instead of the wound in which she was cutting out dead tissue as she talked.

"Ambroise Paré was the most famous barber surgeon of his time, the 16th century. Back then, Surgeons were not Physicians. Surgeons were not doctors. They were barbers. In addition to shaving and cutting hair, there were a few operations that they could do. They pulled abscessed teeth, they removed bladder stones, and, of course, they did amputations. Ambroise

Paré was French, and in time served several Kings: King Henry II, King Francis II, King Charles IX and King Henry III.

The traditional war-time method for treating wounds was pouring boiling oil on to them, to 'cleanse' them. During one battle, there were so many gunshot wounds, that Paré's oil supply became exhausted. He knew of an older Roman method of treating wounds that did not use boiling oil. It used room temperature oil of roses and egg yolk."

Olevia stopped her story for a moment and looked at Robert. "Is my debriding the dead tissues hurting you at all?" she asked.

"No. I can tell you are doing something, as it seems my body is moving a little, or the stretcher is moving, but there is no pain. That is why I keep getting these ulcers, right Doc?" replied Robert.

"Right. Good. To continue my story of ancient methods of treating wounds," said Olevia, "there was a third ingredient that was quite ingenious. Rome had many pine trees. In ancient times, someone observed that if a limb were broken off the pine tree, the tree made a substance that came out of the broken hole in the tree, the hole left by the branch, and that substance helped that open area of the tree to heal over. If the bark were removed, more of this substance came out and could be collected. If this material were purified by heating, then a substance remained that could be applied to human wounds. This type of tree was called a *terabinth*. The substance became known as turps and since it came from a pine tree, *turpentine*. Paré was able to obtain these three materials, yolk, rose and turpentine, and applied them to the soldier's wounds. These soldiers healed faster and had less death from infection than those treated with boiling oil."

Olevia stopped cutting and removing tissue from the buttock wound. "Margaret, can I please have the jar of honey?"

As she poured the honey into the wound, Olevia concluded her story. "After that battle, Doctor Paré never again used boiling oil. He began to practice and teach to keep the wound cleaned of dead tissue, as I just did for you, and keep the dressing simply moist. I am adding honey to your dressing today because it is just so sweet that bacteria will not grow in it. Now if you can keep pressure off this for a week it should start to turn red with new blood vessels and start to heal. Margaret will put on the rest of the bandage and we will see you next week," concluded Olevia.

As Margaret and Johnathan pushed the stretcher slowly out of the treatment room, Olevia noticed who was waiting to come in to see her next. It was Ammon Allred, seated in his wheelchair, holding his painful amputation stump, hardly being able to wait a minute longer to see his Surgeon.

"Dr. Landsmann, you have just got to find a way to get this pain out of my stump. I loved your story about that Dr. Liston and fast amputation. Would that work for me? Can't you just re-amputate my leg a little higher, hope that I live, and your assistants live, through your much slower surgery, and then maybe by starting my healing over again my pain would be gone too?" Ammon suggested hopefully.

Olevia began smiling to herself as she helped him lift himself from the wheelchair on to the exam table.

"Why are you smiling Dr. Landsmann? I saw that little smile. This is not the least bit funny, just moving on to this table has set off the pain," Ammon said, grasping the end of his stump and pulling it up towards his body with a grimace.

"I am smiling because you have just given me a great idea how I can help you with your pain," said Olevia.

"What do you mean," he said, looking up, still grasping his painful stump.

"Perhaps you know that surgery is what we call 'empirical'. Somebody tries something, and if it works, it is done again. Sort of like the story of Ambroise Paré that I just told the patient who just left this treatment room. He got wounds to heal without pouring hot boiling oil on them, and so he continued with that method. He taught others to do the same thing, and here I am today continuing with that teaching," she replied.

"So how does that help me now," he said lowering his leg.

"Today we are introducing science into the field of Medicine and Surgery. Where I went to medical school, at Johns Hopkins University, in Baltimore, Maryland, this introduction of science was our whole approach to solving patient problems, like your pain. In the past, most doctors learning surgery, just followed an older surgeon around for a year or two, and copied what he did for patient care, assuming that it was effective, that it was truth. At Johns Hopkins Hospital, my teacher, Professor William

S. Halsted, created a training program where young doctors stayed for years, gradually having increasing responsibility and learning from several different surgeons. I learned both from Dr. Halsted, THE PROFESSOR, and his best surgical resident, Harvey Cushing. It was Dr. Cushing who stimulated my surgical interest in working with nerves," Olevia explained further.

"Doctor," said Ammon Allred, almost apologetically. "I love your stories, but how is that going to help my painful stump and get rid of my phantom?"

"Ammon, you have given me an idea. This is how surgical progress is made. Instead of cutting off your leg at a higher level, perhaps, I can just cut the nerve that is sending the pain message. Cut that nerve at a higher level," Dr. Landsmann said, sorting out her new surgical research idea.

"Have you ever done that before, Doctor?" Ammon asked quietly.

"Honestly, no. I have not. No one has. Most doctors in the world believe it is wrong to cut out a nerve, that a painful numbness will result, something they call *anesthesia dolorosa*. But in your case Ammon, your nerve has already been cut, and I believe it is now stuck in scar," explained Dr. Landsmann.

"Of course, I have a scar, you can see it plain, right at the end of my stump. And it does hurt if you touch it in certain spots," Ammon Allred, agreed.

"Mr Allred, we all carry scars, some even from childhood," Olevia said, looking away from him, seeming to remember something in the distant past. "Most scars are external, as is yours, but many scars remain deep within us, as memories. How we deal with those scars of our past life determines how we live our future. In your case," she said looking back at him, "your nerve is stuck in your scar, and movement causes the scar to set off pain in your nerve. In particular, the nerve that used to go to your big toe is sending a pain message, and that, I believe is why you think your big toe is still there," Olevia continues.

"Doctor, that would be wonderful, but do you know how to find that nerve sending the pain message about my toe?" asked Ammon, continuing to cradle his stump.

"Mr. Allred, yes, I know where the Phantom lives! It is part of the tibial nerve that ends in the big toe. I think it is now stuck in scar next to an artery which beats against the injured nerve, sending continuing painful messages to your brain. I believe I must cut out that Phantom and relocate your nerve away from that scar into somewhere soft and away from where your wooden leg rests on the skin."

"Doctor, I am willing to be your first patient to have this surgery, as I do not think I can go on living with this pain. My life is almost without pleasure, unless I am sitting still, and doing nothing or just eating and drinking. Would you be willing to operate on me soon?" asked Ammon, now seemingly lifted up with hope.

Dr. Landsmann remembered Jarod Benson, her patient whom she failed to relieve of pain, and who then hung himself. Could she put this man through such an experimental surgery? Could she put herself through another such sequence of events?

"Mr. Allred, let me answer you with another story that illustrates what only you can know for sure. That is, how much pain you are in," offered Dr. Landsmann.

"Reportedly, in a battle near Milan in 1536," Olevia began, "a famous surgeon, who I was describing earlier today to another patient, was asked on the battlefield by a solider if there were anything he, Dr. Paré could do to help two soldiers, two soldiers who were this soldier's good friends. These two soldiers, lying by the soldier who was speaking to Dr. Pare, had been burned by gunpowder, and were in horrible pain. Paré said 'no', that he knew nothing he could do to help these two heal or relieve their pain". Whereupon the burned soldiers' friend withdrew his dagger and slit the throat of each of his friends. Holding the dagger, and turning to the astounded Dr. Paré, the soldier reportedly said, "if I were in that condition, Doctor, I would pray someone would do this same thing for me, slit my throat."

Ammon Allred just looked up at Dr. Landsmann. "Yes, I see what you are saying. It is OK Doctor, even if you fail, please try to help me. You are my only hope?"

As Olevia, looked first into Ammon's eyes, and then down to and touched the scar on his stump, her Uncle Albert's painful wrist suddenly came back into her thoughts.

Halsted's recommendation that "the operating room should be a surgical laboratory of the highest order," crept into her mind. The fear of failure and certain criticism from her Male colleagues lost out to the excitement of discovery and possibility of relieving pain in her patient.

PAIN & COCA

Jennie Ross and Olevia Landsmann were cooking dinner together.

Jennie had invited her new best friend over to her home for dinner. Could they operate on food as well together as they operated on people independently? They each wondered, as they faced the kitchen together instead of the operating room.

Spaghetti and meatballs. Red wine. Garlic bread and olive oil. Grated Reggiano Parmigiana cheese.

But they were alone, now, no surgical scrub tech, no circulating room nurse, no Male surgical resident administering anesthesia, just two women together.

"Olevia, this red wine is from California. They are just starting to produce wine there, and it is pretty good. What do you think?" said Jennie as she handed a glass to Olevia.

Putting her nose into the wide-mouthed glass, and inhaling, Olevia looked at Jennie and said, "Nice nose."

"Are you referring to the aroma of the wine or the nose on my face?" replied Jennie, with a taunting smile.

Olevia then held the glass up to the light and swirled it around, noting how the wine's viscosity allowed it to slowly spiral down the inside of the glass. "Nice legs," said Olevia, now smiling herself.

"Are you referring to the viscosity of this wine or what you imagine you see under my skirt?" replied Jennie, with a wider smile.

Olevia then took a sip of the wine, allowed it to slowly move around the inside of her mouth, and slowly, almost seductively, swallow the wine. "Red fruit forward on the palate. Perhaps I taste ripe cherry," Olevia smiled at Jennie.

Jennie moved closer to Olevia, gently moved the wine glass away from Olevia's mouth, and gave her a soft kiss, directly on her moistened lips. Then Jennie inserted her tongue into Olevia's mouth.

"Yes," said Jennie, as the kiss ended. "Red fruit forward on the palate for sure. I love this type of wine tasting. Think I will pour myself a glass too, and then you can taste me!" she said pouring the red wine into a new glass for herself.

As Olevia watched Jennie pour the wine, all she could picture in her mind, was her Uncle Albert's right forearm, after he had poured the acid on to his own wrist. "Be careful not to spill any of that." Olevia said quickly.

Jennie noted that Olevia's tone of voice had changed from romantic teasing to one of concern. "Olevia, it seems like you are again having a flash back of some sort. What did you just remember," asked Jennie, now reassuming her Doctor role.

"I am sorry, Jennie. It is just that I pictured the red wine spilling on to the beautiful lace cuff of your blouse, and staining your blouse. And that image brought to mind the way my Uncle Albert described the acid burning his wrist," explained Olevia.

"What did he say it looked like?" asked Jennie.

"He said it was irregular in shape. He said that when it first occurred the skin was firm, darkish in color, and then it became dry, extending to a border of lighter pink, that created an irregular oval at the base of the thumb and going up his forearm," said Olevia, completing her description.

"The pain must have been horrible," observed Jennie.

"Uncle Albert said that even though he was having pain, the skin itself was numb. The doctors placed his hand into a splint, and he was given Bayer Aspirin for pain," replied Olevia.

Jennie then tried to change the subject by raising her wine glass. "Let us try an ancient remedy for pain, Olevia. Let us drink some wine, toast to your research into the surgical treatment of pain and start preparing our meal," continued Jennie, toasting with Olevia and they both took a long sip of their wine.

Olevia started slicing onions and garlic to go into the tomato sauce and Jennie added salt and pepper to the ground meat prior to rolling the meatballs, stopping momentarily to put water on the stove to boil for the pasta.

Jennie asked Olevia, "With pain part of everyone's experience, and for some people a daily experience, as we see in our Clinics, why is pain so poorly understood?"

"Jennie, did you ever hear the line attributed to the famous French General Napoleon, about pain?" Olevia asked.

"No. I never heard it. I do know he liked Cognac and had his private label with his symbol, the honeybee, on it," said Jennie.

"Well, we can have some Cognac for desert, or perhaps just another kiss . . . , but to answer my own question, Napoleon is quoted as saying 'It is easier to find men willing to die in battle, then men willing to live with constant pain,'" concluded Olevia.

"Did your Uncle Albert become an alcoholic to relieve his pain?" asked Jennie, coming over and giving Olevia another kiss.

Olevia stopped chopping the onions and returned the kiss.

"Olevia, why are you crying," asked Jennie.

"It is just the onions, silly Jennie, not your kissing," explained Olevia. "But to answer your question, my Uncle Albert did become addicted. Not to alcohol however. He became obsessed with finding the cause of his pain. Pain none of his doctors could relieve."

"Then what did he become addicted to?" asked Jennie.

"Uncle Albert searched through books and scientific writings. He told me he had found a philosophic text by a man named Otto Rank, in Vienna, not far from where we lived in Munich. This Otto Rank was a friend of Sigmund Freud," explained Olevia, as she went back to a rhythmic chopping.

"And," prompted Jennie standing close to Olevia and gently massaging the back of her neck and shoulders.

Between the chopping and the massaging, Olevia's memory was awakened. "Uncle Albert was also obsessed with developing my mind. When we would sit in the English Garden together, he would read to me while having me rub his neck as you are now rubbing mine. He said it would take his mind off the pain in his wrist. He would have me memorize quotations. Here is the one from Otto Rank,"

The key to the creative type is that he is separated out of the shared meanings. He takes in the world as a problem. He has to make personal sense out of it. Existence becomes a problem that needs an ideal answer. But when you no longer accept the collective solution to the problem of existence, then you must fashion your own. The artist is painfully separated. It takes strength and courage the average man does not have.

Olevia turned into Jennie's arms and they hugged and kissed.

The sound of the water boiling on the stove broke the silence, and the embrace.

Jennie turned down the flame under the water and poured the tomato sauce into the pan, while Olevia put in the chopped onion and garlic to simmer.

Jennie put the meat balls onto a separate frying pan to get them started in a little olive oil, and then said, "So, to get back to your story, Otto Rank led to Sigmund Freud, who I know also lived in Vienna. I also know that Freud was a cocaine addict. I am guessing your Uncle Albert became addicted to cocaine. Is that right Olevia?"

"Wow, you are a good detective. And a good kisser. Well then, do you know the story of who introduced cocaine into the medical field?" asked Olevia.

"No. You got me there. Go ahead. I love the history of medicine. It is about how we got to where we are now. We must know the past so as not to relive its mistakes. And that is especially true for Surgeons. And really especially true for us few Women Surgeons, she said giving Olevia a wink.

"Ok. You asked for it, and it is a really interesting story, too," she said giving the pasta a stir, while Jennie stirred the tomato sauce and turned over the meat balls. "The history of science is that in the 1880's Karl Koller, MD, was an eye doctor, one of the first Ophthalmologists. He began his career as a surgeon in Vienna, Austria. He was a friend of Sigmund Freud. Koller knew how painful it was for his patients when their cornea, the outer layer of the eyeball, was touched. Just the way my eyes watered when the acid fumes from the cut onions went into my eyes. Every person at some time has 'gotten something stuck in their eye' and had pain while their body produced tears to wash the offending bit of dust out of their eye. Sometimes it is an eyelash that sets off the pain. What could Koller put into the eye to ease his patient's pain if he were going to operate on their eye? He experimented first with animals, putting various drugs, including morphine, into their eyes, but these medications did not numb the cornea, the surface of the eye."

"Get to the good part already," said Jennie impatiently.

"Getting there," said Olevia. "Sigmund Freud knew well the mind-altering condition induced by cocaine and discussed this with his friend Koller. Freud, in fact, had become addicted to cocaine. Koller tried putting dilute solutions of cocaine on the cornea, on the surface of the animal's eye, and was happily surprised to see that the animals allowed him to touch the eye with a cotton swab."

"Discovery!" said Jennie, drinking more wine, and toasting with Olevia. "What next?" asked Jennie

"Koller decided next to try this on himself. He put a dilute cocaine solution on to the surface of his own eye and noted that he could touch his own eye without it hurting. He noted it also changed the shape of his pupil, the dark spot in the middle of the eye. His pupil grew very large, as it would if he were in the dark. As an Ophthalmologist, Koller knew this meant that the cocaine had changed nerve function, had stopped the light reflex of the pupil," continued Olevia.

"How did Koller get his colleagues to believe him, once he had finished experimenting upon himself?" asked Jennie, now intrigued.

"Great question, and that is how we get cocaine introduced into the United States for medical purposes," said Olevia excitedly.

"What?" exclaimed Jennie, "I do not see that connection at all."

"Well," explained Olevia, "In order to demonstrate to his skeptical colleagues that this was true, and that cocaine could be used to help their patients surgically, Koller went before the Heidelberg Ophthalmological Society in 1884, put cocaine solution on to his own cornea. Then, in an experiment that would be remembered, and have profound implications, he stuck a small pin into his own cornea for all in the audience to witness."

As if to emphasize this point, Olevia took a thin piece of uncooked spaghetti and moved it towards her eye.

As Jennie swiftly deflected Olevia's spaghetti spear away from the eye, Olevia said, "The pin sticks did not cause Koller pain. Reports of this demonstration appeared in the press."

"Oh my goodness. Dr. Koller really did that to himself in public?" said Jennie, now adding the meatballs to the tomato sauce.

"Yes, he did. And, believe it or not, Dr. Halsted, who at that time was in surgery training at Bellevue Hospital in New York City, read of this human experiment in a New York newspaper. This is the same Dr. Halsted who would first teach me about surgery when I was in Johns Hopkins Medical School," said Olevia now plating pasta on to two dishes.

Jennie poured the meatballs and sauce on to the pasta and asked, "what happened next Olevia?"

"Halsted obtained some cocaine solution. To determine if it worked, he injected some into his own forearm. He did this repeatedly until he could determine how strong the solution had to be and how deep to inject it to create numbness in the skin. He experimented upon himself to learn how to help his patients in pain and to identify a way to operate through the skin without that incision being painful. An outcome of his research was that Halsted became addicted to cocaine," concluded Olevia as both she and Jennie sat down to eat.

Jennie poured them each another glass of wine, and commented, "Patients virtually never think of their doctors as putting themselves, the doctor's self, at risk. Patients, logically, only view themself, the patient as being at risk. The patient is sick. The doctor is healthy. Yet for some diseases, the doctor puts himself at risk simply by being there to treat the patient, exposing himself to their infection."

"Yes, that is the most obvious explanation," said Olevia now finally swallowing the first of her dinner. "Hmm, this is delicious.

"Yes, it is," said Jennie. "Maybe we can cook for the Conner Corner Store if we have to give up our Surgical careers," she added jokingly.

"Well, for the surgeon," Olevia went on, while still eating, "the explanation is much more complex. The surgeon must risk himself, I mean 'herself', every time she goes into the operating room. If the surgery is successful, well then, how wonderful. But what if the surgery is not successful? At worst, the patient dies." Olevia now knew too, that when the patient dies, the surgeon then dies a little bit too.

"Jennie, I have not been the same since my patient Jared Benson died. I know he hung himself, but it still seems like my surgical complication," said Olevia, mournfully.

"Olevia, I can relate to this as an Obstetrician," said Jennie, sympathetically, now reaching out to touch Olevia's hand. "When I deliver a baby still born, dead, it is just horrible. And the mother and often the father are right there with me. Horrible. Clearly, I did not kill the baby. But I always feel responsible. Then the next pregnant woman comes to me in labor, and I must just simply go on. Learn from the past, if there were lessons to learn, and then I must try to deliver the next baby. That is the way it is with Surgeons. The next emergency or patient in pain is always out there waiting for us."

"Thank you, Jennie," said Olevia, grasping Jennie's hand.

"Well, Olevia, now we know about Halsted and cocaine," said Jennie, "but how did your Uncle Albert get cocaine to use?"

"My Father, Alexander," said Olevia, "told me that he had been able to get a supply of cocaine through the Bayer chemistry company. He gave it to my Uncle, who diluted it in a weak alcohol solution, and then injected it into his own painful wrist, just above the scar, in line with the thumb. My Father related that a few minutes after the injection, my Uncle Albert's pain was decreased. My Father said that my Uncle then took some more and injected it more deeply into the wrist and thumb joint, and then above the scar in more normal skin in the forearm. My Father told me that a few minutes later my Uncle Albert smiled, for the first time since his acid burn. In fact, My Uncle was able to hug his brother, my Father, using his previously painful right hand," concluded Olevia.

"And that began your Uncle Albert's addiction to cocaine," commented the observant Jennie.

"Yes, it did. And this dinner and wine are going to begin my addiction to YOU," said Olevia now smiling and moving her chair next to Jennie's, giving her a kiss.

Then they toasted to each other again with more red wine. This time, linking their arms around each other and drinking from each other's wine glass.

ORTHO CLINIC

Olevia was on her way into her New Patient clinic, which was held on a different day at the Salt Lake County General Hospital than her Wound Clinic. She arrived early because she had decided to learn more about Orthopedics and wanted to be better acquainted with her Orthopedic colleagues. Orthopedic surgery had several clinics a week for all different kinds of problems, usually grouped according to the anatomy involved. Shoulder clinic. Knee clinic. Foot & Ankle Clinic. Orthopedics as, a surgical subspecialty, was becoming more and more specialized itself.

Today she would find out. Today was a day that both her Wound clinic and an Orthopedic clinic coincided. She walked across the hall to where the sign on the door read "Fracture Clinic".

Just to the inside of the Orthopedic Clinic door was a small conference room, and Olevia saw Levin Randolph MD, the Orthopedic Surgeon with whom she had cared for Edward Cannon, who was injured skiing . Levin was reading a newspaper article on the wall.

Olevia walked up to her colleague, greeting him. "Hello Dr. Randolph. What is in the News today?"

"Oh, hello Dr. Landsmann," he said turning around to see who was greeting him with such a sweet female voice. He was wearing a long white lab coat with his name on it, 'Dr Levin Randolph, Orthopedic Surgery' He noted that Dr. Landsmann had on a similar white lab coat, with pant legs sticking out the bottom. He noted, too, that she was wearing a white, starched shirt, buttoned at the collar. The name on her lab coat said, simply, "Dr. Landsmann". He noted, also, in that first glimpse that she wore no make up, not even lipstick, and her brown hair was pulled back.

Dr. Randolph turned back to what he was reading and said, "Orthopedics posts subjects noteworthy for the patients here, at the entrance to the clinic. This is a group of quotes from our Chief, Dr. Baldwin, who just recently spoke at the Orthopedic Section of the 68th annual meeting of the American Medical Association meeting."

"How interesting," said Olevia. "I know that Samuel C. Baldwin, MD is the first Chief of Orthopedic Surgery at the University of Utah School of Medicine. I have heard that he started as a General Surgeon at the Later Day Saints Hospital here in Salt Lake City and was then so successful at fracture management he was able to focus exclusively on Orthopedic Surgery.

"Yes, quite true, Doctor," said Dr. Randolph. "I am surprised that you would know that bit of local history, but perhaps it is because you too are starting as a General Surgeon but are trying to focus on Peripheral Nerve problems?"

"Perhaps so," said Olevia, and moved up to read the newspaper article. "And it says here that while most surgeons were fixing fractures with glued strips of heavy paper to create splints, Dr. Baldwin learned how to use Plaster of Paris to do this. He learned it from a Doctor Louis A. Sayre, in New York, who is called the Father of Orthopedic Surgery. That is very much like my learning from Harvey Cushing about Peripheral Nerves. I believe one day Cushing will be called the Father of Neurosurgery."

"Well, Dr. Landsmann, the 'news' here is Dr. Baldwin's comments on the new procedures to fix fractures with wires and screws. Perhaps you would like to read it," offered Dr. Randolph with a strange smile.

"Thanks, I will," said Olevia, scanning the article. From Baldwin's first quote, she knew Baldwin was going to be very conservative and NOT in favor of surgery, and particularly NOT by *women*. The quote read:

The more Orthopedic *men* get to using operative procedures to fix fractures, the less cases of fracture they are likely to get to treat. People do not want to undergo an operation if they can help it.

Olevia noted that his second quote again favored a non-operative approach to fracture healing:

With regard to the weight and pulley, I would say there is unquestionably no doubt that a man may pull himself up by his hamstrings; but how many seconds can he hold himself there? A weight attached to the lower portion of a limb, if kept on long enough, will tire out the muscles, allowing, in a large proportion of the cases, for the bones not to overlap, coming into apposition, allowing those bones to heal.

"Dr. Baldwin is seeing patients in our Clinic today Dr. Landsmann, if you would like to meet him," offered Dr. Randolph with a smile.

"Thank you. I would love to learn from him," said Olevia, as she turned away from the bulletin board and walked into the Clinic.

She spotted Dr. Baldwin right away. He was tall, with graying hair, and walking between the examining rooms, clearly in charge. He had an entourage of two young Orthopedic, male, Surgeons and two, female, nurses.

As Olevia walked towards Dr. Baldwin, she heard someone call out her name. She turned to look down and to her right, from where the voice was calling in the otherwise quiet waiting room.

"Doctor Landsmann! Doctor Landsmann!"

She turned to see a young man who looked familiar. He had long black hair, and his left leg was bandaged. He was sitting with crutches. She did not recognize him at first, but he looked familiar.

As Olevia moved closer to the young man, he said, "Do you remember me? You drilled a hole into my head and saved my brain. Now if this darn leg would stop hurting me, I would be great."

"Edward," she said, recognizing Edward Cannon. "Took me a while to recognize you. You have all your hair again." And they both laughed.

"Why do you still come to clinic? Surely your bones have healed a while ago, especially in a young healthy man like yourself," she observed.

"Dr. Landsmann," Edward said, "where they cut the outside of my leg is so painful to touch. When I walk, pain shoots into the top of my foot. It hurts even if I just try to lift up my toes and ankle. I can hardly walk. I have been to therapy and now have to take a lot of pain medicine. The medicine is not helping. I have not been able to go back to work. Even worse, there is great snow up in Alta, and I am stuck here in Salt Lake City," he explained.

By this time, many of the patients in the waiting room were listening to the two people speak to each other, especially since a patient was talking to Woman Surgeon!

Dr. Baldwin noticed the change in direction of the clinic patients' gaze, and that gaze was away from him, and towards a *woman* wearing a white coat in *his* clinic. Dr. Baldwin was one of the surgeons who had established these Orthopedic clinics and was as much a part of tradition at the Salt Lake County General Hospital now as the red sandstone blocks from Red Butte Canyon. He did not like surprises.

Dr. Baldwin walked over to meet this new woman doctor, who was wearing a long white lab coat, like his own. He, in addition to the white lab coat, wore a vest with a gold chain going from a button to a watch in the right vest pocket. He wondered, "Why has *she* come to my clinic?" he said aloud to those about him, or perhaps to no one in particular.

"Hello Doctor, I am Doctor Samuel Baldwin, in charge of the Orthopedic Clinics here and Chief of Orthopedic Surgery at this University. May I help you?" he said introducing himself to Olevia.

"Yes Sir, you may, and I am happy and honored to meet you. I am Doctor Olevia Landsmann, a new Surgeon on the faculty at the University of Utah Medical School."

Olevia noted the perceptible elevation of Dr. Baldwin's bushy eyebrows as she continued her reply. "This young man is both your patient and mine. While your team did a wondrous job with his tibia and fibula fractures, I was privileged to work on one of his bones that Orthopedic surgeons usually stay away from. His skull. The trephination over his right parietal bone relieved the pressure from his acute subdural hematoma, and he awoke to find his leg under weights and pulley traction, organized by Dr. Levin Randolph of your Staff. Mr. Cannon apparently remains under your care."

Dr. Baldwin tried to remain calm and in control. He recognized her formal answer to his question. He also recognized that this Woman Surgeon had given him both a compliment and criticism at the same time, and in front of his staff.

"Dr. Landsmann, thank you for that explanation." Replied Dr. Baldwin, clearly towering over her, despite her own above average female height. Then, in an equally formal tone, he replied, "Mr. Cannon's bones have healed now in perfect alignment, without any need for metal screws. He can ambulate without a problem related to the previous fractures. He remains of great concern to us still because he has severe pain related to an operation. That operation was not required to fix the fracture. It was required due a bleeding complication of the fracture itself. It is the fasciotomy of the lateral compartment where his pain is, and he has recently developed weakness in ankle dorsiflexion unrelated to the pain.

Now Dr. Baldwin paused, and then said thoughtfully, and as a bit of a challenge, "Perhaps since you were successful working on his central nervous system, you could give us advice about his peripheral nervous system, unless, of course, you feel this pain is due to a central nervous system problem, perhaps related to the brain injury," Dr. Baldwin concluded, trying to put the problem back into Olevia's arena.

'Arena', sand, thought Olevia. *Like the gladiators fighting in the Arena at the Circus of Pergamon. It was Olevia Landsmann versus Samuel Baldwin. She had a sword but he held a trident in one hand a net in the other. It was that net he was trying to use to ensnare her now,"* she imagined.

"Dr. Baldwin, perhaps you and I can examine this young man together in one of the examining rooms?" Olevia asked.

"Certainly," said Dr Baldwin, motioning to the nurses accompanying him to move Edward Cannon into the nearest exam room. He then turned to one of the two Orthopedic Residents following him and said, "I believe I saw Dr. Levin Randolph in the back of the Fracture Clinic earlier. Please go and find him. He did a great job on this young man's fracture. He should come and learn why this man still has pain."

"Yes Sir," said one of the residents, and moved away from the group to look for Dr. Randolph.

Once in the exam room, Edward was instructed to get up on to the exam table. He dutifully climbed, painfully, on to the exam table. "Doctors," he said, "this is where the severe pain is," and he pointed to the place along the scar on the outside of his left leg that set off the pain.

At this point, Dr. Levin Randolph and the young resident also entered the room. There were now two Male Orthopedic Surgeons, two Male Orthopedic Residents, one woman nurse and Olevia, along with the patient. Olevia was clearly outnumbered.

Dr. Baldwin moved immediately up to his patient. "I noticed that your leg seemed weak in addition to being painful, young man. Let me examine your motor strength," and with that introduction Dr. Baldwin demonstrated that Edward could not hold his toes and foot out, extended, against even minor resistance, demonstrating weakness in muscles that were not related to the area of his pain, which was the top of the foot.

Olevia then said, "Dr. Baldwin, I seem to recall that one of his fractures was of the fibula. His spiral fracture extended almost to the knee."

"Is that correct, Dr. Randolph?" asked Dr. Baldwin.

"Yes sir, it is," replied Levin Randolph, trying to figure out where this was going. *Is this a 'Witch Hunt?' Is she going to imply that I set the bones wrong and now this man is getting paralyzed?*

Olevia continued, "As of course you know, that region which comes up to the outside of the knee, is where the common peroneal nerve crosses to innervate the muscles that are weak. It may be that the fracture caused pressure on this nerve to result in the weakness you have just demonstrated. His pain is likely where the superficial peroneal nerve is injured or stuck in the fasciotomy scar. Perhaps you have seen similar cases before this one?"

"Bitch," murmured Levin Randolph under his breath, causing the two nearby Orthopedic Residents to turn their head and look at him.

Dr. Baldwin just stood there looking at Olevia. If he heard Levin Randolph's muttered expletive, he did not let on.. "How would you confirm those diagnoses Doctor Landsmann?" he replied, not answering her question.

Olevia then approached Edward's leg and began by touching the top of the foot. "Edward, this will not hurt," she said. "Edward, I am going to touch the top of the foot, and you tell me what you feel, OK?" she asked.

"Yes, go ahead doctor" answered Edward.

As Olevia lightly touched all the surfaces of the top of Edward's foot, he said, "I have no feeling at the top of the foot except between by first two toes."

Olevia looked up at Dr. Baldwin, and said, "As I'm sure you know, Dr. Baldwin, this means his superficial peroneal sensory nerve is not working, but his deep peroneal sensory nerve is still working."

Then Olevia began tapping along the scar from the ankle upwards towards the knee, while Edward just looked at her, as did Dr. Baldwin. Suddenly Edward moved his leg and screamed in pain. Olevia stopped tapping and said to Edward, where did you feel that pain?"

"It shot right down from there to the top of my foot," he said.

Dr. Levin Randolph now looked down. He knew what was coming next.

"Dr. Baldwin, this spot that triggered that pain is where the superficial peroneal nerve is entrapped, and possibly divided to give him a painful neuroma," replied Olevia. Her memory brought back the view she had immediately after the fasciotomy in the operating room, the view that showed the two white ends of a divided nerve. She avoided saying that she knew Levin Randolph had divided the nerve, sparing him embarrassment in front of his colleagues.

Then Olevia did the same thing at the side of the fibula near the knee, and again Edward moved his foot but this time did not scream. "What did you feel Edward?" she asked.

"I felt a tingling go down my leg and into the top of my foot," he replied.

"Dr. Baldwin, tenderness at this spot, near the fibular neck, combined with the motor weakness you demonstrated to me in toe and ankle extension, confirms my diagnosis that this is where the common peroneal nerve is entrapped," replied Olevia.

"Thank you, Doctor Landsmann," said the Professor of Orthopedics. "I see there is much we can learn from each other." He was indeed impressed with her physical examination techniques related to the peripheral nerves; he had never seen these demonstrated before. *He hated to admit that to himself.*

"Now," Dr. Baldwin continued, "what can we do to help this young man get back on to his feet without pain. As far as I know and have read, there does not exist an operation to fix either of the peripheral nerve problems you seem to have just demonstrated."

Olevia realized that he was right.

Olevia saw immediately that Dr. Baldwin had challenged her, again. She had blocked his first throw of the net in the arena of surgical knowledge, but he had just tried to ensnare her again!

Olevia also realized that, at the same time Dr. Baldwin had acknowledged the lack of book knowledge of his own profession about how to deal with the pain problems. He also had acknowledged that he must see these problems quite often in his Fracture Clinic.

Should I accept this challenge? Olevia thought. She immediately saw that IF she went back to the Anatomy Lab to research this problem, and IF she could come up with a surgical approach, that then she would have to take Edward back to surgery. IF she took Edward back to surgery, would Dr. Baldwin come to watch? Would Dr. Randolph try to cut off her finger again during surgery with his huge #22 scalpel blade? Should she even invite one or both of them? And what IF the surgery did not work? What would happen to her reputation? What if she made Edward worse?

To Olevia, Dr. Baldwin seemed to represent the Male establishment of Surgery in general, and, in particular, the Male view of women in Surgery.

"Dr. Baldwin" Olevia replied, knowing she was not answering his question, but wanting a little more time to think about a surgical plan, "I want to thank you for allowing me into your clinic today, and for your time in examining Edward Cannon, together with you and your staff. You and I both have learned a lot and I hope you will invite me back again. It is only through identifying challenging pain problems that we can be stimulated to search for the answers for relieving that pain."

"I look forward to having you come back again and see some other patients with pain," replied Dr. Baldwin. "We have lots of those patients; I have to admit in all honesty. Let us ask our staff to select a date and I can try to bring in a few, as you call them, 'challenging pain problems'," replied the Professor, dropping back into the habit of describing patients by their anatomic problem part rather than as a person in pain.

"Oh, and Dr. Landsmann," Dr. Baldwin added, "what should we do for Edward Cannon's neuroma and nerve compression YOU believe YOU have identified?"

Olevia smiled inwardly as she thought about the research work that would lie ahead of her. "Dr. Baldwin, this will require some thought. To help Edward, it is likely he will need to go back to surgery, and I must do some anatomic research to prepare for that surgery. I will get back to you with these answers and look forward to our next time together in clinic. Perhaps we should establish a new 'joint clinic', and by that I mean YOU and ME, Orthopedics and Peripheral Nerve, not necessarily elbow or ankle joint!"

Now Olevia smiled outwardly as she turned to take her leave of Dr. Baldwin and his Fracture Healing Clinic.

Dr. Baldwin, in order not to let *her* have the last word, said to Edward, who was listening with his mouth wide open, "Edward. I have found these to at least bring some measure of relief, at least to my younger patients at Primary Children's Hospital." With that he put his left hand into his left vest pocket, pulled out some jellybeans, and handed them to Edward Cannon.

HONEY

As Olevia entered the Anatomy Lab to begin the research needed for her to help Edward Connan's leg problem, she heard a small voice, asking her a question.

"Do you look like your Mother?" asked Chipeta.

"And how are you this evening Chipeta? I see it is just you and I and our hidden sources of secrets together again in the Lab," Olevia answered happily.

"I think you must look like your Mother, even though you dress so much like a man," persisted Chipeta.

"Now that you ask, Chipeta, I have been told often that I do look like my Mother. Angelika was her name. It means "Angel", and comes from the Latin, just as your name 'Chipeta', as you told me when we met comes from your native Ute language, and, if I remember correctly means a white bird singing."

"You remember correctly, Doctor," smiled Chipeta, flattered that this Woman Surgeon would remember the meaning of her name. "What part of the body do you want to research today? Can I help you?" asked Chipeta.

"We must learn about some nerves in the leg today Chipeta. Find me a body that has thin legs to make the first dissection easier for us, please," answered Olevia.

As Chipeta walked to the middle of the Lab, and selected a moist, brown-white sheet to pull back from what lay beneath, she continued her questions. "What did your Mother look like?" asked Chipeta.

"Vell, I think she vas beautiful, and I do not really dhink I look like her," said Olevia and noticed that she had slipped back more into her German language roots as she remembered her Mother. Olevia proceeded to put on rubber gloves and to pull up her scarf over her nose. "My Mother was taller than me, with long dark hair to her shoulders. She had a trim, athletic figure. She used to hike and ski. She told me that, when she was a young girl, she wanted to be a doctor, but that women were not allowed to go medical school in Bavaria. That is why she came to work in a chemical factory, in our home town of Munich, and that is where she met my Father," finished Olevia.

"I am glad to learn about Angelika, your Mother. Why do you almost always talk about your Uncle? You do not even talk about your Father very much?" wondered Chipeta, as she too now pulled on a pair of gloves.

Olevia began pulling away the already dissected skin and fat from the right leg to reveal whitish fascia, brownish red muscle, and some stringy white fibers lying loosely on the outside of the leg. Almost absent mindedly, while getting ready to dissect, she said, "My Father worked all the time. Uncle Albert worked, but because of his injured right hand, he could not work all day. Uncle Albert would spend that time with me. He took me on long walks in the English Garden, the beautiful central park of Munich. In the winter, he took me to the Bavarian Alps, Salzburg, just south of Munich, to go skiing. Sometimes we would go to mountains in the summer: it was cooler there. We were often the only two people there," and at this memory, she stood up, took off her scarf, and turned to look out the window at the evening sun.

"What did you just remember Doctor? It seems to have frightened you. Perhaps, you remember a ghost? Our Medicine Man in my village, when I was growing up, would say that sometimes 'even a good memory can leave a bad scar on our insides'," Chipeta stated.

Olevia left the table to go over to some dissecting instruments. She picked up a handful of them and came back to the table. "Chipeta", she said, "Your Medicine Man was correct, at least for me. Some memories were very sweet at the time they happened, but today I look back on them and realize they have left scars in me in places I cannot reach." Olevia now looked at Chipeta. "But Chipeta!! Onwards with our research!"

Olevia pulled the foot of the cadaver back towards buttocks to make the knee bend, saying "Chipeta, please hold this leg in this position. There is a big important nerve that comes from behind the knee, around a thin bone and then the nerve goes to the muscles that lift the toes and the foot into dorsiflexion. When this nerve gets injured, the leg becomes paralyzed. We must learn where the pressure point is on this nerve and how to fix it at surgery."

Chipeta held the leg pulled back in towards the buttock, and she stood on the foot side. "Doctor, so I must guess that when your Uncle hurt his hand, the hand that I saw bandaged, that his injury changed his life, and perhaps yours too?"

"Exactly," sighed Olevia; relieved that she did not have to go further into the specific acts that left those scars. Uncle Albert was the one who spent time with me, taught me, and encouraged me. When his life changed, my life also changed. And, then one day he left me forever."

"But Doctor," said Chipeta, again trying to cheer up Olevia, "He came here and you two will be having some form of spiritual reunion. Perhaps during your research."

Olevia pulled up her scarf and began to dissect.

"Here it is Chipeta, the common peroneal nerve," Olevia said.

"It is as thick as a pencil," observed Chipeta.

"Yes, it is, and round like a pencil, but look what is happening to it as it goes towards this bone, that it must curve around. The nerve is getting a little flatter. And here it dives beneath this group of muscles. Let us cut through them to see what happens to the nerve," commented Olevia.

"Doctor, I see the nerve is still round beneath the brownish red muscle, and then it separates into two smaller branches and then even smaller ones as you follow the nerve down the leg," observed Chipeta while Olevia continued to dissect.

"Now Chipeta, what is just underneath this nerve, as I lift it up?" questioned Olevia.

"Oh Doctor, I see something white and it looks hard," Chipeta said, putting out her finger and touching the white substance. "It is the bone you spoke about!"

"Yes, Chipeta, that is the fibula, and you can see that if that bone were broken, then that nerve could become injured. Now that is one set of observations, on just one cadaver, Chipeta. But in science, we know there are variations, so we must do this again and again and see how often this pattern is true. It is the variations that can make even our friend Mr. Anatomy into an enemy."

Chipeta just looked up at her with wide eyes, and said, "Really Doctor?"

"Yes really, go find another nice leg like this one on another cadaver and I will cover this one," replied the Surgical Scientist.

"Here Doctor, is another thin leg," called Chipeta from across the room.

Olevia did the dissection with the same result, and said, "Two the same, now go and find a third for us to look at."

"This is the same pattern Doctor," observed Chipeta. "Should I find another one?"

"Yes, and then two more," said Olevia.

"Doctor," said Chipeta, as they worked on their fourth cadaver leg. "This one *is* different. When you just cut through the covering of the muscle and the muscle itself, there is still a thick white band covering the nerve."

"Yes, Chipeta, you are correct. This is a major variation. An important one too, because look, as I cut through this new white thick layer, what do you see?"

"The nerve is not rounded, Doctor. It is flattened, and looks like mush, without a pattern," observed Chipeta.

"Excellent Chipeta. This is a compressed nerve. And as I lift up this flattened nerve, what do you see underneath it?" asked Olevia.

"I do see the bone again, but also another white band coming from the side of the bone," observed Chipeta.

"Yes. Now grab that white band that is running down along the nerve, and not across the nerve. What happens?" asked Olevia.

Chipeta did as she was told and watched as the calf muscle moved.

"So Chipeta, you just demonstrated that in this cadaver, there is not only a band across the nerve that holds it close to the bone, but also that the calf muscle, specifically, the lateral gastrocnemius muscle has a thick origin from that bone, and this band lies deep to the nerve," summarized Olevia.

"Yes. I see all of this but what does that mean in simple terms Doctor," asked Chipeta.

"It means that if this person had a leg injury and fractured fibula, then this person was more likely to have a nerve injury to the common peroneal nerve with foot numbness and paralysis. And in terms of treatment, for me, as the Surgeon, I must be aware of this anatomy so that I can remove the extra pressure it exerts on a nerve," concluded Olevia, removing her scarf and going to the window, opening it, to take a break.

"The air smells good," said Chipeta.

"Yes, it does," commented Olevia. "Now Chipeta, I have some good news for you. There is a 3-month course that the Operating Room here has developed to train women how to assist in the operating room. You have been through the Mormon high school system, so you have had enough education to be accepted, if I sponsor you. What do you think?"

"Oh Doctor, I would be so honored. Yes, please let me know what to do next?" said Chipeta excitedly.

"Ok, I will. But for now, Chipeta, let me tell you about the first time my Uncle Albert left me," offered Olevia.

"Doctor, if it is going to make you sad again, you do not have to tell me,"Her new friend said, protectively.

"This is a story about what we are doing now Chipeta. We are working on preserved human specimens. Do you know some of the history of how humans have been preserved?" asked Olevia, now switching from Researcher to Teacher, and thinking how similar the two roles really were.

"I know these cadavers smell and feel like oil and are slippery. I watched this in the embalming place when the new dead bodies come in. They get preserved by injecting fluids into their body. First, they drain out the blood. Then they fill the body with these fluids, then put the body into a refrigerator to wait for us," said Chipeta proud of her knowledge of the place in which she had spent so many years working.

"Yes, excellent Chipeta, but before that, it was known that you could preserve the human body and prevent infection by using something that smelled sweet and tasted good too," said Olevia with a big smile on her face.

"You are telling something not true now Doctor, just to see if you can fool me. I trust you as my teacher, so do not fool me," said Chipeta looking down at the ground now, sadly.

"This is the truth. Only recently I used this ancient technique in my Wound Clinic. The substance is honey, Chipeta," said Olevia.

"Please tell me that story from so long ago then, Doctor," pleaded Chipeta.

"Ok, Chipeta, well suppose," conjectured Olevia, "that a family member from Salt Lake City were to die skiing in the Colorado mountains. Well, the body could be transported home within a day. No problem with deterioration of the body. But what if the body needed to be transported to my hometown of Munich from the Colorado Mountains?"

"Yes, a much greater distance, and I can understand that you would have to preserve the body somehow," said Chipeta with insight into the problem Olevia was presenting.

"More than 2000 years ago, Chipeta, probably before there were Utes farming the Salt Lake Valley, there was a man named Alexander the Great. He was the strongest warrior of his time. He led his people from a part of Europe named Macedonia, in Greece, which was not too far from where I was born. He led his army to conquer the Persian people and took over their Empire. His army then marched into Arabia, where on the shores of the Euphrates river he planned to make the ancient city of Babylonia the capital of his new empire. He died in Babylonia, about 300 years before Jesus Christ was born," told Olevia.

"How could they get his body all the way home back then? There were no airplanes for sure. Just horses and wagons," said Chipeta. "His body would rot, smell and turn to dust."

"Yes, and that is where the honey enters the story," said Olevia. "In order to transport the body of Alexander the Great back home to his native Macedonia, his body was placed into a casket filled with honey. Babylonian doctors knew the medicinal value of honey because it had been described 1500 years before the birth of Jesus Christ. It was described in an Egyptian book, written on papyrus, a form of paper made from plants."

"What language was the book written in?" asked Chipeta.

"Back then, they used symbols, called hieroglyphics. That book contained 700 remedies, among them the use of honey for wound healing," answered Olevia.

"Oh, so did the Egyptians then bury their dead in honey?" Chipeta asked.

"Good question, but no. The Egyptians did research on embalming, on preservation and found a way to remove the insides of people, save the skin, and wrap the body in cloth," answered Olevia.

"Can you explain why the honey worked?" asked Chipeta.

"That gets us back to the first time my Uncle Albert left me. You may remember that my father Alexander and my Uncle were chemists. They said the sugar concentration is just so high in honey, so dense, that bacteria simply cannot multiply and live in that much sugar," answered Olevia.

"What did that have to do with your Uncle leaving you," asked Chipeta.

HARRIET

"As strange as it seems at first to tell the story this way, my Uncle Albert left me for another woman. A woman, who was to influence the rest of his life. A woman, as it turns out, who was to influence the course of my life as well," said Olevia, matter of factly.

"How old were you when he left you for this other woman?" asked Chipeta.

"I was 8 years old. It was 1892," answered Olevia.

"And where did Uncle Albert go to meet this woman? Did she have a name," responded Chipeta, asking two questions in a row.

"My Father and Uncle Albert were asked by their company, the Bayer Company to attend what back then was called an 'Exposition,' which was really just a big meeting. The chemical industry was growing so fast, that meetings of chemists began to take place in Europe, near where I grew up, and then, finally, international meetings of all types of businesses started," Olevia said, and then paused.

"To answer your two questions, Uncle Albert and my Father met Harriet at the Columbian Exposition in Chicago. It was to honor the 400th anniversary of Christopher Columbus's discovery of America in 1492," concluded Olevia.

"I do not believe Columbus discovered America first. My ancestors were already living here!" said Chipeta. "My ancestors would hold tribal councils, in which many tribes would meet, but we did not use a word like 'Exposition,'" she concluded.

"Yes, of course you are right. In my city, Munich, my Grandfather, Jakob Landsmann, went to the first Exposition ever held. It was held in 1854. He represented his company, the Bayer Company. I was told that he had an exhibit on the production of dyes, not from plants or bark, but by a new chemical process. The exhibition was called the *Allgemeine deutsche Industrie-Ausstellung,* which could be translated as the German-speaking, or All German Industrial Show. The next one to be held in Germany was in 1890 in Bremen, but my Grandfather Jakob was then too old to go, so he sent his sons, my Father Alexander and my Uncle Albert," concluded Olevia.

"I understand then that it would be natural for those brothers to travel to the United States together to learn what chemists from the rest of the world were doing," commented Chipeta. "How did they meet this woman, Harriet? Was she very beautiful? Did Uncle Albert want to marry her?" Chipeta again rattled off a bunch of questions at one time.

"To continue my Father's telling of this story, he told me that he and Uncle Albert went to an area called 'NEW APPLICATIONS OF CHEMISTRY TO THE FIELD OF MEDICINE.' The first exhibit there was on an old method of preserving animal and human specimens using alcohol," went on Olevia.

"You mean like whiskey?" asked Chipeta.

"Yes, exactly. The exhibit my Father told me about was so interesting because it began with a historical section. He told me the story about shipping home the body of a famous British Navy officer, Lord Admiral Nelson. Nelson fought against a much larger combined Spanish and French naval fleet of 33 ships. He sailed through the middle of them sinking 22 of their ships and winning the battle. He died however on his own lead ship, which was called the Victory. To preserve his body, his fellow officers soaked Lord Admiral Nelson's body in Brandy. They had plenty of Brandy on board the navy ships. That was not so long ago, in 1805," said Olevia.

"Doctor, please tell me about this woman Harriet," begged Chipeta.

"I am glad you like my stories. So, OK, already. As my Father Alexander described the experience, he and my Uncle Albert rounded a corner at the exhibit. They came face to face with the most beautifully preserved specimen of the human peripheral nervous system that had ever been prepared. It was an expert prosection," said Olevia.

"Doctor, no, now, wait. Are you saying this woman Harriet is dead and preserved?" asked Chipeta in astonishment.

"Yes, exactly, Chipeta. You guessed it," said Olevia. "My Father and Uncle could not believe the sight before them. Beneath the framed anatomy, was the name 'Harriet Cole'. Harriet now 'stood', or, more precisely, 'hung' looking down at those coming into her part of the Columbian Exposition of 1892. Her eyeballs were attached by their optic nerves to her brain. The cranial nerves swirled around where the where face used to be. The spinal cord streamed down from the where the base of the skull would have been and continued down to end in the multiple strands of the spinal cord. She appeared to be standing upon the nerves to the toes. And the whole prosection just sparkled."

"Did Harriet have any skin left?" asked Chipeta.

"No, she did not. And not to make a joke of it, but she just had a lot of nerve!" smiled Olevia, trying to picture that prosection.

"Who did that prosection?" asked Chipeta, "and whatever became of it?"

"My Uncle Albert told me that part of the story," said Olevia. "He said that there was a man next to the framed exhibit. That man introduced himself to my Uncle and my Father as 'Rufus B. Weaver, Professor of Anatomy at the Hahnemann Medical College in Philadelphia.' He told my Uncle that Harriet Cole used to work in his Anatomy Lab and had donated her body for a formal prosection because she so admired the way Dr. Weaver cared for the cadavers in his Anatomy Lab. Dr. Weaver said that after the Exposition, he hoped the University would leave the prosection on display at the Hahnemann Medical College."

"What was so special about the way he preserved her body to make it so different from what we do here at the University of Utah?" asked Chipeta.

"That is exactly what my Father, the Chemist, asked him," replied Olevia. "Rufus B. Weaver, I was told, said that he wrapped a piece of pickling solution-soaked gauze around each strand of nerve immediately after dissecting it. A day later he coated that nerve strand with paint, with a metallic pigment. Finally, Professor Weaver said that he coated each strand with shellac to keep it from drying over time. This also made the nerve shine," concluded Olevia.

"What made your Uncle fall in love with Harriet?" asked Chipeta.

"Uncle Albert told me that after being overwhelmed by Harriet's whole image, he then noticed that on the frame of her prosection was a Gold Medal and Blue Ribbon, indicating prizes Harriet had won. I remember my Uncle Albert saying that these were probably the most beautiful clothing Harriet had ever worn. Then he told me he could not take his eyes off her right wrist," said Olevia, answering the question.

"But Doctor, why her wrist? Was she wearing a beaded bracelet?" asked the Native American who beaded her own jewelry.

"Chipeta, on what used to be Harriet's hands, there were now a series of strings reaching across the wrist and into the fingers. There were nerves exactly where my Uncle Albert's burn pain was located. The nerves went across the wrist! He could not see if they went into the wrist joint itself. Uncle Albert told me that he believed he had found the basis for his persistent pain. It was now right before his eyes on the back of Harriet Cole's hand!" explained Olevia.

"Oh my, what a story. I understand now why Harriet was the woman who changed your Uncle's life," commented Chipeta.

"Yes. My Father told me that on their way home to Munich from Chicago, my Uncle Albert, told him that his new hypothesis for research was that those nerves he saw on Harriet's wrist were injured by the acid that burned him, and that if this were so, anatomic research would lead to the cure of his pain," said Olevia.

She continued, "My Father said that Harriet Cole's memory would last forever, and so would the memory of her Prosector, Rufus B. Weaver, proving the Landsmann family motto, *'Memorandum est vivere in Aeturnum',* 'To be remembered is to live forever,'" concluded Olevia.

"Your Uncle left you to come here to do research. And now you too are here doing research," observed Chipeta.

"Yes, and let's get to work. We have 16 more dissections to complete!"

TISSUE

"It is the right thing to do," Olevia told herself. *After all, their first dinner together was over Jennie's place. Jennie had invited her.* "I must now pay back that invitation," she concluded. She tried not to let herself think about spending 'girl time' with a Gynecologist.

For supper, Olevia thought she might make a dish more traditional, from Munich, from her hometown. "Wiener Schnitzel!" What could be more perfect! Her thoughts were interrupted by a knock on the door.

"What is all that hammering I heard while I was waiting for you to answer the door?" ask Jennie.

"That was just me pounding out the veal into thin pieces for our dinner tonight," answered Olevia.

"Come in. Let me take your jacket," said Olevia, admiring the pink blouse with the ruffled collar that spilled over the open neck, amplifying Jennie's bosom. Below the blouse, Jennie wore a bright red flowing skirt, stopping at her knees, which swirled when she turned, revealing her thighs.

"What are we going to cook tonight?" asked Jennie turning in towards Olevia and giving her a big kiss on the lips. Olevia took in the deep scent of Jennie's perfume.

Olevia blushed, and answered, "We are going to have Wiener Schnitzel, using my Mother's recipe. We will also have roasted potatoes and I have found a wine from Austria, a white wine, a Grüner Veltliner. It was hard to get!" she said, with a big smile.

Olevia was wearing an apron that hung from her neck. Her pale blue blouse was open just one button. She had on just a touch of blush on her cheeks. Tonight, she did not wear pants, but wore, instead a long straight, dark blue dress, whose hem was below her knees. The apron ended just above her knees.

"What can I do to help?" asked Jennie walking up behind Olevia and looking at the food preparation.

"First a drink is in order," suggested Olevia, pouring them each a small glass of the pale-yellow wine.

Jennie lifted her glass to make a toast, "To your Uncle Albert, who has brought us together?" she suggested.

"To Surgery, which has brought us together," suggested Olevia.

"To both then," said Jennie. "And by the way Olevia, can you just tell me how Uncle Albert, came to be teaching Anatomy in Salt Lake City when he started as a Chemist in Munich?"

"OK, if you really want to know. I will give you some brief details while we cook."

"Perfect," said Jennie, moving over to where Olevia was sprinkling flour on to the thin slices of veal.

"You remember that Uncle Albert knew finally that there was a pattern of nerves that were damaged, and you remember that he also knew that injecting cocaine solution on to the nerve allowed relief of pain. He needed a way to combine chemistry with anatomy."

"Yes, I remember those stories you told me, "agreed Jennie.

"Well, this is actually a perfect story to tell you while cooking. Uncle Albert would go to the butcher shop and get a whole chicken, and begin by skinning the chicken, and then removing a leg, just the way you would if cooking, and then separate the muscles from the bones. All the while looking for nerves. But nerves were hard to find in the chicken," said Olevia while continuing to prepare the veal.

"What instruments did he use to dissect?" asked Jennie.

"At first he used a knife and fork," told Olevia, laughing. "Then he began to use instruments from the chemistry lab. Then he went to my Mother Angelika for help."

"What could your mother do to help with dissecting?" asked Jennie.

"Since she worked in the Bayer Company infirmary, My Mother Angelika showed him the catalogue of surgical instruments that were available to buy. Uncle Albert ordered some scalpels, different sized blades, forceps, a large magnifying glass, some instruments called retractors to hold tissues out of the way of the Surgeon, and some little hooks attached to a chain that could also hold tissues out of the way. He was ready to dissect!" answered Olevia.

"And after the chicken, what animal did he try next?" asked Jennie thinking ahead.

"He went back to the butcher. He tried a goose. He tried a pig's leg. He tried the tongue of a cow. He tried and he tried. He just could not find similar anatomy or nerves. He needed human tissue, and he knew the only place he could get it was to go back to school," reported Olevia

"Talking about human tissue, and since you are cooking a 'Wiener', can you stop for a minute and tell me what you are going to do to some man's 'wiener'. I have never had one that was 'schnitzeld'," joked Jennie.

"You are so silly, Jennie. Maybe that is the way women Gynecologists talk! The Wiener Schnitzel is a classic dish of our country, where thin sliced and pounded veal is breaded, and then pain fried to a golden brown. A green salad or potato dish and a lemon slice is traditional," explained Olevia.

"Silly me. Yes, tonight for sure the only 'wiener' we two women will see will be in the kitchen. Now are you going to tell me that Uncle Albert quit the Bayer Company and went back to school? Because, outside of an Anatomy class, you could not get a human body to dissect in Europe except twice a year when a criminal was hung. At those times, the best Surgeon in the city got to do a public prosection for other surgeons!" added Jennie knowingly.

Olevia now took dried bread, toasted it, and crushed it into crumbs, then carefully spread it on to the thin veal that had been dipped in egg.

"Did I tell you this story before?" asked Olevia.

"No," said Jennie, taking a second glass of wine and watching Olevia cooking.

"Well, Uncle Albert went back to his Alma Mater, the school he had graduated from, LMU, the Ludwig-Maximillan University. Albert had studied in the Chemistry

Department there, which was next to the University Hospital; Universitatsklinikum, the hospital for major problems. The Medical School, with its Anatomy Department, was not far away, located on Pettenkoferstrasse, next to the Royal Bavarian University Hospital, in the

Klinikum Innerstadt, the inner-city hospital. Uncle Albert could easily walk there. So, he went to the School of Medicine. He told them he was a graduate of the school of Chemistry, and now wanted to study for a master's degree. Could he do this in the field of Anatomy? Uncle Albert asked."

Perhaps it was her first glass of wine catching up with, because now Olevia's speech became more German, and she assumed the bearing of her stiff, formal German teachers: "Nein". They said. "No". My Uncle Albert hated the word "No", Olevia said. "Uncle Albert persisted. 'Anatomy was not a traditional program of education', he was told. 'Aber', 'however', He was told, he could go to the Anatomy Department and offer to help, and observe, and maybe obtain the knowledge he was seeking in that manner." "Danke", thank you, said Uncle Albert. "Und zo" he did," explained Olevia, speaking again in her German tone of voice and now taking her second glass of the Grüner Veltliner.

Jennie then put down her glass and proceeded to peel the potatoes for roasting. She washed them, put them into some of Olevia's cooking oil, sprinkled them with parsley and put them into the oven. While doing this she continued her questioning; "I hope Uncle Albert found a sympathetic teacher?"

"Not so much sympathetic as excellent," responded Olevia, as she poured oil and some butter into the bottom of a very large iron cooking pan and watched the liquid begin to boil and spatter. "Uncle Albert asked to get a *Magister Artium,* a Master of Arts degree from Professor Nikolaus Rüdinger, MD."

"Why that person? Did he have a reputation for having a good 'wiener'?" said Jennie, kidding around again.

"I actually asked Uncle Albert that question myself," replied Olevia. "Uncle Albert told me that Rüdinger's father had died when Rüdinger was just 3 years old. His father had been a farmer and a butcher. Rüdinger was the youngest of 12 children and went to work at an early age. By age 14 he was apprenticed to a Barber Surgeon with whom he worked for 4 years. From a small inheritance he was able to study medicine. Although his first plan was to become a military surgeon, his brilliance in dissection got him an appointment at the Ludwig-Maximillan University to teach

Anatomy. Rüdinger accepted the position as Prosector. He developed a new technique for embalming, using carbolic acid and glycerin, so that the tissues smelled less, bacteria were still destroyed, and the glycerin rendered the tissues softer."

"Olevia did I hear you say 'tissue'?" asked Jennie, paying more attention to Olevia's face than her words.

"Yes, 'tissue,'" said Olevia.

"Kiss you, why I hardly know you," replied Jennie with a little smile, and gave Olevia another big kiss.

"Ha, ha, and delicious," smiled Olevia, pleased with turning 'tissue' into a kiss. "But Jennie, wait till you learn the rest of this story about Rüdinger."

"OK, but make it short, the Wiener smells delicious," Jennie smiled back.

"Uncle Albert was thrilled that his mentor, Professor Rüdinger had done his PhD research on *The Articular Nerves of the Human Body*. This was published in 1857. In 1882, King Ludwing II promoted Rüdinger to Chairman of the Anatomy Department. When King Ludwig II died, in 1886, it was Rüdinger who performed the embalming and autopsy of the King."

"Are you done yet, Olevia. I came for dinner and to have you as dessert, not for another lecture," said Jennie giving Olevia another hug.

"Yes, Jennie, yes, but there is a dark side to my Uncle Albert's mentor. Unfortunately, Rudinger had a vehement opposition to women entering the field of medicine. He learned this from one of his own teachers, Professor Bischoff. Bischoff concluded, from results of cadaver studies he had done himself on the skull and brain size of men versus women, that women were intellectually incapable of becoming academic professionals."

"Wait a minute Olevia, I think I know about Bishoff," said Jennie. He is well-known in Gynecology because of his research on the rat reproductive cycle. He was the first to link the menstrual cycle to changes related to rat pregnancy."

"Well, I am sure he must have done some good research with rats," replied Olevia. "But Bischoff went on to conclude, and Uncle Albert made me memorize this line, that:

The preoccupation with the study and practice of medicine contradicts and violates the best and noblest side of female nature, modesty, compassion and mercy.

"With that type of thinking being widespread in the Medical Profession where I grew up, it is not surprising that it would not be until 1908 that the first woman was admitted to study medicine in Bavaria," concluded Olevia.

Jennie took the potatoes out of the oven and put some on to two plates while Olevia put some of the Wiener Schnitzel on to each plate and gently squeezed a little lemon juice on to the top of each piece of veal.

"So that is how your Uncle Albert learned how to dissect human 'tissue,'" said Jennie giving Olevia a pretend kiss.

"Yes, Rüdinger gave Albert an embalmed human arm, and asked him to dissect the nerves, to see what he could do. My Uncle Albert injected his painful right wrist and then he could dissect with both hands. He now had real dissecting instruments. He stayed up all night dissecting the nerves of that arm," related Olevia as she began to eat.

"Hmm, I love the supper you prepared, Olevia," said Jennie. "Is there anymore wine left? And what happened when the woman-hating Professor Rüdinger inspected your Uncle's work the next day?"

Olevia got up from the table and opened a second bottle of Grüner Veltliner. "I thought we might need two bottles. How do you like it compared to Chardonnay?"

"I like it about the same. But the Grüner Veltliner is a bit more dry, and medium bodied, sort of the way I imagine you," Jennie said, continuing to flirt with Olevia.

"You may find me not so dry as you imagine," shot back Olevia, "but let me finish this one story."

"OK, more 'tissue' I imagine," Jennie said demurely.

"When Rüdinger came into the Anatomy Lab the next morning, he was astounded to see this beginner's first work. He told my Uncle Albert that his dissection was almost a prosection! It was precise. It was neat. It was a wonderful beginning. Rüdinger accepted Uncle Albert to work with him, and two years later, Uncle Albert received his *Magister Arterium* in

Anatomy, his. Master's Degree, Rüdinger offered him a job as his assistant in Anatomy. Albert was given an appointment as Instructor in Anatomy at the Ludwig-Maximillan University," concluded Olevia.

They ate in silence for a few moments. Jennie knew how that story was going to end. She wanted it to end too, so she stated the obvious, "and then your Uncle Albert left you?"

"Yes," said Olevia quietly. "When Rüdinger died of appendicitis in 1896, my Uncle Albert decided it was time to move on. He would only say that he needed a place to create that was more private. I was 12 years old. I somehow knew that I might never see him again."

Jennie got up from her chair. Went over to Olevia, and put her arm around her, and said, "Well, now you have me."

Jennie then lifted Olevia gently up from the chair and gave her a hug.

Olevia smiled, hugged back warmly and said, "Let us have another glass of wine, with our dessert. I would like to see how you prepare me for dessert using those Gynecologist's clever fingers!"

Olevia and Jennie refilled their glasses and walked into the bedroom.

1st LETTER

Olevia was preparing breakfast. She was wearing just a bathrobe.

"Jennie, how do you want your eggs cooked," asked Olevia.

"Over, just the same way I like you," joked Jennie, coming out of the bedroom, wearing a robe, and combing her hair.

"Olevia, I really want to understand you better," said Jennie seriously. "Now that the wine has worn off, please tell me how you decided to come to America to become a Doctor?"

"When Uncle Albert left," answered Olevia, "I made my first critical life choice. I was filled with the passion for discovery, like my Father Alexander, but not for Chemistry. I decided that my passion was for solving human problems instead of those of chemical molecules. Uncle Albert's search for pain relief led him to Anatomy and me to Surgery. I decided that I would become a Doctor for my life's work," finished Olevia placing eggs on each of their plates.

Jennie was pouring the coffee. "Olevia, you know so much about Philosophy. I wish my education in Canada had included this subject more, but then again you grew up in a culture that created some of the greatest Philosophers. Can you tell me more about their attitudes towards Women as Doctors?"

"Sure. Arthur Schopenhauer is a Philosopher I both admire and hate at the same time," Offered Olevia. "In his early writing, *The World as Will and Representation,* he wrote about what should motivate people. I think it was 1815, he wrote that:

> only compassion can drive moral acts. Compassion alone should
> be the only good of that act. The act cannot be inspired by either
> the prospect of personal utility, or the feeling of duty

"Which I love," commented Olevia, "And yet, in his later writings, in about 1851," Olevia continued, "Schopenhauer expressed his thoughts about women, in an essay appropriately entitled *On Women*. He wrote:

> Women are directly fitted for acting as the nurses and teachers of our early childhood by the fact that they are themselves childish, frivolous and short-sighted. . . Women are deficient in artistic faculties and sense of justice.... woman is by nature meant to obey.

"Olevia, please stop. This is appalling," said Jennie. "Makes me want to throw up, unless that is the Grüner Veltliner!"

"Yes, sickening. That is the part of Schopenhauer that I hate. And where I lived, in Munich, this philosophy quite pervaded current thought. It is why I knew I could not study medicine in my own country," agreed Olevia.

"Oh my. First your Uncle Albert had been forced to leave his native land because he could not educate himself and continue research in Munich's intellectual climate, and then you were forced to leave your country because of its attitudes related to Women in Medicine," summarized Jennie, sipping her coffee.

"Yes, exactly, so I finally had to have a critical talk with my Father Alexander.

"Please share it with me. He must have been so disappointed," sympathized Jennie.

"I tried to ease him into this concept," explained Olevia.

"Father," I began, "Have you heard that a woman won the Nobel Prize in Physics? Marie Curie. She is from Poland but worked on her doctoral thesis in Paris. Do you know she and her husband discovered a new chemical element, and it gives off energy? She has named that energy radioactivity. At the age of 36 she won the Nobel Prize. Obviously, women can do extra-ordinary things, just like men!"

"What did your father reply?" asked Jennie, paying close attention.

"My Father Alexander" replied Olevia, "said 'You are my only child. I have suspected after my brother's injury that your attention and interest have drifted away from chemistry. I am glad to see you are observing what some other women have accomplished in the world. Of course, Olevia, I know women can accomplish much, and especially you, with all your abilities, will accomplish much. Olevia you must follow your heart my dearest. You have the courage and determination now in you that I saw when you were little and climbed those big mountains, and then skied down them too. You are brilliant, coming of course from a brilliant Father, and compassionate Mother,' he added with a smile", said Olevia, remembering her father's answer.

"And you remember every word like it just happened, I can see that," Jennie said, always impressed by Olevia's memory.

"Jennie, how could I forget this conversation?" Olevia emphasized. "My Father said, 'I know the problems facing women here in our own country for advanced degrees. Marie Curie achieved her advances in Paris, France, not Munich, Germany.'"

Olevia continued her memory of her Father's answer to her, " Through business friends in America that I met when your Uncle and I visited the Chicago Exposition," he had said to her, " I have heard that a new medical school has opened in the eastern United States, in a city called Baltimore. It is between Philadelphia and Washington, DC. I have heard that among other unique features of this new school, one of them is that they are more open to accepting women in medical school. I think you should write to them. Give it a try. The school is named the Johns Hopkins School of Medicine. The motto of the Johns Hopkins University is *Veritas vos Liberabit*,' he concluded," said Olevia.

"All right. Go ahead. Tell me what that means in Latin," said Jennie.

"It means 'The Truth shall make you Free'," answered Olevia.

"And you applied, and I know the rest of the story," smiled Jennie now holding Olevia's hand.

"When my letter of acceptance to the Johns Hopkins School of Medicine arrived," said Olevia proudly, "I sat with My Father Alexander and My Mother Angelika. We read the letter together. Then they helped me plan my trip to America to become a Woman Doctor.

II
JOHNS HOPKINS SCHOOL OF MEDICINE

BALTIMORE, MARYLAND, 1910

WELCOME

"Olevia Landsmann", said Florence Sabin, MD, Associate Professor of Medicine at the Johns Hopkins University School of Medicine, it is my privilege to welcome you and give you a little background about the education you will embark upon here in Baltimore."

"Thank you, Doctor," said Olevia, standing in front of Dr. Sabin's desk. Olevia was wearing a straight, slightly tailored, dark blue dress that came down to meet her ankles. Her shoes were black leather, not shiny. The dress buttoned to her neck. Her long brown hair was shoulder length. She wore no lipstick. She held a small navy-blue purse in her left hand. She wore a watch with a black leather strap.

"What did you think of the architecture of this building?" asked Doctor Sabin, smiling.

"I love it really," said Olevia. "The dome with its open observation area is unique, as the domes on buildings in Munich, where I am from, are all enclosed. The color of the red brick seems perhaps unique to Baltimore," observed Olevia, then she stopped talking.

"Yes, you are quite correct. This building was the first to be built. It became the main building of the new Johns Hopkins Hospital, which opened in 1889. The land was donated by the man, Johns Hopkins, himself, in his Will, and given over to the Board of Trustees in 1876, at the time of Mr. Hopkins's death," commented Doctor Sabin, and then she was quiet, seemingly thinking how to phrase the next sentence.

"Olevia, you should know that you are the first 'foreign' woman accepted to the Johns Hopkins School of Medicine," Florence Sabin began again, this time in a gentler voice. "You have been accepted because you have outstanding university grades from Ludwig-Maximillan University, which has a reputation for being a very strict University of the highest standard. You have excellent language skills, and excellent recommendations from your Professors in Munich." Florence Sabin at this point glanced down to read from the folder in front of her. "They said you were compassionate, intuitive, creative, brilliant, serious about becoming a doctor rather than a mother, energetic, and, to be taken as a compliment, 'rather straight-laced'," concluded Dr. Sabin with a smile.

Olevia was undecided as to whether to smile courteously, appear embarrassed by what were probably meant as compliments about her, or to simply keep a straight face. Instead, she chose to say directly, "Thank you Dr. Sabin, I will do my best not to disappoint anyone."

Dr. Sabin replied, "I was asked by the Head of the Medical School Admissions Committee to meet with you, since I myself graduated from this School of Medicine, in 1900, and am the first woman to be appointed as Associate Professor."

Dr. Sabin stopped for a moment then to see what Olevia would say.

Olevia said nothing. Dr. Sabin, deciding to be less threatening, said, "I see you have already published a basic science paper on the conversion of aniline to phtalein. You did this while you were working in the commercial clothing dye industry, with the Bayer Company, where your father worked. I appreciate this as I, too, have published in the scientific literature. My research involved describing the development of the lymphatic system. My research model used pig embryos."

Observing the now perhaps even more distant appearance of Olevia's face, Dr. Sabin tried a different tact.

"Where will you be living while you are in Baltimore, Olevia?"

"My Father, Alexander, learned of a respectable boarding house, run by Miss Susie Slagle on Biddle Street, not too long a walk from the Johns Hopkins Hospital. Perhaps you know of it. That is where I will be staying," replied Olevia.

"I do know of it. Your father made an excellent choice. He also assured the University that there would be no problem paying your tuition, and he has paid the whole first year in advance for you," added Dr. Sabin, reassuringly.

"My Father Alexander has always been generous with regard to my education," replied Olevia, and then, feeling more confident, she asked her first question. "Why did Mr. Hopkins make this donation? Did he have any children?"

"Good question," complimented Dr. Sabin, trying to be encouraging. "Mr. Hopkins had no children. He was a merchant. He was part owner of the Baltimore and Ohio Railroad. At the time of his death, Mr. Hopkins lived about one mile north of where the present-day Johns Hopkins Hospital stands. His home was large for those times, as was the surrounding land, now known as Clifton Park. He also owned this land on which the hospital stands. He donated this too."

Olevia now asked her second question, "Why would he have chosen to build a hospital with his hard-earned money?"

"Mr. Johns Hopkins wrote in his will that 'as best he could see into the future, there would always be the need to heal the sick and to educate the physicians who would take care of the sick.' He left a donation of seven million dollars. Half of this donation was to start a hospital and half was to start a graduate school. It is said that the Johns Hopkins University undergraduate school was developed to educate people well enough to enter the Johns Hopkins graduate school," answered Dr. Sabin, with a little laugh.

Now it was Dr. Sabin's turn to ask a question. "Olevia, do you know why women are accepted into the Johns Hopkins School of Medicine, while most other schools of medicine in Europe and the United States do not?"

"No, I do not," answered Olevia immediately.

"Well, first let me share with you the story of the first woman doctor in the United States," said Dr. Sabin. "Do you know her name, Olevia".

"I do not," Olevia said honestly.

"The first woman to graduate from medical school in the United States was Elizabeth Blackwell, on January 23, 1849," replied Dr. Sabin. "Miss Blackwell graduated from Hobart College, from their Geneva Medical School, in upstate New York. Her admission to the medical school was quite unusual. The Admissions Committee did not know what to do with an application from a woman, as they had never had one. They sent a letter to the full medical student body, 150 men. The letter asked that if anyone objected to admitting a woman to their medical school, to let the

Admissions Committee know, and, in that case, they would not admit her. The male student body thought this was a prank, and no one objected. Elizabeth Blackwell was therefore admitted."

Olevia just starred at Dr. Sabin, eyes open wide, mouth kept shut.

Dr. Sabin resumed her Hopkins history-teaching role. "Although our hospital was built by 1899, and the initial faculty for the medical school were chosen, the medical school could not open. The trustees of the Johns Hopkins School of Medicine were simply out of money, primarily because the stock in the B & O railroad, donated by Mr. Hopkins, had dropped in value," Dr. Sabin paused.

"Had they spent the whole 7 million dollars already?" asked Olevia.

"No Olevia. The Board members of the Johns Hopkins Hospital were not allowed to spend the endowment that Mr. Hopkins, had given to them. They could only spend the interest on that money," answered Dr Sabin.

Dr. Sabin then continued. "To the rescue came four women. Each of these women was the daughter of one of the original Trustees of the new Johns Hopkins University. They were Martha Carey Thomas, Mary Elizabeth Garrett, Elizabeth King and Mary Gwinn, all unmarried, wealthy, well-educated and devoted to the new feminist movement. They would raise the $500,000 needed to open the school and pay for a medical school building, but only if the school would open its doors to qualified women, beginning with the first class. The Board of the Johns Hopkins Hospital accepted this."

Olevia said "Thank you for sharing that history with me. I feel even more honored now that I know this. It is very difficult for women to find a good place to be educated in Medicine, even today."

"Yes, it remains difficult," agreed Dr. Sabin. "Medical education remains a male-dominated field. 'Female Physicians' is the title given to women who do abortions. These women are actually mid-wives, not Physicians. Women of course, in the United States as in Europe, can be nurses, but not doctors."

"I have dedicated myself to become a Woman Physician, and to make discoveries to help with human suffering," stated Olevia, quietly, but with resolve.

"Ms. Landsmann," said Dr Sabin, calling Olevia by her family name for the first time, "You will also be interested to know how selective the admissions process is because of one of those generous women, Mary Elizabeth Garrett. She donated the most money, $350,000. For this she insisted that the entrance requirements to be met by either a man *or* a woman applicant be proof of a bachelor's degree, meaning they had to have already graduated from a University, and to have proficiency in French, German and Latin, and a strong background in physics, chemistry and biology," concluded Dr. Sabin.

Olevia now was so thankful that the tutors her Father Alexander hired for her insisted that she learn these languages. She asked a final question, "How many women were in that first graduating class in 1903."

"There were three, but only one graduated," answered Dr. Sabin.

Olevia, feeling even more empowered now to succeed here, then asked, "What happened to the other two who did not graduate?"

Dr. Sabin replied, "One dropped out due to the curriculum being too difficult. The other married one of her teachers," she said with a distinctly female grin.

THE CREST

Olevia loved the first year of medical school. Her mind and her background seemed perfectly suited for these studies. The first class had been biochemistry, which of course, was already second nature to her. Anatomy, her true love, brought her compliments from her dissecting partners and Anatomy Instructors alike. Histology, using the microscope to look at the parts that made up the human body, gave her the first real look at nerves, and at slices of the brain.

She was obsessed and left herself no time for outside interests. She did take time to write home. Of course, she asked about her Uncle Albert, but no replies about him came. Her Father and Mother were doing well, and sent their love, and some money.

The second year of medical school was her first chance to get close to patients, if you could call examining their body parts in a tub 'getting close'. In the basement of the Pathology Building at Johns Hopkins Hospital were a series of rooms that contained 5-gallon tubs. Each tub contained the organs and other vital parts related to the disease from which that person had died. The deceased person's autopsy number was written in black on each tub. The rooms in the basement were very unsettling. Each student had to go down there with their pathology partner, find the tub that fit with that day's disease, and bring the tub up to the lab for study.

It was while her class was observing an autopsy that Olevia gazed up from the Pathologist who was using a saw to open the skull. As she looked up and away, she caught a glimpse of reddish hair. It was Ezra Maybe, standing on the other side of the autopsy table. He was starring at her. He quickly looked away.

Funny how the human mind works, or at least mine does, thought Olevia. *Our brain distracts us to save us from pain.* She realized that her mind did not want her to see the skull being sawed open, and so it brought to mind, a little joke, about seeing Ezra. A joke based upon his last name. *Ezra Maybe likes me or 'May be' he does not!*

When she and Ezra were back sitting next to each other in the Pathology laboratory, with another tub of body parts, this time from someone who had died of kidney disease, she looked over at Ezra, and tried out her new joke.

"Ezra, I was thinking, 'Maybe' you liked the autopsy or 'May be' you did not?"

"Ha! Ha!, as if I have not heard that a bunch of times before in my life. But, good that you were thinking of me. By the way, I found another mnemonic from Oliver Wendell Holmes, Sr. Do you still remember the names of the bones of the wrist, the carpal bones?" he asked, challenging her intellectually, as he always liked to do.

"I sure do," replied the confident young anatomist, Olevia.

"Take your pen and put the letters of the bones in the correct place on the back of my wrist," he commanded, as if he did not believe she could do it.

Olevia took her pen in her right hand, and grasped his left hand, palm to palm, so that she could write on the back of his left hand. As she did that, their eyes briefly met, and she felt a little chill.

"I will place an N for Navicular here on the thumb side just past the distal radius, then an L for Lunate next to it, then a T for triquetrium, next to that a P just to the underside of it for the Pisiform, which lies under the triquetrium on the ulnar side of the wrist. That is the first or proximal carpal row. Then going back to the thumb side, begin the distal carpal row with a GM for Greater Multangular, then an M for lesser Multangular, then a C for Capitate, and finally, back on the ulnar side, an H for Hamate," completed Olevia with obvious pride.

"Now did you use a mnemonic to remember that, Olevia?" asked Ezra, allowing their hands to stay together, enjoying this form of non-intellectual contact.

"No" she replied matter of factly. "I just remember their Latin and Greek names. What is the memory device that you have to use to remember them," she said, now acting as the clever one.

"Well, some books are now calling the great multangular the trapezium and the lesser multangular the trapezoid, but for the mnemonic I have in mind you are totally correct, and I hope you will find this one more stimulating than my last very proper one on the cranial nerves," commented Ezra.

Ezra then took her right hand in his left hand, and, using his right index finger as a pointer, he retraced the letters she had drawn on his hand, while he said aloud,

"Never Lower Tillie's Pants, GrandMa Might Come Home!"

Then they both had a good laugh, and as their fellow classmates turned, from their tub of organs, to see what was so funny, Olevia and Ezra stopped holding hands.

To end that somewhat awkward moment, Ezra reverted to character and asked Olevia, "I have been wondering why your notebooks have that interesting crest on it, instead of the ones most of use with the Hopkins University Emblem on it, you know the one that says in Latin *Veritas Vos Liberabunt*?"

"Ezra," answered Olevia, holding up her notebook to make the point, "My Father Alexander and my Uncle Albert always had these notebooks in our home, and kept their notes at work in them. My Father sends these notebooks to me. It does save me a little money not to have to buy so many notebooks at the Hopkins Bookstore, and it also reminds me of my family."

"Thanks for sharing that. Now can you explain its symbolism to me, and what it says in Latin? Your Latin is honestly better than mine," admitted Ezra, this time respectfully.

Olevia answered with pride. "Working with fabrics had been in our Landsmann family for generations. My Great Grandfather, Leo, on my Father's side, the father of Grandfather Jakob, created the crest. It hangs over the fireplace now in the Landsmann home in Munich. This crest depicts a golden falcon, representing enlightenment and perseverance. The falcon is landing from the upper left of the crest on to an azure blue lower half with a raguly edge. Blue represented loyalty. That raguly or jagged edge indicated hardship overcome. I was told that my Great Grandfather Leo would describe the life his ancestors had to endure, and, through work, persevere and overcome. Within the family crest, within that field of royal blue, is pair of clasped hands, golden in color. These represent enlightened hands, joined, creating union. Again, I am told that the Landsmann family had helped to form a union of merchants, a guild, in medieval Prussia."

"Great symbolism," commented Ezra earnestly. "Maybe we can talk some more about our families one day, outside of this Pathology classroom."

"OK," Olevia agreed. "Now my turn to ask a question. I understand that most of the people in Utah, where you are from, are Mormon. To the best I can tell, they usually have dark hair or blond hair. What is with your red hair?"

"Excellent question Olevia," responded Ezra. "Perhaps you know there is a big mining industry in the mountains around Salt Lake City. The miners came from all over the world, including your neighbor, Austria. Miners came from Italy, Greece, and even from the Celtic country, Wales. About 10% of the Welsh are redheaded. My grandfather was a red head, William Ryan. He was a miner. He worked in the coal camps of Consumer, Sweets and National in Carbon County, Utah. He married a woman from one of the camps. A Mormon doctor delivered their baby and helped William Ryan through a bad illness. The Doctor sewed him up a couple of times. My Grandfather loved that doctor and converted to be a member of The Church of Jesus Christ of Latter-Day Saints. He changed his last name from Ryan, a typical Welsh surname, to Maybe, one of the more common Mormon names. My father survived growing up in the mining camps and moved to Salt Lake City. He married my Mom, Eliza, and had just one wife. My father told my Grandfather's story about that Camp Doctor so many times, that I became interested in medicine myself. And here I am, red-headed, a Mormon, and on my way to becoming a Doctor."

"Thanks for sharing that beautiful story," said Olevia.

"You are most welcome and thanks for sharing your stories with me," Ezra replied, and then added, "I like talking with you. When do you want to meet outside of class?"

Taken totally by surprise, Olevia just looked down at the desk, demurely.

KICK BUCKETS

"This is NOT what I had in mind when I said I wanted to meet you outside of class," said Ezra, sounding disappointed.

" We are not in our classroom are we?" replied Olevia with a little laugh, as she led Ezra down a dark, somewhat forbidding, stairway.

Ezra and Olevia had to move over to the right and hug the wall as two of their Pathology classmates trudged up the stairs, each holding the handle of a clearly heavy big yellowish bucket, with a number written in thick black numerals.

Ezra moved ahead of her turning the corner and, looking at a sheet in his hand, he said, "Wait a minute. Our path specimen sheet has two different bucket numbers on it, not one. What is going on?" he complained, thinking they were going to have to do twice as much work as the other teams.

"Not to worry, Ezra," said Olevia. "I will get that bucket with the top number and you get the bucket with the other number on it. Meet you back here very soon," she said walking quickly ahead, moving between other medical students who were also looking for their bucket number.

Olevia found her bucket quickly and was standing in the center of the room lifting it with one hand, up and down.

"What are you doing, Olevia?" Ezra asked.

"I can hardly believe there is a whole set of a dead person's organs in my bucket. This bucket is relatively light," she observed, lifting hers up and down with one hand.

"Actually, I must say mine is lighter than usual too," Ezra agreed. "Let's get up to the lab and see what is going on. He led the way up the steps, each of them carrying a bucket containing some part of a deceased person, or so they thought.

Ezra and Olevia reached their desk at the same time. Placed their buckets in front of themselves. Pulled on a pair of rubber gloves. Looked at each other, gave each other a head nod and then opened their own bucket. They looked at each other in surprise.

Each bucket contained an amputated foot, with part of the leg still attached.

"Mine is missing three toes, and the remaining two are black," said Ezra.

"Mine has all the toes, but has a nasty open wound with black edges, and bones exposed beneath the 3rd metatarsal head," said Olevia, the Anatomist.

"Mine has a long incision along the medial side going from the ankle up proximally, with the blood vessels exposed," said Ezra, now examining the specimen more carefully.

"So does mine," commented Olevia.

"What does this mean?" asked Ezra.

"It means that two different pathologic mechanisms resulted in the same need to amputate a leg. We must compare the vessels that are exposed in the two legs and see what the difference is," announced Olevia.

"Yes, that is it! And, in terms of different mechanisms, I must believe that the missing toes plus black toes imply poor circulation as the cause of the amputation, gangrene," said Ezra quickly, not to be outdone by Olevia.

"Excellent thinking Ezra. I like it," said Olevia. "And my patient lost her leg related to infection that was spreading throughout the foot. She has osteomyelitis, the infection is inside of the bones in the middle of the foot," announced Olevia, pleased with herself.

"Why do you say 'her' as if the owner of your leg was a woman?" asked Ezra.

"Oh, come on now Ezra. Your patient's leg is hairy and thin, clearly that of a man. My patient is fat, with pale skin, and no hair. And here, a trace of nail polish!" observed Olevia.

"OK, I get it. You too are a fan of Sherlock Holmes. So, am I Holmes and you are Watson?" asked Ezra.

"Aha! I knew you would have read Sir Arthur Conan Doyle's' short stories. His first was *A Study in Scarlet,* published in Britain in 1887. Of course, you can be Sherlock, the Detective. I will be Watson, the Doctor," smiled Olevia.

"I will agree with you Watson, that your patient, now deceased, was a woman in life," said Ezra, pretending to be holding a pipe in his hand and adopting a British accent.

"Now, Watson, I will name the disease I know what my patient must have had," said Sherlock.

"You are going to say your man was a smoker," said Watson.

"Yes, Buerger's disease is most common in male smokers, and their circulation is very poor," said Ezra the Detective.

"OK, then let's look at the arteries that are exposed," said Dr. Watson. "Buerger's disease is also called *thromboangiits obliterans*, meaning the vessels are inflamed and blocked," added Olevia.

"And just so," remarked Ezra, feeling the artery in the leg with his fingers.

Olevia now got her chance to feel the artery. "It feels like a small lead pipe. And it feels solid. Oh My, no wonder the toes became gangrenous." concluded Olevia.

"Let me see the blood vessels in your patient's leg," said Ezra, reaching across to examine the other leg. "Why these blood vessels are soft, and not occluded. So, no arterial disease, Olevia."

"Infection in the foot of a middle aged, obese woman, with a foot ulcer," said Olevia rephrasing the situation. "Ulcer under the metatarsal head."

"Diabetes" said Ezra.

"Yes, Sherlock, I concur with your diagnosis," said Watson. "What fun. We two, together solved the mystery of the kicking buckets. What a 'kick'!!" said Olevia with a little laugh. They shook hands. Sherlock put out his pipe and put it away.

"Are we done?" asked Olevia. Maybe we can go out and get some fresh air and talk some more, today," she offered.

"Olevia, wait a minute," said an excited Ezra. "Look here at the ankle. We only examined the artery, but there is the tibial nerve next to the artery. The few diabetics I have seen in the Medical Clinic have a variety of foot symptoms that could be from the nerves, and not all attributed to the circulation."

"I have not seen any diabetics yet, Ezra. Tell me what foot symptoms they complain of," asked Olevia, lacking some of Ezra's clinical experience.

"Usually, diabetics complain their feet hurt. Some have burning pain. Others have just numbness and tingling. Always, it is both top and bottom of both feet. Some have balance problems walking, because they cannot feel their feet," answered Ezra, looking up as he was remembering what he had learned in Medical Clinic.

During this same time, Olevia had her eyes almost buried in the ankles of the two patients, where the skin had been opened to see the tibial artery.

"Ezra, look at this! Do you see the same thing I do?" asked Olevia.

"In my patient, the man with Buerger's disease, the nerve looks white and uniform in size. In your patient, the woman with diabetes, the nerve is yellow and swollen about 40% fatter than the nerve in my patient," observed Ezra.

"My observations exactly, Ezra. To the best of my knowledge, this has never been commented upon before," said Olevia. "Perhaps something is going on at the ankle with the nerves in the diabetic that has caused them to swell. We do not know what effect diabetes has on nerves, or at least I have not read it yet."

"Agreed, I have never read anything about the nerves in diabetics. It is always just commented on that their high blood sugar makes it hard for the diabetic to fight infection," Ezra replied.

"Let's return the buckets and go outside. Let's see what our brains make of this relationship of nerves to diabetes and foot ulceration when we have evacuated the formaldehyde from our system," smiled Olevia, leading the way out of the Pathology Lab. "Now we have something really special to talk about Ezra, nerves."

RESPONSIBILITY

Ezra and Olevia sat next to each other in the West Reading room of the William H. Welch Library at the Johns Hopkins School of Medicine. They were gazing up at a large painting named THE FOUR DOCTORS.

"So can you name them from left to right?" interrogated Ezra, as usual, bumping his shoulder into Olevia's in a playful way.

"Always trying to 'one up me,'" said Olevia, bumping him back.

"Is that a 'No' you don't know who they are?" he taunted her.

"The first doctor is Welch, seated on the left. This library we are sitting is named for him. He was the first Dean of the Johns Hopkins School of Medicine and was a Pathologist. To his right, standing, is William S. Halsted, the First Chief of Surgery. He is standing behind a desk and next to a globe of the world. You know, Ezra, I admire him the most in this portrait. Both he and Welch have their hands on books on the desk. To Halsted's right, seated, is William Osler, the first Chief of Medicine, whom, I know you admire the most in this portrait. Finally seated to the far right, is Howard Kelly, the First Chief of Obstetrics and Gynecology here at Hopkins," finished Olevia, satisfied with her identification of the four doctors in the painting.

"Very good," commented Ezra dryly, "but why does Osler have a feather plume in his hand? Did you know it was because he wrote the first textbook of medicine in America in 1895, the *Principles and Practice of Medicine*," asked Ezra, continuing his inquisition of Olevia.

"Yes, or course, and, I already have a copy of his book to read this year, when we first begin to examine our own patients," she said smugly, and then asked her own question. "Who painted THE FOUR DOCTORS and was it painted here in Baltimore?"

"This was painted by John Singer Sargent in 1906, in London," shot back Ezra, proud of his own knowledge of Hopkins history. "Each of the four doctors had to sail to London for this portrait by this world-famous portrait painter.

"Looking at this picture, Ezra, reminds me of a choice you and I are going to have to make soon," said Olevia, turning to Ezra and holding his hand.

"Yes, it is true. This is our third year of medical school. In many parts of the United States today, you can become a doctor in less than 4 years, and still in some medical schools you only have to pay to get in, and not even have finished college," said Ezra. "And especially for you, Olevia. It used to be that when you finished medical school you could just go out and become a 'country doctor', deliver babies, and do whatever surgery was needed, but not anymore," concluded Ezra.

"Both of us are going to have to choose Medicine or Surgery," stated Olevia seriously, and decide soon. We used to sit next to each other in class, Landsmann seated next to Maybe, alphabetically. Now we are on separate learning experiences in different parts of the Hospital," observed Olevia.

Ezra looked back up at the FOUR DOCTORS, "This painting sort of represents that choice, Medicine or Surgery," explained Ezra. "Welch and Osler were medical doctors who did not operate, although you could argue that Welch, as a Pathologist had to use a scalpel to do autopsies. Halsted and Kelly were doctors who operated, though it could be argued that Kelly, as a Gynecologist spent much time in caring for women with problems that did not require surgery."

"Let's go back in the stacks and discus this a little more," said Olevia, standing up and walking towards the FOUR DOCTORS, and then veering right, going through a small gray doorway into a smaller hallway. The hallway had side hallways to the right that had shelves from floor to ceiling. Each shelf filled with books. To the left, the other side of the small hallway, were little study areas, called 'carrels'. The stacks of books on each of the six levels of the library were how, Olevia knew, this area of the library got its nickname, 'The Stacks'.

As Olevia led Ezra along the corridor and down a narrow stairway to the floor below and then back further to a very quiet, more secluded study carrel, Ezra asked, "So what distinguishes the Doctor who choses Medicine from one who choses Surgery, Olevia? Have you thought about this?"

"Actually, yes I have. It is a troublesome question," answered Olevia. "You are almost certainly not going to like my conclusion, and perhaps now is not the time to talk about it," she said, pulling him into the study carrel and giving him a big hug.

Ezra kissed her ear, and said, "Go ahead, I can take it." He sat down in the one chair in the carrel and looked up at her. He noted her dress, tight, dark grey, white collar, long sleeves, belt, her hair back in a ponytail, no makeup. "You are already the Professor and I am your humble student," he smiled. "Please begin."

"The answer may lie in degree of responsibility," said Olevia. "Not degree of responsibility to the patient, as surely all Doctors must have the highest responsibility to their patient," she quickly added. And then went on. "In Medicine, the Medical Doctor can be 'passive', using only his or her brain to solve the patient's problems. In Surgery, the Doctor has to be active, using his or perhaps, in my case, her hands to solve the patient's problem. A simplistic dualism. But of course, nothing is that simple," Olevia added.

Ezra, now sat back, let go of Olevia's hand, seemingly offended. He said, "I know that Surgeons have a bad rap for not being the smartest. You, Olevia, if you become a Surgeon, will clearly not be deserving of that connotation. You must know that historically, all Physicians have been Medical doctors. Historically, Physicians were not Surgeons. Surgeons were not Physicians. Physicians in England, for example were, and still are, called "Doctor", whereas surgeons in England are still called, "Mister". The earliest Surgeons were barbers, not Physicians, they were technicians, having a steady hand and being willing to cut into the human body," simplified Ezra.

Olevia retreated to the entrance of the carrel, as if to leave.

Ezra continued, "The smartest in Medicine listened to the patient's history, examined the patient, added their own knowledge of medicine, came up with a diagnosis, or what was wrong, and came up with a plan of action to correct the problem. The King and Queen of England have their Royal Physician in case they are really sick. If the King or Queen had a "boil", or a "wen", a swollen or inflamed area, then they would call in the

Royal Barber to lance the boil and drain the swollen part," he concluded smugly, having in his mind successfully defended the Medical Profession against Surgeons.

Olevia now stepped back into the room, deciding to engage the enemy, first by co-opting him. "Of course, I know that old joke," she said. "If a Medical doctor were approaching a rapidly closing door, he would put his hand out to keep it from shutting, protecting his head. If a Surgeon were approaching that same door, he would put his head out to keep it from shutting, protecting his hands."

"Ha! Ha!" smiled Ezra. "I think you are appreciating the situation."

"Ezra, let me try to explain it a little differently. I am sorry if my use of 'responsible' came across in a way to hurt you. I respect your mind and you greatly," Olevia said coming close to him, sitting on the little desk, so her knees were up against his chest.

"As a Medical doctor," she went on, "if a patient were suffering from something, you would give that patient some medical remedy. If it worked, then 'it', the drug was what worked. You, the Medical doctor, essentially just did some math. Symptom + Physical Finding = Diagnosis. For diagnosis X give drug A or B or C; for diagnosis Y give drug D, E, or F. If the patient did not get better, it was not really the Medical Doctor's fault. The patient was too sick for drug A to work. If drug B made the patient vomit, or if drug C was ineffective, well then it was not the Medical Doctor's fault. The Medical Doctor gave compassionate care; provided emotional support. If the patient pulled through, all were grateful to the Medical Doctor for the knowledge possessed."

"Ok, Olevia, I follow that reasoning," commented Ezra, putting his hands around her waist.

Olevia went on, trying to explain this difference to Ezra "To be a Surgeon means that you, yourself, the Surgeon, did something to the patient's body with your own hands. Of course, the Surgeon's brain had to listen to the complaint, and the physical examination had to identify the problem, and the Surgeon's diagnosis had to be correct. Then perhaps there would be something, an operation for example, something that could be corrected by your own, your personal, *surgical,* intervention. If the operation failed, the surgeon failed, and all too often the patient died. If the surgeon's operation succeeded, then the surgeon succeeded. The surgeon did it, not an intervening drug. That is what I meant by 'responsibility'," she said, leaning over and kissing his forehead.

Ezra looked her in the eyes, and said, "I agree, if the surgery fails, the surgeon fails."

"Ezra," she said, leaning back, "It is not really Medicine versus Surgery", Osler versus Halsted, brain power versus physical action. No, it is more about a very real personal responsibility for the patient's care and the surgeon's direct, interventional, involvement in that care. This is what I have seen on my Surgery rotations with Halsted and his residents in surgery."

Ezra stood to give Olevia a hug, but they both moved apart at the sound of footsteps coming down the stone hallway floor. They picked up a book simultaneously and pretended as if they were reviewing something together. They heard the footsteps stop about halfway down the hall, and then the footsteps began to descend to the level below them, and grow fainter in the distance.

"Olevia," said Ezra as he gave a quick kiss and then retreated into the little carrel area, "I will probably spend as little time on surgery rotation as I can get away with. So perhaps you can tell me what makes what Halsted does so special, and different from the surgeons who are not at Hopkins Hospital."

"It is both very simple and yet a very dramatic break with the past," began Olevia. "Before he came to Baltimore, Halsted worked at Bellevue Hospital in New York City. He spent many hours doing prosections in his early years as a surgeon, becoming a master anatomist. When he came to Baltimore, he insisted on flawless technique in the operating room. He tied each bleeding vessel with very fine, very thin, suture. He damaged very little tissue. He wore gloves to keep the contamination of his hands from entering the patient. He used carbolic acid in his operating room to make it "sterile", or at least as aseptic, without bacteria, as he could. Instruments were cleaned between patient uses with bichloride of mercury," she explained.

Another medical student now walked past them, and gave them a look, saying "This quiet study area is not the place to be giving a lecture about surgery," and walked on past them.

Ezra grasped Olevia's hand and started leading her out of the Stacks.

"I have a couple more things to say," she said.

"Shhhh", Ezra said holding his finger to his mouth and leading her back up the stairs and towards THE FOUR DOCTORS.

As Ezra and Olevia re-entered the West Reading room of the Welch Library, Olevia said, "Halsted has succeeded in Surgery where many before have failed, and his operations for hernia repair, for removal of the thyroid, and to treat breast cancer will stand the test of time."

She stopped and looked up at Halsted. Ezra stopped and looked up with her.

"Remarkable accomplishments to be sure, if you wish to spend your life as a technician," he said.

Olevia started in with her defense again, "Did you know Ezra that the residency program you will study Medicine in one day began with Halsted introducing it into Surgery training?"

"No, I did not know that," confessed Ezra.

"Prior to the surgery training program that Halsted introduced here at Hopkins, a prospective surgeon would apprentice himself to a 'master' surgeon and learn from him for a few years, and then go out and start his own practice. Halsted believed that a program in which several 'attending' surgeons taught would be more beneficial. Halsted thought that giving the young surgeon a progressive responsibility for operating with the attending present would be the best way of learning.

By now Ezra and Olevia had walked out the front of the Welch Library.

"What are they building over there, right across from us?" asked Olevia.

"That is going to be the new School of Hygiene and Public Health. It will be the first one in the United States," answered Ezra. Then as the two of them turned and walked west on Monument street, Ezra looked north past the Welch Library and pointed to a smaller white brick building on the same block, at the corner of Madison Avenue. "Well, there is building I do not know," said Ezra.

"Ah ha! Gotcha on that one. I have been in there, and hope to work in there one day, if invited," said Olevia mysteriously.

"Really? What is it," persisted Ezra.

"Halsted was a supreme believer in surgical research before surgery on patients," began Olevia, stopping and looking at the little building. "That is the Hunterian Laboratory. Halsted, followed in the footsteps of John Hunter, who was more than a hundred years before him. Hunter was the Father of Scientific Surgery, never doing an operation on a patient he had not practiced on a living animal. At the start of his employment as Surgeon-in-Chief of the new Johns Hopkins Hospital in 1889, Halsted began the Hunterian Laboratory. That little building," concluded Olevia pointing her finger at it, "is a building devoted to surgical research."

"What is an example of what you saw in there?" asked Ezra.

"I observed surgery being done on animals. Anesthesia is used today, in comparison to Johns Hunter's time. Hunter, like Galen almost 1600 years earlier, operated on living animals, vivisection."

"Must have been a lot of loud noises back then," observe Ezra with a shudder. "Sure there was and Hunter used to do the surgery in his kitchen in London. Finally, his wife made him buy a 'country home', so she would not have to listen to the shrieks of the animals, and listen, too, to the complaints of her neighbors."

"We will have no operating in our home, Olevia!" exclaimed Ezra pulling her close and giving her a kiss.

"I will walk you back to Miss Susie Slagle's" said Ezra, leading the way past the Hunterian Laboratory and turning west on to Madison.

"Thanks. You can be my Medical Doctor Guardian," she said holding his hand, then adding, "Giving a sick patient, medicine, medical treatment, of course is important, and valuable, and necessary. But the risk to you, the Medical Physician is not much. Risking a patient's life and death to intervene surgically in a disease process just seems so much more exciting to me. I think I am willing to take the risk."

Ezra, stopped, and held her closely, looking into her eyes, "So you have made you choice?"

Olevia nodded her head in the affirmative.

But she did not tell anybody except Ezra.

INKWELL

"This is the fourth clinical rotation of this year for your medical school class," said the tall, handsome young man addressing the 20 students seated in the classroom in front of him. He wore a dark tweed suit, a stickpin through the collar of his white shirt, and solid wool tie that matched his suit. "My name is John Staige Davis. I was one of Professor Halsted's surgical residents, and now I am part of his faculty in General Surgery. It is my honor to give your introductory lecture in General Surgery," he said. "I know what it is like to be sitting out there, as you are today, as I had the honor of graduating from this school of medicine in 1899."

Dr. Davis, with a kind face but with penetrating dark eyes, looked over the group before him, noting that Olevia Landsmann was the only woman seated before him. He knew that she was one of the 11 women in that year's medical school class. Usually there were 7 or 8 women in the class. In his own class there had been just two, Blance Epler and Sarah Wykcoff. He was unaware of any woman who had ever chosen surgery as a career. Dr. Davis smiled as he said, "This being the 4th rotation, my experience has been that most of you have taken your favorite rotations already, in Medicine, Obstetrics and Gynecology, Pediatrics, and are here because Surgery is part of your required rotations, rather than a subject in the field of Medicine that you thought would interest you."

Dr. Davis looked down at a thick, cardboard sheet on which were photographs and names of the students slated to be in his class. There were 90 medical students in the class of 1914. On his photography sheet were 23 photos. Clearly 3 students had switched out of this class and into some other rotation. His gaze fell upon a youthful round face with a full head of hair and a smile. Dr. Davis spotted him in the second row.

"Mr. Reese, William Isaac Reese," Dr. Davis called out, looking at the young man whose photo he had just seen. "Tell me why this rotation is called 'General' Surgery, and what you would like to do when you leave the Johns Hopkins School of Medicine."

"Sir," replied William Reese, "today a surgeon is trained to operate everywhere on the body that surgery is known to be possible, so I guess we must learn everything in 'general'," he replied, and then sat quietly.

"That is correct, Mr. Reese. And what have you decided you would like to do when you finish medical school?" asked Dr. Davis again.

"Sir, I do want to do some surgery. I have heard the most amazing stories about what Professor Halsted has done. He even operated in a rural setting Sir. My plan is to live in the mid-west of the United States, Oklahoma, probably, and be a Country Doctor. Then I can deliver babies, do surgery, and also practice Medicine," replied Mr. Reese, clearly having thought this all out.

"Excellent plans Mr. Reese. Now, William, there are a lot of stories about our Professor Halsted. Please share with your classmates the ones you are talking about," requested John Staige Davis, politely.

"Sir, forgive me if this is just a 'tall tale', but I have heard it said that Dr. Halsted was called away from Baltimore to travel urgently to Albany, New York to see his mother. She had been growing progressively more ill. It is said that she had severe pain under her rib cage on the right side, and finally was almost not responsive, with a high fever, lying still, and with severe pain," said William Reese, pausing to catch his breath, and looking around at his classmates' faces. They were all looking in his direction, as he continued, "Halsted, I mean Professor Halsted, made the diagnosis of an inflamed gall bladder ready to burst. It is said that the Professor could feel the heat coming through the skin in a very tender spot beneath his Mother's ribs. Halsted, I mean, Professor Halsted, had come prepared with two bags of instruments and sterile towels. He put his mother on to the kitchen table of her home, and, without any assistants, operated on her. I have heard that he gave his Mother a few drops of ether to breathe, and then cut into her side. He removed her gall bladder. And his mother lived!" he said, almost breathless as he completed his story.

"Excellent, William Isaac Reese. Well told, and . . . a true story! Do you have another?" prompted Dr. Davis.

The students were clapping their hands, urging Mr. Reese to tell another Halsted story.

"I do know one more amazing report," offered Mr. Reese quietly.

"Please share it with us then," requested Dr. Davis.

"In this story, the Professor was going to visit his sister. He had been called to her home for the joyous occasion of her giving birth. However, he arrived at the home to find his sister bleeding on floor. The baby had been born and was doing well. Halsted's sister did not respond to Professor Halsted's, her brother's, voice. He found her pulse was weak. She had almost bled to death related to not expelling all the afterbirth. Dr. Halsted, it is said, always traveled with his 'black bags'. He cut into his own arm, withdrew some blood with a syringe and gave his sister transfusions. It is not known how many. Then he opened her belly and stopped the uterus from bleeding. His sister lived," concluded Mr Reese.

Over the sound of the student's applause, Dr. John Staige Davis yelled out, "Also true, Mr. Reese."

As the young medical students became quiet, and looked up at Dr. Davis, he said, "Surgery can be very exciting, rewarding, and . . . heart breaking, if a patient fails to get better or dies from a complication."

These thoughts seemed to settle the class. "Today," Dr. Davis continued, "we begin by letting you know that surgical training as conceived of by Dr. Halsted, takes years of training, under several different surgeons, not just under one surgeon, as in the past. Well, I guess that still today there are young doctors who attach themselves to just one surgeon, as an apprentice, and after a year or so leave to go out on their own. However, today, at the Johns Hopkins Hospital, we have the Residency program developed by Professor Halsted. The first in the United States, and it is becoming the model for all other training programs in all fields of medicine."

Dr. Davis paused here, and, as he did, he saw a hand rise to ask a question. "Yes Ms. Olevia Landsmann, what would you like to ask?"

"Dr. Davis, Sir, I have heard that you, yourself, are starting to concentrate on reconstruction of injured parts of the body, by shifting skin. How is that going to be considered within General Surgery?" asked Olevia.

"Well, what an interesting question. Yes, I am doing that. Our Professor Halsted has identified areas within General Surgery that he believes deserve more attention, and has chosen some of his Residents to, shall we say, 'specialize" in these areas. For example, he has asked Dr. Samuel J. Crowe to develop the field of ear, nose and throat problems, or Otolaryngology. He asked Dr. Hugh Hampton Young to start the field of Urology. He asked Dr. William S. Baer to start Orthopedic Surgery. He asked Dr. Harvey W. Cushing to start Neurosurgery. In fact, Dr. Cushing and I both graduated from Yale University. We just missed being there together, since he graduated in 1891, and I in 1895. You will be spending some time with Dr. Cushing in addition to me during this surgery rotation." Dr. Davis paused, "Now, to answer your question about me, Professor Halsted suggested I look into the new field of Plastic Surgery," answered Dr. Davis.

The classroom was quiet.

"Ms. Landsmann, the women who completed the endowment of this medical school insisted on entering students having a 'classic knowledge of language,' can You tell me then, what a *Plastic* Surgeon is supposed to be doing? " asked Dr. Davis.

After a minute of thought, Olevia said, '*plasticos*' is the Greek word for 'shape or form', so I guess that a *Plastic* Surgeon is a surgeon who restores the person's shape or form by moving skin around!" exclaimed Olevia with obvious pride in herself.

"Yes, yes, quite good. And now, Ms. Landsmann," asked Dr. Davis, "what are your plans for when you finish medical school?"

"Dr. Davis, I must admit I am intrigued by surgery. I am interested in the mechanisms related to pain, and those have to be related to the nervous system," she answered, being sure not to sound too certain about surgery as her real choice.

"Excellent area for research," commented Dr. Davis, and then continued with his lecture on General Surgery, and Professor Halsted's contributions to breast cancer surgery, thyroid disease and removal of the thyroid gland, and repair of groin hernia. As he concluded the lecture, he said, "Tomorrow your lecture will be from my fellow Yale College classmate, Dr. Cushing. While I went to Johns Hopkins for Medical

School, he graduated from Harvard School of Medicine. You will enjoy his lecture for sure," he concluded as he left the classroom.

The next day, when Dr. Cushing entered the classroom, he too carried a set of photographs of the students in the room. He noted that there were just 18 students present, and there was a woman seated in the front row, Olevia Landsmann, he noted, was her name on her photograph.

Olevia noted that Dr. Cushing had the same deep-set, dark eyes as Dr. Davis, but that Dr. Cushing was a whole head shorter, wore a similar dark tweed suit, but was also wearing a vest. She noted that even at his young age he had a receding hair- line. He spoke quickly and was very precise with his words.

"Good day, Lady and Gentlemen," he began. "I am sure you enjoyed Dr. Davis's introduction to General Surgery yesterday. He is both an excellent surgeon and excellent teacher. Today we proceed in a different manner related to how we gain knowledge as Surgeons. You know by now that, at Hopkins, our goal is not only to improve our patients' health, but also to create new knowledge to further advance the care we can give to our patients. And, of course, as we are doing now, to teach. The three pillars upon which your Hopkins education is based are: Patient Care, Research, and Teaching. And please do not ask me which of the three is most important, as we believe each to be equally important," Dr. Cushing paused.

"Professor Halsted believes that once you have finished residency training in Surgery, you must, if you wish to teach, travel to the great centers of learning in Europe, meet the Giants of Surgery and Research in Europe, and bring that knowledge back to Hopkins. I am just back from what they call in Europe, the *Wanderjahre*," and here Cushing stopped, as he noticed a big smile on the face of the woman in the front row. "Why are you smiling at me Ms. Landsmann?" asked Dr. Cushing.

"Forgive me, Sir," said the startled Olevia. "It was not YOU I smiled at, but rather your use of German, my native language. 'Vanderjahre' means 'wandering years'," she replied, and quickly added "Can you share with us who was the most interesting person with whom you studied overseas, while 'vandering'?"

Somewhat taken aback, Harvey Cushing quickly replied, "Of course that person has to be Herr Doctor Professor Emil Theodor Kocher. Did you know he became the second surgeon to win the Nobel Prize, and that was just recently, in 1909. He won it for his work on thyroid disease. That is how Professor Halsted was able to gain entry for me into that famous man's laboratory. Kocher knew of Professor Halsted's publications on thyroid. Indeed, these two men are quite similar. Kocher, using extremely careful surgical technique, similar to the way Professor Halsted operates, reduced the death rate from surgical thyroid removal from 14% in 1884, to 2.4% in 1889, and finally to 0.14% in 1898. The incision used you will see later today, when you see a gall bladder being removed, is called the Kocher incision. However, I was most interested in studying with him related to brain trauma and wound healing," concluded Cushing, "and thank you Ms. Landsmann for getting me started on my lecture today."

Cushing then went on, "Today I want to introduce to you to the interplay between surgery, observations during surgery, research, and improved patient care. The story does not have a good beginning, but I tell it to you because it is how I started, and the way most advances have been made up to now in surgery."

The students were very quiet.

"Professor Halsted wanted me to learn how to operate on the brain. Patients who have brain tumors all die of their brain tumors, many becoming paralyzed, or having horrible headaches prior to death. Many of the first patients I operated on either died during surgery or died shortly after surgery. It was difficult for me to keep trying to remove brain tumors with the knowledge that each of my patients was going to die, but I felt that perseverance was necessary to surgical success. To put patients to sleep, one of the other surgery residents would drop ether through a funnel on to the patient's nose. The surgery resident giving the ether, had to check the patient's pulse and blood pressure to know if the person was awakening or still asleep deeply enough. Taking the blood pressure is a method I learned during my trip to Europe, and introduced here at Hopkins. We learned that during the usual general surgical emergency, related to bleeding, the patient's pulse would speed up and the blood pressure would drop," at this Cushing went to the black board and drew a graph that had time in surgery along the bottom horizontal or x-axis and blood pressure on the y- or vertical axis. The line he drew went from going straight across to suddenly dropping down. He made a second graph, but this time he put pulse on the vertical axis. This line went from horizontal to angling upwards.

Now Cushing turned to face the students. "What do you think happened during the Neurosurgical emergencies prior to the patient dying?" he asked.

There were no hands raised.

"Well then, I will tell you. It is a big surprise. The opposite happens, and he turned to go back to the blackboard and drew another set of lines which showed the pulse slowing as the blood pressure rose higher. He turned to look at the class again, and asked, "What do you see and how would you explain it?" he asked.

Olevia, had seen lots of graphs during her chemistry training in Munich. She understood about pressure transmission in the laboratory glass pipes and vessels. She quickly raised her hand.

"Yes, Ms. Landsmann? Would you like to theorize for us?" asked Cushing.

"Yes, Sir. For some reason, the body is raising its blood pressure, perhaps to force more blood into some part of the body, perhaps into the brain itself," she theorized.

"Good," said Cushing, "and why would the body have to do that," he asked again.

"Perhaps your brain surgery was causing the brain to swell, and the blood vessels did not have enough pressure to get the blood to enter the brain anymore," she further hypothesized.

"Yes, excellent, and correct, but then how can we prove that?" he continued to ask her.

Olevia remained quiet, deep in thought.

"You each know that Professor Halsted established the Hunterian Surgical Research laboratories to honor John Hunter of London, who introduced surgical research by doing experiments on living animals. In 1900, Professor Halsted asked me to take over the Hunterian Surgical Research program. We began this research on living dogs, measuring their pulse and blood pressure. We created a small window of sorts to measure pressure within the skull by removing a piece of bone. We replaced it with glass. We placed a tube filled with mercury under the glass and by raising or lowering the tube we could change the pressure on the surface of the brain. We could see the blood flowing in the vessels on the surface of the brain. That is our research model for this question," he answered. "From this we concluded that there is a reflex between intracranial pressure and the blood pressure and pulse. When we see these lines begin to cross on the patient's anesthesia chart, we now know there is pressure building within the brain. My fellow residents have honored me by calling this phenomenon 'Cushing's Cross", he said stopping for the students to grasp this research finding and its clinical implications.

"To return this research to the operating room, if a surgeon is operating on the brain, what must the surgeon do if the person giving anesthesia tells him the 'the cross has appeared on the anesthesia chart?" asked Cushing.

Olevia could not even restrain her usually polite manner. "You must open the skull immediately to reduce the intracranial pressure or your patient will die," she said jumping straight up from her chair. The class was quiet, and then applause erupted and Olevia shyly sat back down in her seat.

The next day, Olevia was again in the front row, as Dr. Cushing came back to give a second lecture. Cushing described trying to operate on the nerves in the arm and hand. He said these nerves were small and delicate. It was known what the function of these nerves was. For example, the nerve in the front of the wrist that went through a big tunnel alongside 9 tendons was called the median nerve and it transmitted the sensations from the thumb, index, middle, and half of the ring finger to the brain. The median nerve also sent motor instructions from the brain to the thumb that allowed it to move away from the palm and over to touch the tip of the index finger, called opposition. Ability to oppose the thumb is what set the "great apes apart from other monkeys. There was a smaller tunnel next to the big one with a nerve that transmitted the sensation of the little and the other half of the ring finger. It was called the ulnar nerve, and carried motor instructions to the remaining muscles of the hand. Cushing explained that this meant you could ask certain questions to the patient and examine the hand and learn whether the patient's symptoms were from one or the other of these two nerves. Then, you could try to fix that nerve in surgery. Cushing said that while brain surgery was surgery of the Central Nervous System, this new surgery should be called *Peripheral Nerve Surgery.*

"Dr. Cushing," asked Reese Williams, the medical student who wanted to be a country doctor in Oklahoma, "How can you see the little nerves to operate on them if the hand is bleeding?"

"Quite right," Mr. Williams. "I suggest you always carry a rolled up length of rubber with you in your little black bag of tricks. We call that an elastic Esmarch bandage. You begin rolling it from the wrist back up to the elbow then tie it there. This exsanguinates the hand and arm. Then, unravel the distal end where you have to do your surgery, leaving the proximal end tied. If you do not do this, then operating on a peripheral nerve is like trying to fix a watch in an inkwell."

Olevia smiled and said quietly, "Peripheral nerve surgery is possible." Her thoughts extended that possibility to her Uncle Albert, *If my dearest Uncle Albert is still alive,* she thought, *then there is hope that the nerves causing pain at his wrist can be fixed!*

Dr. Harvey Cushing concluded his lecture, "Each year I chose one 3rd year medical student to work in my lab during their 4th year of medical school. To work in my lab as my research assistant, in case any of you are interested, let me know." As he left the classroom, Cushing recalled that he had never chosen a woman medical student for this highly competitive research surgical year.

EMG

Olevia was going to meet Ezra today. She was excited. She had not seen him in about 3 months due to the schedules of the new elective rotations in the medical school. She knew he was going to try one of the new ones, Psychiatry, a field, which had become increasingly popular due to the writings of Sigmund Freud. Everyone was talking about whether young men really were attached to their mothers, until they resolved certain 'deep, subconscious' issues, the so-called Oedipus Complex.

She missed Ezra. She could not deny that she was attracted to him, while at the same time thinking he was self-obsessed, and sometimes even a bit disrespectful. He clearly had his own agenda. But then, so did she. That he did not really understand her was not his fault. She was complex.

She was waiting for him in the usual William H. Welch Library 4th floor study carrel.

As she heard his footsteps on the stairs, she stood up. They gave each other a big hug. It felt good. They had shared a lot with each other. Although she had not shared with him her more intimate experiences with her Uncle Albert in the English Garden or in the Mountains. She had wondered if she could ever trust a man again. Now she found that she had begun to trust Ezra.

Ezra walked into 'their' study carrel, and got right to the point, saying "We need to talk about what we are planning to do after medical school. As you know, we have talked about perhaps working together, since we both like nerves, and perhaps even both going to Utah. You seemed to like the idea of skiing, and that in some place remote like Utah, perhaps the prejudices against women in medicine might be less, right?"

"Yes. That is what we talked about," said Olevia, feeling suddenly hopeful. "How have you enjoyed your new rotations?" Olevia asked showing a personal interest in Him.

"There is just so much to tell you. First of all, I have learned that there is a way now to measure nerve function with electrical impulses shot into the skin and recording with needles from the different muscles. It is called electromyography. EMG is its acronym. This has evolved from the Galvanic electrical stimulation done in Paris on the facial muscles by a Doctor GBA Duchene, and now is being extended to the arms and legs by William Erb in Germany. Erb was in Leipzig but has just been made Professor and Chief of Medicine and Neurology in Heidelberg, a great teaching hospital. Neurology does not even exist yet in America. No one is doing electrical testing yet in America," reported Ezra excitedly.

"Wait a minute" said Olevia, not really knowing what to say, but needing to get a word in. "What is GBA Duchene?"

"Sorry. This is just so exciting to me," apologized Ezra. GBA are Professor Duchene's crazy initials. They stand for Guillaume-Benjamin-Amand. Even Charcot credits him as being the Father of Neurology in France." Ezra then just went right on. "Secondly, a rich man from Philadelphia, named Henry Phipps, has agreed to donate $1.5 million dollars to build a new building to house a new Department of Psychiatry right here at Johns Hopkins Hospital. They are going to put it across from the Pathology Building, on the other side of the tennis courts," continued Ezra.

"Oh, my gosh! That is wonderful," said Olevia, not sure where all this was going. "But there is no one on the Hopkins staff with sufficient interest to run such a department," she then observed thoughtfully.

"You are correct. They are hiring Adolf Meyer, MD, away from Cornell University. He is interested in testing the new theories that psychiatric disorders are related to chemical imbalances in the brain. He will come to Hopkins when the building is complete. The Henry Phipps Psychiatry Building. Previously, Mr. Phipps donated money for the Henry Phipps Tuberculosis Clinic. It is said that he made his money in the steel business with Andrew Carnegie in Pittsburgh."

"How long will it take to build?" she asked.

"Third," Ezra said, jumping ahead, "Due to my interest and excellence in my Medical and Psychiatry rotations, I have been told that they would allow me to be one of the first residents in the new Department of Psychiatry. The building will be open in about two years," he finally said, answering her question.

"And where will you go while they are building?" she asked cautiously.

"Olevia, I do not believe I ever mentioned to you about how many physically impaired young children I saw in Salt Lake City when I was growing up. No one could tell me why there were so many. It was thought that perhaps it stemmed from many Mormons marrying relatives years ago when there were not so many Mormons. Some said there were pollutants in the water that come down from the coal mines. In Paris, Joseph Jules Dejerine MD, Professor of Neurology, is classifying the muscular dystrophies, which is probably what these children back home have. And now, even more good news, a Pediatric hospital is being built in Salt Lake City. It will be called The Primary Pediatric Hospital. These children will have a place to go, to be cared for, to be studied and evaluated to understand what was happening or not happening in their brain to cause their paralysis. When I am done training, I could go and do research there, as well as help the children and provide psychiatric care and support for their families."

"No, you never described this interest of yours, Ezra," confirmed Olevia, "and just what will you be doing while they build the Henry Phipps new building," she asked again.

Ezra now actually looked at Olevia. He tried to figure out why she looked different to him. Yes, she was wearing pants instead of a skirt. Yes, her hair was cut differently, so she looked more like a man. He took her hands in his and looked her straight in the eyes. "I have decided to go to Europe and train at the new centers in Paris and Heidelberg, working with electrodiagnostic testing techniques and learning about muscular dystrophy. Then I can bring this back to America, to Hopkins and the Phipps building, and, finally, to Utah, and to YOU."

Olevia was very quiet, and looked downwards, knowing she was *not* being invited to go to Europe with him.

"Are you happy for me Olevia?" asked Ezra, oblivious to her change in mood.

"Yes, of course, ecstatic. You will be a pioneer in a new field related to nerves," she said quietly, and thinking that here another man has hurt her.

"Oh, by the way. Dejerine trained with Vulpian, whom, to the best that my research can determine, did the first nerve graft!! That should be exciting to you",

Ezra went on, celebrating his own personal glory.

BEQUEST

Olevia looked at the entrance to her room at Miss Susie Slagle's everyday for her mail. She loved mail, but sadly did not get very much. Usually there were announcements from the Johns Hopkins School of Medicine about lectures or other special events.

But today there was a letter from her father, Alexander. She was so excited! Yet even as she carefully opened the envelope, she sensed, intuitively, that this was not going to be good news or her Dad's usually informative letter about the Bayer Company's successes in the world.

The letter had the Landsmann Family Crest at the top. This was the longest letter her Father had ever written to her. It read:

"My Dearest Olevia,

It is with a heavy heart that I must tell you of the death of your Uncle Albert.

I received a letter from the University of Utah, where he was working. Yes, now, I can finally tell you where he has been. He made me promise to keep this from you, so he could continue his research in private, no matter where it led him.

The letter from the Department of Biology at the University of Utah said simply that one of your Uncle Albert's students had come to Albert's laboratory about noon, and found your Uncle leaning against one of his prosection projects.

The letter went on to say, that they were not sure of his cause of death. It seemed he had tried to operate on himself, on that painful part of his right forearm. The letter said that his forearm had been opened deep to the

burn scar. That there were two different nerves that he had isolated from each other, each with a silk suture looped around it. Each nerve lay hanging loosely. Albert, apparently, had divided each of these nerves himself. He was found with a scissors in his left hand. He had apparently been operating upon himself!

The letter went on to comment that there was some blood on the floor, but not that much so they did not think that he bled to death. The letter said that they had found needles and an empty bottle of cocaine solution that he must have used to deaden the pain from the surgery.

Olevia, for this, I blame myself. It was your own Father who supplied your Uncle with cocaine to deaden his pain. As a chemist, I can say, that little is know of the toxic dose in a human, although we do know that it speeds up the heart rate and raises the blood pressure.

Albert had written a letter, which they found in his desk, indicating that he had finished his "major work", his *opus magnus,* and that he bequeathed it to the University of Utah School of Medicine, to be hung in a place in which it could "inspire learning in students and hope for patients in pain".

Albert said in the letter that he left what money he had to the University of Utah to prepare the place to hang this display, and to keep it clean *"in perpetuity"*, which of course, I know with your linguistic abilities, you know means "forever".

Olevia, I must tell you that Albert was working for years on his *opus magnum,* the most complete prosection of the peripheral nervous system. The dissection was carried out even out to its tiniest nerve endings that he could see with his special magnifying glass. All the way to the fingertips, and into the joints. This work had consumed him.

I also knew that he sought in that project an escape from pain for himself. His pain had caused him to use cocaine, and he had become dependent on it. I, myself, used to send him chemicals for his research in embalming, and I would send him cocaine powder that he could put into solution to inject his own nerves.

In writing this to you, I admit that I am partly to blame for the death of my own twin. You must remember that as his mirror image twin I could feel the burning pain in my own left wrist. As his twin, I could only imagine how much worse the pain was for him in his right wrist.

Olevia, Please Forgive Me.

But Olevia, when you become a Doctor, and should you find me in pain, please give me the cocaine that I need. You may know that General Napoleon Bonaparte once said, "It is easier to find men who will die in battle, than a man who will suffer constant pain."

On the science side, Olevia, I do think that Albert did finally achieve his goal before his death. On about the day he must have operated upon himself, my own arm stopped burning. He must have found a way. His plan had been to cut the nerves to stop the pain message. As now you know, that you are studying the human body; pain remains so poorly understood.

Maybe you will work in this area. Surgery of pain.

Think of it Olevia. A new field of endeavor in medicine. Inspired by the love of your Uncle Albert.

Olevia, I know you read Arthur Schopenhauer's philosophy when you were in the University here in Munich. Perhaps you recall his thoughts on creating something new. Please read this again, and prepare yourself, my Dearest Daughter, and, now Surgical Pioneer.

All truth passes through three stages.

First, it is ridiculed.

Second, it is violently opposed.

Third, it is accepted as being self-evident."

Please find time to go to Utah. Find his *opus magnum,* his 'great work". Learn what he learned. Use it to help people. Fear not. Surely you will be opposed. But you must continue what my brother, your Uncle Albert began!

Remember him Olevia.

Memorandum est Vivere in Aeturnum.

Love you,

THE PROSECTOR

Your Father Alexander

IN QUEST

Olevia was back in the Welch Library. She was not in the stacks. She was in the East Reading Room looking through telephone books. It was 12:30PM, and she was on her lunch break from class. Finally she found the telephone book that she wanted. It was the telephone book for the state of Utah.

First the word 'Utah' brought her thoughts to Ezra. Now, 'Utah' represented the place where her Uncle Albert died. It sounded like a wilderness, so different from her civilized München (her brain lapsed back into the German for Munich).

Olevia flipped through the pages until she found what she was looking for: University of Utah School of Medicine. Olevia suspected, that, with her Uncle Albert's great experience in the Anatomy Department at the Ludwig-Maximillian University, he might also have taught Anatomy to the new medical students at the University of Utah.

Olevia, however, could not find Anatomy Department listed. As she kept scanning down the listings underneath the heading University of Utah, finally she found 'Biology Department, Thomas Parks, PhD, Director of Anatomy'.

Olevia then walked down the grey granite steps from the reading room to the main lobby where the telephone was located. *I am going to call the 'U of U'*, she said to herself. *'Nice alliteration'*. She put some quarters into the slot at the top of the phone, and dialed 801-581-7200. She was going to start a new adventure!

"University of Utah," said a melodic, soft-spoken female voice. "How may I help you?" said the Telephone Operator.

"May I speak to Dr. Thomas Parks, an Anatomist in the Biology Department," she said.

"Certainly, Mam. Just give me a moment to look him up . . . . Yes, Biology Department, and within that Department I have found the person with whom you desire to speak. Just another moment while I ring his number," concluded the Telephone Operator.

"Good morning," said a deep male voice, "This is Thomas Parkes, May I help you?"

"Yes, Sir. I hope you can. I believe that my Uncle Albert may have been a member of your Anatomy staff, and I wanted to inquire about him," answered Olevia politely.

"Yes, happy to help. What is your Uncle's full name," responded Dr. Parks.

"My Uncle's full name is Albert Landsmann. I do know that he is recently deceased," said Olevia, more quietly.

"Oh of course I knew Albert Landsmann," replied Dr Parks immediately. "Your departed Uncle Albert was a blessing to our faculty in Anatomy. He was devoted to his dissections. He was clear in his teaching and caring with his students. We will miss him greatly when the next academic year begins. Are you calling from Munich, your voice sounds so clear," Dr. Parks concluded?

"Thank you, Dr. Parks, for those kind words about my Uncle Albert. I have missed him ever since he left Munich to pursue his research. But no, I am not in Munich. Actually I am completing my medical studies at the Johns Hopkins University in Baltimore," she added to see his reaction.

"Wonderful. Wonderful. What an excellent Institution that young medical school has become. A model, really, for the rest of the world to follow. What an education you must be getting there! What is it like, please tell me," replied an excited Dr. Parks?

"Thank you again for those kind words. Yes, Hopkins is a very special place. In fact, the next year I will be doing surgical research with Dr. Harvey Cushing, whom one day the world will learn as having pioneered the field of central and peripheral nerve surgery. I would very much like to follow in his footsteps," Olevia replied.

She had only just learned that Dr. Cushing, against all tradition, had chosen her, a Woman, to be his research assistant in the Hunterian Building. Olevia immediately let Dr. Cushing know that she would accept the great honor of being a student in Surgical Research, under his direction, working in the Hunterian Building. She knew that as his Research Assistant, he would allow her to stand in the gallery and observe him operating. Perhaps he would even let her get closer than the gallery? Perhaps she could administer ether for his patients. Perhaps she could operate on living animals that were anesthetized!

"Wonderful. Wonderful," commented Dr. Parks, interrupting Olevia's wishful thinking. "And then what will be your plans?" he asked, just as Olevia hoped he would.

"I seem to have inherited my Uncle Albert's love for dissection. I find the only way a surgeon can develop new insight into the human body, and especially nerves, is through anatomic dissection," Olevia replied, partly answering his question.

"Yes, that is certainly true, certainly true. The Lord knows we need much better teaching about nerves and what they do in our body. Especially what to do when they are injured." answered Dr. Parks, who seemed, thought Olevia, to like to repeat himself. Perhaps that was part of his approach to teaching! She smiled to herself at that thought.

There was a pause in the conversation.

"Dr. Parks," asked Olevia, "What will you be doing with the special final prosection that I believe my Uncle Albert must have been preparing. And was it completed?"

"Oh yes, yes. Magnificent. Simply Magnificent! No one has seen the like of it. Yes, it must be treasured and placed somewhere special. I must think about that." Professor Parks said.

"What is the subject of the prosection?" Olevia just had to know.

"Why it is exactly as you must have supposed. It is a complete dissection of the human peripheral nervous system, maintaining all its central connections. And the way he chose to display this PROSECTION," paused Parks, "that is a research achievement in and of itself! You must come and see it. It is much too special to attempt to ship it. It is too special to risk damage."

Olevia accepted the offer by saying, "You are most kind, and certainly, Yes, I must make the time to come out there." Then she asked, "Can you tell me, did my Uncle Albert perhaps leave a research notebook that you could look for and send to me so I can begin to appreciate his thought process. He might even have chosen to make those notes in a book that has our family crest on the cover of it," and she went on to describe the appearance of that crest.

"How exciting that you might come out here, Olevia. Exciting, and I will look for those research notebooks and send them to you. Please give me your address."

Olevia gave him her address at Miss Susie Slagle's on Biddle Street, and then asked Doctor Parks, "Professor, I must spend six months here at Johns Hopkins Hospital, doing surgical research. Do you think that if I come to Salt Lake City, you could give me an appointment in Anatomy at the University of Utah, so I could continue my Uncle's research into peripheral nerves?"

"Of course. Certainly. Certainly. A Woman doctor would make a fine addition to my faculty. And, a graduate of Johns Hopkins School of Medicine no less!! YOU would honor us if you would accept," Dr. Parks replied.

"Then I will consider strongly that offer Professor. Strongly," she answered smiling at herself again as she adopted his approach of emphasis by repeating the word 'strongly'. "Oh," she added, "Could you please send me an official invitation in writing on the University letterhead?"

As she hung up the phone, she continued talking to no one in particular. "I will go to Salt Lake City in search of my Uncle Albert and his *opus magnu*m and continue his work. But first I need more skills to become a Surgeon, even if I cannot, as a Woman, enter a formal Surgery Residency program."

PRESERVATION

The Hunterian Building was a three-story building on the southeast corner of Wolfe Street, running North to South, and Madison Street, running East to West. It was made of greying, white stone, had small windows and looked quite short and squat. One of its three floors was underground. That is where the cadavers were embalmed and stored for later use by the medical students. It was a building most people would just pass by without taking notice.

As Olevia walked halfway along Wolfe Street and turned to the left to enter the path to the building in which she would be doing surgical research next year, she closed a notebook that she had been reading as she walked. She looked up to see a young man looking down at her from a second-floor window. "David Siler," she thought to herself. "Not much went on in the research lab that he was not aware of. He was the Senior Laboratory Assistant. Olevia was coming to meet him and learn her place in the lab.

Olevia entered the building, turned her head to the left to see the Anatomy Lab with the tables set for the next incoming class of medical students to dissect, which would be in just a couple of months. Then she turned right and climbed the steps to the second floor, where the research was done.

"Welcome Ms. Landsmann," said a handsome young man, whom she judged to be about 35 years of age. He had newly cut light brown hair, glasses, a mustache, a long white apron covering dark thick pants and a plaid shirt. "We are honored to have you join us next year for research. Dr. Cushing has assigned you a desk at the end, away from the animal cages, so your thoughts may not be bothered by their barking," he said with a smile as he took her to the diagonally opposite part of the second floor. The windows she noted were small, and higher than usual from the floor, perhaps so that no one on the street could observe any of the animal research.

"Thank you," said Olevia, as she put several notebooks on to her new desk.

"Looks like you have already done a lot of research Ms. Landsmann. Are you planning on continuing that work up here in our Lab?" the Senior Laboratory Assistant asked.

"Oh, these are not filled with my research, but that of my Uncle Albert," explained Olevia. "They have just arrived from the University of Utah where he was teaching Anatomy. There are three of them. They arrived yesterday at Miss Susie Slagle's where I am living. I thought, what better place to read them then here in the Hunterian Surgical Research Laboratory," concluded Olevia, spreading out the three books on her small desk.

"Is that the crest of the University of Utah?" asked David Siler, noting the design on the cover of each of the three books.

"No, Sir. It is our Landsmann family crest," she explained, taking off a light-weight, dark grey jacket with long sleeves.

"What research was your Uncle doing," asked David Siler, showing sincere interest in his new student. He noticed that she was wearing dark blue pants, a dark blue shirt buttoned to the collar, no make up, and that her hair was cut short, to just cover her ears. He detected no jewelry, just a plain watch. He could not help but think that she dressed more like a man than a woman.

"Well, Sir, I was just looking at the notebook labeled #1 on my way walking over here. The beginning part is all about how to preserve a prosection so that it would withstand the test of time. Uncle Albert labeled this section "Preservation Approach", and he began by saying he believed he was developing not a 'formula' or a 'secret method', but an approach that future Anatomists could use'" she responded.

"I wonder what he thought was missing from the way we preserve our cadavers today, as I sure you have seen in the basement here," commented David Siler.

"Yes, correct. So my Uncle Albert explained, right here at the beginning what the purpose of his research would be," she said, turning to that page in the book, and reading directly from it, "What, in my view, has been missing from the traditional use of formaldehyde, with or without glycerin for softening the specimen, was a method to remove the fat surrounding the nerves themselves after I have cut away the skin and subcutaneous fat," Olevia paused.

"What a clear handwriting your Uncle had. Left-handed if I am not mistaken?" observed David Siler.

"Oh my, you are quite observant Mr. Siler. He was Left-handed indeed. No wonder you are in charge of research," commented Olevia, clearly trying to start off on the right foot with David Siler.

"May I hold the book closer and read the next part?" he asked, hardly waiting for her reply. He continued Uncle Albert's narrative, "I know that acetone dissolves fat. I have tried putting acetone into a blood vessel, pushing it into the artery and from there throughout the nerve the artery supplied with blood. Then after waiting a day for the fat to dissolve, I would subject the specimen to heat and suction. I know that the ancient Egyptians relied on heat for the mummification process. Acetone is very volatile and evaporates easily. So, I thought a little suction over the specimen would be helpful. I used the suction hood in the chemistry lab. A single body part, like an arm, would fit into that."

"There follows a section on what other Anatomist had been working on for similar purposes," commented Olevia, taking her book back from Mr. Siler. "Uncle Albert comments briefly on the natural specimens of animals and human parts that were collected by John Hunter in London in the 1780s that still remained in good condition. Also, Uncle Albert comments on Charles Darwin's specimens from his trip on the Beagle to the Galapagos Islands, in 1838. These were preserved and endured using various alcohol solutions."

"Here is a section, with color photos glued in," said David Siler, taking the research notebook back into his grasp, and flipping a few pages forward. "It is an approach of a Frenchman," David Siler read, "a brilliant anatomist, who was later deemed to be 'mad'. He claimed to have developed a secret method of embalming, and it involved removing all the skin, then doing the embalming, then somehow removing all fat from the body. Regardless of the chemistry involved, this man, Honoré Fragnonard, had a vision, an artistic vision." Wrote your Uncle Albert.

"What else does it say about this Frenchman. Do you have to be mad to have a vision of the future?" asked Olevia.

Your Uncle Albert's notes revealed that he had studied about this Frenchmen. He notes that Honoré was a Doctor of Animals. A veterinarian. In 1766 he was appointed the first Professor of Anatomy at the École Nationale Vétérinaire de Maisons-Alfort in Paris. In 1771 he was fired from the job. By then he had prepared 700 specimens with his technique, mostly animals. It was not the quality of his work that got him fired, it was how he presented his work. He created tableaux, or scenes. He had a scene in which one monkey was holding a nut in its hand and another monkey clapping hands next to him," David Siler said, showing Olevia the photos that had been glued into the notebook

"Oh my," said Olevia. "These look so real and yet so macabre, almost devilish, at the same time. This photo has a goat thorax with its own head inside its 'chest'. It says, 'Inspired by the biblical scene of Samson fighting the Philistines'. And in this one," Olevia went on excitedly, "Honoré has a standing human being holding the jaw of a donkey, as a weapon, and the human is without skin or fat, just muscle and bone."

"To me," stated David Siler, "Perhaps the most disturbing scene is this one: It seems to depict The Four Horseman of the Apocalypse, with each man sitting astride a horse. Each of the horseman is also posed without skin or fat; just bone and muscle."

"Mr. Siler," said Olevia quietly, "The most outrageous one to me is certainly this small circle of little human fetuses dancing a jig."

"Well as a teacher, Olevia, one must admit these prosections are beautiful and well-preserved, and get your attention. Your Uncle Albert," David Siler went on, "notes that twenty-one of Honoré's specimens can still be observed in the Musee Fragonard d'Alfort in Paris, more than 230 years after they were prepared."

"Yes, I see that," responded Olevia, "and do you see that Latin phrase with which he concluded this section of his notes?" asked Olevia. "That is the motto on our family crest which is also on the front of each of these notebooks, '*Memorandum est Vivere in Aeturnum*'". Olevia felt herself automatically translating the Latin, "To be remembered is to live forever," she concluded.

"Well," commented David Siler, "I would have to agree that Endurance is memory. Preservation led to endurance. A preserved prosection seems to be, for your Uncle Albert, the essence of your family motto", he observed.

"Do you have time to continue reviewing this with me?" asked Olevia.

"Yes, with your permission. My next research experiment does not begin for another hour. These notes seem so private. Perhaps never ever read by anyone before," the Senior Lab Assistant replied respectfully. "It is as if your Uncle Albert is here talking to us.

"Here is his next experiment," stated Olevia. "He named it 'Nerve Visualization' or 'How to get a dye into the nerves to show life!' He wonders about a substance that his Professor at the University had worked on that 'glowed? That gave off light,'" read Olevia. "Uncle Albert writes that he remembers he and my Father Alexander worked on creating new dyes using the chemical phthalein while they worked at the Bayer Chemical Company. Professor Baeyer, also working at the Bayer Company, had taken a dried, acidic form of phtalein, phtalic anhydride, and mixed it with a chemical called resorincol. In 1871 he called his new chemical resorcinphthalein. It would give off a light when light was shown on to it. Uncle Albert notes, that 'Adolf Baeyer's student Emil Fisher, also a Professor of Chemistry at Ludwig-Maximillan University won the very first Noble Prize in Chemistry in 1902, and Adolph Baeyer himself was awarded it in 1905. Uncle Albert then seems to note with pride, 'Two Nobel prizes in the same Chemistry Department. Both to Jewish chemists,'" concluded Olevia.

"Here your Uncle Albert describes his first application of these concepts to a human nerve, with the experiment entitled 'Nerve Glow #1: femoral & sciatic,'" observed David Siler.

"I like the way he describes the specimen. It shows his compassion," commented Olevia, reading the next part. "A miner. Thin. Shot in head. No known relatives. On inspection, both arms with lots of scars. *Injuries, healed memories of a life in the outdoors and underground.* Left leg had no cuts or scars, therefore, disarticulated the leg at the hip, found the femoral artery. Infusing 'new formula' embalming liquid, and at the same time made many parallel cuts in the skin from the thigh to the ankle and stripped off all the skin. After bleeding stopped, cleaned leg, began dissecting. Found arteries to femoral and sciatic nerves and pushed in new formula containing fluorescein mixed with red dye. Then I pushed in acetone into femoral vein. Began grossly removing muscle, bones and obvious fat from leg. After 18 hours of continuous work, femoral and sciatic nerves ready, existing freely in space. Specimen then put it into the large exhaust hood in the corner of lab. Exhaust evaporates acetone and the evaporating acetone takes with it the dissolved fat in the nerve," he concluded.

"A long day in the lab. Probably a full 24 hours," observed David Siler. "Our dog experiments do not take that long. Neither the dog nor the surgical resident would survive," chuckled David Siler. "But look at this date. The very next day he was back to the research. This experiment he calls 'Theory of Display.'"

"Mr. Siler, notice the name 'Harriet'? I think I know where this is going," said Olevia quickly.

"Who is Harriet," asked David Siler, "Did she work with him in the lab?"

"Sort of but not exactly. Harriet was a woman who donated her body for anatomic research and a Doctor in Philadelphia did a masterful prosection of the nerves in her body. It was 'displayed' at the Columbian Exposition in Chicago in 1842, and my Father and Uncle Albert saw Harriet on display there during a business trip. So here, I guess, will be how my Uncle Albert wanted to do something more dramatic than just have nerves hang like strings in the display," she concluded.

"Why yes, Ms. Landsmann. How perceptive you are," commented David Siler again. "It says right here that 'Harriet was flat, two-dimensional, with all wooden pegs being about the same length from the back of the display. Maybe my prosection should have some bones to provide three-dimension. Perhaps the prosection should be positioned as if in motion with one leg in front of the other. Perhaps after Vesalius's illustrations . . .,' and his writing then trailed off, as if Uncle Albert was trying to remember something he had seen.

"Mr. Siler," Olevia said, "Uncle Albert wrote a little more here, "Rufus Weaver's prosection of Harriet is displayed in the same manner that Vesalius's artist depicted the nerves in *Liber IIII, Caput X.*", which Olevia knew meant Book IV or Volume 4, 'Heading Ten' or subdivision 10, in Italian, which came from Latin roots.

"Mr. Siler," said Olevia, "there is probably a copy of Vesalius's illustrations somewhere in the Anatomy Laboratory here in the Hunterian Building. Have you seen it?" asked Olevia.

"Yes, but not an original of course. That book would be very, rare. Let's walk downstairs and have a look," Mr. Siler said as he walked out past the animal cages. The dogs started barking, and wagging their tails, thinking it was feeding time. Mr. Siler, used to these outbursts, walked quickly by the cages, almost bounded down the stairs, and entered a small 'Reference Room' just outside where the cadavers lay on their tables."

"Here it is," Siler said, moving books and folders until he found quite a large one, almost sticking off the shelf due to its large size. "*De Corpora Humani Fabrica, 1543, Andreas Vesalius.*"

"Great. Good job," said Olevia, complementing the Senior Lab Assistant. " It is written in Italian" she now said aloud, "but so much like Latin that I can translate it easily, it means *'The Fabric of the Human Body',* Olevia said, now starting immediately to look at the illustrations which lay without text within the folder.

"Mr. Siler, I think Uncle Albert might have been thinking of something like these poses," Olevia said, showing a series of illustrations to her new friend.

David Siler looked at the pages she was showing him and commented, "The artist depicted the human body in different poses. In this series of drawings, the human body of a man is viewed from the back. The man is standing looking out over the countryside. There are six men lined in a row left to right. The first man, on the far left, has both hands lowered, and all muscles are shown, there is no skin. The second man has the right arm outstretched, and the first layer of muscles have been dissected away. The third man is in the same position, but now has even less muscles. The fourth man has very few muscles left in place, and his hands are outstretched. The fifth man is in the same position, with the deeper layer of muscles hanging off the bones, like pieces of clothing. The sixth man, the one on the far right, has no arms, and has no shoulder bones: He is just part of a skeleton and is kneeling on a block of marble," ended David Siler.

"These illustrations are located in *"Liber II"*, "Book II" or volume 2,"said Olevia. "They do seem to make the anatomy come alive with human purpose," she concluded.

"Ok, then, and now that we have read the Purpose and Methods section of your Uncle Albert's experiment, let us go back and read next his Results and Conclusion sections," instructed David Siler as he headed back up the steps to the again barking dogs.

Olevia reached the notebook first, and turned to the next page, and began to read, "With the nerves attached at top of the wooden box, representing the pelvis, I attached two wooden dowels partway down and at a height about 6 inches away from the back of the box, representing where the knee would be, and two shorter ones further back towards the bottom of the box, representing where the foot would be. Then I attached the femoral and sciatic nerves that dried out overnight in the exhaust hood, to remove the fat. All that remained was pure nerve. Colorful nerve. I then stood back and turned on the bright light to shine on the prosection of the femoral and sciatic nerves. Suddenly the nerves were sparkling. It was the fluorescein I added to the mixture. From the chemistry learned back home in München at Bayer Company. The nerves now had a glow and looked alive again."

"His experiment worked Ms. Landsmann, and what does he say in these little notes just under conclusion," asked David Siler.

"Oh my, it says *'Um größere Abluftlüfter für das Opus Magnum, und die Parkesite'* which means," translated Olevia, 'Get bigger exhaust fan for the Grand Work, and Parkesite.'"

"And you conclude from this what?" asked David Siler.

"His next embalmed prosection would be really big, perhaps a whole human. It will represent his life's work. But I do not know what Parkesite translated as," Olevia said, a bit perplexed about what her Uncle Albert would do next in his own Anatomy Lab in Utah.

PARKES

David Siler then left Olevia to help one of the surgery residents who had just arrived in the lab. He was wearing dark pants and a dark shirt, opened at the neck, the usual garb for a Surgery Resident at the Johns Hopkins Hospital. The two men went over to look at the dogs. The dogs resumed barking, but this time more like growling. This time they were not wagging their tails. Their tails hung straight down. They had learned that dark blue pants meant one of them was going to sleep soon.

Olevia remained at her desk reviewing these precious notebooks from her Uncle Albert. It was strange how touching these books made her feel close to him again, and yet being close to him when she was growing up created such melancholy, often strange, uncomfortable, memories for her. Now Olevia could see from these notebooks that her Father Alexander and Uncle Albert clearly had stayed in contact with each other. Keeping up with the latest in chemistry. She noted that Uncle Albert wrote, "need case to display *opus magnum*." Furthermore, he wrote that he "liked the idea of molding with the newest chemicals." As Olevia opened another of the notebooks with the family crest on it, she was intrigued by an experiment called "Dorsal Radial Pain". She knew now clearly that the region of the thumb, wrist, and forearm that were the source of pain from Uncle Albert's burn was called, anatomically "dorsal", for top or back of the hand, and "radial" for the thumb side of the hand. She was examining this part of her own hand when David Siler came back and looked over her shoulder.

"I got the surgery resident started with his dog. We have been working together for a while. Professor Halsted will not allow a surgery resident to sew the bowel together in a patient until he has done this successfully in a dog. Success meaning that the dog has not developed peritonitis and died!! Now that the dog is asleep and I am not needed for a while, I can come back and work with you. What part are you reading now," asked the Senior Lab Assistant.

"Mr. Siler, to understand my Uncle Albert's research, you need to know that when he was working as a chemist, he burned the back of his right hand, non-dominant hand, with acid. Quite badly burned, down to the wrist bone and thumb joint. The dorsal radial part of his hand. I believe his research was designed to solve the pain problem he had, solve it anatomically. Solve it a way that a Surgeon could then use to help other people in pain," Olevia explained.

"Interesting point of view to create a research hypothesis," remarked David Siler. "Tell me more about his theory, and perhaps we can extend it into something that you can do in the lab during your research year with Dr. Cushing," he encouraged.

Olevia's eyes closed briefly as she tried to both remember, and not remember. "Uncle Albert and I were on a chair lift, skiing when I was about eleven years old. I always sat on his left, so he could hold me with his non-painful left hand. He told me that he had reviewed the line drawings of the earlier anatomists. To help me understand the nerves, he told me they were 'like roadmaps of the human body'. He told me, while on the chair lift, skiing, that trail maps in the mountains were for skiers as road maps were for cars on the road." In her mind, Olevia could both see and feel his left-hand start at her neck, run down across her chest and land in the area between her two legs under the seat belt of the ski lift. He would tell her this represented where the ski lift was located. Sometimes he would tell her the trail was not groomed. Then and he would move his hand around her small breasts is if they were moguls. He would do this several times saying the names of the ski trails. Even wearing her one-piece ski outfit, she hated how this felt. She began to shiver now as she remembered.

"Ms. Landsmann," said David Siler, "you have such an imagination. You are shivering, perhaps you remember the cold chair lift?"

"Lots of memories of Uncle Albert and skiing. Yes, they give me chills," she said, then continued "Actually, Uncle Albert had come now to believe that nerves were the trail maps to the human nervous system. I believe that in this section of his notebook he will be explicit as to which nerves his research has determined are the cause of his pain," she said, and stopped shivering.

"What does this section say? It looks again as if your Uncle Albert is going to record research and is beginning with a little introduction," observed David Siler.

"Uncle Albert writes," read Olevia, "I have read John Hilton's 1863 book, *Rest and Pain*. A compilation of this Anatomist's observations. Rest may help an inflamed nerve, but has not helped the pain I suffer. I suffer from my burned nerves. Scarred nerves. Damaged nerves. Yet in Hilton's 9th lecture, demonstrated in Figure 33 on page 179 the radial sensory nerve (RSN) is shown going to my area of pain. Then, in Figure 36, on page 183, Hilton illustrated the musculocutaneous nerve (MCN) in the forearm forming a loop with the RSN and branches from this loop going deeper down into joints below the thumb. These are the joints that hurt when I move my thumb!" wrote Uncle Albert.

"So now we know his hypothesis Ms. Landsmann. Injury to two nerves that overlap are the source of his persistent, chronic pain," observed David Siler, used to putting surgery residents' thoughts into research projects.

"Here Uncle Albert mentions observations made by his own Professor, Rüdinger, his teacher in Anatomy at the Ludwig-Maximillan University," Olevia continued, fascinated now. "In Rüdinger's doctoral thesis, *Die Gelenknerven des menschlichen Körpers,* meaning *The Articular Nerves of the Human Body*," translated Olevia, Uncle Albert found an illustration similar to the one in Hilton's lecture.

"Look here," instructed Olevia to David Siler. "Here Uncle Albert has written,

'Clearly there are nerves to transmit the skin sensation and there are nerves to transmit the joint sensation. Most obvious, radial sensory nerve," and here he wrote in red, "RSN". His notes continue "RSN comes from the back of the forearm and supplies the skin to the back of the thumb, index, middle and part of the ring finger, and it has little branches into the joints at the base of the thumb."

"Mr. Siler, those are the exact territories of his acid-damaged skin, commented Olevia.

"Your Uncle continues, "Hilton's drawing showed the skin towards the palm side of the thumb at the wrist joint to be innervated by the lateral antebrachial cutaneous nerve," read David Seiler.

"Antebrachial," said Olevia, to herself, again recalling her Latin. "In front of the arm or 'forearm'. Yes Mr Siler, that is the nerve to the forearm skin on the thumb side. Uncle Albert had written that in red too, "LABC". The LABC is the sensory branch of the MSN, the musculo*cutaneous* nerve," she concluded.

"So far, OK, Olevia," commented David Siler, being emotionally detached from this review of the notebooks. "What is the evidence that these nerves innervate those painful joints?" he then asked. "Did the RSN and LABC send branches to the damaged skin and to the thumb joint too?"

Olevia was thinking now. She was an excellent anatomy student. "As I think about this," said Olevia, "I have never seen a drawing of a nerve to a joint in any anatomy book. Now how can that be? Mr. Siler, this must become one of my areas for research. If I can find those nerves, I might be able to help so many people with joint pain, by doing something to these nerves. They must be there, right?" She asked herself. "How would we know a joint hurt if there were no nerve in the joint to send our brain that information?"

"Ms. Landsmann," Professor Halsted has proven that an alcohol solution of cocaine can put skin and nerves to sleep. Does this suggest a method of proving your theory about nerves and joints," suggested David Siler, again using his experience at Hopkins to help a new researcher focus.

"Why of course," smiled Olevia. "That solution can be injected into or near a nerve. Injecting the nerve itself might injure the nerve," she offered. "If the joint pain stopped then you would know which nerve went to the painful joint," she paused, and then added, "Uncle Albert knew all about cocaine, and would regularly inject himself. So he must have known the answer to this question," she concluded.

"Ms. Landsmann," persisted David Siler, "What would the Methods section say for this experiment that your Uncle Albert wanted to do? What would it say for your Methods section if you chose to work on this subject?"

"I think I can see the direction this research should take," responded Olevia. "If Uncle Albert could find the nerves to the skin that are damaged, and to the joints, he could just have those removed to stop his pain. A surgeon should be able to find those nerves and remove them, so that should be the next step," she offered. Then quickly added, "But I do not believe anyone has yet cut out a human nerve to treat pain."

"Great job Ms. Landsmann. You are on your way. When you are ready, and have Dr. Cushing's approval, bring the research to me and I will help you set it up in a Canine model. I just heard the surgery resident calling me to check out his bowel anastomosis in one of the dogs. He has been using Professor Halsted's technique which prevents the bowel connection from leaking," and David Siler turned and left.

Olevia sat there smiling, stunned, excited about the research ahead of her, and, a little frightened at the same time.

As she rose to leave her desk, her arm turned over a page in one of the notebooks. Something caught her eye, and she looked down. There she read a portion of a letter from her Father Alexander to her Uncle Albert. It had been glued on to the notebook page;

There is a class of compounds being worked on now called polymers. Repeating units of the same structure, one attached to another in a long chain. This gives chemicals special properties. In fact, Adolf Baeyer had discovered the first form of this in Munich in the Chemistry Department. He combined formaldehyde with phenol in 1872 but did not realize some of the properties of the product that formed. This fell to Leo Baekland, a Belgium-born chemist who had moved to the United States. He combined formaldehyde with phenol under certain conditions of increased pressure and acidity and created a resin that could then be poured into a mold, heated, and it would take on the shape of that mold. It was the first thermoplastic compound. The first *plastic*. Baekland called his new substance "Bakelite" after himself. This chemical also had the property that it did not conduct electricity, so it could be used in different shapes around electric wires as insulators.

A new "plastic" has been identified. Pioneering chemistry work done in Birmingham, England. In 1856, Alexander Parkes, was dissolving plant fibers, which are cellulose, with nitric acid. If he then added alcohol to this product, he had a polymer that also could be heated and transformed into different shapes. He demonstrated this at the International Exhibition in London in 1862 and won a Bronze Medal. He called his new compound "Parkesite". The material was clear but pigments could be added.

NOW OLEVIA KNEW WHAT Parkesite was and that her Father Alexander must have sent some to her Uncle Albert. He would then have the necessary chemicals to prepare the display case.

"I can hardly wait to see this finished "opus magnum" of my Uncle Albert when I go to Utah, thought Olevia.

As Olevia approached the dogs they seemed peaceful, looking at one of their group sleeping on the floor of its cage, slowly wagging its tail. A portion of hair from its abdomen was shaved off. The surgery must have gone well, thought Olevia. She turned to see David Siler watching her.

"Mr. Siler," she said. "Is the Anatomy Lab open at night?"

"Well Ms. Landsmann, yes, the door to the Anatomy Lab is unlocked, but the Hunterian Building is locked," he saw her mouth turn down in disappointment. "Why do you ask?"

"Surgical residencies are not open to Woman, as you must know. I would like to come in at night and practice the surgery that I see from the observation gallery in the operating room. I must find a way to get some actual experience. Indeed, I would like to get permission for my research year to have my own cadaver, so I can practice cutting through the skin and finding the organs through small incisions as they do in real surgery," she said calmly.

"Ms. Landsmann," replied David Siler, "I am the Senior Laboratory Assistant and I will see that you get a key to the building. Now what else has been on your mind today?" he said with a little smile, excited to see someone looking forward to surgical research.

"Doctor Halsted and Cushing, and in time, their residents, take the living body apart, then attempt to put it back together again. The awake patient after surgery is the judge and jury of the surgeon's skill and knowledge. Each success making the surgeon more full of self-esteem, and more embolden to operate again." Olevia explained.

"Yes, and your question or concern is?" he asked politely.

"And each failure?" Olevia asked. "What would that do to a surgeon? If Uncle Albert's embalming technique failed, or if he cut a nerve during a prosection, well, he could just get another specimen and start over. What could the surgeon do if this happened to a living patient?"

"Ms. Landsmann," commented David Siler philosophically, "You are beginning to realize that Surgical Knowledge comes at a price. A price measured out in human suffering and anguish, in anger and frustration. The surgeon has to make mistakes to gain knowledge, and through knowledge will come the wisdom to not make the same mistake when doing the same operation again. And with surgical education, with the training of the next surgeon, this information will be transmitted. Then comes progress and improved patient care. Here in the Hunterian, we help you take those first steps, even if it begins with Dog Surgery."

Olevia blinked. "What a process. Having to fail in order to succeed. Is every success paid for by previous failure?" Olevia asked, rhetorically. She felt something she had not often experienced. Doubt in herself. It was enough to try to repeat what the men surgeons where doing. Did she have the courage to identify the hidden mysteries locked within the human body, and then apply them to help people? Would people even let her operate on them?

NERVE IN MUSCLE

Olevia was waiting with Mr. David Seiler near her desk in the corner of the Hunterian Building. They were standing next to a blackboard on which there was a diagram that showed thick white line going to a piece of skin. The line came from rough scheme of the spinal cord. Near the skin, a red "X" went though the while line and there was a red ball at the "X". David and Olevia both heard the dogs start to bark. They looked up to see Dr. Harvey Cushing walk into the Research Laboratory.

"Hello David and Olevia," said Dr. Cushing. "I am ready for your presentation. Have you decided upon a research project of your own Olevia?"

"Yes, Dr. Cushing. I want to investigate an important aspect of a surgical approach to a painful peripheral nerve," answered Olevia, quite seriously.

"Perfect. Very little is known about that aspect of the Peripheral Nervous System. Please proceed," said Dr. Cushing.

Olevia turned to the blackboard, "We know from the work of August Waller in 1850, who used the frog for his experimental model," began Olevia, "that if you injure a nerve by cutting it in half, the distal part degenerates over a period of about 3 weeks." She illustrated this by taking blue colored chalk and placing dots along the part of the white line that ran between the "X" and the skin.

"Yes Olevia, we now all agree with that. When Waller looked at what happened to the nerve that was between the cut and its target tissue, the axon part of the nerve clearly degenerated, while the connective tissue, the supporting tissue remained. That is why we can still see a nerve lying in the subcutaneous tissues even when that nerve is not sending a message anymore. It is the proximal part of the nerve, the nerve left attached to the central nervous system that sends the message of pain from this nerve," replied Cushing, taking the red piece of chalk and drawing and arrow that pointed to the spine, pointing from the red "X". "Olevia, what is the question you want to answer in YOUR research?"

"Dr. Cushing, I just want to state one more observation before I tell you the question I want to answer," explained Olevia.

"Ok, Olevia, this will be like the INTRODUCTION part of the paper you may write about this research one day," said Dr. Cushing with a smile of encouragement.

"Thank you, Sir," said Olevia. "Many people get their skin cut and therefore their nerves cut, but these people do not seem to have pain. The people who do have pain, for example after a cut, a burn or a crush, may have that live end of the nerve become stuck in the scar to cause a painful neuroma," said Olevia taking the red chalk and enlarging the round ball along the white nerve at the "X". "Would you agree with that Dr. Cushing?"

"Yes, that is correct Olevia. So,…. the question to research is what can a surgeon do to relieve the pain of a nerve stuck in a scar?" at which point Dr. Cushing took an eraser and erased the red "X", symbolically making the pain go way. "Go ahead now Olevia, with the question YOU want to research," asked Dr. Cushing again.

"Dr. Cushing, we also know that if that nerve transmitting the pain message from the painful neuroma is divided, cut again, the nerve will regenerate, and the pain will return," said Olevia, taking the red chalk and drawing a new "X" on the white line closer to the spinal cord. "Dr. Cushing, I want to do an experiment in a Canine limb to determine what can be done to that proximal end of that nerve to prevent it from growing back and forming a painful neuroma again. I want to investigate a method to treat or prevent that problem, using a dog instead of a human for the experiment," answered Olevia.

"Excellent research project, Olevia. Here is what has been tried already. As Dr. Halsted has shown, a cocaine infusion can stop the pain, and that proves the pain is due to that certain nerve that has received the cocaine. I have cut such nerves and the pain is gone for a while, as you say. In most of these patients the nerve seems to grow back to some degree and their pain returns. I say "to some degree" because the part that the nerve used to go, that skin remains numb, even though the patient experiences pain in this area," he explained, again using the diagram on the blackboard. "This phenomenon has been termed *"anesthesia dolorosa"*, when it occurs," He answered.

"Painful numbness" is what that means. *Dolorosa* from the Latin for 'pain', and *Anesthesia* from the Greek for 'without sensation'," Olevia added. "A strange term."

"Yes," Cushing said. "Now Olevia, tell me what your proposed treatment will be in your experimental model"

"Dr. Cushing, as you know, I come from Munich, and I try to read the recent German publications as they might relate to what we do here in your laboratory. I found a paper recently written by a Doctor W. Moszkowicz. He reported taking the live end of a nerve and implanting it into a muscle, to keep the nerve from growing back to the skin," replied Olevia eager to see Dr. Cushing's reaction.

"There is some logic to this, I suppose," replied Dr. Cushing. "How many people did he try it with and how did the results turn out. Where did he publish this?" Cushing asked her.

"Sir, He reported just two patients. This was in a recent article in the Central Journal of Surgery. The paper was entitled *"Zur Behandlung den Schmerzhaften Neurome"*, which can be translated as "The treatment of the Painful Neuroma", she responded.

"I assume then, Olevia, that placing a nerve into muscle is the project you would like to pursue here in the lab. This would be worthy of basic science understanding Olevia. How would you proceed to study this? Now tell me the Methods section of your future paper."

Olevia had been planning for this question with Mr. Siler, who was intently observing the interaction between his newest researcher and his boss.

"I would take several dogs," began Olevia, "put each to sleep with ether anesthesia, cut into the skin of a forelimb, divide a nerve to the skin of the forelimb, and leave the end of the nerve nearby just under the skin. In another group of dogs, I would do the same thing, but in this group I would put the live end of the nerve into the nearest muscle so the nerve could not grow back to the skin. I would observe the dogs, making notes each day on how they walked and how they used the limb that had surgery."

"What would your assumption be Olevia? What is your hypothesis?" asked Dr. Cushing.

"I would assume that if the forelimb were painful, then the dog would limp. I could test this hypothesis by touching the piece of numb skin with long instrument and see if the dog responded as if in pain or responded but did not withdraw the leg in pain. I would do this for three months, because it might take the nerve a few months to grow back," replied Olevia confidently.

Cushing smiled. "I am so pleased that you not only have a plan, but it is a scientific one in which you create a hypothesis, and then test it. If successful, then we can try this approach in a series of patients. How will you determine what has happened to the end of the nerve in the muscle?"

"Sir, with your permission, I would excise a piece of the muscle with the nerve end implanted into it, and also excise the painful neuroma from the dogs in which the nerve was not implanted into muscle. Then I would do histology to study what happened at the end of each nerve, similar to the way August Waller looked at the nerves from the frogs. After I studied those nerves under the microscope and formed my own opinion of the nerves, then I would review the findings with a Pathologist," replied Olevia thoughtfully.

"I approve this project. Please begin as soon as possible, because you only have 6 months left in this academic year," said Cushing. "Mr. Siler will assist you in this surgery." Dr. Cushing paused, and then added, "and I would like you to participate more in my own surgery. Olevia, you should try to observe me in surgery whenever you can. As long as you are operating on nerves in living dogs, instead of cadavers, you should see what they look like in living people too."

"Yes Sir," she said. "Thank you. I will be there tomorrow to observe you in Surgery."

Dr. Cushing turned, winked at David Siler, and left.

David Siler looked at Olevia, smiled, and whispered "Let us start planning this research in detail right away."

SURGICAL SCIENTIST

Olevia went into the operating room to observe Dr. Harvey Cushing at work..

She was just amazed by what she saw.

First, he had to make the correct diagnosis of what was wrong with the patient. She had seen Dr. Cushing examine his patient in the Surgical Clinic. He had the keen powers of clinical observation that she noted also in Dr. William Osler, the Chief of Medicine. Here in surgery, Cushing was so precise, just as his teacher, William Halsted, Chief of Surgery. Cushing used tiny silk sutures to tie blood vessels. He was gentle with the tissues so as not to damage them.

He was now opening the skull to work on a "tumor", of sorts. A metal tumor. A bullet! He knew its location because of the physical findings and symptoms of his patient. But to be sure, Cushing was looking at an x-ray that an assistant was holding up to a light for him. Olevia knew this story. Another Hopkins legend. With his own money, Cushing bought the first x-ray machine for the Johns Hopkins Hospital. Having seen these machines while they were being developed in Europe during his *Wanderjahre,* he wanted there to be one at Hopkins Hospital. Cushing himself took the first x-ray ever done at Johns Hopkins Hospital, and it clearly showed a bullet inside the skull.

While Cushing was gently moving the brain aside a little, an assistant constantly dripped a solution on to the brain to keep it moist. Cushing himself, in the Hunterian Laboratory, had developed this salt solution to match the same degree of acidity and to have as much salt in it as the fluid usually surrounding the brain.

The surgical resident administering the ether for anesthesia, wrote down the pulse and blood pressure every few minutes on a chart. It now was officially now called the "anesthesia record". Dr. Cushing himself had invented this form of charting. Charting in surgery was something Dr. Cushing also brought back from his trip to Europe, where he had seen for the first time the blood pressure cuff, officially called the "sphygmomanometer". Dr. Cushing used a modified form of these pressure recordings in the Hunterian Laboratory to record the pressure inside the skull of animals.

In this operating room in the Johns Hopkins Hospital, Olevia was not permitted to "scrub in". She stood on an elevated platform to observe. She wore the exact same outfit as all the men who were scrubbed in, except for gloves. With her mask on, she could pass for any one of the male surgical residents.

It was clear that Dr. Harvey Cushing had brought into existence here at Johns Hopkins the concept of the Surgical Scientist. Olevia right there and then decided that this was going to be what she would strive to do. As she thought about this concept, she decided that the surgical scientist must record observations and results. Yes, of course. But, the moral imperative must drive her to go beyond this. To apply these results to help people do more than survive their surgical ordeals: To triumph above them. For her, that would mean applying the research she developed through her anatomic dissections into operations to help people in pain.

She only wished that she could have developed this in time to have helped her Uncle Albert. She had come to realize that she both loved and hated him. He left scars within her body, starting from her early childhood. These scars made her afraid she could never trust a man again, even a relative. And yet, she felt so strongly that her desire to help people in pain came from trying to help her Uncle Albert. She wondered, "Was cutting into people to help relieve their pain to be just another way to retaliate for the way she had been hurt? She was not sure. She just had confidence that in time she would work out all of these conflicts

Now Olevia looked around the quiet operating room. The entire team wore pants, of course, as not one woman, other than herself, Olevia, and the nurse assisting Dr. Cushing with instruments, were present. Olevia realized that she must find a way to "fit in" with this male dominated surgery system. Perhaps if she appeared less feminine, she would attract less attention. Perhaps this would help her as she entered what she suspected would be an even more male-dominated society in Utah than it already was in Baltimore.

The next day Olevia went back to the laboratory. With the help of David Siler, she gave a dog ether, and operated upon one of its forelimbs. It was sort of the same as a human forelimb, the hand and arm. By the time she did the second forelimb of the same dog, she was able to identify the nerves she would use for her research. Dr. Cushing had an entire room full of healthy dogs, often, stray dogs that the city of Baltimore would bring to him. Here the dogs had warmth, food and water, someone to care for them, and their lives contributed to helping their fellow living, human creatures through a compassionate approach to learning, research. By the end of the first week, Olevia had completed the project, which she had outlined for Dr. Cushing. At least, she had completed the surgical part.

The next week she went to Pathology to learn Histology, how to take tissue, fix it in formaldehyde, then embed it into wax, then slice it quite thin, finally remove the wax with a series of chemicals, then stain the tissue to identify nerve from muscle. She became a Histologist. Then she would look at the stained, fixed, tissue the same way she and Ezra used to do in Pathology class together. She learned to tell a normal nerve from a neuroma, and normal muscle from a nerve placed into a muscle.

She wondered about Ezra in Europe. Was he learning electrical stimulation of muscles and nerves, at the same time she was working with muscles and nerves? Romantic thought! Or was he meeting exciting new women! Was he forgetting all about her? Would she ever let a man touch her again the way her Uncle Albert had touched her?

Olevia thought, and fully expected to meet Ezra again in Salt Lake City in the future. How would they relate to each other then?

The next week Olevia took another dog, and harvested nerve and muscle tissue and practiced her histology techniques. This took lots of practice. Soon she would have very valuable specimens that she had to handle exactly right to learn the results of her experiments.

Then she went back to histology. Now she had to learn what type of chemical stains were necessary to identify nerve fibers. The processes were very hard to master. Silver stains. Gold stains. Very difficult. She practiced.

Then it was time. It was 6 weeks after the first dog surgery. At first both groups of dogs limped, at least for the first week, due, she wrote into her notebooks, surgical pain. She had now switched back to the notebooks with the Landsmann Family Crest. She would cut out a copy of the Johns Hopkins University emblem, with the flag of Maryland on it, and glue it to the lower right corner of each of these notebooks. After all, she was a Landsmann at Hopkins.

By the third week after surgery both groups of dogs were walking almost normally, and she noted this. By the 6th week however, one group of dogs was back limping while the other group of dogs, those in which the nerve had been implanted into muscle, was walking still normally.

"Oh my gosh," observed Olevia to herself. "The surgical implantation of nerve into muscle is preventing the pain from returning."

She could hardly wait for Dr. Cushing's next visit to the Hunterian Lab, and that would be tomorrow. She decided to ask someone else in the lab, who was not involved in this experiment, to observe the dogs and give her their assessment.

She did, and they made the same set of observations. All dogs in one group limped. All dogs in the other did not limp.

Dr. Cushing came into the lab. He went up to Olevia and said, "How have you enjoyed coming to the operating room?"

"It is inspiring to observe your judgment and surgical technique," she answered, telling quite the truth, while thinking it sounded like she was just praising him for its own sake. It is however, a little difficult to see your exact technique from so far away," she answered, continuing to be truthful.

"Thank you," he modestly replied. "You have done well in the operating room. You have been present but not disturbing, and forgive me for saying this, but, for an attractive women, you have dressed so as to not be too distracting."

Olevia just stood silent.

Dr. Cushing just stood there silent, looking at her.

Finally, Olevia said, "Thank you Dr. Cushing. There is just so much to learn."

"Yes, and what have you learned here in the lab with your own experiment," Cushing inquired.

"Please look at these two groups of dogs while I encourage them to take a few steps and see if you observe a difference between the two groups," she asked of Dr. Cushing.

"Well, excellent Olevia. I certainly hope the group walking normally is the experimental group with the nerve implanted into muscle, and the other group is the control group with the nerve cut but left underneath the skin," observed Dr. Cushing.

"Professor, it is only six weeks, but your observations are correct, and I am very encouraged by these early results in these few animals," said Olevia humbly.

"Ms. Landsmann," said Dr. Cushing with a smile, "now we await the results of the histology. While we wait for you to harvest the specimens and do the staining of the tissues, I invite you to scrub in on my next few surgeries."

PRESENTATION

Olevia had one more research item to complete before she cold leave Baltimore and Johns Hopkins Hospital. "What should I wear", she wondered. She observed that since there were no women in surgery, she looked very different from the men. Clearly, she was a woman. She loved being a woman. She looked forward to seeing Ezra again one day in Salt Lake City. But she had made a decision to de-emphasize, is the way she now thought of it, to de-emphasize her "womanhood". Olevia chose pants and a jacket to wear to the Hunterian Lab today, her big, day.

Dr. Harvey Cushing sat before his researchers in the conference room of the Hunterian Lab. It was the end of June, the end of the academic year. The end of Olevia's last year in medical school. The end of Olevia's research year.

Olevia rose to present the results of her research, entitled "Does Nerve implantation into Muscle Prevent Painful Neuroma Formation?"

David Siler sat in the front row, smiling encouragingly to Olevia. Seated behind him were many of the Surgery Resident's from Professor Halsted's General Surgery residency program.

Dr. Cushing stood up, and said, "Ms. Landsmann, please make your presentation.

Even the dogs became quiet.

Olevia had planned to begin her talk with a review of the clinical problem that initiated this research work. "Thank you, Dr. Cushing, for this opportunity, and thank you Mr. David Siler for your invaluable assistance in carrying out this research which I will now present."

Just at that moment, the door to the conference room opened, and Olevia observed that Dr. Johns Staige Davis, Assistant Professor of Plastic

Surgery at Johns Hopkins Hospital, had entered the room, and sat in the last row.

Olevia paused, took a deep breath and began her presentation (she had no notes in front of her), "If a nerve to the skin, a sensory peripheral nerve, is injured in an accident or as a complication of surgery, the proximal end of the nerve, the end still attached to the spine continues to be "alive", while the distal end, the end closest to the fingertips, if it is in the upper extremity, will "die". The proximal end still has its cell bodies alive in the spine in the dorsal root ganglia." Then she turned to the screen behind her, and David Siler got up and turned on the projector.

Olevia continued, picking up a pointer and pointing to the dorsal root ganglia in the illustration she had prepared for this lecture. "Therefore, the proximal end of the nerve will regenerate towards its original skin territory. We know the distal end degenerates due to the research published by August Waller in 1850, using a model in the frog."

At this point she stopped, turned to face the seated surgeons, to see the expected look of surprise in the eyes of her listeners. Some laughed quietly. "I do not know why Dr. Waller, from London, who published his work in the *Philosophical Transactions,* worked with frogs. Perhaps because he was first a neurophysiologist before he became a medical doctor. We know that legs of frogs were used for the early Galvanic stimulation studies on muscle function and reflexes."

The residents, seemingly impressed by this choice of a research model, stopped looking at each other and gave her their full attention.

Getting back to her own research, Olevia continued, "In the Canine surgery that I did, the skin is always cut but those nerve endings to the skin are quite small. When one of the larger nerves is injured, such as the radial sensory nerve, the one that I transected in the forelimb," she nodded to Mr. Siler to insert the next slide. "the end still attached to the spine will try to grow back towards the skin it used to innervate by linking up with its former distal end. In many people with this type of injury, they remain numb in the area that that nerve used to go, and it becomes painful at the site of the injury, with the brain perceiving the pain in the numb area from the neuroma that forms at the end of the regenerating nerve. This neuroma is just the regenerating ends stuck in scar." She nodded to Mr. Siler who put in the next slide. "The subject of my research was to evaluate the theory, the hypothesis, that if a live end of a sensory nerve is placed into a normal muscle, then, the nerve in the muscle will not form a painful ending. It will not form a painful neuroma."

One of the Surgery Residents of Dr. Halsted, who was attending this research session, asked. "That is a fascinating concept, young Dr. Landsmann," he said, granting Olevia her medical degree a few weeks early. "Can you share with us how you arrived at that theory?"

"Certainly, I can," Olevia answered. "Pain after a nerve injury has been a subject on my mind ever since my Uncle Albert sustained such an injury at work. He lived with pain in his wrist and forearm on the thumb side, and it altered his life and that of our family who loved him. Obviously, it has altered my life. As I studied here at Hopkins, I continued to read the German scientific literature, and found a report by a Doctor Moszkowicz, of two patients in pain who had their injured nerve placed into muscle. Their pain went away. There were just two patients treated in that way. There was not research; there was no control group. Yet Doctor Moszkowicz's idea might be correct. I believe those first clinical observations deserved further investigation. Dr. Cushing agreed. And so," she said with a polite smile, "Here we are."

"Please continue on, Ms. Landsmann. That was a good Introduction," encouraged Dr. Cushing, resuming control of the research presentation.

"The Method used to evaluate this hypothesis was to have two groups of dogs," she nodded to Mr. Siler, and he promptly put in the next slide. "Five dogs in each group. One group would have the radial sensory cut and implanted into one of the forearm muscles, one that did not have much movement, an accessory wrist extensor, the brachioradialis muscle was chosen for this purpose. The other group of dogs had the same nerve divided with the proximal end allowed to lie in the subcutaneous fat, just above the wrist."

"Both groups of dogs were allowed their normal amount of activity in their cages and given the same diet. An independent observer, Mr. David Siler, who did not know which group of dogs had which operation, observed the dogs' ability to ambulate for the next six weeks," Olevia said, and paused.

Now a different surgery resident raised his hand. "How did you judge if a dog was in pain?" he asked, and why did you decide you needed an independent observer?"

"Well, clearly I am biased. I am both the Surgeon and the research investigator and would like my hypothesis to be proven true. Therefore, someone who did not know which group was which was needed. To answer your second question, Sir, my assumption upon the effect of pain on ambulation, based upon observing patients with a painful foot, was that the dog would put less pressure on the painful foot and would limp," she explained.

"Please move on to the Results section, now, Ms. Landsmann," requested Dr. Cushing.

"Yes Sir," went on Olevia, "We observed that all ten dogs limped immediately after surgery, most likely from the pain of the surgery. Then by the second to third week, all ten dogs walked more normally, and we believe this was because the surgical pain was gone," here she again turned and nodded to Mr. Siler, who put in the slide with the graph showing walking without limping by both groups of dogs. "By the 4th week after surgery, the group that had the nerve implanted into muscle continued to walk more normally and continued to walk normally until the 10th week after surgery, when the observation period ended. In contrast, the group with the nerve left to regenerate into the scar, had progressively worse and worse walking behavior. By the 6th week, some dogs in this group refused to stand at all. Both the independent observer, Mr Siler, and I, agreed exactly with these findings and the rating of walking ability. As you can see from the graph, these observations continued through the end of the study."

Then she continued. "At 10 weeks after implanting the nerve into muscle, the dogs were put to sleep again, and the specimens harvested for histologic evaluation."

Olevia turned to Mr. Siler, and nodded her head. A series of sections of nerve and muscle appeared.

Olevia continued, "I chose a Mallory Trichrome Stain to evaluate the histology, because it stains the muscle red, connective tissue like collagen, blue, and nerve pink. The white, as you probably know is the way fat appears with this stain," Olevia explained further.

"As you can see," Olevia said pointing to the screen, "This slide is from one of the dogs in the group that served as the control group, where the nerve was left beneath the skin to grow as it normally would. The pink nerve end is swollen, the blue collagen scarring is extensively present, and there are bundles of pink nerve fibers disorganized throughout the scar. This is the histologic appearance of a neuroma using the Trichrome stain. Of course, histology alone cannot tell us if these were painful. But these neuromas were found in the dogs that limped." She turned and nodded to Mr. Siler. The next slide appeared on the screen.

"In contrast to that neuroma, the histology you are seeing now, from one of the dogs where the nerve was placed in muscle, demonstrates small pink nerve fiber groups in between red muscle fibers, with little blue scarring, and therefore with no neuroma formation. To remind you, these are from the dogs that did not limp."

Dr. Cushing now stood up and said, "Excellent work Olevia, are there any questions from the audience?"

One of the Surgery Residents raised his hand, was acknowledged by Dr. Cushing, and asked, "Dr. Landsmann, what type of control did you use to prove that you had actually denervated the skin over the dorsum of the forelimb, meaning, that you really divided the radial sensory nerve?"

"Thank you for that question. That of course was important to prove. At the 6th week and the 10th week after dividing the radial sensory nerve, the skin on the top of the forelimb, which was the target skin territory, was touched with a warm piece of metal, heated by hot water. This metal rod was put into the cage. The heat did not cause the dog to move its leg on the side that had the surgery. On the side that did not have the surgery, the dog moved its foot away from the painful hot rod. This demonstrated that the nerve that I divided was in fact divided."

Dr. Cushing stood up again and said, "Dr. Landsmann, Excellent demonstration of the scientific method. Now, what is your conclusion, and how should we surgeons take this new information back into the operating room to help our patients in pain?"

Olevia could not have been happier. There seemed to be complete acceptance of her research by her laboratory group, and by her most famous Dr. Cushing. What a way to end her time at Johns Hopkins School of Medicine!

"Thank you, Dr. Cushing, for this opportunity," Answered Olevia. "My Conclusion is that, in this experimental model of the dog forelimb, implantation of sensory nerve into muscle prevents formation of a painful neuroma and permits recovery of limb function. It is up to those reviewing this information as to whether they wish to try this now on people with a painful neuroma."

Now Dr. John Staige Davis stood up from the back row. "With all due respect to you and Dr. Cushing, Ms. Landsmann," he said, "You did NOT show that putting a nerve in muscle could treat a painful neuroma. I suggest that your conclusion should be that placing a nerve in muscle may prevent painful neuroma formation. To prove you could treat a painful neuroma in the manner which you suggest, you would now have to take those five dogs who remain in pain from your surgery, back to surgery, resect that painful neuroma, and then place its proximal end of the radial sensory nerve into muscle. Then, once again, observe the dog's ability to walk." He then sat down with a concerned look on his face.

Dr. Cushing smiled at his colleague's comments, "Dr. Davis, excellent comment. Really excellent." Then turning to Olevia, Dr. Cushing said, "Olevia, before you leave Baltimore to go on with your life as a Surgical Scientist, I know you will take time to stay in Baltimore and complete the additional research that Dr. Davis has suggested."

The room was quiet, and all eyes looked at Olevia.

"Yes sir. It will be an honor to continue to work in the Hunterian Laboratory, and perhaps while I am here, as a Surgical Scientist, Dr. Davis would permit me to scrub in with him on some of his surgeries, as you have been so kind as to permit me to do, so that I may gain more actual surgical experience?" she lowered her head a little as she asked humbly for this honor.

Dr. Cushing turned to look at Dr. Davis, and gave him a smile and a wink, acknowledging his approval of this request. Then, Dr. Cushing had one last word for Olevia, "Oh, and finally, Ms. Landsmann, please send me a written report so that we may submit your completed research to the Bulletin of the Johns Hopkins Hospital for publication. As I am sure you are aware, Mr. Siler's name and mine should be included in the authorship. Oh, and include the name of the Pathologist, with whom I assume you have reviewed your histology conclusions."

After everyone had filed out of the room, and David Siler asked her to return tomorrow to begin the next phase of her research.

Olevia then followed the Surgery Residents out of the laboratory floor, past the now barking dogs, went down the steps and out the door of the Hunterian Laboratory. She took a breath of the Spring air, heard the birds tweeting, and turned to walk back "home", at Miss Susie Slagle's.

She now needed to ask for a 6 month extension of her stay.

2nd LETTER

As Olevia started up the white marble steps at Miss Susie Slagle's, she saw the Mailman walking up to her residence. He clearly had some mail in his hand.

Olevia just had a premonition that there might be a letter to her. "Do you have one for me?" she asked as the Mailman approached her, "A letter for Miss Olevia Landsmann?"

The Mailman stopped on the step next to her and scanned the mail in his hand. "Why yes I do! Were you expecting something?" he asked, handing her an envelope, and continued up the stairs.

"Well, sort of. I am graduating from the Johns Hopkins School of Medicine and thought I might receive a letter of congratulations soon from my family," she replied, following him up the steps and into the lobby of her residence.

Olevia looked at the envelope. No, it was NOT from Munich, not from her Father Alexander. It was from the University of Utah, Department of Biology, from Dr. Thomas Parks, Director of Anatomy.

"Hello Olevia," said a classmate coming down into the lobby from the second floor. He rested his hand and arm on the large dark wooden banister, watching the mailman depositing the mail on to the old desk in the front lobby. "Did you get another check from back home? Time you took us all out for a drink to celebrate your graduation," he suggested to her with a big smile.

"No it is not from my parents, but I think it may be worth more than another check from them.....it may be a job offer!! In which case I will still take you out for a drink. Maybe someone will even offer you a job when you graduate, though I doubt it," she replied, giving it right back to him.

"Nice, quick, read the letter, I can hardly wait. Who wants YOU anyway!!" he continued to joke with her.

"OK. I will share it with you. It is a letter of invitation from Professor Thomas Parks. He invites me to be on his faculty as Instructor in Anatomy at the new University of Utah School of Medicine. He says that if I send him a copy of my Johns Hopkins School of Medicine Diploma, then he will help me to obtain surgical privileges to operate at the Salt Lake County General Hospital!" she said with a smile, and ran up the steps past him, giving him a punch in the arm.

She stopped at the top of the landing and reread the letter. Dr. Parks also wrote that he had spoken to the Chairman of the Board of Trustees of the hospital, The Honorable Gary Lord Clarke-Smith, Esq., who had accepted her Uncle Albert's bequest of the peripheral nerve prosection. It would be hung in the hall where the Surgery Department held its clinic, to inspire young surgeons in anatomic dissection.

Olevia was overwhelmed. She beamed. She cried. She would send a copy of this letter to her Father Alexander.

She could hardly wait to complete her Hunterian Laboratory research and get to Utah.

III
SALT LAKE CITY, UTAH, 1916

HAROLD

As Olevia walked up to the Salt Lake County General Hospital, she paused. She stopped and looked around. She had come down State Street to 2100 South Street, the corner at which was located the hospital for the new University of Utah Medical School. This old hospital was a beautiful structure. It was made from some of the same marble that had been quarried in Little Cottonwood Canyon to build the Mormon Tabernacle.

Dr. Parks had come through for her. Now, she was an Instructor in this new school. She could work in its Anatomy Lab, and today she was on her way to her very own Surgery Clinic.

She remembered the first day that Dr. Park brought her here. He had been successful at having Mr. Gary Lord Clarke- Smith, a lawyer and one of the hospital's Trustees, get permission to hang her Uncle Albert's *opus magnum* in the hallway that led into the clinic area of the hospital, to "inspire" those who walked by.

Olevia decided that today she would behave as a new patient going into the Surgery Clinic, to experience what they might feel.

As Olevia walked into the wide corridor, she found herself surrounded by patients coming in to be seen. The first arch in the hallway was clearly marked "Medical Clinic", with the name David J. Grafton, MD, Chief of the Department of Medicine, listed on the wall. She knew that the Medical doctors usually did not think much of a Surgeon's diagnostic ability. To the Medical "people", the Surgeons were like Cowboys of the Old West, always shooting things up. A Surgeon was a Maverick, often making as much or more of a problem for a patient and the Medical team than the help they gave to the patient they were supposed to be caring for.

Olevia couldn't help but wonder at the unusual collection of names and backgrounds here in Salt Lake City. "Gary Lord Clarke-Smith", she guessed was a man from an English background, probably a family that had been "knighted," a meaning that a member had been elevated to be a "Lord", and married now into the Smith family. There were sure a lot of Smiths in Salt Lake City. She knew "Smith" was a common Mormon name.

As Olevia approached the next hallway arch, clearly marked "Surgery Clinic", she could see the name "Elijah Willis, MD, Chief of Surgery," listed on the wall. She, also, could see a line of patients alongside the wall on the left. There was another line and a desk on the opposite side of the hall, similar to that on the medical side. She knew what was on that left side of the hall that was so interesting. Patients were lined up to see it. It was "Harold". Her Uncle Albert had given his prosection a male name to match the "Harriet" that had so inspired him and set off his quest for pain relief. Olevia walked up and took a position at the end of the line, pretending to be a patient.

As patients moved along, past the display, many would stop, and raise their right hand high and forward, as if giving the display a "high five" or a friendly wave.

As Olevia got closer she could see the prosection. From this perspective, it looked like it was a demonstration of the arteries and veins of the human body. Olevia, however, knew that what at first appeared to be vessels were really nerves. Those in the right arm were hanging at the right side. Those for the left arm were raised and positioned slightly forward, as if the left hand were outstretched. Those for the legs were positioned unusually, too. The left leg was positioned forward, and the right, more towards the rear, as if the person was in motion, taking a step out of the display case to greet you, left foot going first.

Olevia remembered Uncle Albert's drawings in his notebook. He had created a pose for his prosection quite different from that of Harriet, in which all the nerves were hanging straight downward. Uncle Albert had created something more like the illustrations in Vesalius' *De Humani Corporis Fabrica,* just as he had written in his notebook. He created a body in motion, depicting action, depicting life, not a static appearance.

Harold's left hand, as her Uncle Albert's left hand, was up in action, the right hand depicted without movement at his side.

Olevia could clearly see now, as she got closer, the reason the nerves appeared to be vessels. It was because there was a hint of red along each of them, this was where Uncle Albert's chemical preservation technique had added the fluorescein dye.

The nerves were highlighted by just the presence of a few bones, to make up the left foot, the bones of the right forearm, and a couple of ribs to suggest a thorax.

"How often have you been to the surgery clinic," Olevia asked the person standing in front of her. "This is my 6th visit, Mam. My stomach keeps bothering me. They think I have a gall stone or an ulcer," the woman answered.

"Why do people raise their right hand to put it in front of the left hand of that anatomy display?" Olevia asked her, just to see the lady's response.

"For me, it is just for 'good luck'," she answered, and then continued, "but I have asked some of the other patients who come here and do this. They think too that is for luck, or perhaps something spiritual. You know this place is run by the Mormons, and they believe in Angels, so, maybe some of the Mormon patients get special meaning from this 'Supreme Healer'."

Being next in line, Olevia could now look on with amazement. Yes, she was still amazed even though she had already spent many hours studying this PROSECTION at night when this hallway was empty. This was the most detailed prosection of the nervous system she had ever seen. And it was accurate, of course. It had to be truth. It came directly from a cadaver dissection.

She had taken notes about the details that she could see related to nerves that were not in any anatomy book she had ever seen. Then she had gone to the Anatomy Lab, done more dissections, and confirmed to herself that these nerves were really there! Especially about nerves to the joints. This prosection was truth. Truth she could rely on to help the patients she might see who had pain related to injured nerves.

Today, since Olevia was pretending to be a patient, she raised her right hand and put her palm against the display case. It had been created from some thin form of plastic. This was the Parkesite, the clear plastic created from the chemicals her Father Alexander had send over to her Uncle Albert.

Olevia's right palm went directly against, or so it seemed, the left palm of the prosection. Just the same as when she was a little girl and she held her Uncle Albert's left hand. There seemed to be warmth between her palm and the prosection. She smiled as she again pictured her Uncle Albert creating this. She knew, however, that the warmth was just from the friction of all those hands that had preceded hers on this piece of plastic. Or was it something else?

Olevia now looked at the bronze plate fixed to the base of the display. It read,

Harold;

Prosection by Albert Landsmann, 1909.

Olevia continued walking towards her clinic. She took off her outer coat, revealing now her white lab coat as she entered the clinic.

As she walked towards the secretary's desk to see who would be her first patient today, she heard some call her name, "Dr. Landsmann, remember me?"

She turned to see Edward Cannon, with his crutch, sitting in her clinic. "Of course, I remember you. How is your head, any headaches from that hole I put into it?" She asked with a smile.

"My head is great. Dr. Baldwin, the Chief of Orthopedic Surgery, whom you met that day in his clinic, sent me to see you. It is 6 months after my compartment release surgery, and my pain is the same and I cannot walk without the crutch. I am still on pain medicines and cannot work," Edward explained. "Dr. Baldwin said that you may have a new operation figured out to help me. If you do, I want you to do it right away. Otherwise, I want Dr. Baldwin to amputate my leg. I have gotten pretty good at walking with a crutch," Edward finished, and looked up at Olevia expectantly, hopefully.

"Well, let me examine you again today, and we will make a plan," Dr. Landsmann replied, and walked back to see her first patient, already waiting in the examination room.

The first patient was a 37-year-old woman, Martha Pratt, referred to her by her friend, Jennie, the Gynecologist. Martha told her, "Your Doctor friend operated on me to remove my uterus, which would bleed a lot every month. It had tumors in it. I already have 5 children, so it was OK with me to remove it. The bleeding was so bad I was turning pale from loss of blood and getting weak."

"Thank you for sharing that with me," replied Olevia, "and who is this handsome young man with you?" she asked.

"This is one of my sons. He is a smart one. I want him to listen to what you got to say to me, 'cause I may not remember it right by the time I get home," she replied humbly.

Olevia remembered this story. Her friend Jennie told her that she was sending a patient over to her who had a painful scar. "Yes, Dr. Ross told me she was sending you to me. Show me where you have the pain."

The woman, who was lying down, lifted up her long skirt until the area below her belly button and the top of her underpants was visible. Her son turned his head. "The pain is right here, in this corner of the scar," Martha said pointing to the area in the pubic hair in which the scar ended."

Olevia gently touched the right side and compared it to touching the left side in the same place.

Martha said, "that right side is sort of dull, like you are touching me through my clothes, but I feel it real well on the left."

Then Olevia pressed in, on that right side a little harder this time, and Martha let out a little "Ouch, that is right where the pain is. It hurts when I sit because by belly pushes it in. And it hurts if I try to tighten a belt or wear a girdle," she said, taking deep breaths to control her pain.

"Yes, I can see that, Martha," said Dr. Landsmann confirming her findings.

"I now know how to find the nerves that are causing your pain, it is like the nerves that cause pain after a hernia repair. If you wish, I can remove those nerves for you," explained Dr. Landsmann to Martha Pratt."

"Yes, Doctor, please plan to do this soon, so I can get back to caring for my children.

After Olevia saw two more patients, she walked into an exam room to find Edward Cannon sitting on the table with his pants leg pulled above his knee. Olevia examined him and again found the spot at the outside of the knee that sent tingling down his leg to the top of the foot, the spot in the scar from the fasciotomy that was so painful to him, and the numbness over the top of the foot except for the skin between the first two toes. "The findings are the same as last time I saw you," said Dr. Landsmann.

"What can you do to help me, Doctor? I really do not want my leg amputated. I can tell my leg is getting weaker. I have trouble now lifting my toes. I think I am getting paralyzed. I am willing to try anything, even if it is some new operation you have invented," stated Edward quite bluntly.

"You are correct in that there is an operation that has developed from my anatomy research. You remember Dr. Baldwin and I discussed that a nerve, the superficial peroneal nerve, was," Olevia hesitated for a minute, trying to choose the best word. She wanted to say "injured" but was now beginning to think about Lawyers. If she said "injured" it might expose Dr. Levin Randolph to a lawsuit. Well, she thought again to herself, "Perhaps that would not be a bad thing!" However, the word "stuck" might be a better choice than the word "injured", implying no blame to the Orthopedic Surgeon.

"Edward," Olevia finally continued, "That nerve is *stuck* in the scar. My new operation will remove the damaged, painful part of the nerve. Since your foot is already numb on the top, it will stay numb, and I will move that live end of the nerve into a muscle, to keep the nerve from growing back," she explained. "Also, up near your knee, the bigger nerve, from which this stuck one arises, is also stuck or compressed against the bone that was broken. I must operate up there too, and remove the scar tissue to decompress that nerve, called the common peroneal nerve. It is this entrapment that is making your leg get weaker."

"Have these operations ever been done before?" asked Edward, his voice trembling a little.

"Edward Cannon, you would be the first person to have these operations," she said looking him straight in the eye. "We both will have to be brave," she answered truthfully. "Now where did you hear about my doing operations that I invented?"

"In the Orthopedic Clinic. Dr. Baldwin was telling other surgeons about his conversation with you and how you examined me. He seemed impressed. He told me to tell you that if you made me better, he had lots more patients to send. But the other doctors, were looking down, one was even angry, saying something about Women should stay out of surgery, and no one knew what would happen if you operated on nerves," continued Edward. "Honestly, Dr. Landsmann, it all worries me too, but I am in such pain. What else can I do?" Edward Cannon then repeated, "I do not want an amputation, really. I do not want to take drugs the rest of my life. I do trust you, Dr. Landsmann, even if you are a Woman and even if you have never done this before."

FIBROID

Olevia caught up with Jennie Ross going into the elevator of Salt Lake County General Hospital. Jennie turned, smiled at Olevia, gave her a big hug, and said, "History today Olevia. Two Women surgeons are going to be together in an operating room at the same time."

"Unheard of!" said Olevia with a big smile on her face.

As the elevator started up to the top floor, where the operating rooms were located, Jennie looked at Olevia thoughtfully, and said, "Wonder who the first woman surgeon even was, or if anyone even knows?"

"When I was interviewed by Dr. Florence Sabin, for the Johns Hopkins School of Medicine, I did ask her that question," responded Olevia. "Dr. Sabin told me that while she did not know for sure who was the very first woman surgeon, she had heard of a woman doctor who worked as a surgeon in the Civil War, her name was Mary Edwards Walker,"

"Bet she had an interesting life," commented Jennie. "Do you know anymore about her?"

"Yes, I do. I wanted to impress Dr. Sabin, so I did some library research on her. Mary Edwards Walker was born in New York State, and went to medical school in Syracuse, New York. She was only just out of medical school when the Civil War started. She volunteered for the Union Army, and even though women were considered unfit to serve as doctors, she was allowed to work as a nurse. She was present at the first Battle of Bull Run. She must have been very brave, as she asked for permission to be a spy. Finally, she was given a job as an assistant Surgeon at a field hospital in Washington, D.C. She was the first woman ever to be employed by the U.S. Army. She did work behind the enemy lines and was captured and imprisoned as a spy. Four months later she was traded back to the Union, a prisoner swap, for the release of a Confederate Colonel, a male surgeon. For her courage, she became the first woman to be awarded the Congressional Medal of Honor," concluded Olevia, just as the elevator door opened.

Jennie walked out of the elevator ahead of Olevia, and turned towards her and said, "Amazing story, and I bet almost no one knows about it."

"Her story is not well known," Jennie. I have decided that I will teach about Mary Walker, her bravery deserves to be remembered forever. After all, *Memorandum est Vivere in Aeturnum,*" Olevia said with a smile.

Jennie now led the way to the operating rooms, and said, "Of course you should, and one day," she said giving a little laugh, "someone will teach about you and me."

"Tell me about the surgery that I am going to be observing you do today, Jennie," asked Olevia.

"You are going to watch me do an operation that Gynecologists do almost every week; remove the uterus. It can be removed, for lots of reasons. Usually, for bleeding. Usually for tumors that are benign, not cancerous, just big and uncomfortable. Tumors pushing against the bladder or the rectum, causing pain," explained Jennie.

"That means no more babies for this woman," Olevia said, stating the obvious.

"Right," commented Jennie. "Olevia you know from your Latin that '*uterus*' meant "womb". No uterus no babies. We never remove the uterus to prevent pregnancy. 'Hysterectomy' however, is Greek, *hustra* for "womb" and the suffix *"ectomy"* meaning "out from" or excision. Like an Appendectomy, removal of the appendix," concluded Jennie.

Olevia smiled to herself since language was so much fun. "Jennie, here is a little joke for you then, since you are getting so deep into language. The Appendix is really a Latin word, meaning "to add on" and its real name was the *vermiform appendix* meaning a "worm-like" piece that was "added on" to the large intestine. So, linguistically, an "appendectomy" was "removing and add on"," laughed Olevia, amused by her own cleverness. She would have to remember that one to tell Ezra when she next saw him. He, too, would surely think it was so clever.

Olevia and Jennie were now entering the locker room, the same one used for the nurses. There was no separate locker room for women surgeons.

Mable Ryan, RN, the circulating nurse who was in the room for the surgery that Olevia and Levin Randolph did together on the leg with compartment syndrome, was just finishing putting on her scrub clothes. She looked up as the two Women Doctors walked into the dressing room. She smiled and stood politely in front of them. "My name is Mable Ryan, and I have the great honor to be the Circulating Nurse in the operating room with you two today."

"I remember you Mabel, your eyes anyway. And now seeing your whole pretty face, you remind me so much of someone," Olevia observed.

"Yes, thank you, Doctor. You probably know my mother from the Emergency Room, Hannah Ryan," Mabel replied.

"Yes, of course, I see the resemblance," observed Olevia.

"Doctor Landsmann, if I may say," said Mabel quietly, and looking around to see that no one else was in the locker room with them, "I saw how Dr. Levin Randolph almost cut you with that large #22 scalpel blade he likes to wield around. That was horrible of him."

"The operating room is a dangerous work environment Mabel. We all know that," said Olevia, trying to avoid the accusation against Dr. Randolph.

"Yes, Doctor it is a dangerous place. But, Doctor, many of us have overheard him talking to other Surgeons in the operating room about the Woman Surgeon, and he means you. For some reason, Dr. Landsmann, you have really threatened him." Nurse Ryan concluded.

"Thank you for sharing that with us, Mabel. We will be on the look out. See you in the OR," said Olevia.

Nurse Ryan left the dressing room.

Olevia and Jennie each got undressed. Olevia was wearing a white neck high collar shirt without buttons made of cotton. Jennie just pulled the surgical gown on over her bra. Jennie asked, "why do you wear that undershirt to surgery? Are you cold?"

"Modest perhaps," Olevia said. "In surgery, even in medical school, I noticed how the men would stare down the front of the women's surgical covering. So, the less distractions the better, even for someone like me, who is not as well endowed as you are Jennie, in the breast department that is," she commented with a smile.

"You have a great figure, Olevia", commented Jennie, "If you do not mind my saying so."

"Thanks," said Olevia, blushing, "I am not used to getting compliments from men or women about my appearance."

Olevia was proceeding to put her short hair into a surgical cap and observed Jennie working much harder to include her longer hair into the hat, pushing in several clips. "Why don't you wear your hair shorter?" asked Olevia, "Although I admit it would be a shame to cut it. You have beautiful long dark, thick hair," Added Olevia, somewhat to her own surprise.

"The long hair is a lot of work," agreed Jennie.

Jennie led the way out of the dressing room and into the corridor with the operating rooms. They could both smell the ether. They each pulled up their surgical masks and began to scrub their hands at the scrub sink. A male surgeon across the hall, at another sink, turned to look at them.

"I think the long hair makes me more attractive, and so I just have to accept working harder to take care of it," Jennie finally commented.

The two of them then entered the operating room to see that the Circulating Nurse, Mabel Ryan, had shaved the pubic hairs, and scrubbed the lower abdomen with iodine. The Scrub Nurse, who was really not a nurse, but a Scrub Tech, was placing sterile drapes around the lower abdomen.

Olevia looked at the Scrub Tech, and said, "One of my associates has been training to be a Scrub Tech. Her name is Chipeta. Do you know if she has started to work here in the operating room yet?"

"No Doctor," replied the Scrub Tech. "If she is here working, I have not met her yet. Here at the University, many women come and go. Hard to keep track of them all," she replied.

"Thank you," said Olevia and decided that from now on she would call the Scrub Tech a Scrub Nurse, out of respect. The Scrub Techs actually worked harder during an operation than the Circulating Nurse, who, however, had more responsibility.

Now, both Women Surgeons wearing sterile gloves and gowns, stood facing each other on opposite sides of the surgery table. They looked at each other over the surgical masks, and the each could see the other one smiling back, eyes twinkling.

"Here we go," said Jennie. She was right-handed and stood naturally on the patient's right side. She took the scalpel, with the smaller #15 blade, in her right hand and with a firm single long movement cut through the skin and into the fat from the left side to the right side just above the pubic bone. As the blood began to ooze out on to the area, both doctors placed sterile towels on the skin edges and pressed for a few minutes, giving Jennie a chance to teach.

"You were trained in General Surgery to make an up and down incision from the umbilicus to the pubis, and then separate the muscles going straight in. As you know, this takes a while to recover from and you have all the intestine in the way. This incision, transverse instead of longitudinal, has been popularized by one your own countrymen. But you probably never heard of him. Joseph Pfannenstiel?"

Olevia started laughing. "You must be telling a joke Jennie. You must know that *Pfannenstiel* mean a "pan handle" in German, reverting to her German accent."

"No joke, but it is funny. Dr. Pan Handle, then, was Secretary of the German Gynecology Society and was Editor of the German journal Archives of Gynecology," she replied, then stopped and looked over at the Circulating Nurse, Mable Ryan.

"Mabel, remember our discussion of how dangerous an occupation surgery can be?" asked Jennie.

"Yes, Dr. Ross, of course I do, it was just a little while ago in the dressing room.

"Good. Let me share with you and Dr. Landsmann how Dr. Pan Handle died. His finger was cut while removing and infected Fallopian tube. He died from that infection in 1909," Dr. Ross said quietly. "Gynecology lost one of its true pioneers from an injury in the operating room."

Now that the skin had stopped bleeding, Olevia was looking through the fat. "I do not see those ilioinguinal or iliohypogastric nerves at this level yet," she said.

Jennie then proceeded to open the thick white connective tissue that covered the muscles. Each time there was bleeding she would stop to place a thick black silk "tie" around it. "That is the same gentle technique that

Dr. Halsted introduced us to. It is wonderful to see that surgical knowledge is spreading," commented Olevia, giving Jennie a compliment. "It is important once one surgeon identifies something as being true or helpful that this information can be shared with the other surgeons, even though this may take years."

"Yes, I agree," said Jennie now making the next deeper cut to go below the muscles and into the pelvis where the uterus would be found.

"Jennie, look, there they are!" called out Olevia, pointing to two small nerves, one of which was just one or at most two millimeters in diameter. They were just little white lines, curving on the surface of the red muscle and then going down and into the tissues on the other side of the incision, going towards the pubic bone."

"You have sharp eyes, Olevia. I have never noticed them, and certainly would not have thought of those as important structures to save," said Jennie.

"You now know how, even if they are not directly cut by your incision, they can get stuck in the scar related to healing, and cause pain with numbness in the pubic hair area. And, you now can see my plan for finding the ilioinguinal and iliohypogastric nerves to treat pain after hernia surgery. Or even now after hysterectomy, like in the patient, Martha Pratt, who you just sent to see me," said Olevia, triumphantly.

"Great, and what will you do with the live end of the nerve, Olevia?" Jennie asked what seemed to be the question on everyone's mind.

"Let's have a root beer to celebrate this discovery, Jennie. Let's go down State Street a little where there is a General Store, and we can sit. I will tell you about my research putting a nerve into muscle," suggested Olevia. "Now let's get that uterus out!"

Two hours later they were sipping their root beer. Smiling at each other. Sharing successful surgery stories and their shared new experience.

"Olevia, I love that research story, putting nerve into muscle. I hope it will help these patients in pain, and now I have a story to tell you," said Jennie.

"One more observation first," said Olevia. "If I may say so, Jennie, I have had much more fun with you today than I have ever had with my male colleagues. Or even with any man."

"Thank you said Jennie," now having it be her turn to blush. "And that is sort of what I wanted to tell you. "I believe you know there is a new hospital for children that opened here in Salt Lake City. Some of my patients have been using a new Pediatrician from there to take care of their babies. He has been doing a great job, and he wanted to meet me. So, we met. He told me that there is another new doctor working there." Jennie paused to see Olevia's reaction, and then continued. "A doctor who trained in the new field of Psychiatry and Childhood Neurology. He said the doctor has brought with him a device to study electrical activity in nerves."

Olevia almost jumped up from her chair. "Ezra Maybe is here now?"

"Well," said Jennie, now more quietly, "Prepare yourself. He still has red hair. But besides his electrical equipment, he also has something else new," and Jennie paused.

"Well, go on tell me," demanded Olevia.

"He has a wife. Your Ezra is married," said Jennie quietly.

"Oh my," said Olevia, quietly, sadly. "You know Jennie, when I was back in medical school, I thought I loved Ezra. Now, I know I love surgery," continued Olevia, musing. "Yet I must see him, and so I will schedule an appointment to see Ezra at the Primary Children's Hospital. I can hardly wait to see Ezra again, whether he is married or not."

ETHER

As Olevia walked towards the operating rooms, she knew that today there would be two challenges. She would do two operations never done before by any Surgeon, no less a Woman Surgeon. Edward Cannon and then Martha Pratt would each have a new surgical approach to treat painful nerves.

"Dr. Landsmann?" asked the tall handsome man in a surgical scrub outfit.

"Yes, I am," replied Olevia. "Will you be working with me today?"

"Yes. My name is Ether Helaman," he replied with a smile. "Yes, I have heard the jokes, 'Helaman, great name for a doctor.' Or how about, 'so you only heal men, not women patients?' Dr. Helaman went on, making fun of his last name.

"Well Doctor, I must admit I have never heard either your first or last names before," said Olevia politely.

"They are both Mormon names, Dr. Landsmann, as yours is German," explained the doctor, his blue eyes smiling down at her. "Perhaps you know there is the Book of Ether as part of the Book of Mormon. Ether was a prophet, a seeker and teacher of truth. Helaman was also a Mormon Prophet," he explained.

"Doctor Helaman," commented Olevia with a sly smile, a perhaps intuitively knowing smile, "You are here not just to assist me in surgery, but to be a seeker of truth." Now Olevia knew she had three challenges today. Edward, Martha, and Ether. She knew that Ether would be reporting back to the Chief of Surgery, Dr. Willis on how she did today in surgery.

Looking down a little, more at the floor, instead of directly at Olevia, Dr. Helaman said, "Actually I am here to give your two patients anesthesia.

Now, please, let us not get started on joking about my first name, Ether, as that is the form of anesthesia I will use today," he said.

Both doctors laughed, relieving the tension of their first encounter.

"I will see you in the OR, Doctor," said Dr. Helaman, as he turned to go.

"I will just mark the site of my incision on Mr. Cannon's leg, and then come and join you," Olevia said turning to go on down the hall in the opposite direction.

Turning from the hallway into the patient pre-induction room, Olevia said, "Good morning Edward," and walked over to the where Edward Cannon was lying on the stretcher with a nurse in attendance. The nurse, in a white skirt and blouse, with a small white cap pinned to her long blond hair, clearly appeared different from this Woman surgeon, who wore dark blue pants and shirt, with a white undershirt showing at the neck, and her short brown hair uncovered.

"Good morning doctor. I can hardly wait for you to take away my pain. I have prayed all night for God to guide your hands," said Edward.

"I will do my best. And Edward, I want you to know, that I do believe that God does guide my hands. Now show me the exact spot along that long scar where you have the horrible pain that shoots into the top of your foot," directed Olevia.

"It is right here," said Edward, not hesitating for a minute, pointing to the spot.

"I will mark it with this pen so I can find it in surgery," she said drawing on his leg.

"Ouch," said Edward pulling his leg instinctively away for the doctor.

"I am so sorry that hurt you," Olevia said, and turned to go. Looking at him over her shoulder she said, "See you in the operating room soon, Edward."

As Olevia, her hands scrubbed, and dripping water, walked into the operating room, Dr. Helaman lifted his eyes from the head of the operating table, looked up at her, smiled, and said, "Your patient is asleep Doctor, you may begin whenever you are ready."

"Thank you, Doctor," Olevia said, and turned to face the Scrub Nurse to put on her gown and glove.

"Good morning Doctor," said a smiling Chipeta, the Scrub Nurse.

"Why good morning Chipeta. I learned that you graduated at the top of your Scrub Nurse class. I was told you were best at Anatomy, not a surprise there!" Olevia said, happy to see her friend from the Anatomy Lab now working in the operating room.

As Chipeta helped Olevia put on her gown, and then her gloves, Olevia turned to Ether, and said, "Tell me Doctor Helaman, where did you do your surgical training," she asked.

"Right here at University of Utah, under Professor Elijah S.F. Willis, Chief of Surgery," he answered.

It was quiet for a few minutes as Olevia looked over the available surgical instruments with Chipeta, drew her proposed incision to cross over the painful spot she had marked prior to surgery, and then said, to Chipeta, the Scrub Nurse, "Here we go. May I please have the Esmarch bandage?"

"Yes, Doctor, here it is," said Chipeta handing the bandage to Olevia.

Just as she wrapping the leg, Dr. Helaman spoke up. "Doctor Landsmann, the surgery you are doing is listed as 'excision of painful neuroma of the superficial peroneal nerve and implantation of the nerve into muscle. I must say that none of us has ever heard of this operation. Can you tell us what it is you are planning on doing and why?"

"Ether, may I call you Ether?" asked Olevia, trying not to sound annoyed as clearly this doctor was planning to live up to his name, and be a "seeker", perhaps an actual spy for Dr. Willis, her Chief of Surgery.

"Certainly. Call me 'Ether'. Ether is my name, and dropping ether today is my game," he chuckled dropping some more ether into the funnel over Edward Connan's nose.

Olevia took the Esmarch rubber bandage that Mable handed to her and began wrapping it, starting at the toes, working her way up the leg up to the knee. She replied to Dr. Helaman as she was wrapping the elastic bandage, "When Doctor Levin Randolph, the Orthopedic Surgeon whom I am sure you know, operated to release the pressure in Edward's leg after the fibular fracture had been reduced, the fasciotomy incision cut through the nerve, which you correctly named."

Olevia then began unwrapping the Esmarch bandage from the toes to the knee, effectively pumping all the blood out of the leg. Now as she prepared to open again the incision made for the fasciotomy, there would be no bleeding and she would see the nerves. As Dr. Cushing had said, "You can't fix a watch in an inkwell."

"Scalpel please, Chipeta, #15 blade," requested Olevia returning the Esmarch to the Chipeta.

As Olevia was cutting into the scar, Dr. Helaman spoke up again, clearly trying to disrupt her. "Doctor Landsmann, will you please demonstrate the painful neuroma to us once you have found it. None of us has ever seen one before?"

"Certainly. And, here it is, right exactly at the spot where Edward said his worst pain was and where I marked the pain location prior to coming into surgery." Olevia, now moved away from the incision, and demonstrated the swollen rounded mass, the size of a grape.

"How do you know that is a painful neuroma," asked Dr. Helaman.

"Let me prove this to you, Ether. You see as I dissect this mass proximally that it is attached to this white structure. That is the superficial peroneal nerve." She emphasized this by pulling on the grape-like structure: its attachment to the superficial peroneal nerve became quite obvious.

"Ok, I must agree with you that you have demonstrated something new to me," he replied going back to the head of the table and dropping some more ether.

"Now, Ether, let me show you something new in anesthesia." Olevia turned to Chipeta, the scrub nurse, and said, do you have that special solution that was brought into the room for me?"

"Yes, Doctor. Here it is," Chipeta said, handing a syringe filled with fluid to Olevia.

"What is in the syringe," inquired the curious Dr. Helaman.

"Ether, you are aware probably that both the famous Professor of Surgery William Stewart Halsted at Johns Hopkins Hospital, where I trained, used cocaine, as a cocaine solution to achieve local anesthesia. My Father, Alexander is a chemist. He sent this to me from Munich the newest local anesthetic. You may know that cocaine is a class of chemicals called "esters". The chemists have produced a new ester in this class that is not a narcotic like cocaine and cannot get anyone addicted. It was synthesized in Germany in 1905, and a Doctor Einhorn was the first to use it for an amputation of the leg. Because it was new, Einhorn had named it *Novo*caine, or "new caine," answered Olevia, finding her chemistry background useful.

Dr. Helaman looked on in amazement as Olevia injected the nerve going into the grape-sized neuroma. "Why are you doing that, Doctor? The patient is asleep and can feel no pain," the anesthesiologist questioned.

"Yes, quite so. His conscious brain is asleep now so that even if a pain message is sent it will not be perceived. But when he awakens, this nerve will send a pain message from my having cut off the neuroma. But if I inject this nerve with a local anesthetic, his brain will not know that I am cutting this nerve, and when he awakens, for at least a few hours, his brain will not receive a pain message from this nerve," she said as she cut the grape-sized neuroma from the nerve, and handed it to Chipeta, saying "This specimen should go to Pathology, label it 'neuroma of right superficial peroneal nerve.'"

"That is an interesting new concept also, Dr. Landsmann," commented Ether.

"Ether, I suspect there is a clever woman out there waiting for you. And, like this anesthetic, her name will be 'Ester,'" joked Olevia.

"Could be a very peaceful relationship, Ether and Ester. We will each put each other to sleep," Dr. Helaman picked up on the joke.

Then, anticipating Dr. Helaman's next challenge, Olevia took the offensive and said, "Ether, you see this small nerve, about 3 or 4 mm in size? To prevent this from regenerating and causing Edward's pain to come back, I am going to take the live end of the nerve and put it deeply into the underside of these muscles."

She thought to herself, these muscles might be small, but there they were, and she had no experience with how big the muscle had to be, so she implanted the nerve into muscle, just as she had done while doing research on dogs in the Hunterian laboratory.

"Seems like a good idea, but I have never heard of such a surgical approach," observed Dr. Helaman. "Now what are you going to do up at the knee?"

Olevia next made a new smaller incision at the side of the knee where the fibula fracture had been. "Edward's common peroneal nerve is under a lot of pressure here, causing his foot to become paralyzed. He has trouble lifting up his toes and ankle. He is developing a foot drop," she explained.

"I have seen men lifting their foot high above the ground, to clear their toes, taking a "steppage gait" or high-stepping walk related to foot drop," commented Dr. Helaman, "but there has been no known operation to treat it, or prevent it from getting worse," he continued to challenge this Woman Surgeon.

"Ether, come over and watch. I have been practicing this approach in the Anatomy Lab, on cadavers, and have learned where the pressure point is."

Dr. Helaman again left the head of the table, and came, and watched over Olevia's shoulder. Ether's head was so close to her that she could smell the ether fumes that clung to his mask. She did not like him being that close to her, and moved her shoulder away from him saying, "You will see better if I just move a little to the left."

After moving away from Ether a little, she said, "This is the tight white fascia that is pressing on these muscles overlying the common peroneal nerve. Now as I pull these muscles to the side, and Chipeta holds the retractor, you will see the large common peroneal nerve. This nerve is easily one centimeter in diameter and white and round before it enters the region of fibular head, above where the fracture was," Olevia said, pointing out these structures.

"Now, I carefully lift the nerve from the bone, where it is stuck, scarred, and you can see the nerve becomes flattened and yellow in color. Clearly this is where the compression is," Olevia said, pointing this out to Ether.

"Yes, Doctor Landsmann, I can actually see that," said Dr. Helaman.

"I am glad Prophet Ether that you are here to be witness to this truth. I believe that this is the first time this nerve has ever been decompressed. I wish that we had asked a cameraman to be here to photograph this," commented Olevia. She loved the discovery that seemed always to be part of surgery.

Then she let the Esmarch bandage down. She smiled at Chipeta, and said, "You see Chipeta, just like you and I observed it in the Anatomy Lab."

Olevia and Chipeta stood for about 15 minutes, holding the moist towels over the incisions, waiting for the bleeding to stop. They just quietly smiled at each other, and Olevia took her right hand and gently patted Chipeta on the arm, as if to say, 'Well Done'.

When most of the bleeding had stopped, Olevia began tying off the remaining bleeders with thin 5-0 silk sutures. As each suture was tied, Chipeta quickly moved her hand in, holding a small scissors, and cut the suture for Olevia. "Just like weaving and beading," she said with a smile.

Finally, Olevia sutured the skin neatly, the way she had watched Dr. John Staige Davis do it for his Plastic Surgery patients back at Hopkins, during those extra 6 months she had worked in the Hunterian Laboratory.

"Chipeta," thank you for your excellent assistance.

Olevia turned to Dr. Helaman. "Thank you for that excellent anesthesia, she complemented him.

"You are welcome, thank you for teaching me. I will be sure to tell Dr. Willis what I saw," he said as the patient coughed a few times and woke up. "I will see you back in here soon for your second case.

Dr. Landsmann then walked back to the holding area, where Martha Pratt was waiting for her on stretcher, just as Edward Connan had been. "Hello Martha," greeted Olevia.

"Oh, I am so glad to see you Dr. Landsmann. My family and I have been looking forward to you making my pain go away. They want their "Mama" back," Martha said.

"Martha let's review exactly where the pain is, so I can put a mark on that spot," said Olevia, pulling up the white sheet to reveal the pubic hair and the red, thickened scar.

"Here is the worst spot, just at the right end of that ugly scar that Dr. Ross made," responded Martha. "This pain keeps me from doing so much every day, Doctor. I have confidence you will find the injured nerves and remove them."

"Yes, let me put a mark there with my pen. Now my memory says that the pain can be set off from up here, away from the scar, by my pressing where I know these nerves are coming from. Let us just check that again," said Olevia as she placed her hands in a different location.

"Oh Yes. Ouch! Yes, I feel the pain go from where your hand is right down to this spot," observed Martha.

"Perfect. Then Martha my incision will be up here away from that scar. This is where I know I can find the little nerves that are stuck in the scar," said Olevia, drawing a 2 inch line, her proposed incision.

"And Dr. Landsmann," said Martha, while you are in the operating room and I am asleep, could you cut out that ugly scar and close it up again. Make it look better?"

"OK, Martha. First my goal is to get rid of your pain. If there is time in surgery, then I will cut out the scar and make it look nicer for you. I did do some training in Plastic Surgery," replied Olevia, now turning to walk back to the recovery room.

On the way she passed the space that had Edward Connan in it. His nurse was giving him a sip of water. His eyes looked dazed. His Mother was sitting there next to him, holding his hand, and looking quite anxious.

"Mrs. Connan," said Olevia. "The surgery went very well. Let us see how his leg is doing at this early point," she said as she pulled up the sheet to reveal his foot.

"Edward," said Olevia loudly, "Lift up your toes and your ankle."

Edward looked down at his foot and willed his foot to move. And it did!

"Oh my, Doctor Landsmann," said Mrs. Connan. "His paralyzed foot is moving!"

"Yes, it is," said Olevia smiling. "Now let us try touching the place that used to be so painful," she said taking her hand and pushing against the surgical site, the place she had marked with an 'X'.

Edward remained expressionless.

"Does your leg hurt here anymore?" asked Olevia.

"No, it just feels numb," he said.

"Perfect. Edward you are going to do great. I will see you later," she said turning to go the operating room.

Mrs. Connan got up and gave Olevia a hug. "Thank you, Doctor. Edward told me you were very brave, and that this surgery had not been done before. God bless you, Doctor."

"You are most welcome. I did the best I could. Tell Edward that God guided my hands," Olevia said, as she completed her turn and walked down the hall to the operating room.

MARTHA

Olevia put on her scrub mask, scrubbed her hands and walked again into the operating room.

"Doctor, your patient Martha Pratt is asleep and ready for you," called out a more friendly Dr. Helaman.

"Thank you Ethe", Olevia said smiling through her mask at Ether.

" Chipeta, are you ready for another fun peripheral nerve surgery?" asked Olevia.

"Yes, Doctor," she said helping Olevia into her gown and then into her gloves. Finally, Chipeta handed Olevia the marking pen.

"Scalpel please," requested Dr. Landsmann.

Chipeta handed her the scalpel with a #15 blade.

Olevia took the scalpel, observed that a #15 blade was in place, looked at Chipeta and smiled, realizing that Chipeta knew her preferred instrument already.

Then Olevia took the knife and cut into the skin near the right iliac crest, about 6 inches from the previous, lower abdominal, thick red scar.

Once the blood stopped, she cut along the lines of tension in the thick white top layer of fascia, called the external oblique.

Chipeta handed her retractors, and Olevia used them, pulling this layer upwards and downwards, searching for a little white nerve.

"Dr. Landsmann, if I may ask again, just what type of operation are you proposing to do now?" asked Dr. Helaman.

"Ether, of course you may ask, and I may even answer you," she said with a little smile under her mask, looking at him and giving him a little wink, a gesture that could be seen with a scrub mask on. "Dr. Jennie Ross, a Gynecologist made this Pfannensteil incision during a hysterectomy. Most often the wound heals well and without pain. In this case, as you can see, a thick scar formed, a painful scar. The source of this pain is, as with the last patient, an injured nerve. A nerve to the skin is stuck in that painful scar. The goal of this operation is to remove at least one, and possibly two nerves to that skin region, thereby relieving her of her pain."

"Yes", there it is," Olevia said aloud, as she saw the thin white ilioinguinal nerve down below her. "Would you like to see the culprit, Ether? It is much smaller than that superficial peroneal nerve you saw in the last patient."

"What is that red muscle?" questioned Dr. Helaman as he looked over Olevia's shoulder, again standing threateningly close.

"Ether, please be careful not to contaminate me by touching my sterile gown," she cautioned him.

"Sure, sorry," Ether said, stepping about 6 inches further away, and looking into the wound to see the nerve.

"Here, retracted, is the white external oblique fascia. The red is the internal oblique muscle. Now I will inject this nerve with Novocaine," which she did, "Divide the nerve. Grasp this proximal end and start dissecting it so I can drop it back deep below these muscles, so it cannot grow back up into the skin again," which she did.

"If you permit another question, Dr. Landsmann. How do you know that you have removed the correct nerve?" Dr. Helaman asked.

"Now let me show you a little trick I have been working on. Pretty simple really. Watch what happens when I pull on the remaining, distal end of the nerve." Olevia now grasped the other end of the nerve and pulled on it vigorously several times. "Notice what happens to the thick painful scar!" commanded Olevia.

Both Chipeta and Dr. Helaman exclaimed simultaneously, "It is moving. The painful scar is moving."

"That is the proof that we got the correct nerve, the ilioinguinal nerve," said Olevia encouragingly, looking around the room.

Suddenly, Olevia, became still and quiet. Across from her was a metal pole from which hung the bag of fluid going into the patient, the salt water, the sterile saline bag. It just hung there, like a man hanging from the limb of a tree. The memory of the young man, who hung himself after her surgery that failed to relieve him of his groin pain, came back to her. She could see him. She opened and shut her eyes. What had she learned from her cadaver prosections since then?

"Doctor, what do you need from me next?" prompted Chipeta, realizing that Olevia, who had been a blur of continuous purposeful movement, was just standing there staring at the IV pole.

"Chipeta, I need those eagle sharp eyes of yours to help me find the second nerve. The iliohypogastric nerve. Normal anatomy is my guide. But abnormal anatomy can be my worst enemy. The nerve may be in an unusual place, and I cannot give up until I have found it," said Olevia.

Olevia spent about 15 more minutes now, quietly, moving the white fascial covering around, searching, while Chipeta held the retractors, and looked intently into the wound.

"Chipeta, I cannot rest until I find the second nerve. I know that God will guide my hands, as he knows you and I worked so hard to learn where that nerve may be hiding," said Olevia quietly so that just Chipeta could hear her.

"Doctor," whispered Chipeta. "What is that small white line?"

"Yes, Chipeta! There it is," Olevia said with relief.

"That nerve is so small, Doctor!" said Chipeta.

"Yes, just about 1 mm in size. You can see now how it would be impossible to find if I tried to look for it in the original white scar," commented Olevia as she injected the nerve with the Novocaine.

"Dr. Landsmann," interrupted Dr. Helaman, one more time. "What happens if you pull on that little nerve?"

"Ether, come and see," Olevia encouraged. When he was next to her, she pulled on the nerve.

The same painful area of the scar moved again.

"All right, Doctor Landsmann, you are two nerves for two pulls on the scar," observed Ether.

Olevia was thrilled.

"Congratulations," said Chipeta.

"These two nerves overlap," she said, not to anyone in particular. "There will now be two different specimens to send to Pathology," she said to her Scrub Nurse. "Label one the ilioinguinal and the second the iliohypogastric nerve."

"Can I begin to awaken the patient now?" asked Ether.

"Dr. Helaman, let her stay asleep a little longer. I am going to grant her request, and cut out the poorly healed scar and close the skin again," Olevia said.

"Why is that worth doing?" asked Dr. Helaman, continue to question Olevia's motives.

"My teacher, John Staige Davis, MD, taught me that if a patient is not pleased with some aspect of herself, and you can change it with some degree of certainty, then you should try. I believe the reason this scar is so ugly is that the retractors pulled too hard on the skin damaging the edges, and there was also probably some bleeding. I believe I can get a better result for her now using a gentle technique. It will not take me much longer," explained Olevia encouragingly.

"Does this mean you are still experimenting in the operating room, Dr. Landsmann?" asked Dr. Helaman, in a somewhat threatening tone

"Experiment in the operating room?" she asked aloud as she quickly cut out the thick scar. Then, as she gently pressed on the skin edges so they would stop bleeding, she said, "Yes this is how surgical progress must be made. You try in surgery with the best knowledge you have. If you fail, you must go back to the Anatomy Lab. The truth is there. Find it. Go back to surgery, and, the next time, use the experience of failure to propel surgery forward. That is what we did today, Ether," remarked Olevia forcefully, taking another look at the IV bag, swinging slowly from the IV pole, remembering her first operation doing this. The surgery she did on Jared Benson.

"Suture please Chipeta," requested Olevia. Then, as she was sewing, "to quote another of my surgical mentors, Professor William Stewart Halsted. He gave a lecture to the graduating medical students at Yale University. His lecture was entitled, 'On Training in Surgery'. He told the medical students that 'The operating room should be a laboratory. A surgical laboratory of the highest order'. "

"Chipeta, bandages please," said Olevia, completing the scar revision. "I think both Doctors Davis and Halsted would be proud of what we did in the operating room today." Then, as she remembered her Surgical Scientist research, she added, "Dr. Cushing too would be proud to see a peripheral nerve be placed into a muscle in human, instead of a dog."

Olevia turned, headed to the door of the operating room, stopped, then turned and looked back. "Thank you everyone for your help. Ether, I wish I could be there when you, the Prophet, report to your Chief, Dr. Willis, about the surgery you saw here today.

As she exited the door to the operating room, she murmured under her breath, "And please do not be a False Prophet.

"Olevia could hardly wait till tomorrow to learn how Edward and Martha would be doing.

REUNION

Olevia walked out of the Salt Lake County General Hospital and got into a cab.

"Please take me to the new Primary Pediatric Hospital," she said to the cab driver. "Do you know where it is?"

"Yes, Mam," replied the driver. "It only opened earlier this year. It is a pretty building and is located on the same grounds as the University of Utah, on Drive," he completed his answer and headed off towards the new hospital from this older hospital. "It is not really very far. Is it an emergency? Do you want me to rush?"

"No rush, this time, I will be half an hour early. Gives me some time to look around," Olevia answered.

"It is sort of a sad place," commented the cab driver. "Lots of children being wheeled around. So many paralyzed. I hope the doctors in this new building can help them," he said, his voice trailing off.

"I am going to see a friend of mine. He is a doctor who has just come back from specialized training in Europe, and I, too, am hopeful, he can help them. There will be a special team assembled here to look into the problems of these children," offered Olevia, as they pulled up in front of the new Primary Pediatric Hospital after the short drive.

As she got out of the cab, she looked up at a new, white stone building with big windows. It was just three stories tall. A bright shiny sign with the hospital's name hung over the front door. A caretaker was pushing a wheelchair past her as she walked up to the hospital entrance. The little child was thin, with legs that seemed to go off in different directions, and arms that were flexed at the elbow. The child had short hair. Olevia could not tell if this child was a boy or girl. There was a bib around her neck and the child was drooling.

In the lobby, Olevia was saddened to see so many children with various forms of paralyzed limbs, some also with the appearance of being retarded. Yet each child was with a caregiver. The whole lobby was well lit, with uplifting artwork.

She walked up to a large sign on the wall. She looked at the list of Doctors with offices in the new hospital. There it was! She spotted Ezra Maybe, MD, Pediatric Nerve Problems. Room 246.

OIevia saw the stairway and walked up the one flight to Ezra's office. The door was closed. She hesitated a minute, and then knocked on the door.

His secretary let her in and offered her a seat. Olevia gazed up at the wall to see something very familiar. Hanging, in a beautiful wooden frame, was the Diploma of Graduation from the Johns Hopkins School of Medicine. It looked just like hers. Then hanging just beneath it was the Certificate of Completion of Residency in Psychiatry from the Johns Hopkins Hospital. It was signed by Adolf Meyer, MD, the person Ezra told her was coming from Cornell to be the new, and first Chief of Psychiatry in the new Henry Phipps Psychiatry Building. "Time passes so quickly," she thought to herself. "When I was last at Hopkins, that building did not even exist.

Then her eye caught a photo on the other wall, opposite the wall with the Johns Hopkins diplomas. There was a photo of Doctor and Mrs. Maybe. She was a little shorter than Ezra, had blond hair and was very pretty!

Suddenly the door behind the secretary's desk almost flew open and a burst of energy, with red hair entered the room.

"Olevia!" "My gosh! So wonderful to see you again, and in Salt Lake City!" shouted out Ezra, full of enthusiasm.

They gave each other a hug, although, Olevia thought, a little less warmly than when they had their last hug in the study carrel on level 4 of the William H. Welch Library.

Ezra guided Olevia into his rather spacious office with a view of the Wasatch Mountain range. They each sat down and looked at each other. There was a different photo of Doctor and Mrs. Maybe on his desk.

Ezra spoke first. "You look so different! Your hair is cut short, you are wearing pants, and you seem taller when I hugged you last. But that is probably due to those boots you are wearing? What happened to skirts and longer hair, Olevia?"

Immediately put on the defensive, Olevia could only answer truthfully, "For a Woman involved in the Male's world of surgery, dressing in a less feminine way seems simply more practical." She knew she looked "männlich", as they would say in Munich, more like a man.

Ezra just plowed along, "There is so much to share with you. This new electrical testing is going to revolutionize our ability to tell what is happening with a peripheral nerve."

"Yes" she answered. "It may well do that. But I believe once you give the electrical shock, the recording site responds to the first energy to reach it, and the test result will say the measurement is normal. At least that is from what I have been reading. Only today, in surgery, where one can observe the nerve, I found the common peroneal nerve narrowed, and yellow, clearly compressed near the knee related to a fractured fibula. If your test said the nerve was in trouble, then fine. But what if the new electrical testing said the nerve was still in the 'normal range'. Might your new electrical device say 'normal' even if only some of the fibers were not working, even if those few injured fibers created pain and weakness?"

"Well, Olevia, as I am a doctor in the new field of Neurology, my first examination is still a clinical test for muscle strength and I examine whether the patient can feel movement, or hot or cold sensation. But as you know these are mainly subjective tests. We just believe that what the patient tells us is true. Now, in contrast, this electrical testing is objective, you can do it on an unconscious patient. This testing will become the standard for the future, and that is what I am teaching, now, "replied Ezra, the Pediatric Neurologist.

"Perhaps Ezra," suggested Olevia, "I could send you some of my Adult patients to you, and you could test them. We could correlate my *subjective findings* with your *objective findings* and then compare them with what was found in surgery, and after the recovery process from surgery. Dr. Maybe, *maybe* we can do some research together?" she said making a little joke, to break the tension already building between them.

"You mean, Olevia, that even if I said the patient had a normal test result, you would still operate on them?" asked Ezra, sounding concerned.

"Yes, of course. If that nerve was tender when touched, and if there were motor weakness, then even if your test said the nerve was normal, I would operate. How else can we learn the truth? That is what we were taught at Hopkins, remember?"

Ezra did not answer right away. He just was uncharacteristically quiet. Then he said, "Olevia, I must tell you two things that I know will make you quite unhappy. Even though we have not seen each other for two years or so, I still view myself as one of your closest friends. I must try to alert you."

"Alert me about what?" asked Olevia, taken by surprise.

"First, about your Uncle Albert. You know I have completed Psychiatry training. I am sure that you, being from Germany, are well versed with Sigmund Freud. Well, to make a long analysis short, I have thought of you often. When we were together you spoke so often of your Uncle, rarely of your Father, and almost never of your Mother. Freud believed that boys go through an Oedipal phase, loving their mother, and worrying about losing their penis, since their Mother did not have one. Boys develope "castration anxiety", while looking for their true identity. Girls, Freud believed, realized there was a difference too. Their Father had something their Mother did not have. Girls developed "penis envy". Freud believed that if this does not resolve appropriately, the girl remains attached to her Father. This is called, by Jung, another Psychiatrist, "The Electra Complex". It is thought that the girl will become increasingly manly, to emulate her Father. In your case, Albert was your Father's twin. I worried about you while I was away, and here you are dressed like a man," Ezra concluded his analysis.

Olevia did not know what to say at all. Finally, to break the silence, she said,

"What does Jung predict will happen to someone you say is like me, someone with the Electra Complex?"

"Well, perhaps you recall in Greek Mythology, Electra kills her mother, Clytemnestra, for having driven her father, Agamemnon, away. Clearly this is Mythology. Jung predicts that in our times, the person with the Electra complex will become a Lesbian."

"Oh my gosh, Ezra, I am worried that you need psychoanalysis yourself!" Olevia exclaimed standing up. An image of a voluptuous, almost naked, Jennie Ross, changing into her surgical scrub clothes in the locker room, flittered through Olevia's mind.

After Olevia had calmed herself down a little, she asked, sitting down again, "What is your second bit of bad news for me?"

"Olevia, you know you were my first love. I cannot stand to listen to anything bad said about you when I know how hard you work to create relief of pain," Ezra managed to stammer out. "I hear surgeons, of course they are all Men, talking when I am making rounds, or having a meal with them. They talk of a new Woman Surgeon, who seems to believe she can relieve pain in patients when her male colleagues have failed. They say she is operating on people with newly created operations. They say she is experimenting on her patients."

"Ezra," Olevia said standing up again. "You know me better than that. But you also know that I base my operations on anatomic research. Yes, I am developing new operations to relieve pain caused by the surgery of others. Those 'Others' are Men. What other reaction would you expect from those Surgeons, gratitude to me?

"I see your point Olevia, but you must know there is mounting jealousy and anger in our Hospital Community about you," Ezra responded.

"Ezra, I saw your wedding photo on your desk. I wish you and your new wife a life of health and prosperity," said Olevia standing up to leave. "You, too, were my first love. I would still like to do research with you, if you do not consider it experimenting on your patients, or mine. Thank you for these warnings."

Olevia then turned, and, with a heavy heart, and a deep sign, left Ezra's office.

Olevia had trouble sleeping that night after her meeting with Ezra.

This was unusual for her, as she was usually exhausted. Two thoughts moved in and out of the forefront of her thoughts.

First troubling thought: "Of course I am obsessed with my Uncle Albert. How he touched me as a child left a deep scar within me. A scar is permanent. A scar represents a healed wound. It is a memory of being injured. My Uncle Albert injured me, but I still love him. Did my love of my Uncle Albert turn me into a woman who, deep inside, due to that scar, now hates men. Is that why I dress like a man? Am I really going to spend my life loving women instead of men, as Ezra suggests?

Second troubling thought: "My anatomy research and new surgical procedures are too challenging for the medical establishment, for the Male-dominant medical society that I am in. Should I heed Ezra's warning and change what I am doing?" Exhausted now, her mind allowed her to drift off to sleep. Tomorrow would be another day for her to think through all of this.

DISBELIEF

As she entered the Surgical Ward at Salt Lake County General Hospital to see her two post-operative patients, Edward Cannon and Martha Pratt, she passed the Chief of Surgery, Elijah Willis, MD. "Good morning Dr. Willis," she said. Since she did not think he considered her as a friend, and since she was always respectful, she just called him "Dr. Willis."

"Good morning, Dr. Landsmann", he replied walking past her. Then he stopped and turned back towards her. "Are you coming to see your two patients from yesterday?"

"Yes, Sir," I am. "What are your thoughts about the surgery that I did. I suppose Dr. Ether Helaman gave you a complete report.

"May I come and visit them with you? As I viewed the OR schedule yesterday, I noticed you were doing peripheral nerve surgery that I have never heard of before. Yes, Dr. Helaman briefly told me about the surgery that you did. Honestly, he was too shocked by what he saw to be able to discus it. All he could do was report it to me. It would be of great interest to me to see how your two patients are doing this morning."

"Of course, Sir. It will be equally interesting for me to see how they are doing?" she responded. She now knew the False Prophet Ether Helaman had reported his observations as "experimental surgery" to his Chief, Dr. Willis.

As Olevia and Dr. Willis entered the Male Ward, she heard her name called out. "Dr. Landsmann," she heard Edward call. "I am over here."

Olevia and Dr. Willis walked towards the voice, which came from behind a group of nurses helping a patient with his leg in a fracture frame.

"Good morning Edward, you seem awake and energetic this morning. I would like you to meet Dr. Willis, our Chief of Surgery at this hospital.

"Hello," said Edward quietly, appropriately impressed by the large man with the big beard, standing next to Dr. Landsmann.

"Dr. Willis, this is Edward Cannon, whom Dr. Baldwin referred to me," said Olevia, completing the introductions.

Then she reviewed for Dr. Willis, Edward's history. How he had been injured skiing. How Dr. Levin Randolph set Edward's leg in traction while she drilled the hole in his skull to drain the acute subdural hematoma. Then the subsequent surgery by Dr. Randolph to relieve pressure in the leg related to compartment syndrome. Finally, how, during the fasciotomy to release the pressure, the superficial peroneal nerve was injured creating a painful and disabling neuroma. Furthermore, during the time of the fracture healing, the common peroneal nerve became stuck and compressed at the knee, near the fracture site, leading to the foot drop, the paralysis of the right foot and toes. Then Olevia described what she did at surgery the day before.

"Well young man," said Dr. Willis, after listening to Olevia's presentation, "How are you doing today?'

"It seems like a miracle, Sir," Edward said. "Now when I touch the side of my leg, I just feel some pain from the surgery, but the shooting into the top of my foot is gone, and I can move my paralyzed foot without pain. I even think I can control my toe movements more," Edward concluded demonstrating his ability to lift his toes and ankle while he was talking.

Olevia smiled, and said modestly, "A good start Edward, this is what we were hoping for. I see very little drainage on your bandage. We will start you walking every 2 hours today, just around the ward, to let the common peroneal nerve glide so it does not get stuck again at that old fracture site."

Dr. Willis said "Wonderful beginning son. Dr. Landsmann's surgery was pioneering in spirit, appropriate for the "Old Wild West", but let us know how you are doing three months from now, will you?" he said ending on a possibly doubtful note.

Olevia realized that Dr. Willis was raising the possibility that her "early'" surgical success might not prove lasting.

Olevia and Dr. Willis then left the Male Ward and entered the Female Ward, across the hall. Olevia looked for and found Martha Pratt.

"Dr. Willis, this is Martha Pratt, referred to me by Dr. Ross," and then Olevia told Dr. Willis Martha's history and physical examination and what had been done at surgery. "Martha had a hysterectomy for uterine bleeding and related fibroids. Although she recovered from the pelvic surgery, she had disabling pain from the surgical incision site itself. This pain is similar in my experience to the pain men have after inguinal hernia surgery. My plan at surgery was to remove the injured nerves in that area."

"Well young lady, how are you doing today?" Dr. Willis asked Martha directly.

"My stomach muscles on the right side hurt a lot, but that is where the surgery was done. Of course, Dr. Landsmann told me to expect that. But what's amazing, is that after all this time since my hysterectomy, the sharp pain down here near my old scar and pubic bone is gone," Martha said demonstrating with her hand where the pain used to be. "There is no longer a knife sticking into me. I feel like when these muscles calm down, I will be able to sit normally again, and hope to go back to playing with my 5 children, and be their Mother again."

Dr. Landsmann smiled.

Dr. Willis looked skeptical.

"There is a little blood on your bandage, Martha. Let us change your bandage and then Dr. Willis can see the incisions," said Olevia motioning to a nurse to bring over the dressing cart.

Olevia now put on a pair of gloves and removed the dressings to reveal two bright pink incisions.

"Dr. Landsmann," said Martha in an excited voice, "my old incision looks beautiful. How did you do that? And the new incision is so small! Thank you Dr. Landsmann."

Now it was Dr. Willis's turn. "Dr. Landsmann, why are there two incisions?" he asked.

"Dr. Willis, I believe that when failure to help patients with groin pain after hernia repair has occurred, it is because surgeons tried to find the hurt nerve within the old scar. The nerve is just 1 to 2 mm and white and the scar is white. An almost impossible job! My anatomy research proved to me that if I make a new incision in this location," Olevia said, pointing to the shorter incision, "near the anterior superior iliac crest, then I can find the nerves lying on red muscle beneath the external oblique fascia. That is the location I cut the nerves, then move them deep to the muscles so they cannot grow back into the original scar," explained Olevia.

"Then why did you re-operate down here," Dr. Willis asked, trying to understand her logic.

"Martha just hated the way that scar looked, hypertrophic and red. I excised it and closed it gently, hoping to get better healing this second time," explained Dr. Landsmann, wondering if that explanation made any sense to Dr. Willis.

"Martha," said Dr. Willis, looking directly at the patient's face now, instead of her abdomen, "I am hoping for the best for you. I also hope that when the new scar heals that it, too, does not become painful. Please get back to us in three months and let us know how you are doing," Dr. Willis concluded, and then looked to Olevia, as the nurses were putting on a new dressing.

Olevia could see Dr. Willis' continued disbelief. As they moved away from Martha's bedside, he said, "Thank you for sharing your experiences with me. Everything you have shown me today is new to me. I am not sure what I really think of it. What you are doing is not within the tradition of General Surgery, and you are on my staff. This is going to require some thought on my part," he concluded, as he turned to go.

Then, Dr. Willis, stopped, turned back to Olevia and said, "Dr. Landsmann, may I have another word with you?"

"Of course, Dr. Willis," Olevia said and then turned to Martha saying "I will see you later today."

The two surgeons walked into a small consultation room just outside the surgical ward, a room that could be used for a Doctor to talk to a patient's family.

"Olevia, I must take a few minutes to talk to you," said Dr. Willis. " You are in an unusual position. For example, you are here in a *Surgery Ward*. Yet you have never done a surgery residency. You operate here, and, again, you have never completed a formal surgery residency training. Of course, few if any of our older "surgeons" did a residency because residencies did not exist when they finished medical training. So here you are. You equally could be in the Department of Medicine. We are new Departments here at the University of Utah and are sorting things out. I am excited, with your scientific background from Johns Hopkins School of Medicine. However, I have already received information that one of your first patients committed suicide because you *failed to relieve his pain*. I know surgeons learn from past mistakes. What did you learn from that patient's surgery, which obviously failed?

Olevia was inwardly very disturbed by this interaction and had already tormented herself with these very questions. She looked Dr. Willis directly in the eyes, and said, "Dr. Willis, you are correct in everything you said. After learning that my patient, whose name was Jared Benson, was not relieved of his pain, I went back to the Anatomy Lab. It turns out that two nerves can go to that exact area of pain that Jared Benson had. Even Gray's Anatomy Book, which you know we all consider as Truth, the last word on Anatomy, does not show this overlap. In the Anatomy Lab, I realized that my surgical approach for Jared Benson, going through the old scar, could not help me find both nerves. However, what I discovered was that if I made a new incision, and went higher, I could find both nerves in tissues not previously operated upon. Yesterday, during Martha's surgery, I proved this. I found that second nerve, iliohypogastric nerve, and pulled on it. The same area of Martha's painful scar moved as it did when I pulled on the ilioinguinal nerves. To answer your question, what I learned from that tragic failure with Jared Benson was more about the anatomy, and that now we must think that two nerves must be removed to relieve that pain. To do this we must create a new incision. And yes, Martha's improvement right now is not proof of a long-lasting result, but it is a good start," explained Olevia.

"That is excellent, Olevia. I must warn you, however, Medicine is such a conservative field, as it should be. New knowledge, especially in Surgery, when combined with complications, is especially difficult to incorporate and to tolerate in our staff. Please keep careful records, and document everything. I suspect that a "review" of your work is going to be requested," he said ominously.

Dr. Willis turned and left.

Olevia headed down the hall to her surgical clinic.

HUNG

Olevia walked by Harold and the line of patients waiting to give him a "high five", and then walked into her clinic.

The secretary told her that she had two new patients today referred by Dr. Baldwin, the Chief of Orthopedics.

As Olevia entered the exam room, a tall, handsome man stood up from his chair, extended his hand. He took a few steps towards her. She noted that he had, a limp and a cane. She also noted that he was wearing a suit with a vest. "Hello, Dr. Landsmann," he said, "I am so glad to meet you. My name is Jedediah Smith. I have had pain in my right knee ever since a skiing accident. No bones were broken, fortunately, but my ligaments tore enough that my knee would not support my weight. Dr. Baldwin immobilized me with weights and a pulley for 6 weeks. My ligaments healed and are strong again, but," here Jedediah Smith paused, stopped shaking Olevia's hand, and said" I have very bad knee pain every time I bend my knee and bear weight on it."

Olevia smiled at him, and said, "Thank you for that history Mr. Smith, please sit down. I can tell your knee is still hurting you."

As he sat down, Jedediah Smith said, "Yes it does still hurt. I have seen three different Orthopedic Surgeons in the Wasatch Valley, and they all say the same thing, 'give it time, and do more therapy'. They say they know of lots of patients like myself with knee pain, but they just have nothing else to offer me."

"Yes, that seems about right from the Orthopedic, point of view, Mr. Smith. Yet Dr. Baldwin, Chief of Orthopedics did send you to see me. There must be some hope for you, perhaps related to nerves instead of the ligaments?" offered Olevia.

"Yes, Dr. Landsmann, that is exactly what Dr. Baldwin told me. He told me that you actually believe that there are nerves in joints and that you know how to find them. If this is true, then please help me," entreated Jedediah Smith looking up at her earnestly from his chair.

"Mr. Smith, from the way you presented your problem and manner of speech, it appears that you have had an excellent education. Do you mind telling me a little about yourself," asked Olevia taking a personal interest in this new patient.

"Thank you for the compliment. I am trained in analysis and presentation of complex material and matters. I am a practicing attorney. But please let's not talk about me. Tell me about these nerves in joints. How do you know they are really there? Why do YOU think they exist, and the Orthopedic Surgeons do not know of their existence?" Jedediah Smith Esq., the lawyer, began his questioning.

"May I call you Mr. Smith?" Olevia asked, intrigued, and trying to decide how to answer his questions. She now suspected she would have to answer many more questions like these.

"Please call me "Jed", Jedediah replied.

"Jed, you have the perfect training for me to explain this to you," began Olevia, starting with some philosophy. "To the best that I have been able to determine, and forgive me if this sounds like a criticism, I have been told that Lawyers do not necessarily deal with truth, but with winning. Doctors, by contrast, must start from what is known as truth, and try to care for patients, even if all is not known about what that care must entail."

"I would agree with your reasoning here, Dr. Landsmann," said Jedediah Smith, "but I do not see yet how this is leading up to nerves."

"Jed," continued Olevia, "for Lawyers, you have previous cases that have been decided, which you call "case law", going back to medieval times in England, right?" Olevia asked him.

"Yes, true again Doctor, but again, what does that have to do with nerves?" Jed the lawyer answered, seeming to grow concerned that she was not answering his question

"Jed, let me continue please. We Doctors, especially those of us who call ourselves Surgical Scientists, have Anatomy, whereas Lawyers have Case

Law." At this point Olevia went over to a bookshelf on the surgical clinic wall and took down a book.

"Jed," she said showing him the book, "This book is Gray's Anatomy, written in 1858 in England. It has already been reprinted many times because its illustrations are considered so authoritative. So now I ask you, what do Lawyer's do if there is no case law to use to settle a complaint? Now, before you answer, let us extend that to what you think a Surgeon should do if there is no answer in the Anatomy Book to a question that should deal with Anatomy?

"Ok, Doctor, that is a good analogy," admitted the Lawyer, with a calmer tone of voice.

"Jed, the Anatomy book is truth to a Surgeon. This book in my hand shows not even one nerve to the knee joint. In fact, not one nerve to any joint in the arm or leg. What do you think that means?

Jedediah Smith was used to Debating Contests and cross-examination, but rarely had he been put on the "witness stand", as Dr. Landsmann now seemed to be doing. He liked her spirit. Since Dr. Landsmann had stopped talking, it was clearly his turn to respond.

"A Judge can give a ruling in such a new type of legal dispute. The Judge thereby creates a "precedent". If the "losing side" still is not satisfied, this ruling can be appealed, and a 'higher judge' can overturn the lower court's decision. And so it goes in Law, up to the Supreme Court of the United States of America. I do not know what you would do if the answer you seek to help a patient is not in an Anatomy book, Dr. Landsmann," Jedediah Smith answered.

"And Jed, that is the point of my doing research. By Anatomy research on the human body, in a cadaver, I can ask today the questions that Anatomists hundreds of years ago never even tried to answer," replied Olevia.

"Are you telling me, Doctor Landsmann, that there are no nerves shown to the knee joint in that Bible of yours, but that you have found them during your research in the Anatomy Lab?" asked Jed Smith, now resuming the role of hopeful Patient, instead of doubting Lawyer.

"That is correct, Jed. There is not one Anatomy book anywhere that I know of that shows a nerve to any joint in the human body. Now Jed, I am just going to guess that you go to Church. Do you think God forgot to put nerves into the joints?"

"God does not forget anything, Doctor. And let me tell you, I cannot kneel to pray in Church. I sit when the rest of the congregation kneels. I have prayed to God to let me kneel to pray to him again," answered Jedediah Smith seriously. "Doctor, perhaps your new knowledge will be the answer to my prayers."

Olevia smiled. She liked how he spoke. She liked how he analyzed information. She liked HIM. "Jeb," Olevia said, "did you pass that PROSECTION that is hung in the lobby to our Surgery Clinic, the one displaying the nerves in the human body as you walked in today?"

"Yes, I did. Is that what the display is, nerves?" he answered. 'There was too big a line waiting to see it. Looked like a bunch of blood vessels, to me as I passed it by."

"Jed, my Uncle Albert did that PROSECTION before he died. He named it 'Harold'. Harold now hangs in perpetuity to give potential answers about peripheral nerves to those in need of hope for their pain. If you look closely at Harold on your way out today, you will see those are nerves. If you look really closely at the knee, in fact at any joint, you will see there are nerves to the joint. Uncle Albert died before he could publish his observations. I have now gone back to the cadaver lab and confirmed for myself the existence of the nerves to the knee," replied Olevia.

"Oh My Gosh!" commented Jed excitedly. "Do you know how to find those little nerves and remove them?" he asked quickly, still processing the information and what would need to be done to help him.

"Yes, Jed, I believe I know how to find them, and remove them and reposition them so that they will not grow back into the knee joint. When I have time, I will begin to write down these observations for the scientific publications, perhaps publishing them in the literature, in a journal called *Journal of Bone & Joint Surgery,* so that the doctors who most need to know this information can have it available to them. This journal was begun in 1889 and is being read by those surgeons interested in this area of the body.

Jed now painfully stood up and looked Olevia directly in the eyes. "So, truth for you Dr. Landsmann comes from research. That research for you as a Surgeon comes through anatomic dissections," he summarized thoughtfully.

"Exactly, Jed," Olevia replied.

"How many people with knee pain have you helped so far, Doctor," Jed, now the lawyer again, asked hopefully.

"None," replied Olevia honestly. "You may be the first if you wish," she said confidently.

"Really. You have never done that operation before, Dr. Landsmann?" the lawyer asked?

"Correct," she replied. "Mr Smith, Someone has to be first for each new operation. Even if it has to be a Lawyer!"

Jed sat back down, with a grimace. He was quiet for a few moments.

"Dr. Landsmann, then as best you can imagine, what would the surgery be like, and what would the recovery be like? Please explain it carefully to me, so I can be informed, and consider my options, other than living with knee pain for the rest of my life," requested Jedediah Smith, continuing to be a Lawyer.

SKIING

Olevia and Jennie were finally skiing together
It had been so hard to co-ordinate their schedules. They only went up into Little Cottonwood Canyon part way, to allow more skiing time and less driving time. The chair lifts were now open, and they could sit, and share. They sat close together.

Olevia, staring down the mountain, suddenly realized that the trails before her seemed to outline something else. "Jennie", she said, figuring it out, "Perhaps I spend too much time with cadavers and thinking about nerves. But, as I look down there, I see peripheral nerves, coming from the top of the mountain, and branching off into more and more distal nerves. And down there, to the right, where a tree has fallen across that small trail, I picture an injured nerve. These ski trails are like the trail map of the human body. Or, better to say, *'nerves are the trail maps of the human body.'*" Olevia said, completing her thought.

Jennie grasped Olevia's gloved hand in her own, gloved hand, and looked at her through her goggles. "Olevia," for sure you are obsessed with nerves, your research, discovering truth. It is OK. It is what I believe you were meant to do."

"Jennie, let me tell you a new patient that Dr. Baldwin just sent to me. This young man was injured in a mining accident. A sharp heavy piece of granite fell, smashing his right forearm, breaking both bones just above the wrist. Even though the bones were in several pieces, Dr. Baldwin managed through 3 months of weights and pulley traction to manipulate them back into position and they healed. But this young man cannot touch the skin that the rock crushed and cannot bend or flex his wrist or thumb without horrible pain. He keeps his right hand wrapped with a moist towel. Like the causalgia pain described by Dr. Silas Weir Mitchell in the Civil War soldiers who were hit with those round bullets they used to use back then."

"Oh my, what do you think is going on?" asked Jennie.

"He has the same sort of injury my Uncle Albert had. I took Novocaine, the local anesthetic, and blocked the two nerves that go to that skin. Then he could move his thumb and touch the skin. He smiled, but still could not bend his wrist."

"That means to me that you found the nerves to the skin but not the nerves to the wrist joint itself" explained Jennie, trying to understand the anatomy.

"Yes, exactly, Jennie," complimented Olevia. "From Uncle Albert's prosection of Harold, I saw there was a nerve just to the back of the wrist joint, and I have found this in my cadaver dissections, too. So next I blocked this nerve, the posterior interosseous nerve, it is called. Then the young miner could suddenly move his wrist without pain," Olevia explained demonstrating by moving her own wrist. "I told him that when the block wore off, he was not going to be very happy. His pain would be back with a vengeance."

"Wonderful diagnostic techniques. So will you operate on him?" asked Jennie.

"Yes, I hope he comes back again to see me so we can discus the surgery." "I do hope he comes back then too," Jennie said.

"Thank you for your reassurance." Olevia was happy to have someone supporting her work. "How is Martha Pratt doing, the woman who had the painful lower abdominal scar after you removed her uterus?"

"Martha is so happy, Olevia. She sings your praises. I am now discussing this case with my colleagues to see if there are more patients like Martha that we can send to you," answered Jennie with further reassurance.

"Wonderful. Now we just must hope that this pain relief lasts more than six months. Then we can begin write a report about this new approach. Perhaps even Dr. Willis will then believe that removing those nerves will relieve groin pain.

"Now Olevia, stop talking about nerves and let us talk about MEN. Tell me about your reunion with Ezra," asked Jennie.

"Olevia told her, including the parts about other doctors seemingly gathering together to close in on her, and about how Ezra thought that she might be more interested in being with women than with being with men."

"Olevia, you will have to learn to live in this world of men who are jealous of your newly acquired reputation and professional success. They do not like to be challenged and will look for ways to discredit you. Be careful. Keep careful records,"

said Jennie looking at her. Olevia, I do love you, but in a way different than the way I love men," she said as she slid off the chair lift followed by Olevia.

They both skied to the top of the next trail and stopped.

"Jennie, what were you saying about your loving men?" asked Olevia.

"Be happy for me Olevia, I have a new boyfriend," shouted Jennie as she took off down the slope.

ALEXANDER

Olevia received word that her Father, Alexander was not well.

She had not been back to Germany to visit him in, how long? Three years? She had been so busy. Research. Patient care. Surgery, after surgery. Developing new operations.

How could she have forgotten her family back in Munich. *Memorandum est Vivere in Aeturnum.* If no one remembers you, you are effectively dead, even if you are really alive. If you are dead, and someone remembers you, even if you are dead, then you are effectively alive.

Olevia worried, "Who would see her patients if she stopped and went back to Munich?" She would just have to ask someone to do this for her. If she had been hurt herself on the ski slopes, someone would just simply have to take over her patients.

She knew that most doctors just can't believe they are expendable, that someone else could ever fill in for them. But of course, that was hubris and simply not true.

Olevia went back to Munich. Her Father Alexander was very old, and simply wearing out. He had retired. He had outlived his wife, Angelika. He had outlived his twin, Albert. Olevia, finally, had come to visit him. She knew it was just in time.

Olevia held her father's right hand. He was lying on the couch in the family living room, looking up at the Landsmann Family Crest.

Olevia realized that her Father's left hand felt identical to the way her Uncle Albert's left hand felt when she used to hold it.

Father and daughter were reunited. But it felt strange to Olevia. She had always felt more like her Uncle had been her Father. Her father worked all the time. Just the way she was working all the time now.

"Olevia," her Father Alexander said softly, "Come closer so you can hear me," he requested, with a deep German Jewish accent. "Thank you for taking time from your 'verk' as a Doctor, as a 'Voman' Surgeon in America. Thank you for coming to see me."

"Of course, Father. I should have come back to visit more often. Just as you were so busy as a Chemist, so I am also so busy as a Doctor," Olevia offered as a poor excuse.

"Olevia, you remind me of a philosophy problem I have been trying to deal with. What do you believe is the difference between choosing Chemistry as a Profession and choosing Medicine as a Profession, and especially, Surgery?" asked Alexander in a moment of clarity.

"Yes Father. This puzzled me when I was working in your laboratory and trying to decide if I should go into Medicine, motivated of course by Uncle Albert's pain," Olevia said, trying to think how best to answer this difficult question.

Alexander tried to sit up on the couch, but coughed, and weakly lay back down. Olevia put her arm beneath him, to help him lie back down.

"What did you decide is the difference," Alexander persisted.

"In Chemistry, physical rules determine outcome. In Medicine, art is applied to knowledge. The Physician, and especially the Surgeon, risks himself with a decision, and the patient's life changes as the outcome. Medicine involves more personal involvement than Chemistry. We still have so many things to learn about the human body," concluded Olevia.

Alexander murmured something, but Olevia could not hear him. She put her ear close to her Father's mouth. "Your Grandfather Jacob, who, you know, was also my Father, told your Uncle Albert and me, when we were old enough to remember, that at the moment we were born, we were holding hands. Holding hands, just like in the Landsmann Family Crest. You know this Olevia, Yes? Our Family Crest shows two hands holding each other?" Alexander said, pointing with his right hand to the wall in the living room.

"Yes, I know about this, of course, Father," she reassured him.

"Your Great Grandfather, Leon, developed the Landsmann Family Crest. How could he have predicted two hands holding each other? Everything the Landsmann's have overcome through hard work, the meaning of that jagged edge in blue on the Crest. And you are there Olevia. Do you see the Golden Eagle, the symbol of enlightenment and perseverance? How could he have known? My grandfather, Leo, what a vision he had......"

It was quiet for a few moments, as Alexander's voice trailed off.

Olevia looked at the crest. She listened to her Father Alexander's deep breathing. Then she heard something else....her Father Alexander, was speaking again.

"Tell me 'vhat' your 'verk' is like Olevia, my daughter, the Doctor. Finally, there is a Medical Doctor in the Landsmann family! Tell me what you do at 'verk', Doctor Landsmann?" he asked his daughter.

Olevia told her Father stories about America, and her work, and her excitement. She thanked him for giving her the start in life, the principles and training that created her. She cried softly as she could feel his grip weaken on her hand.

"Olevia, said her Father. You are the last of the Landsmann Family. You know this. I 'vorry', Olevia, about how our Family will be remembered. *Vas denkst du?*" Alexander asked.

"What do I think? You ask me in Yiddish, Father?" replied Olevia. She of course understood Yiddish. A combination of Hebrew and German, spoken in the Ghettos where the Jews were kept confined in Europe since the Middle Ages.

"Yes *Schöne*", Yes my beautiful one," he responded, more quietly, again in Yiddish.

"Father, you have not called me 'beautiful one' since I was a very little girl," she said. "You used to call me *'Schöne Punim'*, beautiful face," remembered Olevia.

"Vell?" he replied. "About time to call you that again." he said, grasping her chin with his hand. And then he was quiet for awhile . . . . "How 'vill' the Landsmann Family be remembered if there are no grandchildren for you Olevia?

"Vell," she said, adopting some of his Yiddish, "Uncle Albert will be remembered, and his name, your twin brother's name will be remembered for ever, Father. His *opus magnum,* his amazing PROSECTION hangs in the entrance way into the Clinics at the University of Utah, and will be there forever, with his name on a bronze plaque on the wall."

"And you *Schöne*?" he asked. "How 'vill' you be remembered? I know part of the answer, *Schöne*. You have already published a scientific paper with your mentor, Professor Doctor Harvey Cushing, putting a *Gid* into *Fleish*!!! One day every surgeon will put a nerve into muscle to help a patient in pain who has an injured nerve. If only you could have finished your research in time to help your Uncle Albert," her Father said, and slowly closed his eyes.

"Father, you are so funny the way your mind is now mixing thoughts as you are so tired," Olevia said, knowing that her Father Alexander had taken the first word *Gid* from the Hebrew, *Gid Hanasheh,* the sciatic nerve from the biblical story of Jacob fighting with the Angel, from the Torah, from Genesis. She remembered the story from when she was little; When the Angel could not defeat Jacob, the Angel moved Jacob's sciatic nerve, behind his hip, causing him to limp forever thereafter. And then, her Father had mixed the Yiddish word for meat, *Fleish,* to create a "nerve put into muscle", which was the subject of her research in the Hunterian Lab at Johns Hopkins University.

Alexander opened his eyes again. "Olevia, of course you 'vill' publish much more that will let 'Landsmann" be a name *Vivere in Aeturnum.* But Olevia," Alexander continued, "Vill you marry and have children?"

"Oh Father," Olevia replied, not knowing how to answer. "Would you like that?"

"Yes, *Schöne. Aber Schöne,* do not change your last name! Remain a Landsmann. *Und Ihre Kinder, müssen den zweiten Vornamen Landsmann haben.* And your children must have the last name of Landsmann. *Memorandum est in Aeturnum,"* Alexander concluded, now mixing German and Latin.

"Yes Father, if I have children, their middle name shall be Landsmann," Olevia replied obediently, and the Landsmann named will be remembered forever, just as you wish."

Olevia felt, instinctively that her Father Alexander had one more thing to say. She put her ear next to his lips.

"*Gute Nacht Albert, bide bald"* Alexander whispered.

"Good night Albert, see you soon," Olevia continued her translation.

Then, slowly, still smiling, and holding Olevia's hand, Alexander drifted off into eternal sleep. He was 66 years old.

She kissed him on his bald *koepe,* his head, as a tear fell from her eye to his forehead.

She looked up at the Landsmann Family Crest.

She decided to pack it up and bring it back to America with her. It belonged with the last of the Landsmanns.

3rd LETTER

Work has always been the best way to block out an unhappy memory or event. When Olevia returned to Salt Lake City from Munich, she dove right back into her work. She went directly to her Surgery Clinic.

Olevia was pleased to observe her almost 'visceral' reaction to the handsome man sitting in front of her in the examination room. Then as a peripheral nerve doctor she realized it was not 'visceral' but 'autonomic'. Her heart had skipped a beat. She hoped the nurse standing in the exam room with them did notice her blush.

"Dr. Landsmann, I am here today for you to prove to me that my knee pain is coming from nerves that do not exist in the Anatomy Book, but do exist in Harold," said Jedediah Smith, the lawyer in the suit.

"How nice to see you again, Jed" Olevia replied. She noticed that his clothing was more relaxed at this visit. He had on a striped shirt, with open collar, and rather loose, almost baggy pants.

"Dr. Landsmann, I did exactly as you suggested the last time, I saw you. When I left here, I walked to that 'prosection' as you called it. The one displaying the nerves. The one labeled 'Harold", he continued.

"Yes, Jed, I know which one you mean. The only one you can possibly mean," she said with a kind smile. "And what did you observe there?"

"It is amazing in detail. I saw perhaps what you are referring to, a little structure going to the inside of where my mind imagined the knee joint would have been. Also, since you have been gone, I have been asking "around" and learned that you have some new chemical anesthetic you put into a nerve to learn if putting that nerve to sleep will relieve pain. Am I right?" Jedediah Smith, Esq. asked.

"Yes, Jed, you are correct 'on all counts'," she jokingly replied in legal language. "Do you give me permission, then, to proceed with the injections?" Olevia asked.

"Yes, please do so," said Jed, giving his permission, and rolling up the loose pants to above his knee.

"First I have to examine the areas where I know the nerves can be located, and you must tell me what you feel as I press on these areas," instructed Olevia.

"OK. Go ahead. I am ready," he said.

First Olevia pressed over the medial side of the knee just below the vastus medialis muscle.

"Ouch, wow, that is very tender. How did you know exactly where to touch my knee?" asked Jed.

"Anatomy, Mr. Smith, Anatomy," she replied, marking the spot with a pen.

"Tell me what happens when I press here," Olevia said, moving to a spot just below the vastus lateralis, on the other side, the outside of the knee.

"Ouch. You are two for two, Doctor," pointed out the lawyer.

Olevia now marked that pain point, and said, "Those are the spots where I have learned, through cadaver dissections, these nerves are located.

"Are you going to inject those spots next?" he asked.

"Yes, but first let me clean the skin with some alcohol, which will feel cold.

The nurse, who had been standing quietly in the corner of the exam room, now stepped forward handing Olevia a bottle, which she poured on to the knee and rubbed vigorously with a cloth, also handed to her by the nurse. Jed was sitting on the edge of the examination table.

Then the nurse handed Olevia a syringe and a small bottle.

"This anesthetic is called Novocaine," Olevia said. "Now just hold still and I will put each of these nerves to sleep," she said as she injected the Novocaine. "Now tell me if you feel anything like the knee joint pain you have as I put in the local anesthetic, so we can know that we have located the nerve," she instructed.

As Olevia began the injection on the lateral side of the knee, Jed said excitedly in a higher voice than usual, "Wow! Ouch! That is it. I feel that right inside my knee. You found that nerve Doctor."

The nurse applied a small bandage where Doctor Landsmann had injected.

"Great. Sorry it hurt. And now to do this to the other side of the knee," Olevia said moving slightly to get a correct angle for the injection. She then injected the medial side of the knee.

"You got it again, Doctor. Congratulations," Jed said, now giving a deep sigh.

Olevia sat down on a chair across from her patient, as the nurse applied another bandage.

"Jed, it takes a little while for the medication to work. Sometimes even big strong men, like yourself, faint after an injection. The nurse and I will just stay and talk with you for a little while before we have you stand, walk and try to kneel down.

"OK," he said. "Perhaps I do feel a little lightheaded."

Olevia noted that he was turning a bit pale, and sweating, signs of a vasovagal response, the medical name for fainting. She grabbed his hand and felt his pulse, at the same time she said, "Jed, just put your head down on the table. Just lie back. You will be over this reaction in just a minute."

"OK Doc, thanks," he said lowering his head.

"Tell me a little about your self," Olevia encouraged, to keep him awake and focused. She continued holding his hand and monitoring his pulse. The nurse brought over a moist compress and put it on his forehead.

"Well Doctor Landsmann," Jed said, his voice sounding a little stronger, "like what do you want to know about me?"

"Whatever you feel like sharing she said, sitting up, clearly noting his color coming back.

"I am part of a big Mormon family of Smiths. Many are lawyers, married and have lots of kids. Not me though. Not yet anyway. Still single. I like to ski, and outside of that I just work all the time...... except when I am at the hospital seeing Doctors," he said, looking up with a smile.

"Ok Jed. Moment of truth! Your face is pink again. Safe for you to sit up," said Olevia letting go of his hand and getting up.

Observing that Jed could sit and remain pink, Olevia said, "Now stand up, and take a little walk, and then come back in here. The nurse will walk with you. I will be completing my charts in here," she instructed again. "Oh, and Jed, start out using your cane. Olevia busied herself writing in his chart.

"Hey Doc," Olevia heard just a few minutes later. She looked up from her charts to see Jed walking briskly into the exam room, without using his cane.

"Look at me! No limp! No cane!" exclaimed Jed triumphantly.

Olevia smiled, and then watched quietly as he stood in front of her.

"So far so good, Jed. Now, try to kneel on the floor," requested Olevia.

Jed did as asked and knelt down on the floor on his "bad" knee. He looked up at her, and for some reason her mind imagined a suitor in love proposing to his beloved.

"Kneeling does not hurt either," Jed said with a huge smile.

Olevia just smiled. Finally, she said. "The nerve block was a success. Two nerves are causing your pain, the medial and lateral retinacular nerves."

"I'm a believer Doc. Sign me up. If my pain goes away, you will have a convert on your hands," said Jed jokingly, surprising language for a Mormon, and a lawyer.

"Well Jed, we have a lot to talk about first," said Olevia.

"We sure do," replied Jed. If those two nerves are not in that Anatomy book, how come you know their names. I would have thought you would have named them yourself, like 'Landsmann knee nerve #1 and Landsmann nerve #2'?"

Before Olevia could answer Jed, there was knock on the exam room door. Olevia turned to see a hospital messenger standing there with an urgent look on his face. "Dr. Landsmann, I have an urgent letter for you," he said.

"Excuse me Jed, I will be right back," said Olevia getting up to get the letter.

"Now what," she thought, signing for the letter. The last letter told of her Father Alexander's declining health. He had died. Now what? Letters seemed to have been so pivotal in her life, and this letter looked very official. Olevia turned to Jed and the nurse, saying "Excuse me, again, I will be right back." She stepped outside the clinic to the little consultation room to read this in private.

The letter had the Scales of Justice symbol at the top in gold. Below that, in dark bold type, it stated,

The State of Utah informs you of the case below,
filed against you, entitled,
Jared Benson (deceased) and Benson Family
versus Olevia Landsmann, MD
Case #4,261

Olevia realized that her hands were shaking, and she sat down.

She could not bring herself to read any further.

After a few minutes, she folded up the letter, and walked back into the exam room.

"Is everything OK, Doctor?" asked Jed, you look concerned.

"Jed let's finish what needs to be done for you," Olevia began. "If you wish me to remove the nerves, this is what you need to know about the surgical procedure," and she went on to explain it in detail. "There is no 'precedent' for this surgery, to throw in a legal phrase. As with any surgery, I cannot guarantee the results of surgery would be the same as what you are feeling right now, with the nerves asleep from the nerve block. However, theoretically, the results of the nerve block should be a good predictor of success. Often in the human body nerves overlap, and that if you got a lot of relief, but one spot still hurts you, then I may have to look for another nerve that might be involved, which might mean that another operation would be necessary."

"Dr. Landsmann, I understand that. I have written down some other types of questions for you to answer for me," Jed said.

He asked the questions and Olevia did her best to answer them for him. "Dr. Landsmann, you are the only one who has offered me any hope. I do believe that it is only through new knowledge that we can advance, really in all fields, but especially in the field of Medicine. And when you have made me better, then you can rewrite the Anatomy Books, so that people, and Orthopedic Surgeons in particular, will know that God did not forget to put nerves into our joints."

"Thank you, Jed," Olevia said humbly.

"Doctor, when can we do the surgery and I will clear my calendar," Jed said, with enthusiasm.

"All right then, Jed. You can go out and chose a date with the scheduling secretary," replied Olevia. "We can do it pretty soon, if you wish," she said turning to leave. As she did, she murmured to herself, "I better go back and do a few more knee dissections before I operate on HIM!"

"Dr. Landsmann, one more question, please," she heard Jed say and she turned with a smile and a little sigh.

"I am pretty good at 'reading' people's reactions. Is there anything I can do about that message you just received," he offered kindly.

Olevia turned to the nurse, and said to her, "Thank you for your help. We will just be here talking for a few more minutes. You may attend to another patient,"

When the nurse left the exam room, Olevia turned to Jed, and said, "Ok then, Mr. Jedediah Smith, it was a legal letter. Maybe you can tell me what this letter really means," she said handing him the letter. Then adding quickly, "But I trust you will keep what it says strictly confidential."

"Of course, I will," said Jedediah Smith, Esq, who now read not only the first page, but read also enough of the following pages so that he knew what this letter was about.

Olevia watched his eyes as he read. They were so alert, so attentive. So handsome. She should not be thinking about that; he was her patient, and now,....perhaps her lawyer!"

He finished reading and looked up from the letter to Olevia. He looked at her with concern, knowing what was in store for her.

"Dr. Landsmann, I am deeply sorry to have to interpret this legal language for you, but apparently there was a young male patient of yours, who is now deceased. His family has found a very prestigious Salt Lake City law firm, and they have today served you with these papers."

"And what do these papers say I did," Olevia quietly asked, already knowing.

"These papers allege that due to your negligence in performing new and unproven, investigational surgery, and failing in that surgery, that, directly as a cause of your negligence, your patient took his own life." Jedediah

Smith, Esquire, then concluded, "The Benson Family allege this is your fault. Dr. Landsmann. The family of the deceased has sued you for malpractice."

SMITHS

Olevia walked her patient Jed out of the clinic, noticing how well he was still walking after the nerve block. "She turned to him and said, "Now it is time for you to give ME some advice. Let's go into this consultation room and talk a few minutes more, before your knee pain returns and you decide you hate me."

"OK," Jed said. "My knee still feels great." He sat down and took up his lawyer tone of voice. "Dr. Landsmann you have just been served with legal papers. These indicate that you are being sued for malpractice. Malpractice is actually a pretty new type of crime, and there is not a lot of precedent for how these cases proceed, but one thing is certain," he paused. "You need to get a lawyer to defend you."

"Whom do you recommend," asked Olevia.

"Remember I told you that the plaintiff's lawyer, your patient, Jared Benson's lawyer, that is, your former patient's family's lawyer, is part of a prestigious law firm? That firm is The Smith Law firm, founded by Gary Lord Clarke-Smith, Esquire."

"Oh my gosh," said Olevia, "He is Chairman of the Board of Trustees of this Hospital, Salt Lake County General Hospital!"

"Yes, he is," said Jed. "He is also my Grandfather," he added quietly.

Olevia almost physically took a step back from Jed.

Then Jed added, "To make things worse, the lawyer representing the plaintiff, is Elam Smith, and he is my first cousin," continued Jedediah Smith, Esq.

"Do you work for that same law firm?" Olevia asked.

"No, but I cannot represent you and still be your patient, and I want you to fix my knee pain. Our firm does have excellent lawyers, and I will be happy to talk to one to see if he would like to take this case, said Jedediah Smith, Esquire.

"Thank you, Jed, then please do ask for someone to represent me," instructed Olevia.

"Dr. Landsmann, I know that whoever represents you will have a difficult time with defense because of the new scientific approach you bring to surgery. They will want to know if there is anyone who could stand up and testify in your behalf, to defend your work with nerves," questioned Jedediah Smith, Esquire.

Jed, there are two people here in town. One is another woman surgeon, Jennifer Ross, MD who knows and respects my work. The other was a student with me at Johns Hopkins School of Medicine and specializes now in nerves, here in Salt Lake City. Although here in Salt Lake City he is working with nerve problems in children. His name is Ezra Maybe, MD," replied Olevia proudly.

Now it was Jedediah's turn to be quiet for a minute.

"What are you thinking about?" inquired Olevia.

"Does Doctor Ezra Maybe have red hair?" Asked Jedediah Smith, the Lawyer.

"Yes, he does have red hair," said Olevia. "How did you know that?"

"You now just have one witness, Doctor Ross," stated Jed. "Ezra Maybe is married to another of my first cousins, the daughter of my Uncle, another Smith who is a lawyer. Your Doctor Ezra Maybe married a Smith!

Olevia just sat starring at him in disbelief. The Mormon community was very tightly intertwined, and she was getting trapped in the net that was the Smith Family.

As Jedediah got up to leave, he said, "Try not to worry too much, Doctor Landsmann. Schedule my surgery, and I will try to find you a defense lawyer." Then he walked out without a limp, the Novocaine was still working. He smiled at her reassuringly.

After a few more minutes, Olevia got up and went back to the Surgery Clinic secretary. They selected a surgical date for Jedediah Smith, Esq., and then Olevia asked, "What is on my schedule for the rest of today. I think I need to take a walk."

"Dr. Landsman, go for an hour's walk. Have lunch, and then you have a 2PM meeting just added to your schedule today. You are to meet with the Chief of Surgery, Dr. Willis, in his office.

Olevia now was seeing warning signs at every turn.

She left and walked outside for a while. Not hungry at all.

Dr. Elijah Willis wanted to meet with her. Perhaps he was married to a member of the Smith family as well! Perhaps he had something good to tell her, but as she knocked on his office door, she suspected this was not going to be a friendly chat.

"Dr. Landsmann," you are a few minutes early, said Dr. Willis's secretary. He is here and will see you shortly.

Olevia sat down.

"Dr. Landsmann, come on in, and have a seat," said the Chief of Surgery in a welcoming voice.

"Thank you," she said and sat down. She was wearing pants and a jacket, a white blouse, and no make up. She felt she looked appropriately non-feminine, and perhaps therefore less threatening.

"I do have some bad news for you Dr. Landsmann, and very little advice. I have never been in this situation before," said Elijah Willis, MD, Chief of Surgery, his voice becoming solemn.

"I have been told that complaints have come to the Board of Trustees of this Hospital, Salt Lake County General Hospital, about you. I am told these complaints say that you are operating on patients using a diagnosis that does not exist. The complaints say that you are using patients as experimental animals," Dr. Willis relayed the message.

"Can I be told who made these complaints?" Olevia asked.

"Mr. Gary Lord Clarke-Smith, Esq., the Chairman of the Board, would not tell me the names of your "accusers". He says the information was given to him in "confidence". Nevertheless, he feels these complaints must be investigated, and has asked me to form a committee to investigate your medical records here at our hospital. I have appointed therefore David J. Grafton, MD, the Chief of the Department of Medicine, as an "independent" person to Chair this committee. He has tasked for review everyone of your hospital charts, especially the ones related to surgery, with very special attention to the ones related to peripheral nerve surgery." Then he paused.

Olevia sat quietly, just looking at him. She felt as if her life were ending. A *Male MEDICAL* doctor oversaw the committee. Now she knew she had no chance.

"Dr. Landsmann, beginning the first of next month you will lose your hospital operating privileges. I want you to complete your obligations to patients already scheduled. You can still see patients for follow up and do wound care in your Surgery Clinic. You can still do Anatomy dissections and teach Anatomy. But after the first of next month, you can only operate on cadavers, as these people can no longer be injured by your surgery," Dr. Willis concluded.

QUO VADIS?

It was the coldest day of the year so far.

Olevia chose to go skiing.

She chose to go alone.

She had a 45-minute car ride to think about the events of her life so far.

When she arrived at Alta, and put on her warmest clothes and skies, she chose the ski lifts that would take her to the very top. Well, almost to the very top.

She would have to hike her way up to the very top of the mountain on her skis, and hope that the gusts of winds did not blow her off the mountaintop.

Or maybe she should hope that they did blow her off the top.

She was in a dark mood.

It was rumored that more than one adventurous skier in the past had been blown off the mountaintop and died. Some never to be found again in the deep valleys bellow.

"Who would even know I was gone?" she thought to herself, sitting on the chairlift. "Who would miss me? Certainly not any family members, there were none left. Certainly, not Ezra, he had a new wife and busy job. Jennie Ross might realize I was gone, but now she has her own new boy friend to occupy her thoughts and her time. No one would miss me," she concluded.

"There would be many that would be happy if I were gone, never to be seen near an operating room. Certainly Dr. Willis and Dr. Grafton, Chiefs of Surgery and Medicine, would be happy. Certainly, Levin Randolph in Orthopedics. Would be happy. Probably Ether Helaman would not miss me either", she thought.

Olevia's mind jumped ahead to the courtroom. When the time came, when the Judge called the role to begin the Malpractice Suit against Dr. Landsmann, the Bailiff would notice that there was no one responding in the courtroom. "Then people would realize I am gone," she thought. "Probably they will believe I have escaped back to Munich to avoid my conviction. Surely, they will believe I am guilty. "They will not even search for me." Perhaps someone will go to Chipeta and ask her when I was last seen. Yes, Chipeta will be the only one to miss me. Perhaps in the Spring, when the avalanches thaw, my body will be found," she thought. "Ironically, I will be preserved, in the cold. No embalming fluid necessary."

As she continued up the mountainside, Olevia looked down. Sure enough. Those ski trails were trail maps of the human body. She could see the ski marks going down from the chair lift like the different branches of the brachial plexus, then dividing into the final big runs, the median and ulna nerve runs going down one side of the mountain and the radial nerve run going down the backside of the mountain, just as those nerves did to the front and back of the arm.

"Am I losing my mind?" she thought. "Certainly, Ezra thinks I have an abnormal Psyche. He thinks I am Electra! Instead of killing my mother though, I killed a patient, or so the lawsuit alleges. And now I am thinking of another murder, a self murder."

"No, I am not Electra," her more rational self fought back. "Electra liked women, even though Electra was a woman. Thanks to Ezra's psychiatric evaluation of me, I doubted my own sexuality. But only I know that I am fighting the scar deep inside me, the scar that Uncle Albert left there. That scar created any sexual misgivings I might have," she concluded.

"I did love Ezra. I do love Jennie. I think I am attracted now to Jedediah, but I will probably never get to live out that reality for at least one very good reason, having nothing to do with my sexuality. I have to operate on him! And what if that surgery fails?" she continued to question herself.

She slid off the chair lift and polled her way to the very top of the mountain.

The wind gusted up to 40 mile per hour, or so it seemed.

She could not see out of her goggles.

What had her life been about?

To become a doctor. I have.

To become a surgeon. I have.

"What is left for me now that I am a Surgeon but no longer have operating privileges? Am I a Surgeon if I can't operate? Am I a doctor if my patient is already dead?" she continued to question.

"I can still dissect, and I can do research on cadavers," she thought a little more positively. "I loved finding these secrets to answer questions about the living. Is this enough for me?"

"I have so much more I want to do to help those suffering in pain. Is simply doing a PROSECTION, getting it drawn or painted or photographed and then getting it published enough?"

"I know the answer. 'No, it is not enough', she said aloud into the gusting wind.

By now she had hiked from the chair lift to the top of the mountain. She stood at its edge, at the precipice.

She continued talking into the wind. "If I cannot translate my research into helping patients myself, using my own two hands to accomplish that relief, not just writing theoretical papers, then "No", then that form of a life in medicine would not be enough for me."

"I might as well have stayed in Munich and become a chemist. Nothing risky there, as long as you don't burn your self with acid," she said ironically.

"Burned or deeply frozen? perhaps not much difference for me now," she thought.

A big gust of wind now came at her from behind, throwing her off balance, and almost off the precipice.

As she recovered her balance, a little whiff of wind, hit her goggles, just enough to clear them. Suddenly she had a new vision.

"*Quo vadis?*" Back in her teaching mode, she muttered, "Latin for Where are you going now?"

She pivoted 180 degrees on her skis and plunged down the black diamond in a tuck position.

She had a new vision.

Uncle Albert would be proud of her.

LOSE YOUR NERVE

The knee was just lying there, shining white like one of the snow-capped peaks in the Wasatch Range. The overhead operating room light gave it that appearance, making everything around the surgical site look darker, and fade into the distance. Allowing the surgeon to focus.

The knee was waiting for Olevia. Its injured nerves were sending out cries for help as if coming from below the avalanche of white.

Olevia was scrubbing her hands at the scrub sink prior to going into surgery. She was ready. She had done several more prosections on the nerves to the knee. She knew she could find them. And they had to be found today.

Today was the last day she would be allowed to operate at Salt Lake County General Hospital until the Special Commission, Chaired by David J. Grafton, MD, Chief of the Department of Medicine, concluded their review of her patients' medical records and decided if she was "worthy" to continue operating. "Imagine," she thought, "a *MEDICAL* doctor deciding if I am worthy to operate?" Surely Dr. Willis, Dr. Grafton and the venerable Gary Lord Clark-Smith were old friends. Probably all graduates of Brigham Young University, and all attending services on Sunday at the Tabernacle. Of course, they would all be supporting each other in this Old West version of a New England Witch Hunt.

As she finished scrubbing and turned to use her buttock to push open the door to the operating room, she said to herself, "Today is going to be the highlight of my surgical career, even if it is going to be the last day I ever operate again here, in this hospital."

"Good morning, Dr. Landsmann," said Chipeta, the surgical scrub nurse. "Today you have three peripheral nerve operations, what fun this will be," she added with a smile.

"Yes, thank you, Chipeta. And each will be different, and I hope each will continue the path to proving there is a place for peripheral nerve surgery for pain," Olevia replied putting on her gown and gloves.

Olevia now looked over the "anesthesia screen" to see if Ether Helaman were here today, spying on her again. But it was a different Surgery Resident dropping the ether. "How is our patient doing," Olevia inquired.

"Fine Dr. Landsmann. You may proceed with your peripheral nerve surgery," he replied not even looking up at her.

"He probably knows this is my last day and he thinks he won't have to deal with me again in the future," thought Olevia. "Well, he is going to be proven wrong, she said to herself.

"How did you decide to start with this knee surgery case first?" scrub nurse Chipeta asked, innocently.

"This is the most difficult surgery of the three. It has never done before. I am going to denervate this knee," she answered aloud. Inwardly, she thought," Yes and the surgery is made all the more difficult in that my patient, Jedediah Smith, is a lawyer. A relative of a lawyer who is suing me! Jed is also someone I have come to admire. He is helping me through my own medical problem, the Jared Benson lawsuit! But now I must focus on this surgery."

The knee was impersonal. In surgery it was a knee. The patient's face was shielded from the surgeon. The surgeon just concentrated on the knee. The shiny white knee in the glare of the operating room light.

Olevia injected the Novocaine local anesthetic along two lines, each 3 inches long, that she had drawn, one on each side of the knee. She began with the knee bent. Then, standing to the left side of this patient to operate on the left knee, she made the transverse cut into the skin and then down into the fat, and pressed the skin so it would not bleed.

"Why did you choose not to wrap the leg with the Esmarch bandage, Doctor, as you usually do?" asked Chipeta, used to Dr. Landsmann's usual approach to extremity nerve surgery.

"Today, I am not using the Esmarch bandage to exsanguinate the leg," replied Olevia, "because the nerves I am looking for are small but are always located next to a small artery. I will use the blood in that artery to help me find the nerve," she explained to Chipeta, and anyone else who was listening.

As Olevia carefully opened the thick white covering overlying the muscle, the vastus lateralis, she looked just past the muscle, and YES, there it was. The small, one millimeter artery, the lateral recurrent geniculate artery. "This is the small artery I was looking for she said to Chipeta. It supplies blood to the outside of the knee joint, and it is an extra artery, that is what its name, 'recurrent' means," she explained.

"Now," thought, Olevia, "for the support I will need in the contests and research papers to come" She looked over to the corner of the operating room where a man had been standing quietly. He held a large black box in his hands. He too was wearing a scrub gown, cap, and mask.

"Photographer, this is a view I would like to take a photograph of," she said to the Department of Biology photographer who was used to working in the Anatomy Lab and photographing biology projects.

"Doctor Landsmann," the photographer said, "Please move that overhead light out of the way, as it distorts the true colors, and could you please put a small metal probe underneath the nerve, to distinguish it from all the surrounding structures."

"Thank you for those suggestions," said Olevia, as she did as he asked.

"Perfect," said the photographer. "Now my first photograph will be from further away so it shows that it is you, Dr. Landsmann, doing the surgery. Next, I will come in closer and photograph to show the knee and surgical site. Then I will switch lenses and shoot a close up to emphasize the nerve."

"Thank you for those photos. Now wait just a minute and you can take one more close up," said Olevia. Then she injected the nerve, cut out a piece to send to the Pathologist to identify it as a nerve. Then she pulled on the nerve and placed it deeply into an area behind the knee, as this nerve came under the hamstring tendon from behind the knee. "Now just photograph this piece of nerve on the skin to show it is no longer going into the knee," she instructed the photographer. Then she closed the white connective tissue layer and closed the skin.

"Now rotate the knee towards me," Olevia asked, as Chipeta allowed the knee to rotate outwards, externally rotating the knee so the leg was almost flat. Oliveia then proceeded to do the same operation on the medial side of the knee, finding again the nerve to this side of the knee joint. "Now take a photo of this nerve so that we can see, in distinction from the other side, that here the nerve first innervates the overlying muscle, the vastus medialis, and then, although the Anatomy books show the nerve ending in the muscle, the nerve actually comes out from under the muscle to innervate the knee."

After this was photographed, Olevia instructed finally, "Now take a photo of me implanting the end of this medial retinacular nerve into the vastus medialis muscle." Then she began sewing up that side of the knee.

"Chipeta," said Olevia, as she sewed, and Chipeta cut the sutures, "We just found in a living person the same nerves that my Uncle Albert found and demonstrated in his prosection, the one he named Harold."

"Dr. Landsmann, if this nerve is not in an Anatomy book, how do you know what name to call it?" asked the perceptive scrub nurse, Chipeta.

"Well the naming is the privilege that goes to the Anatomist that discovers the nerve." She now remembered that the 'owner' of this knee, Jedediah Smith, asked her that exact question. "These nerves might one day be called the medial and lateral Landsmann nerves," she said with a little laugh. "But I just named them anatomically." She concluded putting on the bandage.

Then Jedediah and his knee were wheeled out of the operating room.

As Olevia scrubbed her hands for the next patient, she felt very positive and very close to her family history. Today she would do the operation that her Uncle Albert needed, and for which he had found the anatomic information necessary to solve his own problem. These nerves, too, were demonstrated in his Harold PROSECTION. Uncle Albert died trying to operate on himself. He was not only his own Surgeon. He also was his own Anesthesiologist. Sadly, he overdosed with the cocaine solution he injected into himself for his local anesthetic.

Olevia knew that her Uncle Albert died trying to relieve his own pain through peripheral nerve surgery. "Uncle Albert," she said softly to herself as she turned and backed into the operating room, "Today, I will do 'YOUR' operation on a young man injured in a mining accident. I know you are up there observing this surgery."

"Dr. Landsmann, can you tell us something about this next patient whose hand you are going to operate on?" asked Mabel Ryan, RN, the Circulating nurse.

"Certainly, Mabel," answered Olevia. "Dr. Baldwin, the Chief of Orthopedics sent him to me, because no one else knew what to do for him. This miner's hand was crushed in an accident while he was working. Dr. Baldwin corrected the broken bones, but the man is in so much pain he has asked for his hand to be amputated. He cannot touch the skin over the back of the hand on the thumb side and he cannot bend his wrist without severe pain. He keeps his hand covered with a moist towel. Even wind blowing on it causes him to cry out in pain," Olevia answered.

"Dr. Landsmann," observed Chipeta, "I have seen these nerves in the cadavers in the Anatomy Lab with you. But have you ever done one of these operations before?" asked Chipeta, handing Dr Landsmann the Esmarch bandage.

"No, I have not," said Olevia as she rolled the bandage from the fingers to the elbow, turning the pink hand white in color. She looked down at the hand and wrist, lying out on a table next to the stretcher, and, as she began to sit down next to the table she again was amazed at the view. The overhead operating lights shown bright white light on to the chest and the arm, looking just like the trail map Olevia imagined from the chair lift, while skiing.

"Doctor Landsmann," asked Mabel Ryan, who had overheard the conversation between Chipeta and Olevia, "How do you prepare to do an operation that was never done before? You must be so brave."

"Mable, I practice the surgery in the cadaver lab," she said as Chipeta handed her the #15 blade and scalpel. "I must be certain of the Anatomy. 'Brave?' Perhaps. I risk everything doing this surgery. If the surgery fails, then what explanation must there be other than either I have made the wrong diagnosis or I did not understand the anatomy well enough," Olevia explained."

"Why do you take this risk," asked the young circulating nurse, watching Dr. Landsmann open the skin going from behind the thumb and up the forearm.

"If I can understand the anatomic basis for the patient's pain, then I have come to believe it is my duty to advance knowledge, to offer hope for those in pain. You see the photographer here. I plan to publish the results of this surgery so that other surgeons can learn the operations I have developed. Time, not a Court of Law, will be the True Judge of my work," Olevia answered philosophically.

The photographer came over and stood behind the seated Olevia. He observed that quite easily in fact she isolated two different nerves deep to the damaged, crushed, skin. She placed a probe under each of them, and then said, "Photograph please. Do that long view first to show me with the hand and forearm."

The photographer took the picture.

"Great, now take the close up to show both nerves," directed Olevia. "Great. Now take a photo of me injecting the nerve with the local anesthetic. Great. Now pull back and show that I am pulling on these nerves and skin and thumb are being pulled back, demonstrating that these nerves go to this painful area. Ok. Thanks. Now take a photo of these two small pieces of nerve removed, disconnecting the nerves. Great."

Olevia then had to decide into which muscles to implant these nerves. She had considered this in the Anatomy Lab. The closest muscles were the little ones that made the thumb lift as if hitch-hiking. But, these muscles moved too much and were too close to the surface of the skin, and they were small. Both nerves, the ones her Uncle Albert labeled RSN (radial sensory nerve) and LABC (lateral antebrachial cutaneous), in his notebook for his experiments, she knew came down to the wrist after crossing the elbow quite near a muscle that was actually an almost useless muscle in humans. It is the brachioradialis muscle. In lower animals it used to extend the wrist, but with evolution it moved back, hooked to the forearm bone, the radius and now was an extra elbow flexor instead of a wrist extensor. In fact, it was the same muscle she had used to implant the nerves in her Canine research in the Hunterian Lab, a time that now seemed so long ago. Olevia then made a new incision near this brachioradialis muscle at the elbow, then pulled on the nerves near the wrist until she saw them move in this new incision. Then she pulled the two nerves out of the wrist area and up into the elbow area, had another photo taken, shortened these long nerves by cutting off another piece of each of them, and, finally, implanted each of them deeply into the underside of the brachioradialis muscle. "Photo please".

"Are you done now Dr. Landsmann?" asked Chipeta.

"No," Olevia answered. "Those two nerves fixed the pain in the skin and thumb movement, as the first block in my clinic did. Now I must remove the nerve to the back of the wrist joint, she said making a new incision."

Olevia moved the tendons out of the way, and said, "There it is, the nerve to the back of the wrist joint. Photo please," she said, placing a probe beneath the 2 mm white nerve. "The Anatomy books show this nerve ending after it innervates those hitch-hiking muscles. But, as you can see, this nerve continues into the back of the wrist joint." Then she injected this nerve with Novocaine. She removed a piece of the nerve, and handed it to Chipeta, saying, "label this specimen as 'posterior interosseous nerve.'" Finally, Olevia implanted the proximal end of this nerve into the underside of the bigger muscles that extend the fingers. "Photo," she called. Then sutured the skin closed and was done.

As Olevia scrubbed for third, and last surgery of the day, she anticipated Mabel Ryan's question.

"This will be our easiest case of the day, Mabel. I have done this type of surgery before, and it worked, the second time I did it," Olevia said, putting on her gown and glove.

"What surgery did this woman have before?" asked Chipeta.

"This patient was sent by Dr. Jennie Ross, and excellent Gynecologist. Dr. Ross removed this woman's uterus, but the wound healed poorly, leaving this painful scar," replied Olevia.

The bright overhead light revealed a white flat mesa, with a purplish thick line going across it, like a raging river. On each end of that line Olevia had marked in ink the sites of the pain. "Photo please," she said. Then she began on the right side, as she had done before in other patients.

"Here they are, the ilioinguinal and iliohypogastric nerves," commented Olevia, "these were not hard to find at all! Photo please." Then she injected the nerves, relocated them well away from the scar, back deep beneath the abdominal muscles. Closed all the layers, repeated this on the left side, and said "done."

"Done with surgery for today. Hopefully, though, not done with surgery for the rest of my life," she thought.

Olevia turned to those in the operating room who had helped her today, and said, "Thank you for your help Peripheral Nerve Team."

As she changed her clothes in the dressing room, Olevia thought again about her new plan for a life without operating privileges.

"I am going to write up my research and try to get it published," she said, closing the door to the Women's dressing room, and leaving the Surgery floor.

DEFENSE

Olevia was wearing a long dress with a white blouse, buttoned up almost to her neck, and a long scarf around her shoulders. Her only jewelry was a wristwatch. In truth she had no other jewelry.

"Olevia, I would like you to meet Jarvis Greer, Esq., a member of our law firm. He will be handling your Defense in the malpractice case against you," said Jedediah Smith, Esq., wearing a suit, vest and tie, and being quite formal.

Olevia noticed that Jedediah was looking at her in an entirely different way than he had in the clinic. Perhaps it was because of how different she looked dressed like this.

Olevia turned now to look directly at her new lawyer. "I am happy to meet you," said Olevia. "Wish the circumstances were different. Usually, I am the one being asked to help someone else."

"Mr. Smith, will excuse us now Doctor, and you and I will sit in our conference room for a while. He already knows everything I am going to say, and in case we have to call him as a witness in your defense, that is if the surgery that you did for him actually works, then it would be better for him not to participate in the discussions we are about to have," explained Mr. Greer.

Olevia turned to watch Mr. Smith go away. "Jedediah," she called, reverting to her more familiar doctor/patient role.

"Yes, Doctor," Jedediah said, turning back to look at her.

"Thank you for organizing this. And I notice that you do not have a cane with you today," said Olevia.

"Then you are doubly welcome, Doctor, as I find I need it less and less," said Jedediah, and gave her a wink. "My knee pain is just about gone, thanks to you," and continued walking down the hall, away from them.

Mr. Greer now began. "Doctor I have read the charges against you, as I assume you have. Is that correct?"

"Yes, that is correct." Olevia answered.

"I have a copy of your records, from Salt Lake County General Hospital. They are just a few pages in number. There is just the consultation report from the first day you saw your patient, Jared Benson, in clinic. Then there is the report of the operation. Then there is the report of the day he came back to get his sutures removed. Then there is nothing. Do you have anything else to add to this file?" asked Mr. Greer.

"No, Sir, I do not." Replied Olevia.

"Do you know much about Malpractice Lawsuits, Doctor?" Mr. Greer asked.

"No, Sir, I do not," she replied.

"Well let me tell you, no one knows much about them. Until a few years ago, there almost were none. Then as Orthopedic Surgeons began to do more and more fracture work, and, as you might expect with any new form of surgery, they had complications. Examples might be one leg being shorter than the other, or the foot being crooked on the side of the fracture, or an infection or failed bone healing requiring amputation. Between 1835 and 1860, lawyers began the process of claiming that the treating doctor did not care for the patient properly, creating sort of a crisis in malpractice litigation. Now there are lawyers, like myself, who defend the doctor, and there are lawyers like Elam Smith, Esq., that attack the doctor," Mr. Greer explained.

"Do I have to prove I am innocent, or do they have to prove I am guilty?" Olevia asked innocently.

"The Plaintiff, the side accusing you, has the burden of proof. It has become quite strict. They must prove four things. First, that you had a duty to the patient, which clearly you did, as you accepted him to be your patient. Second, they must prove that a "breach" of that care, occurred. This means that you treated the patient below the "standard of care."

"What does that mean, Mr. Greer?" asked Olevia.

"The 'standard of care' can be defined as the level of care that would be provided by a reasonably prudent physician in the same circumstances that you found yourself in. Now this is getting a little ahead of the story here, but this can work for or against you, because no one else has ever done this surgery, so in that sense there is no "standard of care" other than just letting the patient suffer without doing anything."

"Thank you for that definition," Olevia replied.

Jarvis Greer then went on, "The third thing the Plaintiff must prove, is that your 'negligence' resulted in harm to the patient. We must consider whether your not relieving the patient's pain is 'negligent'? Is failure to achieve the desired result 'negligent' in and of itself? That is an interesting question."

Olevia just remained silent. She did feel responsible for Jared Benson's death, but she certainly did not kill him. He did not die even in the hospital, no less the operating room.

"Finally," continued Jarvis Greer, Esquire, "the fourth thing the Plaintiff must prove is that damage resulted from your negligence. Now clearly there was damage, the patient is dead. But did YOU cause that damage?" Lawyer Jarvis concluded.

"Thank you for that clear explanation, and now I guess you need to work on how to get those ideas of yours, and mine, lined up to make a good defense," Olevia said hoping for the best.

"To proceed," replied Mr. Jarvis Greer, I must find witnesses that give an opinion on each of these subjects, and I must take a deposition, which is the legal term for a formal interview, of the "plaintiff", which is impossible because Jared Benson is dead. Therefore, I will have to interview his relatives and try to learn the facts as they have presented them to their lawyer."

"What can I do to help myself, Mr. Greer?" Olevia asked.

"Who referred this patient to you, and what were his complaints," asked Mr. Greer.

"No one referred him to me specifically. Mr. Benson just came to the Wound Clinic to see if anyone could help with the pain. He told me he had a hernia repair the year before by a surgeon in town. The hernia bulge stayed away but beginning right after surgery he had a similar but worse type of pain, going from near the right hip bone down to the base of the penis and into the top of the scrotum and to the pubic hair. The pain kept him from sitting normally as he could not stay flexed at the hip. He was unable to have sexual intercourse with his wife. He could not play with his children, and he was unable to work due to pain. Taking medications did not help his pain. The original surgeon said he had seen a case like this once before but did not know what to do help Jared Benson with his pain. Mr. Benson was getting depressed. He could not support his family. He told me that his wife was talking about taking the kids back to live with her parents," Olevia recalled from memory.

"Now Doctor, you have some of that documented in your records, but not the part about Mr. Benson's family thinking they would leave, or his not being able to support his family. Are you sure you remember that and why did you not write it down?" Mr. Greer asked.

"There is only so much time between the patients in Clinic, Mr. Greer. As you can see, what I have is all handwritten, and it is written clearly so it can be read. It takes time. But I remember him because he was a patient quite early in my time in that Clinic, and I wanted to help him so much," Olevia explained.

"Dr. Landsmann, did you tell the patient you had never done this surgery before on anyone?" asked Mr. Greer, accusingly.

"No, I did not. He did not ask me. He asked if I could help him. I told him there was a nerve that went in that direction that can become trapped or injured in the hernia repair. He asked me if I could remove it. I told him that I could look for it and remove it if I found it. He just said to do whatever I had to do, because this pain was ruining his life," explained Olevia.

"Is it correct that you have not documented that conversation anywhere?"

"Yes, that is correct," she replied.

"Have you read about the operation that you did in any surgery textbook, or ever seen it done before?" Mr. Greer asked.

"No, I have not," said Olevia, honestly.

"How did you know what to do, then?" Mr. Greer asked, while writing away the whole time on his long, yellow, note pad.

"I had decided that my professional contribution to surgery was going to be to develop operations to treat pain due to injured nerves. I knew where the nerve was. I practiced the surgical approach to find the nerve in a cadaver. My plan was NOT to reopen the hernia repair itself, because that surgery was successful, but rather to go through the same incision, find the nerve before it went into the hernia repair," Olevia explained her thought process.

"Dr. Landsmann, why did your surgery fail?" Mr. Greer asked next.

"I now know why," Mr. Greer, but no one knew this at the time I operated on him. I now know that there are two nerves that can be involved in this pain. The ilioinguinal gets involved by the reconstruction of the tissues damaged by the hernia itself, while the second nerve, with a similar name, the iliohypogastric nerve, gets stuck in the suturing that closes the skin," Olevia answer the best she could.

"Can you bring me appropriate drawings of all this so I can understand it better and we can explain it to a jury? Also, these drawings will be invaluable when you have your deposition," said Mr. Greer.

"Who is going to do what to me?" questioned Olevia.

"Mr. Elam Smith, Esquire, will be contacting you to set up that interview I was talking about, a deposition. It is for him to discover what you know and what you do not know, and what he can use against you if this goes to court," explained Mr. Greer. "Now we have another important set of questions. Who can come to defend what you say about nerves and nerve surgery, or just to support your character in general?"

Olevia had been thinking about this for a while now. "You can look for a general surgeon who will say that about 10% of hernia patients develop disabling pain and there so far has been no treatment. He might agree that it made sense to remove the already damaged nerve. You might ask my fellow surgeon, Doctor Jennie Ross, a Gynecologist to testify. I have done this operation now on two of her patients. In each, with the lesson I learned from this first patient, I removed two nerves at surgery, through a new incision, not the original hernia repair incision. Both of these women have each had good relief of their groin pain. You could ask my Department Chairman, Dr. Elijah Willis, he has seemed supportive of me, although I am not sure of what he says or does behind my back. Finally, there is a former classmate of mine from Johns Hopkins Medical School who is out here in Salt Lake City now. His name is Ezra Mabey. He is interested in nerves, although in children, and he could testify perhaps that my examination and thought processes were appropriate to solve this clinical problem." Then she added," there is a chance that some of my research may be published prior to this case going to court, and if that happens, it will give you something to prove my intent to investigate and solve difficult nerve problems."

"Yes, that gives me us a good place to start. One last thing, as I asked you earlier, can you try to get me some illustrations of these nerves?" asked Mr. Greer.

"Yes, I will work on this. I might even have to have someone in the Biology Department draw them," replied Olevia.

"Doctor Landsmann, that is enough for today. I have a lot of work in front of me. Is there anything you would like to ask me?"

"Yes, there is," said Olevia. "Have you done this type of malpractice law before and if so, how successful were you?"

"Good for you Dr. Landsmann. Perfect questions. Yes, I have and I am 4 for 4," answered Mr. Greer smugly. "But," he added, Elam Smith, the Plaintiff's lawyer is older than me, and his record is 10 wins and 2 losses. He makes a lot of money on these types of malpractice cases. My fee, Dr. Landsmann, which you did not ask, is $20 per hour, and I will ask you for a $400 down payment if you don't mind. I promise to work as quickly as I can to minimize your costs."

"Do you have any other questions for me Dr. Landsmann?" Jarvis Greer asked.

"Yes, I do. One last one, although I think I know the answer, I just have to ask."

"Go ahead then," said Jarvis Greer, standing up from behind the conference table. "Ask away!"

"Mr. Jarvis Greer," said Olevia, also standing up, "Are you related to any 'Smiths'?"

"Ha! Ha!, and No, I am not," he replied, escorting Olevia to the conference room door.

PUBLISH

Olevia was standing outside the entrance to the Anatomy Lab. She was waiting for Dr. Parks to arrive. She saw him walking up the pathway to where she was standing. He was tall, slim, had a long white beard and was wearing his usual long white laboratory coat.

"Hello Olevia," said Thomas Parks, PhD, Professor and Director of Anatomy at the University of Utah. "First of all, I must say how sorry, how sorry I was to learn that "The Lord", Mr. Clarke-Smith, our Chairman of the Board here at Salt Lake County General Hospital, has taken away your Surgical privileges. I know that Dr. Willis, the Chief of Surgery, never did give you an office in the Department of Surgery with all those Male Surgeons! It is, however, my honor, my honor to give you an office here in our Department of Anatomy, where you are making so many contributions," he concluded, shaking her hand and giving her a warm smile.

"Thank you for all your many kindnesses, Sir," said Olevia following Dr. Parks down the hallway, and remembering from her first phone conversation with him his proclivity to repeat himself.

"You are welcome," he said, continuing down the hall. "Well, here is where MY office is. My office is right here," he said pointing for emphasis at a huge office. I am hopeful that you have taken time to read all these historical writings on the wall about 'our profession,'" Dr. Parkes said, pointing around him at the walls.

"Oh yes, Sir. Early in my time here, Chipeta, brought me in and introduced me to them. She has a keen mind and great curiosity," replied Olevia.

"Yes, and that is something else remarkable that you did Dr. Landsmann, which I am sure no one knows about. You inspired her to go from a *Janitorial position,* here in our Department of Anatomy to being your Research Assistant, and now, my Gosh, to being a Scrub Tech in the operating room! You are indeed, Olevia, an inspiration, a true inspiration to those who know the real you," complimented Dr. Parks.

"Thank you, Sir. I only wish the Male Surgeons could be as open and free from professional jealousy as you are," Olevia said quietly.

"Well, then, here is room, a small room, but a room, that you can use for your writing," Dr. Parks said, opening a door to a small office near the end of the hall. It looked out upon a brick wall of another building. There was nothing on the walls. There was a small desk and one chair. There was also one filing cabinet.

"Thank you, Sir," said Olevia, "This will be a perfect place for me to write."

"And how have your scientific publications been coming along?" Dr. Parks asked.

"The best news is that the Bulletin of the Johns Hopkins Hospital has finally published my research on nerve implantation into muscle, or '*Gid en Fleish*', as my Father Alexander would say in Yiddish. The publisher just sent me 50 free copies of that article too. I will get one from my house and give it to YOU. You will get the first reprint of the article," Olevia said excitedly.

"How nice, how nice," Dr. Parks answered, "and who else will you give them to? That is important, I believe, for you to do. Not to brag about yourself, although no doubt some of your detractors will take it that way, but to publicize your accomplishments among our staff," he suggested.

"Hmm. Good idea, even from a political point of view. Then I am thinking I will give one to Doctor David J. Grafton, Chief of Medicine and Doctor Elijah Willis, Chief of Surgery, even though I suspect they either will not read it or will just simply tear it up. I will give a copy to my friends Ezra Maybe and Jennie Ross. I will give one to my lawyer Jarvis Greer. And while I am at his office will give one to a patient of mine, who is also a lawyer, Jedediah Smith."

"Sounds like a good starting place. If you will take my suggestion, give one to Doctor Samuel Baldwin, Chief of Orthopedics. I believe he has referred patients to you," said Thomas Parks.

"Yes, thanks, of course, and perhaps I will put one up on the wall of the Surgical and the Wound Clinic where I still see patients," added Olevia.

"And while you are at it with those walls, how about one for the entrance way to our Anatomy Lab and give one to Chipeta," Dr. Parks continued.

"OK, OK, already. I wanted to save a couple for myself!!!!!," Olevia said shyly.

"Now Dr. Landsmann, what are your next publication plans," her Director of Anatomy asked, looking towards the future.

"I am now writing a paper on the innervation of the knee joint. There is a relatively new journal, the Journal of Bone & Joint Surgery," she replied. "Where else do suggest I might submit the article?," Olevia asked thoughtfully.

"I see your reasoning," replied Dr. Parks. "Since you have had one acceptance, and therefore some credibility as a researcher, with the Johns Hopkins Hospital Bulletin, you might try to submit this knee denervation paper to that journal," he concluded.

"Thank you, Dr. Parks," I will try that and maybe they will expedite the publication since there are so many people with knee pain.

"And after that paper, Dr. Landsmann, what is next?" he asked.

"I am sending a paper with Jennie Ross as a co-author. This has the intra-operative photographs of the two patients whose pain has been helped by resecting both of those groin nerves," she replied.

"Great. To which journal will this research be submitted?" he asked.

"This is an easier decision. To the journal, Surgery Gynecology and Obstetrics. As you know, this is a leading journal in surgery, having started in 1905. Best of all, Dr. Harvey Cushing, my mentor, is on its Editorial Board," she replied.

"I am so impressed, Dr. Landsmann. Impressed. Are you tired of this question? 'What is next on your list'?" asked Dr. Parks.

"Ha! Ha! I love writing. Even more than skiing, but ...not as much as operating, Dr. Parks," Olevia replied a little sadly.

"If I had to make a bet, an actual bet, a money bet, I believe your surgical career is just starting," said Thomas Parks, encouragingly. "So, what is next?"

"Next I want to write a paper on the dissections Chipeta and I have done on the yellow color and swelling seen in obese patients in the tibial nerve in the tarsal tunnel. I have found there are really four tunnels to consider for decompression instead of just one. To which journal would you suggest I submit this research?" Olevia asked.

"Hmmm. This research might be published in a Medical journal or even a Pathology journal, instead of a Surgical journal. There is now a lot of interest in diabetes, diabetes," suggested Dr. Parks.

"Thanks, and I know your next question," said Olevia with a smile.

"What is next for you to write up?" complied Dr. Parks.

"Another clinical case in which resecting an injured nerve has been successful at relieving pain," Olevia answered.

"Really? Can you tell me just a little about that one?" Dr. Parks asked.

"Sure, when I was in my Wound Clinic last week, I was so happy to see back a young man whose right wrist was crushed in a mining accident, damaging the nerves to the skin and the joints, giving him a useless and extremely painful hand. He asked for it to be amputated. As you noted earlier, he was sent to me by Dr. Baldwin, in Orthopedics, after the broken bones had healed. In the surgery that I did, I removed the two nerves to the damaged skin and denervated the wrist joint."

"Wow, great. Really Great. Was it the radial sensory and lateral antebrachial cutaneous nerves that you removed?" asked the Professor Anatomy.

"Yes, Professor, and the terminal branches of the posterior interosseous nerve, that innervated the dorsal wrist capsule," Olevia added.

"You MUST write that case up. Write it up right away. No one even knows there are nerves to those joints," stated Dr. Parks.

"Sir, if you permit me one correction? The man who did the PROSECTION you have hung on the wall in the Hospital on the way to the Surgery Clinics knew of these nerves. He may have been the first to demonstrate them in a prosection. If you look carefully at Harold, you will see these little nerves to the joints of the wrist, as well as the nerves to the knee joint," stated Olevia.

"Really? Then I must go and have another look in more detail at Harold," here Dr. Parks paused, as if sensing that something special was going to happen. "Olevia," he continued after the pause, "that PROSECTION was done by Albert Landsmann. I have often wondered if you two might be related." Surmised Dr. Parks.

"Yes, Sir. Albert Landsmann is, or was, my Uncle Albert," she answered.

"Oh my Gosh. My Gosh," said Dr. Parks, "I should have known. Perhaps skill at prosecting may prove to be an inherited trait."

"Thank you for that compliment, Dr. Park. Now, to get back to the final paper I am working on for publication, the miner with the painful wrist and joint problem. This was the same problem, by the way, that my Uncle Albert had. It was the problem he was trying to solve when he operated on himself. As you know, he died trying!"

"Such a shame. A shame. So how did that patient do when you saw him back in your Clinic?" asked Dr. Parks.

"He did great. I had a photographer meet me in Clinic at the 6th post-operative week. She took pictures of him touching the injured right forearm with his left hand and smiling. Then she had him photographed while making the hitch-hiking sign with both hands at the same, as this demonstrated the ability for joint movement. She then photographed him again flexing and extending both wrists, which he could now do equally well," Olevia concluded.

"What will he do now Dr. Landsmann?" Dr. Parks inquired.

"I have given him permission to return to work at light duty in the mine, but only AFTER he returned to see Dr. Samuel Baldwin, to demonstrate to the Orthopedic Surgeons that he had been helped greatly both in terms of pain and hand function," she replied feeling quite proud of herself.

"And where will you submit this paper for publication?" asked Dr. Park.

LANCINATE LIGAMENT

Olevia was still allowed to operate on the Dead.

Even though Jared Benson was dead, still she was getting sued by him, or at least by his family. This was strange. She wondered if the lawyers would even figure out a way for the relatives of a cadaver to sue the prosector!

As Olevia walked into the Anatomy Lab, she thought, "Uncle Albert had an *opus magnum*. What would hers be? *The relationship of nerve compression to diabetic symptoms.' A great place to start*, she thought.

Olevia remembered back to that day in medical school at Johns Hopkins when she and Ezra "kicked the bucket" together. She was Dr. Watson. He was Sherlock Holmes. They made a critical observation. But both had been too busy doing their medical schoolwork, to follow up on the relationship of nerves in the diabetic patient to diabetic foot symptoms, and subsequent ulceration and amputation. She saw too many amputations in her Wound Clinic and Surgical Clinic.

"Hello Doctor Landsmann," greeted her secret research assistant and friend, Chipeta.

"Hello Chipeta," said Olevia. I am so glad you have enough energy to come and help me today. Did you have any trouble getting time off from the Operating Room to come and help me with this research?"

"No problem, Doctor. This is how we learn the secrets from the departed to help the living who visit us in the operating room," Chipeta replied philosophically.

"Chipeta, today I need your special knowledge of these cadavers" said Olevia. "I am interested to learn if I can find tightness around a nerve at the ankle, the tibial nerve on the inside, or medial side of the ankle. Today we are going to do an experiment, and I need your help," said Olevia.

"Yes, Doctor. What do you need me to do?" she said smiling.

"Chipeta, my hypothesis, my theory is that the nerve at the inside of the ankle goes through some tunnels. If a person has been injured, the nerve might be tight in the scarred tunnel. If the person had a disease, like diabetes, that might affect the nerve, then the nerve might be a different color than it is in the non-diabetic, where the nerve is usually white," explained Olevia.

"What do I have to do to help you," asked Chipeta.

"Chipeta, I want you to uncover every cadaver in the room. And YOU decide, not me, if you see signs of the ankle having been injured, like scars on the skin, or the foot at a funny angle. I want you to see which cadavers are fat, because the fat ones might have had diabetes, compared to the skinny cadavers. Then I want you to write down what you think the color of each tibial nerve is within the tarsal tunnel, because you have excellent eyes and are very good with colors," said Olevia.

"And what are you going to do Doctor, while I am working so hard?" Chipeta said jokingly and with a smile.

"The Anatomy books show this tibial nerve going through just one tunnel, covered with a ligament, called the lancinate ligament. From my preliminary prosections, I believe that there are many more tunnels in this location. I want to describe them and see how they might cause pressure on the nerves to give pain in the feet," answered Olevia.

"Doctor, this sounds too easy. How can research be so easy?" asked Chipeta.

"There is still so much to learn from the human body. The research does not have to be difficult. We just must be clever enough to ask the right questions of the dead. Perhaps they will give us the answers we need," concluded Olevia.

Chipeta began immediately to remove the covers from each cadaver. She took a paper towel the students used to dry the formaldehyde, and put it on the fat cadavers, and the ones whose feet had ulcers or amputations, to mark them for Olevia.

Olevia just took the nearest skinny cadaver and began to dissect the tibial nerve, starting just above the ankle, and following the nerves down into the foot.

Chipeta finished her job and came over to watch Olevia. "What have you found so far?" she asked the Doctor.

"Well, this seems all too simple, as you said," replied Olevia. "Look, Chipeta, here is the tarsal tunnel, one big tunnel, quite loose, with the important tibial artery and its two veins, and here is the rounded tibial nerve, under no pressure. But look here as the nerve starts to go into the bottom of the foot, it splits and goes through two new tunnels, and these are quite tight. And here is another little tunnel with this little nerve to the heel."

"Dr. Landsman, so there are four tunnels not one?" Chipeta asked.

"Yes Chipeta. And what color do you say this nerve is?" asked Olevia.

"Well, sort of white. Some brownish discoloration, from the formaldehyde. Whitish-brown I must say," concluded Chipeta.

"Ok, good. Now let us see one of the cadavers without a toe or with an ulcer. Did you find any Chipeta?" asked Olevia.

"Yes, I did. This fat cadaver down in this corner, is like that," said Chipeta leading the way.

"Now you observe while I dissect," said Olevia, bringing her dissecting instruments down near the ankle.

"Doctor," said Chipeta. "I can see already this nerve is much bigger, swollen almost compared to the last nerve."

"What else do you see Chipeta," said Olevia opening another tunnel, more down towards the foot.

"The nerve is a different color, and that nerve is very swollen just going into that tight tunnel," observed Chipeta.

"Yes, I agree," said Olevia. "And how would you describe the color of this swollen nerve, Chipeta?" asked Olevia.

"More yellow. Almost like the nerve is full of fat," replied Chipeta.

"I agree with your observation," said Olevia, smiling at Chipeta.

"What does it mean Doctor?" asked Chipeta.

"Well, I will tell you that after we do this to all the rest of the cadavers in this room, making notes as you have done as to which cadavers are fat, which are missing toes, and the color of their nerves," said Olevia.

"Oh my, Doctor, a lot more work, and I have already been cleaning for hours," said Chipeta, trying not to complain.

"Yes, lots of work. Fortunately, we have all night and nowhere else to go!" said Olevia.

"Oh Doctor, this research is exciting, but tiring," Chipeta said as she went off to get the next cadaver ready for the Doctor.

"Chipeta! When we are done with this research, I am going to write a report for the scientific literature. You are going to be named as a co-author. You will be the first Ute Nation person to be published in the scientific literature.

"I am just happy to help you, Doctor. But thank you. It will be a big honor for my People," said Chipeta as she got back to work.

DEPOSITION

"Dr. Landsman, I am Elam Smith, the lawyer representing the deceased and his family. You are here today to give testimony in this matter. We have to your left the court reporter, who will record everything we say, so speak slowly. She may need to ask you how to spell certain medical terms at the end of the deposition. If at any time I say something that is not clear to you, please do not hesitate to ask me to repeat it. Please do not reply by nodding or shaking your head, as a verbal response is required. Do you understand?" asked Elam Smith, Esquire.

"Yes," said Olevia. She had been instructed by her lawyer, Mr. Greer, to answer with the shortest possible, yet complete answer and to give no information that was not directly asked of her.

"Dr. Landsmann," commanded the court reporter. "Please stand. Raise your right hand. Do you solemnly swear to state the whole truth and nothing but the truth, so help you God?"

"I do," answered Olevia, wearing a long skirt, white blouse, a man's style jacket, and no make up. She wore flat simple shoes and her one piece of jewelry, her watch.

"Dr. Landsmann, Please tell me your relationship with Dr. Ephraim G. Gowans," asked Mr. Smith.

"I did not have a relationship with Dr. Gowans. He was the first Chairman of Anatomy at the University of Utah. He died shortly before I arrived here," she answered, and realized that she had given too long an answer.

"Then whom did you relate to in the Anatomy Lab?" Mr. Smith asked.

"Professor Thomas Parks," Olevia answered exactly to the point.

"Dr. Landsmann, Please tell me about your relationship with Ezra Maybe, MD," asked Mr. Smith.

"He and I went to the same medical school, and we were in the same class," she answered.

"Dr. Landsmann, Please tell me about your relationship with Jennie Ross, MD," asked Mr. Smith.

"She is a Woman Surgeon, a colleague of mine at the Salt Lake County General Hospital," she answered.

"Dr. Landsmann, Please tell me about your relationship with ....:

And this continued on and on, Olevia, thought, until there was no one left that she knew in Salt Lake City, that Mr. Elam Smith did not ask her about.

"Doctor Landsmann," Mr. Smith now began in earnest, is it true that you practice surgery at Salt Lake County General Hospital?"

"Yes," Olevia answered.

"Doctor Landsmann," he asked next, "is it true that you never did a formal surgery residency training?"

"Yes, however I did spend a great deal of time in surgery working with two of the greatest Surgeons of our time" Olevia replied. She could already see where this was going.

"Doctor Landsmann was that time you spent observing in surgery considered by your teachers as a formal residency at the Johns Hopkins Hospital?" asked Elam Smith in rebuttal.

"It was not considered a formal residency," she answered truthfully.

"Doctor Landsmann is it true that you operated on the deceased, Jared Benson?"

"I do not understand your question, Mr. Smith," she answered. "I operate on living people. I dissect dead people," she continued, again realizing that she was talking too much.

"Dr. Landsmann, I am sorry for the confusion my question caused you. Did you operate upon Mr. Jared Benson, while he was still alive?" Mr. Smith now asked.

"Yes," answered Olevia, succinctly.

"Dr. Landsmann," is it true that you, a doctor who never trained in surgery, did an operation that has never been done before on Mr. Jared Benson?"

"Yes," it is true," Olevia answered, becoming now actually distressed. Her own lawyer, Mr. Greer was sitting right next to her. Shouldn't he object or something on her behalf?

"Dr. Landsmann," is it true that you, a doctor without formal surgery training, did an operation that had never been done before, and following that operation, that patient of yours, Mr. Jared Benson, took his own life due to the severity of his persisting, unrelieved pain?"

Now Olevia saw some light. "It is true that he took his own life," she answered, "but we do not know why he took his own life."

"Dr. Landsmann, you have been instructed just to answer the question, not to ask me questions," he said bullying her. There was a pause as Mr. Smith considered his next question.

"Dr. Landsmann, is there any witness who can corroborate that you say my client, my deceased client, your dead patient, Mr. Jared Benson, gave you permission to do this surgery?" Mr. Smith then asked.

"No there is not. We were in the examination room when we had this discussion,. There were no witnesses," Olevia answered honestly.

"Dr. Landsmann, is it true that you never told this man that you had never done this surgery before?" went on Mr. Smith.

"Yes," sighed Olevia.

"Dr. Landsmann, did you tell your patient the risks of the procedure including failure?"

"No," replied Olevia, thinking, *If I ever do get to operate again, I am going to have a witness with me and write down these risks.*

"Dr. Landsmann, would you agree with me that your surgery was a failure?"

"Yes," Olevia said quietly.

"Dr. Landsmann, speak up, the court reporter could hardly hear you," Mr. Smith said quickly. "Was your surgery a FAILURE Dr. Landsmann?"

"YES, it was," Olevia answered, louder this time.

"Dr. Landsmann," Mr. Smith was getting ready to ask another question, and looked down at his notes.

Olevia thought to herself, "I never thought I would get so sick of hearing my name spoken."

"Dr. Landsmann, is it true that you do not operate any more?"

"I object to that line of questioning," said her lawyer, Jarvis Greer."

"He is finally speaking up for me," Olevia thought to herself.

"You can object if you wish Mr. Greer. This line of questioning goes to whether Dr. Landsmann has remained in good Medical Standing in her own medical community, and I submit the Judge would allow the question.

"Dr. Landsmann," Mr. Greer looked at his own client now, and counseled quite sternly, "Mr. Smith asked you a "yes" or "no" question, Dr. Landsmann, which you may answer, "yes" or "no"."

Sensing that somehow this question had some deeper meaning than she could perceive at present, Olevia asked, "Mr. Smith, can you repeat the question please."

"Certainly, Doctor. Let me ask a different question first, to better lay the groundwork for my question to which Mr. Greer objected just now."

Mr. Smith, thought for a brief minute, and then resumed. "Dr. Landsmann, is it true that your surgical privileges have been suspended at Salt Lake County General Hospital pending a review of your clinic and operative records?"

Mr. Greer stood to say something, and then sat down. Looking at Olevia, apparently this was surprise information to him.

Olevia looked at Mr. Greer, and said "Yes, that is true."

The deposition went on for another half hour. Mr. Smith went through her educational background, why she left Germany. "Did you leave Germany because you weren't good enough to get into the Ludwig-Maximillian University?" he even asked. He questioned her about how she could do research on animals. He asked, "Didn't animals have feelings. Don't animals suffer too?"

Mr. Elam Smith even got into accusations of drug abuse, by asking, "Dr. Landsmann, you studied at Johns Hopkins Hospital, where Dr. Halsted, formerly from New York City, taught. It is well known that Dr. Halsted, while in New York City, introduced cocaine as a local anesthetic. Do you know of his work with cocaine, Dr. Landsmann," Mr. Smith asked?

"Yes, I do," answered Olevia truthfully.

Dr. Landsmann, I now show you and put into evidence, this published paper of YOUR teacher, Dr. Halsted. Do you recognize this published paper Dr. Landsmann?" Mr. Smith asked, shoving some printed material stapled together at the upper left hand corner.

"Yes, I do," she said, after reading the title, which was, "Practical Comments on the Use and Abuse of Cocaine," authored by William S. Halsted, and published in The New York Medical Journal, 1885, page 284."

Dr. Landsmann, do you use local anesthetics?" Mr. Smith said suddenly.

"Yes, I do," answered Olevia truthfully.

"Dr. Landsmann, are you addicted to cocaine?" Mr. Smith asked.

"No, I am not addicted to anything, and I use no medication at all," Olevia answered, giving her longest reply. She saw her lawyer, Jarvis Greer, look up at her reprovingly. She again had given too long an answer.

"Dr. Landsmann," Mr. Smith continued relentlessly, "Are there scientific writings you will rely upon in the opinions you have expressed today?"

Olevia was ready for this question. Her lawyer, Mr. Greer, told her this question would be coming and if she did not get this information in now, into the record, it could not be introduced later in the trial unless someone else introduced it. She knew she was not allowed to say more than "yes" and "no."

"Dr. Landsmann, your answer please," Mr. Smith badgered her.

"Yes, there are, Sir," Olevia began her response, feeling tired now, "They are the scientific paper published by William S. Halsted, in 1889, titled "The Radical Cure of Hernia", published in the Bulletin of the Johns Hopkins Hospital, and, also, the Gray's Anatomy Textbook."

Mr. Smith pursued this, with "Any other materials or illustrations, Dr. Landsmann?"

"Yes. There is an illustration from an anatomy paper on the innervation of the groin, in humans, that has been prepared for submission to a journal. There is also a research paper that has been submitted to a journal related to the management of a painful nerve. Finally, there is a manuscript in preparation related to the treatment of the painful scar after hysterectomy," Olevia concluded.

"Very well then, Dr. Landsmann, I will expect Mr. Greer to get photocopies of those texts and illustrations and papers to me as soon as possible," said Mr. Smith looking at Mr. Greer.

"We will copy those critical parts and deliver them to you Mr. Smith, within the next two weeks," said Mr. Greer.

And then, just like that, Mr. Smith stopped calling her name.

The deposition was over.

Olevia, walked out quietly with her lawyer.

"Dr. Landsmann, you did an excellent job in there. How do you feel?" asked Jarvis Greer, in a supportive tone.

"How do I feel, Mr. Greer? I feel assaulted. Worse. Violated! Nothing about my life is private. That Smith lawyer could expose any part of me he wished," answered Olevia, angrily. Clearly being happy she could now talk again in complete sentences and say whatever she wished.

"Yes, I know. The usual reaction from a Doctor being deposed for the first time," replied Jarvis Greer, Esq. "Doctor, if you would not mind, I would like to review some of that deposition with you now in my office," stated her lawyer.

"With all due respect Mr. Greer, I have just had just had all the lawyer questions and beatings I can deal with for one day. And this was in private. I do not know how I will be able to do this again in public, in front of Jury of My Peers, what ever that means. And in public in front of whatever friends I have left. I apologize. I am going home," Olevia said, apologetically, and left.

S G & O

DURING THE MONTH AFTER that deposition, Olevia met with her lawyer, Jarvis Greer, every week. He went through her "temporary" loss of operating room privileges at the Salt Lake County General Hospital. He offered to intervene legally in this matter if she wanted him to do so. They decided together to wait and see what happened. If the Committee investigating her recommended formal loss of privileges, then Mr. Greer said he could appeal and file a Civil Lawsuit against the hospital.

Olevia just felt she was getting deeper and deeper into legal troubles. If nothing else, she would run out of money soon. She would have to start taking money from the funds that her Father Alexander had left to her. She did not want to use those funds. They were for an emergency. But if she could not operate, she could not earn a living as a surgeon here in Utah. That would be an emergency!

She did not want to earn her living changing bandages in a Wound Clinic and telling people in pain that there was no hope for them. She wanted to go back to relieving pain by removing the nerves that were changing these patient's lives.

She could now, in a strange way, relate the pain in her life caused by legal matters, to the pain in the lives of patients, where that pain changed their lives.

She knew her research and clinical translation of that new knowledge into patient care could change and improve lives everywhere. To do that, she needed to operate again. Furthermore, she needed to be in a position where she could train other doctors to do the operations that she invented.

Olevia had calculated that if she was the only one doing the surgery to treat patients in pain, then only so many patients could be helped. If she trained ten surgeons how to do the surgery, and they each trained ten more surgeons, then thousands of lives could be changed. This was now her vision.

Meantime, she was in the Anatomy Lab, and she was writing. She was also waiting, and checking her mail each day.

Then good news finally arrived. The journal Surgery Gynecology & Obstetrics sent her a letter. It was written by Harvey Cushing, MD, Assistant Editor for the journal, SG&O. It read,

"Dear Doctor Landsmann, The Editorial Board of SG & O, upon review of your clinical report, has determined to accept your paper for publication. Please find enclosed your manuscript, which needs a few corrections as noted by my hand writing in the margins. Once you have sent this manuscript back to us, we deem it of sufficient importance to our readers that we will place it into the next issue of SG & O., sincerely,

Harvey Cushing, MD, Professor of Surgery at Harvard Medical School, Boston, Massachusetts."

Olevia had been following the progress of her mentor, Dr. Cushing. After he successfully proved that he could operate to remove brain tumors of the pituitary gland, he was able to show that this gland secreted a hormone, which he called "growth hormone." Too much growth hormone, and a person became a giant. Too little and the person did not grow, and the person became a dwarf, or just a short person. For these accomplishments, Cushing was already being acclaimed, not only as the first Neurosurgeon and the Father of Neurosurgery, but also as the first surgeon to start a whole new Medical field, Endocrinology, the study of hormones secreted in the human body. Cushing left Johns Hopkins Hospital at that point in time and moved to Harvard University and the Massachusetts General Hospital, in Boston.

Olevia knew that she would treasure this letter of acceptance for the rest of her life. She would have it framed. Maybe she would even bring it to court to be used as an exhibit! That is, if her lawyer agreed. There were so many rules as to what could be admitted as "evidence".

Olevia got out her writing tools and new paper and set about making the changes required of her newly accepted paper, entitled,

"Relief of Post-hysterectomy Scar Pain by Resection of both the Ilioinguinal and Iliohypogastric Nerves," authored by Olevia Landsmann, MD and Jennie Ross, MD, from the University of Utah School of Medicine, Salt Lake City, Utah.

At least she could still write University of Utah as her address. The University of Utah had not kicked her out, yet.

As she looked at her paper one more time, she smiled at how short the bibliography was. Three references. One to Gray's Anatomy, on the ilioinguinal nerve. One to the textbook *Operative Gynecology* written by her Hopkins Gynecology Professor, Howard A. Kelly, MD, on the approach used for hysterectomy. And her very own first paper, "Implantation of Sensory Nerve into Muscle Prevents Painful Neuroma; Result in the Canine Forelimb," by Olevia Landsmann, MD, David Siler, BA, and Harvey Cushing, MD, published in the Bulletin of the Johns Hopkins Hospital.

She smiled again. The Bulletin of the Johns Hopkins Hospital. William Stewart Halsted was one of its editors and had personally written the letter of acceptance to her for this paper. That letter was framed already, and on her wall at home.

THE LORD

"Dr. Landsmann," I have some important new information, about your case," said Jarvis Greer, Esquire, as Olevia entered the glass enclosed conference room in the law offices.

Olevia was more relaxed today and wore a springtime colorful dress. On the advice "of counsel", she had let her hair grow longer, and it was almost down to her shoulders. Mr. Greer said this would make her look more "sympathetic and appealing" to the members of Jury when the time came.

Mr. Greer handed Olevia some papers to read, and asked, "What do you think of the Mom and Dad's answers to me regarding their son Jared Benson's state of mind before you operated on him?"

Just then, Jedediah Smith walked by the glass window, looked in and waved. Then he knocked and stuck his head in the door. "You know I am a Lawyer named "Smith", but I am not spying," he said. "Just wanted to say hello and say to my Doctor how nice it is to see you wearing something colorful." And then he was gone.

Olevia just could not help herself. She smiled, gave a little wave to Jed, and blushed.

Jarvis Greer, Esq, now somewhat annoyed, repeated, "What do you think of the Mom and Dad's answers to me regarding their son's state of mind before you operated on him?"

"As a Doctor, but knowing I am not a Psychiatrist, I would say Mr. Benson's answers are those of someone depressed. If he has to live with pain and give up his wife and children, due to being out of work, lack of sex, and his wife constantly asking him when he was going to get better, then Mr Benson did not wish to continue to live. Mr. Benson's parents' testimony proves how badly he was hurting, and, as he viewed his life, he had no choice left but to end it. The parents even admit that he asked them if they would look after his family if something were to happen to him."

"I agree with you exactly," said Jarvis Greer, Esquire. "What this means in legal terms is that you can not be found guilty for "causation," his pain was there before you operated on him. You did not increase his damaged condition. You did not improve it. You did not worsen it, so even if found "guilty," there are no damages. You might get asked to pay funeral expenses," said Mr. Greer dryly, but with a smile.

Olevia saw now that Mr. Greer's plan was to turn the parents' testimony in favor of the Defense.

"What is my biggest weakness in this case, as you view it?" Olevia bravely asked.

"It is not what you think, Olevia. I am most concerned about these nebulous charges that seem to have been trumped up by a group of men who are jealous of your early success, and fearful of where your success might lead," Mr. Greer said.

"You are talking about the Hospital Special Committee investigation into "unnecessary surgery," being carried out at Salt Lake County General Hospital," Olevia said, seeing his point immediately.

"Yes Olevia. Even if they have not decided against you, just the knowledge of that hanging in the air will convince the Jury that you are a "bad doctor". The Jury of your Peers has nothing to do with your peers in practical reality. Your true peers are people like Ezra Maybe, MD. Dr. Landsmann, you truly have few peers. While I am worried that Ezra will be a serious witness against you, according to his deposition, I believe I have developed a strategy for him when I get to cross-examine him on the witness stand. However, Olevia, we must bring this "Investigation" by the "Committee" at the hospital to a close immediately."

Olevia looked at him. Constantly amazed at the turns and twists within the legal system, and how clever the best lawyer had to be to win. A Lawsuit was a game, and who ever knew the rules best, would win. Whoever had the best Lawyer would win.

"OK," said Olevia, "I follow that logic, but how can I do anything to move the Hospital investigation along?"

"Surprise, Doctor," said Mr. Greer with a grin. We have a meeting in half an hour with 'The Lord'."

Mr. Greer stood up and opened the door for Olevia.

With her mouth still open, Olevia got up and followed Mr. Greer down to a waiting taxi.

The taxi drove them both to the Salt Lake County General Hospital. They exited the taxi, entered the Hospital, and took the elevator to the top floor. They walked down a long corridor coming to a large conference room at the end of the hall. The sign on over the door said Wasatch Conference Room. On the door hung a sign, "This room reserved 2 to 4 PM, Chairman of the Board of Trustees, conference."

Mr. Greer knocked on the door.

"Come in," said a deep, strong voice." The voice of 'The Lord'.

"Best wishes to you Mr. Clarke-Smith," said Mr. Greer, extending his hand.

"Pleasure to see you again Mr. Greer," said the tall man, with grey hair, standing, partly blocking the breath-taking view of the Wasatch Mountain Range, which was seen through the large window behind him. This was Gary Lord Clarke-Smith, Esq., the current patriarch of the Smith Family Law Firm, Chairman of the Board of Trustees of the Salt Lake County General Hospital, a High Priest in The Church of Jesus Christ of Latter-Day Saints. He had an impressive grey beard.

"The Lord" turned and looked down upon Olevia. He was at least a head taller than she was.

"It is a pleasure to meet you finally," said The Lord, stepping slowly from the window towards Olevia.

"Sir, first, let me thank you for your initial support of my application to join the Anatomy staff of the University of Utah, and for my Hospital privileges here at your hospital," Olevia said humbly, looking up at him, holding her ground.

Now the Doctor part of her observed the Chairman of the Board walk towards her. He walked slowly. His feet were slightly spread apart. And, considering how well he was dressed, his shoes were strange, sort of square shaped at the tip and they appeared soft, not made from shiny leather, as she would have expected.

"Oh no," she said to herself. "Sherlock Holmes and Watson have no place in this Board Room today. Or do they?" Then her thoughts were interrupted.

"You are most welcome, and those honors seemed deserved at the time and were championed by Doctor Thomas Parks in the Anatomy Lab, who surely needed your help and who continues to send glowing reports. Please, both of you have a seat," he said as he took the large chair at the head of the table, with the Wasatch Range behind him.

"Mr. Greer, you requested this meeting. The floor is yours Sir," said the Lord.

"Thank you. The Committee investigating my client, Doctor Landsmann, the Committee chaired by Dr. David J. Grafton, Chief of Medicine, has had 3 months to review just a hand full or so of short medical records. The loss of operating room privileges is preventing many patients in pain from getting the care they need at YOUR hospital. There is no one else on the staff, even on the whole West Coast, who is qualified to help these patients whose care is entrusted to your hospital. Given this situation, and the fact that my client has been denied even seeing the name of one person who has accused her, I am here to ask, under the "due process of law", that you request a committee report from Dr. Grafton. If the Committee is done with its investigation, then we need to know the results," Mr. Greer said, completing his opening remarks.

"Mr. Greer, of course I understand your position and your very reasonable request. Indeed, in preparation for this meeting, which, truthfully could be about only one or two things, the Investigation you mentioned, or the Lawsuit against the good Doctor Landsmann, I made inquiries of the Committee," responded the Lord, shrewdly.

"Thank you, Sir, and pray tell us, what did you learn from the Committee?" asked Mr. Greer, most politely.

"Doctor Landsmann, I am happy to inform you that the Committee actually found your charts were better documented than a similar set of charts from surgeons from the same time frame at our Hospital," the Lord said, smiling weakly.

Before Olevia could even begin to reply, Jarvis Greer, Esquire quickly said, "Mr. Clarke-Smith, that is welcome news. May I assume, then you will issue a letter to Dr. Landsmann that her operating privileges have been restored, and that no issues remain under investigation?" asked Mr. Greer hopefully.

"Well, not exactly so. There are still concerns voiced about Dr. Landsmann's doing unnecessary surgery," The Lord said, going back to his position of authority. "And you must remember Sir, that while you and your client may view me as preventing her from giving care to those in need of whatever her "unique" skills are, I also must uphold my fiduciary trust responsibilities to see that no harm comes to the patients of our great hospital."

"Mr. Clarke-Smith, am I to understand that based on complaints that we can not be allowed to learn, you will continue to hold my client in a position of punishment?" questioned Mr. Greer.

"Yes, that is one way to express what is still going on," said The Lord now trying to appear beneficent.

"Then Sir, I must tell you my next intent. First, I have prepared a lawsuit, and it will be filed within 48 hours if we do not get a clear letter restoring my client's operating privileges and freeing her from all investigations of this Committee. The lawsuit accuses you personally, and Salt Lake County General Hospital, of failure to grant "due process" to my client. Even in Utah, Sir, a person is required to receive due process under the Law, as you well know."

"Mr. Greer, of course you may institute as many lawsuits as you wish. You are *still* a lawyer in good standing in our state of Utah," said The Lord, almost threateningly.

"Mr. Clarke-Smith," said Mr. Greer, undeterred, "It is also my understanding that you are close friends with Elijah Willis, MD, Chief of Surgery, who feels, apparently, threatened by this new Woman Surgeon on his staff and is looking for a way to end this threat. Through the collusion of Dr. Willis, Chief of Surgery, and your other close friend David J. Grafton, MD, Chief of Medicine, you have concocted these charges from "unknown" persons. The lawsuit will also allege "restraint of trade".

The Lord now interrupted. "That is simply preposterous, and threats will not be tolerated."

"It is not a threat, I assure you, Sir. The papers are right here in my briefcase, ready to be filed, depending upon the outcome of this meeting, and now, please, let me tell you the second part of what I came to disclose to you," said Mr. Greer in a very quiet but persuasive tone.

The Lord was quiet, but attentive.

"You, yourself, just mentioned the malpractice action going on against Dr. Landsmann. That malpractice case is being prosecuted by your Grandson, Mr. Elam Smith. Mr. Elam Smith somehow knows about your Hospital Committee's confidential investigation because he brought it up during his deposition of Dr. Landsmann. Now, how would he learn about such an "internal" hospital investigation? Furthermore, Mr. Elam Smith, plans to use a Doctor Ezra Mabey as a star witness against my client, as evidenced from a recent discovery deposition we had. Now I know, and you know, Mr. Clarke-Smith, that despite Dr. Mabey's last name, he is married to your grand daughter, the cousin of Elam Smith," said Mr. Greer.

"Where is all this going, this family tree business, Mr. Greer, really," said The Lord.

"This family tree business means, Mr. Clarke-Smith, if you will remember your legal background, that Mr. Elam should have recused himself from this case. My plan will be to lay out your entire family tree and collusion in an attempt to win a monetary award for your Grandson, and to placate the "Old Guard" on your hospital staff without regard to one new staff members' integrity, and her desire to improve the management of difficult pain problems. I will lead, personally, the call for your resignation from the Board of Trustees of this Hospital, and for a mistrial of the malpractice suit being prosecuted by your Grandson," said Mr. Greer.

The Board Room was silent for quite a while.

Mr. Clarke-Smith was thinking. "Elam certainly should have known better, why that youngster is just getting too greedy. Though I must say there are so many Smiths now it is truly hard to know when one is required to recuse himself. The Lord smiled inwardly. On the other point, being a High Priest in the Church, he had come to learn that miracles were happening through medical research at the University of Utah. Research was the future of Medicine. Those Old Timers on the staff are just having a hard time adjusting to change. Heck even he was having a hard time adjusting. Maybe he was just getting too soft in his old age, although he quickly rejected that later thought.

Then The Lord stood up. "You will have a letter in your hands within 48 hours restoring Dr. Landsmann's operating room privileges," said the Lord.

JUDGEMENT

"All rise," called the courtroom Bailiff.

Olevia stood and inwardly smiled, as one of her self-defense mechanisms came into play, a retreat into academic knowledge. "Bailiff" from the Latin, *bajulus,* to oversee or manage, as in today's Courtroom affairs.

"The Honorable Judge Fletcher Weber, presiding," continued the Bailiff.

Once the Judge, in his black robe, took his seat, the assembled people in the courtroom also took their seats.

The Judge then said, "In the matter of 'The Deceased, Jared Benson and Benson Family versus Olevia Landsmann, MD', will the attorney's representing both parties approach the bench."

Olevia watched as Elam Smith, Esq representing her deceased patient, and Jarvis Greer, Esq, her lawyer walked up to the "bench" in front of the Judge. Olevia observed the three men, huddled together whispering for a while. She assumed they were getting some early legal maneuvering organized.

Olevia was left sitting by herself on the right side of the courtroom, as she faced the "bench", while an older couple, the deceased's Father and Mother, sat on the left side at a table, like hers. They looked at her, giving her very incriminating, cold stares. Their looks seemed to say, "You killed our son!" Olevia glanced away and turned her head slightly so she could see behind her, the right side of the isle, the Defendant's side of the courtroom.

She saw three women seated closely together, and recognized Dr. Jennie Ross and two of Jennie's patients, each of whom, Olevia had operated upon. She recognized Martha Pratt but could not remember the other woman's name. "Maybe I am under more stress than I realize," Olevia thought to herself. The three women sitting behind Olevia smiled encouragement to her. Olevia breathed a little sigh of relief. At least there were some people here on "her side" of the isle.

She could not turn her head further without being too obvious. The jury was sitting on the left side, all facing her, and many were now observing her. Jarvis Greer, Esq. told her that the Jury would be watching her intently. Olevia was supposed to appear interested, make no facial grimaces or smiles, always appear serious, and to look straight ahead!

Olevia could not help herself. She was just too curious. She now turned her head to the left, the left side of the isle, the Plaintiff's side. She was startled to see a tall, handsome man walk briskly down the outside of the isle, as if he were late, and take a seat on that left side. Briefly he looked over at her. It was Jedediah. He smiled and winked, and then sat down on the Plaintiff's side of the isle. "Oh well," thought, Olevia, "he is a "Smith" by blood, anyway. "

Then, she sat up a little straighter to see better. Jedediah sat down next to another tall man. An older man. A man with a long beard. He sat down next to his Grandfather, The Lord, Gary Lord Clarke-Smith, Esquire.

As her gaze was returning towards the Jury Box, her vision caught a glimpse of red. Red hair. "Oh no, she thought, recognizing Ezra Mabey, MD. He was on the Plaintiff's side too. She hoped he would testify in her behalf. He was NOT looking in her direction. *Oh well*, thought Olevia, *He is a 'Smith' by marriage, now, anyway. And a "Neurologist.* Olevia turned to face forward as she sensed movement in the courtroom.

The lawyers left the bench and returned to their seats. Judge Fletcher Weber then said, "The Trial will begin with opening arguments, with Mr. Smith, for the Plaintiff, going first."

Mr. Elam Smith arose and walked directly to the jury. He spoke slowly, looking directly into the eyes of the 10 men and 2 women seated there. Olevia noted that all twelve of the jurors appeared somewhat similar, blond or brown hair, well groomed, men with beards, sitting up straight, attentive. Probably most of them were members of The Church of Jesus Christ of Latter-Day Saints, as was her deceased patient, a Mormon.

"Members of the Jury, I represent the deceased and his family. This trial, this case, is brought before you for you to determine whether Dr.

Landsmann, the *Woman* you see seated at the defendant's table over there," he said turning and pointing an accusing finger at Olevia, "that Doctor Landsmann, who had a moral commitment "to do no harm" to her patient, Jared Benson, as stated in the Hippocratic Oath, which every Medical Doctor takes upon graduation, which Dr. Landsmann did take. That Dr. Landsmann had the moral imperative "to do no harm", and yet she did do harm. Irreparable Harm. We will prove to you that Dr. Landsmann did knowingly and deliberately violate the standard of care of a Doctor for her Patient. We will prove to you that Dr. Landsmann performed investigational and experimental surgery on her patient, Jared Benson, the deceased, just as she had done in the past on her experimental animals, Dogs. Dr. Landsman, the Plaintiff will prove, had some training in Dog Surgery, but no actual training as a Surgeon of People. She will testify herself, that she did NOT do a Surgical Residency Training."

Here Elam Smith, Esquire, paused for effect. Then, he continued, "As a direct result of Dr. Landsmann's experimental surgery, *HER* patient, Jared Benson, had such severe and incapacitating pain, that he took his own life. In doing so, and as a direct result of Dr. Landsmann's negligence, he left his wife and 5 little children destitute. We ask that you bring forth a verdict of "Guilty", and find for the Plaintiff, the deceased Jared Benson, and the deceased's family, the Benson Family. In doing so, we ask that you give an appropriate monetary award to satisfy the damages that Dr. Landsmann caused. A monetary award that must consider Mr. Benson's young age at the time of his death, and the money required to raise and to educate his 5 children. Thank you, members of the Jury." Mr. Elam Smith then walked back to his seat, and quietly sat down.

Olevia mentally crawled under the table at which she was sitting, crawled into a little ball. She seemed doomed.

Olevia heard, as if from a distant voice, "The Defense may proceed with its opening argument to the Jury."

Mr. Greer got up from his seat next to Olevia and approached the jurors. "Members of the Jury, I am Jarvis Greer, the attorney representing Dr. Landsmann," Olevia heard, still as if from afar. She was still mentally curled into a protective little ball.

"The Defense will prove to you that the deceased, Mr. Jared Benson, had a complication that occurs to about 10% of men who have a hernia operation. Pain in the groin. To many of these men, their hernia is fixed, but they remain disabled, unable to work or have relations with their wives, or even to play with their children related to pain. This is what happened to the deceased, who was Dr. Landsmann's patient. Dr. Landsmann did not cause the pain that caused her patient to take his own life. It is true, that Jared Benson, is no longer with us. It is true that Dr. Landsmann is profoundly sorry for Jared Benson and his family. However, Mr. Benson could find no relief for his pain with medication. The surgeon who fixed the hernia had no idea what to do for him. The Defense will show that this suffering man, Mr. Benson, sought help from 4 other surgeons, before coming, out of desperation, to the Wound Clinic at Salt Lake County General Hospital. There, by chance, he met Dr. Landsmann. Dr. Landsmann studied at the Johns Hopkins School of Medicine, which is one of the leading Medical Institutions in this country. Johns Hopkins School of Medicine is dedicated to taking patient problems into the laboratory. Her training was as a Surgical Scientist. She spent one year in the most famous research surgical laboratory in America, the Hunterian Laboratory. It is named for John Hunter, an English doctor, who is the Father of Scientific Surgery. He never would do surgery on a patient, until it was perfected in the Anatomy Laboratory, through anatomic dissection and until he had done this surgery first in an animal. Only then would he try it on a patient. Ladies and Gentlemen of the Jury, Dr. Landsman spent one year doing research on nerves and their relationship to pain in the Hunterian Laboratory. That research has been published, preparing the way for that surgery to be introduced to help people in pain, people like Mr. Jared Benson. Dr. Landsman spent two years of her medical school training observing Dr. Halsted and Dr. Cushing operate. These are the two leading surgeons of our times. The Defense maintains that Dr. Landsmann did have appropriate training and anatomic dissection skills at the time she operated on her patient, Jared Benson. This man was in severe, chronic pain, and was depressed and probably suicidal, as his own parents will attest. That is how he was at the time he saw Dr. Landsmann for help. She did not create this pain. He told her she was his "last hope". Dr. Landsmann did try an operation not done before, that is true enough. She simply tried to remove the nerve that she knew was stuck in the hernia repair scar. Dr. Landsmann did not create that first scar. Dr. Landsmann tried her best to relieve Jared Benson's pain, but, sadly, her operation, well conceived as it was, did not relieve his pain. The patient took his own life. Dr. Landsmann did not kill the deceased. It is our hope that you, the Jury, after considering all the facts, will find Dr. Landsmann "not guilty". Thank you for your attention," concluded Mr. Jarvis. He then turned and returned quietly to his seat.

Olevia felt herself uncurl from beneath her table and sit up straight and look confident again. She knew, however, the Plaintiff was getting ready to call their first witness to testify against her.

The Judge now spoke loudly, "The Plaintiff may call the first witness."

Mr. Elam Smith stood up. "The Plaintiff calls Doctor Ezra Mabey to the stand."

The red-haired first witness, stood up from the Plaintiff's left side of the isle and walked to the witness chair which was directly in front of Olevia, but up closer to the Judges' bench. As Olevia turned to watch Ezra, her former confidant, her first true love, rise to attack her, her eyes seemed to meet those of Jedediah again. His eyes looked confident, and he winked at her again, as if encouraging her to hang in there.

The Bailiff swore in Doctor Maybe, who did promise "to tell the truth, the whole truth and nothing but the truth."

"Doctor Maybe, please tell the court about your medical training," asked Mr. Smith.

"I graduated from the Johns Hopkins School of Medicine, where I became interested in the nervous system. Upon completion of medical school, I traveled to France and Germany to learn the latest diagnostic approaches to testing peripheral nerves, for examining children born with problems within their central nervous system. Then I came back to Baltimore, where I became the first Resident to complete the new program in Psychiatry," Ezra answered succinctly.

Olevia was thinking that he seemed more modest than usual.

"Doctor Maybe, do you hold yourself out to be an expert in the Nervous System of the Human Body?" asked Mr. Smith.

"Yes, I do," Ezra said.

"Doctor Maybe, are you what is now sometimes referred to as a Neurologist?" asked Mr. Smith.

"Yes, I am," Ezra said.

"Doctor Maybe, have you reread the medical records of the Defendant in this case, Doctor Landsmann, as they relate to Jared Benson, the deceased?" asked Mr. Smith.

"Yes, I have," Ezra said.

"Dr. Maybe, what was the diagnosis that Dr. Landsman wrote down as the reason she was operating on her patient, the deceased in this case?" asked Mr. Smith.

"A neuroma of the ilioinguinal nerve," answered Ezra.

"Doctor Maybe, would you agree with me that Doctor Landsman at no time used any type of special equipment to make the diagnosis of neuroma of the ilioinguinal nerve?" asked Mr. Smith.

"I would agree with you, Yes," said Ezra.

"Now Dr. Maybe, please read to us what this report, exhibit #5, says. As you can clearly see at the top of the page, this is the Pathology Report that was made on the specimen that Dr. Landsmann sent from the operating room," prompted Mr. Smith.

"The Pathology Report" says "normal nerve", read Ezra.

"So, Dr. Maybe, to summarize what you have just said, as an expert in the field of Neurology, would you agree with me Sir, that Dr. Landsmann, without any special method of making a diagnosis of neuroma, took a man to surgery, and removed a normal nerve. Is that a fair summary of what you just said?" prompted Mr. Smith.

"Yes it is," replied Ezra looking down at his shoes, never once looking at Olevia.

"Thank you, Doctor Mabey, that is all I have to ask you at this time," said Elam Smith, Esquire.

The Judge now looked over at the Bailiff and looked at his watch.

The Bailiff stood, and said. "Court will recess for lunch. Be back at 1:30PM. No eating in the courtroom! All stand for the Honorable Fletcher Weber."

Jarvis Greer, Esq, turned to Olevia and whispered something into her ear, "I am concerned about the time of this lunch break. Normally the

Judge would have let me proceed to do my cross-examination while Dr. Maybe's testimony was fresh in their minds, and they could understand me attacking it. The Judge clearly wants them to be thinking about Dr. Maybe's damaging testimony to our case during their lunch break."

Olevia just looked at him, dismayed. He had told her ahead of time he would not be talking to her during the breaks, as he had to focus on his own questions.

Jarvis Greer, Esq. got up and walked out. The whole courtroom emptied.

Olevia sat there, looking down, not around. She had no appetite. The Courtroom became quiet. Everyone had left for lunch. Olevia then got up, found some water, and drank a glass. Then she just sat down again and closed her eyes.

PRO-SECTION

"All rise," said the Bailiff, as Judge Fletcher Weber entered the courtroom and returned to his seat.

"Doctor Mabey is recalled to the witness stand. May the court remind the Doctor that he is still under oath," said the Judge.

As Doctor Mabey returned to the witness stand, the Judge continued, "The Defense can begin its cross-examination of Doctor Maybe."

"Doctor Mabey, I am Jarvis Greer, representing Dr. Landsmann. I would like to ask you some questions about the statements you made while you were being questioned by Mr. Elam Smith for the Plaintiff," said Mr. Greer, in a friendly tone.

"I am ready," replied Dr. Maybe.

"From what you have said, you and Dr. Landsmann were classmates in medical school. At the time of graduation, what were your relative class rankings?" Mr. Greer asked.

"I graduated first in the class. Dr. Landsmann graduated fourth. I was the smartest one going into the field of Medicine. She was the smartest one going into the field of Surgery," Ezra said.

"Now that is more like his old egotistical self," thought Olevia.

"Doctor Maybe, with your extensive training in the nervous system, do you know a specific way that a neuroma of the ilioinguinal nerve can be diagnosed?" asked Mr. Greer.

"No, I do not know of any," answered Ezra.

Olevia tried not to let herself smile. Ezra just said something helpful to her!

"Doctor Maybe," you have the honor of being the first at the famous Johns Hopkins Hospital to go through a new training program that may provide a basis for training Neurologists...." Jarvis Greer, Esq. paused here for emphasis. The courtroom was very quiet. "Doctor Maybe, is there anywhere in the United States of America, or Europe for that matter, that you know of, where a Woman Doctor can receive formal surgical residency training?"

"Doctor Mabey was quiet for a moment or two, as if thinking this through, thinking about the implications of what he said, one way or the other, and then he said, "No, Sir. There does not exist such a surgical training program. Surgical residency training programs currently are only for men, to the best of my knowledge."

Olevia was smiling inwardly again. Ezra was giving testimony that was actually helpful to her side of the case.

"Thank you Doctor Maybe, the Defense has no further questions for you."

Once Ezra had returned to the Plaintiff's side of the isle, Mr. Elam Smith said, "The Plaintiff now calls Doctor Landsmann to the stand.

Olevia startled at hearing her name, she thought she would not be called until much later in the case. She rose, walked to the witness stand, adjusted her jacket and the collar of her white blouse, then sat down, and pulled her long skirt well below her knees.

The Bailiff now rose from his seat. "Dr. Landsmann, would you stand and raise your right hand, and repeat after me. Olevia did so, and the Bailiff swore her in. Olevia promised, "to tell the truth, the whole truth and nothing but the truth so help her God."

"Doctor Landsmann, I am Elam Smith. "I represent your *deceased* patient and his family. Do you admit that Jared Benson was your patient?'

"Yes, Sir, I do," replied Doctor Landsmann.

"Dr. Landsmann, do you admit that you had a duty to give him the best possible care and to do him no harm?" Elam Smith, the lawyer asked.

"Yes, Sir, I do," replied Doctor Landsmann.

"Doctor Landsmann," asked Mr. Smith, "You have been operating at the Salt Lake County General Hospital is that correct?"

"Yes, Sir, it is" Olevia replied.

"Doctor Landsmann," Mr. Smith now attacked, "What did you do wrong to lose your surgical privileges there?"

There was a deadly silence in the court room.

Olevia seemed perplexed, was quiet, and then said, "Mr. Smith, excuse me, I do now have full surgical privileges there." Olevia tried to keep a straight face, at what she knew would be surprise information to Mr. Elam Smith, the Plaintiff's lawyer.

"Excuse me, Doctor Landsmann? Excuse me!" Elam Smith, Esquire, now walked over to his desk, retrieved a thick document, thumbed through it till he found what he wanted and returned to stand in front of Olevia. "In your sworn deposition, you said you had lost your surgical privileges, and that you were under investigation," stammered Mr. Smith. "Were you lying to me at that time, during your deposition Doctor Landsmann?" he said trying to put an evil spin to this that would benefit his side of the argument.

"Sir, I said I was being investigated, and had *temporarily* not been able to operate. Yesterday I received a letter, and I hope your office did too, from the Chairman of the Board of Trustees of my hospital, the Honorable Gary Lord Clarke-Smith, Esq, indicating that my case has been resolved. My records were accurate and up to date, and my full operating privileges have been restored. I am planning to be operating again next week." Olevia responded, trying to keep the joy from her voice.

"Why was I not informed of this prior to trial?" Mr. Elam Smith said angrily, turning to Mr. Greer.

Judge Fletcher Weber, witnessing a very disturbing phenomenon erupting in his usually orderly Courtroom, said, "Will both lawyers approach the bench please."

As Mr. Smith and Mr. Greer walked to the bench, and conferred with the Judge, Olevia finally allowed herself to look out into the Courtroom. Mr. Greer had told her to keep looking at the Jury, and not really at Mr. Elam Smith. The Jury needed to see her sincerity. She now had an opportunity to look around.

As Olevia looked out into the Courtroom, she was positively stunned. First, of all, the room was packed. She just could not look at the left side, the Plaintiff's side of the isle.

As her gaze swung towards the right side of the isle, her side, the Defendant's side, she could not miss her dear friend, Dr. Ross. She was sitting with her two patients, smiling up at her. She flashed ahead to these two patients being called to the stand. They had previously had the same type of pain that the deceased, the Plaintiff in this case had. Olevia had perfected her operation for this type of pain, and now could teach that two nerves, not just one had to be removed. The surgeon must have confidence to move on through failure, to learn from failure. Get additional knowledge through anatomic dissection, PROSECTION. Persevere. Succeed. This is what her lawyer must bring out into the public in this Courtroom, when the trial continues. Mr. Greer will ask the right questions, she was sure of it, when his time came again.

Olevia turned and looked at the Judge and the two lawyers. Something very difficult was being decided. They were having intense, animated, talks. Olevia looked back to her side of the isle. The right side. She was on the *right side*. She was in the *right*.

On the right, sitting now just slightly behind where she was sitting, where she certainly could not have seen him, was Jedediah. Jedediah Smith, Esq., wearing a bright, red-striped bow tie. He winked at her. *He was now on her side* of the isle, the *right side*. She allowed herself to give him a small smile. Suddenly she knew that he would be called to testify that her new operation relieved his knee pain. This would open the door, after this trial ended of course, to offer this operation to many more of Dr. Baldwin's patients.

And there, further back, seated in the middle, hard to believe, the clear outline and smiling face of Dr. Samuel Baldwin, Chief of Orthopedic Surgery. Sitting next to him were two men, both smiling. She recognized Ammon Allred, the man with the painful leg amputation stump that she had operated on. She recalled burying those painful neuromas into the muscles higher up in the stump, so he could be fitted with a prosthesis. As Ammon Allred saw her looking at him, he leaned away from Dr. Baldwin, and with both hands lifted his thigh, showing her that he was able to wear his artificial leg. The man next to him stood and gave a thumbs up sign, and with one hand pointed to head and the other pointed to his leg, which he lifted and put on the bench in front of him. Now Olevia recognized him as Edward Cannon, the man whom she had operated on twice. First with the burr hole in the skull and second for the painful leg after his compartment syndrome.

Heads in the courtroom turned to see this unusual sight. A man holding his artificial leg high in the air and the man next to him pointing to his head with one hand and his leg with the other hand.

Then someone got up from behind this man, walked towards the man, raised his hand to Dr. Landsmann, and waved. It was the man whose wrist had been shattered by that mining accident. Dr. Baldwin had sent him to her to fix his wrist pain. She flashed back to her Uncle Albert, who had the same type of pain. Prosections by her Uncle Albert and herself had helped her to create a surgical approach to help this man in pain. This young man was now back at work. Today, *he was here to help her*. He kept waving to her with that right hand, and he too gave her a "thumbs up" with the thumb he previously had been unable to move due to pain.

Her patients' relief from pain, she realized with pride, was the proof of her research. Proof that what she had learned from dissection of the dead, helped improve the lives of the living. And would for generations to come. Her work would be remembered, *Memorandum est Vivere in Aeturnum*, as it said on the Landsmann family crest.

"Order in the Courtroom! Order in the Courtroom!" the Bailiff yelled out loud.

Judge Fletcher Weber now pounded his gavel on to his desk. "This Courtroom will now come to order. We have concluded our deliberations at the bench," he said.

"Dr. Landsmann," said Judge Fletcher Weber. "You may step down from the witness box and return to your seat."

Olevia looked to her lawyer, Jarvis Greer, for advice.

He motioned to her to come back to the table next to him.

The Courtroom was very quiet. The Jurors looked to the Judge. The Plaintiffs, Jared Benson's parents, and their Lawyer Mr. Elam Smith, looked up at the Judge. The Defendant, Olevia and her lawyer, Mr. Jarvis Greer, looked up at the Judge. All eyes, and ears, were trained on the Judge.

The Judge was very solemn, clearly trying to find the correct way to explain what he was going to say next. Judge Fletcher Weber knew that probably many people in Salt Lake City already knew that the lawyer for the Plaintiff was the Grandson of the person in charge of the Investigation against the Defendant, the Honorable Gary Lord Clarke-Smith, who was sitting out there in the courtroom. The Judge could not even begin to explain, even to himself the reasoning of Clarke-Smith in *not* sending a copy of that letter restoring operating privileges to Dr. Landsmann, unless, ... Unless he wanted to teach his grandson and important lesson.

The Judge knew there was only one course to take that served justice, and he now knew how to explain his decision to the people in His Courtroom.

Judge Fletcher Weber now rose. "This Court has received information that was just discussed at the bench, as you saw. That information leads me to make the following ruling in this case," said the Judge, pausing for a few seconds. "I declare, in the case of the Deceased, Jared Benson, and the Benson Family versus Olevia Landsmann, MD, I declare this case to be a mistrial."

As loud voices arose throughout the courtroom, the Bailiff rose, and banged his gavel down on the desk, and said "Order, Order in the courtroom, or we will have you all cleared out. Judge Weber has not finished speaking,"

The room quieted. People sat down. The Judge, still standing said, "Thank you" to the Bailiff. "He turned to face the courtroom. The basis for this Mistrial is that the Plaintiff's Attorney, Mr. Elam Smith, had knowledge, through familial connections, about parallel proceedings related to the Defendant, Dr, Landsmann. Knowing this, the Plaintiff's Attorney, Mr. Elam Smith, should have recused himself from this case. Regarding the Plaintiffs, the Benson Family, you are able to find a new lawyer and try this case again, if you wish to do so. Mr. Elam Smith will meet me in my office after this case adjourns, so we may discus his knowledge of when a lawyer should not accept to try a case. Now, the Jury is dismissed, and Thank You for your service. Court is adjourned."

Judge Fletcher Weber turned and walked out.

The Jury stood, and then filed out.

Olevia, not quite comprehending what just happened, extended her hand, and thanked her lawyer, Jarvis Greer, Esq. for his brilliant maneuvering.

Olevia turned then and looked around the Courtroom. Her gaze stuck upon a tall figure, a man with a beard, walking slowly, with a wavering step, leaving the building. With a cane in his hand, and with the whole left side of the courtroom following slowly behind him, he seemed to Olevia to resemble Moses with his wooden staff in his hand, leading his people out of Egypt.

Then, Olevia was surrounded by those on the "right". Her patients were walking towards her smiling, and Jennie was giving her a big hug. She could see Jed standing next in line to give her a hug, too.

She was looking forward to that hug.

TRIO

Jarvis Greer, Esquire, her lawyer, waited his turn. He watched with a warm smile as Dr. Landsmann's supporters came up and congratulated her. It was as if they thought she had won, that she had been acquitted. But she had not. She was in limbo. It was his task now to tell her that.

Jarvis Greer, Esq. saw that Dr. Landsmann and Jedediah were standing closely together just talking to each other. Relaxed, finally. "Dr. Landsmann," said Jarvis Greer, "Perhaps you and Jedediah and I can go back to my office and discus what happened here today.

"Certainly," said Olevia. "I had planned to spend several days sitting on that hard wooden chair with you. The plush chairs you and Jed have in your office will be a pleasure," she added as the three of them walked out the door.

Jed took Olevia's arm as they walked down the courthouse steps. As if she might faint. As if she needed his help. She allowed him to assist her.

Olevia looked up at Jed and said, "Thank you for switching sides of the isle to be on my side when it was going to count," she said with a grin.

"Family first! The Smiths were taught from the time we were little," Jed said, trying to explain his initial choice of where to sit in the courtroom. "Now you are sort of like family, the Family Doctor!"

"I hope the Honorable Gary Lord Clarke-Smith will not cast you out of the Smith family, Jed," Olevia teased him.

As they got into a taxi, Jarvis Greer sat up front, allowing Olevia and Jed to sit in the back seat together.

"Olevia, speaking of 'The Lord', which is what I know people call Grandfather, out of respect of course," I couldn't help but notice how you stared at him as he was leaving the courthouse. Do you actually hate him that much?" asked Jed.

"Oh Jed," Olevia said with a soft sigh of sadness. "How dreadful you must think I am. No, I do not hate him. He has so much responsibility. He must answer to so many different groups of people, and weigh what is best. In that way he is like The Lord above. I was looking at him as a Doctor. Have you not noticed how he walks? Notice those strange shoes? What is going on there, Jed, do you know?"

"Honestly Doctor," Jed replied. "I just thought Grandpa was getting old, a bit unsteady on his feet. Last year he began to use the cane, afraid he might fall down the steps he said. This year, over Christmas, sitting around the fire, he told us his feet were buzzing about all the time, and his feet hurt to touch the wooden or stone floor, so he got special shoes and fat padded slippers. You know he is about 68 years old. He seems ancient to us grandkids," Jed replied.

"Jed, that is what I was concerned about. I have been doing some research on those symptoms as being related to the nerves in the feet getting compressed. I believe The Lord is at risk for getting a foot ulcer!" explained Olevia.

"Here we are, you two," said Jarvis Greer, paying the taxi driver and hopping out of the front seat. He headed up to the office building.

As Olevia got out of the taxi, she thought the neighborhood looked familiar. Then she realized why. Across the street was the new Primary Pediatric Hospital, the one in which Ezra worked.

"Wait for us Jarvis," called Jed, as he and Olevia hurried to keep up.

"About time you slow pokes showed up," said Jarvis with a big smile, sitting in the conference room, his tie off, and his feet up on the table.

"What next you two legal eagles?" asked Olevia.

"Dr. Landsmann, THIS case is over. Your future in this matter remains however unclear. Jared Benson's parents may get over their anger, and just grieve. You after all, did not kill their son. He killed himself. You tried to help him and failed. Failure to achieve the desired result from surgery is not grounds for malpractice. They may seek another lawyer to take their case and try to take you to court again. Perhaps the new lawyer will advise them that they have no grounds for a malpractice case. Perhaps they will find a "hungry" new lawyer, with nothing else to do who will take the case. If that occurs, you and I will start all over again."

"Mr. Greer, you have been wonderful to me throughout this horrible situation. Jed, I thank you deeply for suggesting Mr. Greer to me. Mr. Greer, if they come after me again, I will be right back at your door asking for help and hoping you have not doubled your hourly fee! If you do however double it, then, I will find the money to pay you. You are worth it," she said standing up to leave.

Jarvis Greer, Esq. got up, shook her hand, thanked her for her kind words.

Mr. Jedediah Smith, the lawyer-turned-patient, stood up, and said "Just so you know, Dr. Landsmann, I would have testified in your behalf if Mr. Greer had invited me to be a witness, but, since I did not have a chance to do that, may I offer you an invitation to lunch?" he said.

"Jed, now that you are no longer my patient, and your knee is doing so well, how about I accept your lunch invitation, and you call me Olevia from now on?" she said with a wink.

As they exited the law office building, they faced the Primary Pediatric Hospital. Jed spotted Ezra first. "Olevia," Jed said pointing out the redhead getting out of a taxi across the street. "Let us go say hello. You may have picked up on the fact that he did not say anything against you on the witness stand. He told the truth and remained a gentleman and friend to you," at least that is my interpretation of the proceedings," continued Jed as he just about had to pull the reluctant Olevia across the street.

Olevia smiled and said, "Not bad moves for a guy who was crippled with pain and using a cane a few weeks ago," she said as she tried to keep up with Jed crossing the street.

"Ezra," called out Jed. "Ezra, wait up. We want to talk with you."

Ezra, halfway to the hospital entrance, heard his name and turned around. His eyes opened widely in surprise. He just stood still.

"Cousin-in-Law," said Jed putting his arm around the shoulder of the shorter Ezra. "We wanted to talk to you for a few minutes."

"Ezra," on high-alert after his day in court, just said, "Hello cousin. Hello Olevia . . . Olevia, I did the best I could for you in there today," he finally said looking at her.

"Indeed you did, Ezra. I knew you would, even though I am not part of the Smith family," she said with a little laugh. "Ezra, 'family' is what we want to talk to you about. Have you had a chance to watch your Grandfather walk, and see those shoes he wears, and now he uses a cane! Ezra, Jed and I are concerned about him," said Olevia trying to explain why they were there.

Ezra did not know really what to say. He just stood looking at the two of them. Finally, he said, "You know, I just think of him as my Grandfather. I do not analyze him physically. To me, he is just one big brain, with so much responsibility. I know how he comes across. That is largely a 'defense mechanism'. Oopps! Sorry to get Freudian again Olevia. What are you thinking is going on with my Grandfather?"

"Ezra, remember in our Pathology class, the 'Kick Buckets'?" Olevia asked.

"Sure, what fun. What does that have to do with my Grandfather?" he asked, "He still has both his legs".

Jedediah Smith just looked on and listened.

"Ezra, this past year or so, I have gotten back to the observations you and I made in Pathology class at Johns Hopkins Medical School. In the Anatomy lab here in Utah, I have found that the obese cadavers have yellow tibial nerves in their tarsal tunnels, which probably gave them sensory symptoms in the bottoms of their feet. One of these feet had an ulceration. Perhaps this would have led to an amputation," Olevia tried to explain.

"Well, Grandfather did have a wide based ataxic gait today and clearly needs the cane for balance. That can come from loss of sensation," conceded Ezra.

Now it was Jed's turn to contribute. "Ezra, you may not have heard him tell some of us this past year, over the Christmas Holidays, as we sat around the fire. He was rubbing his feet. He said they burn or feel cold. They tingle and buzz and it was disturbing to him. I asked him about his new shoes, and he said that he could not stand his feet to touch the floor without something soft on them."

"Diabetes!" said Ezra. "Oh my gosh. I missed the signs of this in my own family. Thank you for telling me, Jed. We must get him on a strict diet, avoid sugar and most carbohydrates. He is going to hate it. I must go to see him right away," and he turned to leave.

"Hey, wait a minute, lab partner," said Olevia. "I am going too, and so is Jed."

"The three of us going to see him together?" exclaimed Ezra.

"Yes" Olevia and Jed said together, "We are."

"We are going to gang up on him, Ezra. Make him take off his shoes and socks so you and I can both examine him together", said Olevia by herself. Then you can use your magical electrical device and see if you can find a nerve compression or neuropathy.

"OK," said Ezra, feeling himself getting co-opted into something he was not sure he really wanted to be part of. "And if you and I agree and confirm that he has a nerve problem, then what?" asked Ezra.

"You will give him the best medical advice about his disease, and if there is evidence of a nerve entrapment, then I will operate and decompress his nerves!" she said with confidence.

While Ezra sat down on the curb and held his head ,Jed suggested, "Lets go see him right now!"

EXAMINATION

"Come in," said the deep voice of The Lord.

The Honorable Gary Lord Clarke-Smith, Esquire rose from his chair behind his huge desk, and walked forward with his cane to meet his two of his Grandchildren and one of his Salt Lake County General Hospital Surgeons, a Woman Surgeon.

"Thank you for making time to see us today, Grandfather, and on short notice," said Ezra, clearly wanting to be in charge. He carried a small suitcase with him, which he set down next to his chair.

"Sit down, please," said The Lord, as he walked back behind his desk. "Is this about the trial that just ended?"

"No sir, it is not," said Ezra. "It is about your own health. It is about your feet and what your symptoms mean. It is about the way you are walking and if anything can be done to help you," replied Ezra, as if presenting a case to a Judge in court.

"What do you mean asked the Grandfather?" now assuming a more relaxed pose, as he knew this was not another legal matter.

"Grandfather" said Jed, "can you please come sit in this chair and take off your shoes and socks so these two doctors, with their differing approaches, can examine your feet. They are looking for evidence that your symptoms are coming for a nerve compression at your ankle or a medical problem like diabetes, or both."

"How interesting. What fun," said the Grandfather, moving to the front of the desk where a remaining empty chair was located. "Ezra are you packed to leave town in case you are wrong in your diagnosis?" he chuckled.

"Grandfather, this is the electrical testing apparatus I brought back from Europe to test the children with nerve problems, but it can be used in Grandfathers too," he said with a smile.

"Sir," interjected Olevia, "May I examine you first, because once Doctor Maybe finishes with his electrical device, you may not want anyone else to examine you!" she said giving Ezra and apologetic smile. "Please take off your shoes and socks," she asked politely.

"Certainly, Doctor, proceed," encouraged The Lord. "And I did bathe them this morning, so you do not have to hold your nose," he commented with a smile.

Olevia moved her chair in front of her new patient, bent over and gently put The Lord's foot on her knee. "I am now examining your pulse on the top of the foot and behind the ankle," she said, and then commented, "Your pulses are strong and full, suggesting that your symptoms are NOT related to your arterial system, which means your symptoms are related to your peripheral nerves."

"That is good news, I suppose," said The Lord. "I won't get gangrene."

Olevia now took out a small engineer's measurement calipers from her pocket. "These have blunted points and do not hurt, Sir. This is so we can know if you have enough nerve fibers still working in the toes to determine if I am touching you with either one or two separate blunt points," explained Olevia.

As Olevia was explaining this device and what she was going to do next, Ezra said, "Olevia you might find it interesting that while I was traveling in Germany, studying, I went through Leipzig, where Ernest Heinrich Weber taught Psychology and Anatomy and Physiology. He died in 1878 so I did not get to meet him. But his two-point discrimination test, the one you are doing now on Grandfather, is quite popular there among Neurologists. It is hardly known however here in America," Ezra concluded.

"Thank you, Ezra," said Olevia, lifting her head to look at him. "You will probably become the youngest Professor of Medicine at the University of Utah." Then she lowered her head to focus on the test she was doing. "Sir," she said to The Lord, "just tell me whether you can distinguish if I am touching your big toe with either one or two blunt points."

As Olevia repeated her test moving the two prongs of the caliper to different distances apart, The Lord kept saying "One, One, they all really feel the same. Are you doing something different each time?"

"Well, Sir," answered Olevia. "You cannot distinguish one from two points even up to 15 mm apart, which means that many of your nerve fibers for detecting touch and pressure are no longer working." She paused for emphasis. Then said, "Let me try moving-touch instead of pressure. Now, Sir, do you feel this at all?" Olevia asked as she took her fingers and moved the prongs along the bottom of his foot, trying to tickle him.

"Well, I can tell something is moving on the bottom of the foot, but I hardly feel it," he responded. "I used to be quite ticklish on the bottom of my feet."

"Grandfather," said Ezra, "that loss of feeling, that Dr. Landsmann just demonstrated with her examination, is why you have poor balance, and, I am sorry to say, it means you are now are likely to develop what is called a neuropathic ulcer in your foot, or an infection that will lead to an ulcer. It is important that you always protect those toes and feet. It is important that you did get those special shoes."

"Sir," said Olevia, bringing the discussion back to her examination. "What do you feel when I tap over the inside of your ankle."

"I feel you tapping there," replied The Lord.

"That is good. Now I will tap a little harder and tell me what you feel next," Olevia instructed, as she tapped harder on the place behind his medial malleolus and his calcaneus, between the ankle bone and the heel bone.

"How strange," said The Lord. "Why I can feel that shoot out to my arch and to my big toe," He explained.

"Olevia, may I try that examination please?" requested Ezra, who almost pushed Olevia out of the way to repeat the examination.

Ezra got the same response from his Grandfather on both the right and left foot. When the nerve was tapped in the tarsal tunnel, The Lord could feel sensation go into his toes.

"Ezra," said Olevia, "Please see if his common peroneal nerves are tender at the fibular head."

Ezra tried this, and those nerves were tender too. When tapped sensation went down towards the top of the foot.

Ezra turned and looked at Olevia. He nodded. He had confirmed her findings. There were compressed nerves in these locations.

Ezra turned to his Grandfather and said. "Grandfather, your exam demonstrates you have severe nerve problems in both feet, most likely with nerve compressions at your knee and ankle. I would like to learn if my new electrodiagnostic testing can identify this as well," he said moving to open his suitcase.

"Ezra," said The Lord, "what can be done to help me with this problem?"

Ezra now set about connecting a bunch of wires and little connectors to his Grandfather's leg and to connect them to the device that was in the suitcase. "Grandfather, the most likely cause for this is Diabetes. In Medicine, currently, we know only that Diabetes is a problem with how your body handles sugar. You have too much of this sugar in your blood, and your body gets rid of it in your urine," he replied.

As he continued to hook up his device, Olevia, encouraged Ezra: "Ezra, tell your Grandfather how our Professor of Medicine at Johns Hopkins, Dr. Osler, would make the diagnosis of Diabetes."

"Yes, Grandfather. This is true. Perhaps you know that urine is sterile and has no bacteria. Well, our Dr. Williams Osler, who wrote the first textbook of Medicine in America in 1895. It is titled, *The Principles and Practice of Medicine*. Osler would dip his finger into a patient's urine and then Osler would lick his own finger. If the urine tasted sweet he would make the diagnosis of Diabetes!" replied Ezra.

"Well Grandson, those painful electrical shocks you are giving me are making me feel like I have to urinate. Stick out your finger, and I will give you a sample to taste," The Lord said, as his leg gave another convulsion.

Jed got up from the sofa where he had been watching all of this and stood behind his Grandfather, placing one of his hands on each of his Grandfather's shoulders, offering support, through what was clearly a painful examination. As Jed did so, he looked at Olevia, and just sadly shook his head, not approving of this new electrical way of making a diagnosis that was so painful to the patient.

Olevia watched Jed's actions, realizing how empathetic and loving he was towards his Grandfather.

Ezra ignored his Grandfather's pain and just kept moving along, shocking one spot after another on his Grandfather's leg, and recording the responses on a strip of paper that was coming out of the other side of the electrodiagnostic device. "Thank you for that offer, Grandfather, but no, I do not want to taste your urine sample. And we are almost done here," said Ezra.

Jed who had been silently watching all of this now said, "Ezra, what do all those squiggles being recorded on the strip of paper mean?"

Ezra looked up from studying his results. "This testing shows severe slowing of the electrical impulses, especially across the ankle. Every nerve tested is abnormal. And it is abnormal in both feet to the same degree. hisT test must be interpreted as showing a disease of all the nerves, a neuropathy it is called. Common, in about 50% of people with Diabetes, but also present in about one-third of Grandfather's age who do not have diabetes."

"Ezra can your testing detect a localized nerve compression at the knee or the ankle in either the left or the right side?" asked Olevia, which was the critical question for her, as a peripheral nerve surgeon.

"No, Olevia, my test results do not show individual entrapped nerves. To be perfectly honest, the nerves may be 'too sick' for me to be able to demonstrate nerve entrapment even if it were there. From our physical examination today, clinically, I agree with you that there are compressed nerves, but the electrical testing cannot confirm that," concluded Ezra.

"Ezra," replied Olevia, "You know this was my concern from the first time you ever discussed electrodiagnostic testing with me, that either early with a sensory nerve problem, or late with a sensory nerve problem, as with your Grandfather, the clinical findings might suggest a compression, but in the early nerve compression your testing might say there was no compression, and in the late stage, your testing would show neuropathy but no nerve compression. This will likely create problems with diagnosis and treatment decision making between Neurologists and Peripheral Nerve Surgeons for a long time to come."

"Yes Olevia, I agree with you," said Ezra. "What you and I have experienced together today is not a good for my new field of electrodiagnostic testing. Hopefully in time we will develop either better electrical testing or better ways of interpreting what it means," commented Ezra honestly.

"Doctors, then what am I to do?" Asked Gary Lord Clarke-Smith. "Suppose I have Diabetes and Neuropathy. Those are names. My feet are in pain all day and all night, ever day, and at night now. I am losing my balance. What treatment can help me get relief?" asked The Lord.

"Grandfather," said Ezra, "all we know is to have you continue to exercise to keep up your strength, get on a proper diet to help your metabolism, and to protect your feet from injury or infection that could lead to amputation, with those special shoes you are wearing."

Gary Lord Clarke-Smith, Esquire was very good at evaluating information, and reaching a conclusion to help other people. Now he had to do this for himself.

The Lord looked directly at Olevia. "Dr. Landsmann, has your nerve research in the Anatomy Lab found anything that may offer me relief from my pain and my risk of ulceration and . . . amputation?"

"Yes Sir," answered Olevia. "Nerve decompression surgery. This surgery has rarely been done for a nerve compressed by an injury, like a crush or fracture. It has never been done for someone with Diabetes. You would be the first person on whom it was done. There cannot even be an estimate to give you on your chance for success. The surgery may be a complete failure, with no relief of pain. Or, if I injure a motor nerve doing the surgery, you may awaken paralyzed," she said, having learned a lot from her legal experience with Jared Benson.

The room was very quiet, for a while. Elam and Jed, and the new Doctor in the Family, Ezra, all sat, looking at The Lord.

"Grandfather," asked Jed, who had been observing all these interactions quietly, standing behind The Lord, "What are your thoughts now after all of this examination and diagnosis?"

The Lord finally looked up at the two Doctors, Ezra and Olevia. "From what you tell me, my future holds increasing pain and loss of function if I do nothing, even if I am very good with my diet and ugly shoes," stated The Lord. "Already I am fearful going up and down stairs because I have no balance. Walking on the ice in winter now terrifies me, as I am concerned that I will fall and break my hip. For sure, I cannot play in the yard with my many great-grandchildren anymore."

"Grandfather," those are important observations," said Jed. "I know it is very difficult for you to admit this to anyone. You have always been so independent."

"Yes, Jedediah, that is true," commented The Lord. Then, turning to Olevia, The Lord said, "Doctor Landsmann, I have one more question for you."

"Yes Sir, what is it?" she replied.

"Will you operate on both legs at the same time?" asked The Lord

TEST TICKLE

As Olevia stood in front of the scrub sink, scrubbing her hands, preparing to operate, she thought about the amazing and rapidly changing political climate of the past months. In deed, scrubbing next to her was Elijah Willis, MD, Chief of her Department of Surgery.

Dr. Willis turned to Olevia, and said, "Dr. Landsmann, I wonder what you make of the events of the last few weeks?"

"What do you mean specifically," she asked?

"Well Doctor, our Salt Lake County General Hospital formed a committee to evaluate your patient's medical records because you were accused of doing experimental surgery on your patients. Which, of course you know you were doing. To your credit, you do keep good medical records, so the committee could not find anything wrong in your patient charts. One of your patients, however, committed suicide because you were unable to relieve his pain. It is true that your scalpel did not directly cause his death. You had a malpractice suite against you, which is also a black mark on the reputation of *MY* Department. You lost your hospital operating privileges. Yet here you are again, Doctor Landsmann, ready to do experimental surgery on someone no less than the Chairman of our Hospital Board, and . . . a very dear friend of mine," concluded Dr. Willis.

"Those are the correct events that have happened to me, Dr. Willis. I am who I am, however. I am here as a Woman Surgeon whose work is based on research to help people in pain. If I do not try to help your good friend, with this operation, then I must give up anyway what I have trained myself to do," Olevia answered her Chief of Surgery.

"Dr. Landsmann," said Chief of Surgery Elijah Willis. "I am here as the witness. If you fail today, you will never set foot in another operating room again, as long as I have any persuasion over other surgeons."

Olevia stopped scrubbing and turned to go into the operating room. Dr. Willis turned to follow her. "Dr. Willis, the journey I have been through related to prejudice against Women in Medicine, prejudice against creating new knowledge through Anatomic research, exemplifies the times we live in. All I can do is proceed with what I believe is best for my patients based upon surgical science. That is what I plan to do today, and, Sir, I appreciate your taking time to scrub in, and see the anatomic basis for our patient's symptoms," she concluded and walked into the operating room, followed by her Chief.

The room was perfectly quiet. The Scrub Nurse, Chipeta, offered the first gown and gloves not to Olevia but to the Chief of the Department of Surgery.

The silence was broken by the Circulating Nurse, Mabel Ryan. "Good morning, Dr. Willis and Dr. Landsmann. We are all excited to work with you this morning."

Olevia looked around and, smiling beneath her mask, said, "I am thankful that our top Peripheral Nerve Team is here for this special operation. Dr. Ether Helaman, on Ether Anesthesia, Mable Ryan, on Circulation, Chipeta on Surgical Instruments, our Photographer on Camera," she concluded as if she were the Lead Singer introducing her backup Band members at a Musical Concert.

"Which leg are you going to operate on today, Dr. Landsmann, you don't want to operate on the wrong leg," said Dr. Willis her Chief. "You already know most of the large Smith family of lawyers that will be in the waiting room to learn the results of YOUR surgery."

"Of course, Sir, we have marked the left leg, which is the one draped. This patient does need the surgery on both feet, and if we are successful on the left, he can have the second one operated on as soon as 6 weeks from now," answered Olevia.

"Why not operate on both today, Doctor, that is what your patient wanted, as I understand it," the Chief of Surgery replied.

As Olevia proceeded to outline an incision near the outside, lateral side, of the left knee and the inside, the medial side, of the ankle, she said, "Yes he did want both sides operated on at once. I explained to him that he would need one leg to carry his weight, as I will allow him to start walking right away, so the nerves do not get stuck in scar tissue during the healing process. Also, since this is the first time this surgery has been done, should the surgery not prove to be helpful to him, we would not have operated on both legs, and failed in both legs," said Olevia, explaining her reasoning.

Olevia stood so she could directly see the knee where she was operating. She pulled the leg up and flexed the knee. Chipeta stood across from her, and Dr. Willis stood directly behind Olevia where he could observe everything.

Olevia wrapped the leg from the toes to above the knee with the Esmarch bandage, and then unwrapped all except the portion above the knee.

"Knife please, Chipeta," requested Olevia.

"Yes Doctor," replied Chipeta who already had the #15 scalpel blade in her hand.

Olevia took the scalpel, and began to make her incision.

"I understand you did this part of the procedure once before, Doctor Landsmann," remarked Dr. Willis, who had clearly been checking up on her.

"Yes, Sir. That patient was Edward Cannon. He sustained a compression of this common peroneal nerve after a ski accident in which he fractured the fibula. His leg was becoming paralyzed. After the decompression surgery, He walks quite well now," she answered.

"One for one," remarked Dr. Willis.

"There, Dr. Willis. Do you see this white band compressing and running across this large yellow structure?" asked Olevia, pointing into the open wound.

"Yes. That looks like an ordinary fatty tumor, a lipoma. Do you think that is the cause of the nerve compression Doctor, a lipoma?" the Chief Willis asked.

"Photographer, please," requested Olevia, as she and the Chief stood back and watched the photograph being taken.

"Dr. Willis, I am quite concerned that this yellow structure is not a fatty tumor, but rather, this is the sick appearance of this diseased common peroneal nerve in this diabetic man," she said as she released the white constricting band. "Now, Dr. Willis, observe as I lift this yellow structure from its site of compression."

"Amazing Dr. Landsmann. I do agree that is the nerve. And now I think I see some red filling the vessels in the previously compressed area, restoring circulation," the Chief observed.

"Yes. I agree. I just wish now that we had invited Ezra in to observe these nerves," sighed Olevia.

"He can see my photographs," chimed in the Photographer, happily.

Olevia looked at Chipeta and winked. Then said, "This is just like the finding our research in the Anatomy Lab demonstrated, Dr. Willis," and then she wrapped a moist towel around the knee, and explained, "Your observation was correct: the compressed area has not enough oxygen, that is why the patient perceives tingling. Sometimes this buzzing can stop soon after surgery. More blood will flow in the nerve once we let the Esmarch bandage down. The nerve can begin to function quite quickly if not too many fibers have died. Now we will switch sides of the table. As she did this, Olevia allowed the leg to straighten out.

"Knife please, Chipeta," requested Olevia. "Chipeta, please use your left hand to push the toes this way, externally rotating the leg, so I can get to the tarsal tunnel."

"Yes, Doctor," said Chipeta, doing as she was asked.

Olevia used the knife then to open the skin over the tarsal tunnel, and then used scissors to open the lancinate ligament, covering the tibial nerve and the blood vessels.

"Dr. Landsmann," said the Chief, who was observing the surgery closely, "I believe that tibial nerve is also swollen and yellow, right there beneath the blood vessels."

"Yes Sir, good observation. Photographer, please," Olevia said moving right along.

"Are we done then?" asked the Chief.

"No Sir, there are really three more tunnels down here. You probably noticed that there was not much tightness here we released the lancinate ligament to get into the tarsal tunnel. Let me show the other tunnels to you. This is where the real pressure is upon the nerves," she offered opening the medial and lateral plantar tunnels and removing the tissues between the two tunnels.

"How did you figure this out, Dr. Landsmann?" asked the Chief.

"All through doing cadaver dissections and comparing the nerves in the skinny cadavers to the nerves in the obese cadavers. This information is the subject of the current research paper I am writing," Olevia offered proudly. "Chipeta, who works in the Anatomy Lab, and who is our Scrub Nurse today, assisted me with that research."

Dr. Willis looked at Chipeta with new appreciation but did not say anything. He just commented, "I can see those tunnels are tight," as Olevia finished releasing the nerve to the heel.

"We are removing the elastic bandage now," said Olevia, "Chipeta, please put a moist towel over each wound and apply pressure for a few minutes to stop the bleeding."

While that was happening, Olevia looked at the Anesthesia person, "How is our patient doing Ether?" she asked.

"Doing great, considering his age," Ether replied.

Chipeta handed a needle holder and suture to Olevia, who began to close the ankle incision.

"Dr. Willis would you be kind enough to close the skin at the knee incision?" Olevia asked, treating him now more like a colleague than a boss.

"Thank you. Happy to help," the Chief said quietly. Then lifted his head to look at Olevia. "Dr. Landsmann, I must tell you that your surgical technical skills are excellent. You are very gentle with the delicate tissues. I am most impressed with this anatomy, which, honestly, probably no one except you, and Chipeta, has ever seen before."

"Thank you, Sir. That is how I learned to operate watching my teachers, Drs. Halsted and Cushing, at Johns Hopkins Hospital. They were amazing to watch. I only hope to honor them and continue their tradition," she said completing putting on the bandage.

As Olevia left the operating room, she turned and said, "Thank you Peripheral Nerve Team," smiled and walked out, followed by Dr. Willis.

"Let us go talk to the family," said Dr. Willis as he led the way.

Then, at the entrance to the room marked Family Waiting Room, Olevia saw the Chief of Medicine, David J. Grafton, standing talking to a medical resident. Dr. Willis saw him too, and left her side, saying, "You go on Dr. Landsmann and talk to the family. You are the Surgeon. I will say hello to my friend, Dr. Grafton, and tell him that diabetic nerves are yellow. He should get himself into the operating room some day and learn something from us Surgeons!!"

Olevia smiled at Dr. Willis, turned her head to smile at Dr. Grafton, and opened the door to the Family Waiting Room.

"Hello David," she heard Elijah say to his good friend Dr. Grafton. "I have some surprising news for you about the color of nerves in a diabetic, and how those nerves are swollen. I just saw them myself in surgery with Dr. Landsmann."

Olevia, stopped at the door to the Family Waiting Room, and quietly listened.

"Oh, sure," said the Chief of Medicine to the Chief of Surgery. "I bet you had great fun watching a Woman Surgeon butcher a person with diabetes. Cutting into a leg that may never heal in order to prove her theories. I can tell you I will do whatever I can do to prevent further unnecessary surgery on the leg of a diabetic. The treatment of Diabetes is medical, not surgical!" emphasized David J. Grafton, MD.

Olevia just shook her head, and continued walking into the Family Waiting Room, realizing that even if today she did win over some of her Male Surgical colleagues, she now had a new army of enemies, Medical Doctors.

There was hardly room for Olevia to enter the waiting room. The large Smith family occupied almost the whole room.

"Here is the Surgeon," she heard someone say, and the room became quiet. Everyone turned to look at her. She spotted Ezra's red hair right away. Standing near him, the taller head of Jed stood out. Just to her right was Elam Smith, Esquire, who had been Jared Benson's lawyer against her.

With all eyes upon her, Olevia said, "The Honorable Gary Lord Clarke-Smith has come through the surgery well. There have been no problems. We found what we expected, which was large, swollen entrapped nerves, and these were released from pressure."

"Is the surgery successful?" a voice called out from somewhere in the room.

"Time will tell us to what extent he recovers the use of this leg. But I am very hopeful this recovery will happen. Your prayers will be most welcome," Olevia replied.

"When can we see him?" asked another person.

"Your relative is waking up now in recovery. I can take a few of you back with me now, to see him if you wish," Olevia offered. "Mrs. Clarke-Smith would you please accompany me?" Then Olevia added, "Dr. Ezra Maybe, Jedediah Smith, and Elam Smith I know three of you, and would request you come with me, too.

She turned to leave the Family Waiting Room, and the relatives she had requested followed her, down the hall and into the Recovery Room.

"If you four would wait here for just a minute, I will check to see if he is awake enough yet for you to greet him, "Olevia explained, and walked back towards where the nurses were standing next to Doctor Ether Helaman and Chipeta.

Olevia walked quickly towards them, concerned that something was wrong. "Is he doing Ok?" she asked quickly.

"Perfect," reassured Dr. Helaman. "He is smiling and asking for some Wasatch Valley water."

"He is also asking for his wife," added Chipeta.

At just this moment Dr. Willis and Dr. Grafton, Chief of Surgery and Chief of Medicine, also walked up to the bedside.

"Dr. Landsmann," said Dr. Grafton, "I am Mr. Clarke-Smith's Medical Physician. He has diabetes you know. Surgery can be quite risky for a diabetic, so I am here if he needs me. I am sure that is fine with you Doctor?"

"Certainly. We all appreciate your concern," said Olevia, knowing what his ulterior motives.

Olevia walked over to the head of the bed. She could see from her patient's eyes that he was still awakening from anesthesia. "Your surgery went really well, Sir. You should make a great recovery. Does anything hurt?" she asked The Lord.

"I can't tell yet, Doctor, can I have some more water, please?" asked The Lord.

As the recovery room nurse helped him with a sip of water, Olevia looked at Ether and Mable, and winked. She went to the foot of the bed, where the big bandage was exposed on the left foot. Drs. Willis and Grafton were both watching Olevia. As Ether and Chipeta watched also, Olevia gently wiggled her fingers on the bottom of his left foot.

"What was that?" asked The Lord with surprise, sitting up.

"Everything is OK, Sir. I was just checking your bandage," replied Olevia.

Olevia winked again, this time at Mabel, and said, "I will be right back with his wife and some other relatives. She turned and waved to the four people standing up the hallway and walked to meet them.

Dr. Willis and Grafton were intently talking to each other. "You see David, that yellow swollen nerve is getting blood flow again, and sensation is coming back into his numb foot," said Dr. Willis, the Chief of Surgery to the Chief of Medicine, saying something positive about the surgery's early result.

"Come on now, Elijah," said the Chief of Medicine scornfully, "This patient probably cannot even tell you his own name yet, after just waking up. But if time proves this observation to be correct, you and I will be able to help a lot of people. "But I am still very skeptical about what we are watching. You know the patient wants the surgery to work, and so do the Surgeons," he said patting his friend on the shoulder. "This is still just one patient's observation at one point in time."

Olevia watched as The Lord's Wife, Ezra, Elam and Jed got closer to her. She said to them, "Mr. Clarke-Smith is doing well for so soon after surgery. He has asked for water from the Wasatch Valley, and for his wife. A good sign," she said and led them next to the bed.

It was very crowded in the small recovery room space around The Lord's stretcher. Jed moved in very close to Olevia, his shoulder touching hers.

After greetings to the patient from Ezra, Jed, Elam and from his wife, everyone turned to Olevia, as if to ask, "what now?"

"Mr. Clark-Smith, are you in much pain?" Olevia asked the question again, this time to a more awake patient.

"My foot has this horrible buzzing and tingling still," said The Lord. "Does that mean the surgery failed?" he asked.

Dr. Grafton now looked knowingly at Dr. Willis, as if to say. "The surgery has been a failure, as I would have predicted."

It was very quiet. All eyes turned back towards Olevia. Jed moved even closer as if physically lending his support.

Then Olevia asked, "Which foot are you talking about Sir?"

"My right foot is killing me still," The Lord replied.

Smiles migrated around the recovery room stretcher.

"Well, Sir. We operated on your left foot. What does that left foot feel like now?" Olevia asked.

"Gosh darn it. Lord Almighty," said The Lord sitting up. "My left foot does not hurt anymore!"

Everyone standing around The Lord starting clapping their hands. Including Elam and Jed, Ether and Chipeta and the recovery room nurses. Ezra, the Neurologist, just stood there, mouth slightly open. Drs. Willis and Grafton just looked at each other, realizing a new horizon was opening for the care of their diabetic patients in pain.

Now Olevia looked at Ezra, "Doctor Maybe, as a Neurologist, would you be so kind as to take your fingers and wiggle them vigorously on the bottom of Mr. Clarke-Smith's previously almost anesthetic, left foot?" requested Olevia.

Ezra went over and applied a moving touch stimulus to the bottom of his Grandfather's foot.

Gary Lord Clarke-Smith, Esquire, Chairman of the Hospital Board, gave out a huge laugh, and pulled his foot up and away from Ezra's stimulus.

Ezra, shocked by this response, simultaneously pulled his hand away, and stepped back. "What happened Grandpa, what did you feel?" asked Ezra.

Still laughing, The Lord answered, "I can feel my foot. That tickled!!"

Ezra turned to his former classmate, remembering her sense of humor, and said, "Dr. Landsmann, we need a name for that new medical exam that I just performed. Do you have a name to suggest?"

"Of course," said Olevia with a wink to Ezra, "That exam technique hence forth will be called 'The Test Tickle'.

Those surrounding The Lord's stretcher were mostly either covering their mouth with a smile on their face, or were just laughing out loud, "Test Tickle" they were saying out loud. "Testicle"!!!

David J. Grafton, MD, Chief of Medicine was *not* laughing along with everyone else. He turned to Dr. Willis, the Chief of Surgery, and said, "Elijah, please, for The Lord's sake, ask Dr. Ezra Maybe to do that same test on the foot that did not have surgery. Are we all going to be hoodwinked, tricked, made fools of by this Snake Oil Sales Woman!"

"Dr. Maybe," said Dr. Willis, "in the interest of Science, would you please do that same amount of sensory stimulation to the right foot, the foot that did NOT have surgery, so we can observe the effect of that stimulation on this patient who is just now awakening from anesthesia."

"Certainly, Sir, I will do that right now," said Ezra, taking his fingertips and wiggling them against the bottom of The Lord's right foot.

"Why is the room suddenly so quiet?" asked The Lord, not moving the right foot at all. "Please someone, rub the bottom of my left foot again. I want to have that feeling again?" the patient on the stretcher said quite loudly.

"Of course, we can do that again Sir," said Olevia, looking at Ezra, with a modest smile and raised eyebrows.

Without saying a word, Ezra reached out and tickled the bottom of The Lord's left foot.

"Lord Almighty," said The Lord, laughing out loud, and pulling his left foot away from the stimulus that Ezra had just given him, "My left foot is coming back to life again. It is a true Miracle, Praise the Lord who is deserving of Praise. . . .. And may we all give thanks to Dr. Landsmann, perhaps the bravest Surgeon I know."

There were cheers and applause all around.

Even Dr. David J. Grafton clapped his hands together, as he tried to figure out what all of this would mean to the many diabetics he had in his Medical practice.

Olevia smiled, said 'Thank you' to the Honorable Gary Lord Clarke-Smith, Esquire, and said to everyone around her, "Let us give him a little time alone with his wife now. I will return to see him later tonight," and turned to walk out of the recovery room.

Jedediah Smith, who had been standing slightly behind Olevia, now found himself standing face to face with her.

"How about a root beer to celebrate?" he asked putting his arm on her shoulder, directing her to the exit.

Don't miss out!

Visit the website below and you can sign up to receive emails whenever A. Lee Dellon, MD, PhD publishes a new book. There's no charge and no obligation.

https://books2read.com/r/B-A-UTNT-URGYB

BOOKS 2 READ

Connecting independent readers to independent writers.

About the Author

A. Lee Dellon, MD, PhD graduated from Johns Hopkins School of Medicine, completed his Plastic Surgery residency at Johns Hopkins Hospital in 1978, and was a central figure in developing the specialty of Peripheral Nerve Surgery. He began the Dellon Institutes for Peripheral Nerve Surgery, and has won research prizes in Anatomy, Immunobiology, Neural Regeneration, and Treatment of Chronic Nerve Compression. He retired from surgery in 2022. He has written five surgical texts in use worldwide. THE PROSECTOR is his first novel.